MAUS

A SURVIVOR'S TALE

PENGUIN BOOKS

AUS

A SURVIVOR'S TALE

I

MY FATHER
BLEEDS
HISTORY

II

AND HERE
MY TROUBLES
BEGAN

art *spiegelman*

Thanks to Ken and Flo Jacobs, Ernie Gehr, Paul Pavel, Louise Fili, Steven Heller,

Deborah Karl, and Mala Spiegelman, whose appreciation and support

have helped bring this book into the world.

And thanks to Françoise Mouly for her intelligence and integrity,

for her editorial skills, and for her love.

PENGUIN BOOKS

Published by the Penguin Group
Penguin Books Ltd, 80 Strand, London WC2R 0RL, England
Penguin Putnam Inc., 375 Hudson Street, New York, New York 10014, USA
Penguin Books Australia Ltd, 250 Camberwell Road, Camberwell, Victoria 3124, Australia
Penguin Books Canada Ltd, 10 Alcorn Avenue, Toronto, Ontario, Canada M4V 3B2
Penguin Books India (P) Ltd, 11 Community Centre, Panchsheel Park, New Delhi – 110 017, India
Penguin Books (NZ) Ltd, Cnr Rosedale and Airborne Roads, Albany, Auckland, New Zealand
Penguin Books (South Africa) (Pty) Ltd, 24 Sturdee Avenue, Rosebank 2196, South Africa

Penguin Books Ltd, Registered Offices: 80 Strand, London WC2R 0RL, England

www.penguin.com

Maus, Volume I first published by Pantheon Books, 1986
Maus, Volume II first published by Pantheon Books, 1992
The Complete Maus first published in the United States of America by Pantheon Books 1996
Published in Great Britain in Penguin Books 2003
10

Maus, Volume I copyright © Art Spiegelman, 1973, 1980, 1981, 1982, 1983,
1984, 1985, 1986
Maus, Volume II copyright © Art Spiegelman, 1986, 1989, 1990, 1991
All rights reserved

Chapters one to six of Maus, Volume I and chapters one to four of Maus, Volume II first
appeared, in a somewhat different form, in Raw magazine between 1980 and 1991.
'Prisoner of the Hell Planet' originally appeared in Short Order Comix #1, 1973

The moral right of the author has been asserted

Printed in China by South China Printing Co Ltd.

ISBN-13: 978-0-141-01408-1
ISBN-10: 0-141-01408-3

It was summer, I remember. I was ten or eleven...

LAST ONE TO THE SCHOOLYARD IS A ROTTEN EGG!

...I was roller-skating with Howie and Steve....

...'til my skate came loose.

OW!

HEY! WAIT UP FELLAS!

ROTTEN EGG! HA HA!

W-WAIT UP!

SNK, SNF

My father was in front, fixing something...

ARTIE! COME TO HOLD THIS A MINUTE WHILE I SAW.

SNRK?

WHY DO YOU CRY, ARTIE? HOLD BETTER ON THE WOOD.

I-I FELL, AND MY FRIENDS SKATED AWAY W-WITHOUT ME.

He stopped sawing.

FRIENDS? YOUR FRIENDS?...

IF YOU LOCK THEM TOGETHER IN A ROOM WITH NO FOOD FOR A WEEK ....

...THEN YOU COULD SEE WHAT IT IS, FRIENDS!...

MAUS

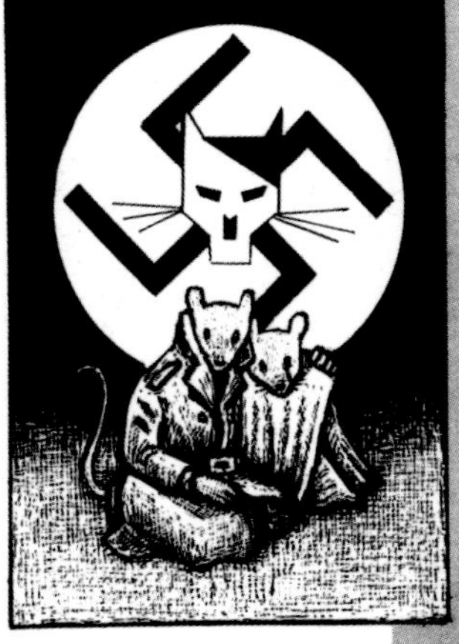

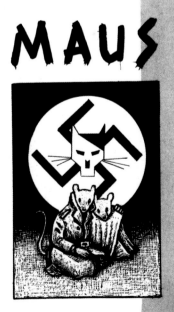

FOR ANJA

MY FATHER BLEEDS HISTORY

(MID-1930s TO WINTER 1944)

CONTENTS

"The Jews are undoubtedly a race,

but they are not human."

Adolf Hitler

CHAPTER ONE

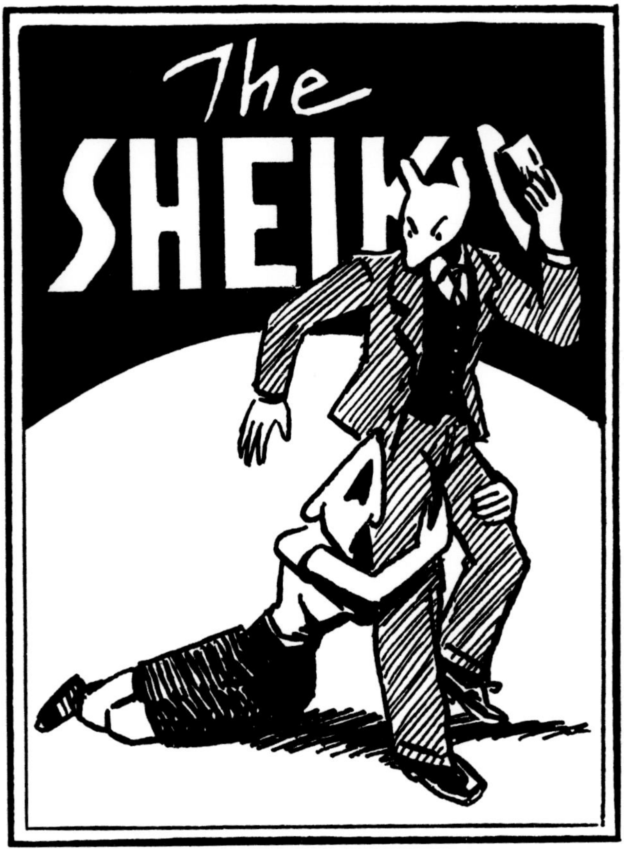
The
SHEIK

I went out to see my Father in Rego Park. I hadn't seen him in a long time- we weren't that close.

POPPA!

OI, ARTIE. YOU'RE LATE. I WAS WORRIED.

IT'S A SHAME FRANÇOISE ALSO DIDN'T COME.

UH-HUH. SHE SENDS REGARDS.

He had aged a lot since I saw him last. My Mother's suicide and his two heart attacks had taken their Toll.

MALA! LOOK WHO'S HERE! ARTIE!

He was remarried. Mala knew my parents in Poland before the war.

She was a survivor too, like most of my parents' friends.

HI, ARTIE. LET ME TAKE YOUR COAT.

THE DINNER IS ON THE TABLE.

ACCH, MALA!

A WIRE HANGER YOU GIVE HIM! I HAVEN'T SEEN ARTIE IN ALMOST TWO YEARS- WE HAVE PLENTY WOODEN HANGERS.

They didn't get along.

After dinner he took me into my old room...

COME—WE'LL TALK WHILE I PEDAL...

IT'S GOOD FOR MY HEART, THE PEDALING. BUT, TELL ME, HOW IS IT BY YOU? HOW IS GOING THE COMICS BUSINESS?

I STILL WANT TO DRAW THAT BOOK ABOUT YOU...

THE ONE I USED TO TALK TO YOU ABOUT...

ABOUT YOUR LIFE IN POLAND, AND THE WAR.

IT WOULD TAKE **MANY** BOOKS, MY LIFE, AND NO ONE WANTS ANYWAY TO HEAR SUCH STORIES.

I WANT TO HEAR IT. START WITH MOM... TELL ME HOW YOU MET.

BETTER YOU SHOULD SPEND YOUR TIME TO MAKE DRAWINGS WHAT WILL BRING YOU SOME MONEY...

BUT, IF YOU WANT, I CAN TELL YOU...I LIVED THEN IN CZESTOCHOWA, A SMALL CITY NOT FAR FROM THE BORDER OF GERMANY...

I WAS IN TEXTILES—BUYING AND SELLING—I DIDN'T MAKE MUCH, BUT ALWAYS I COULD MAKE A *LIVING*.

14

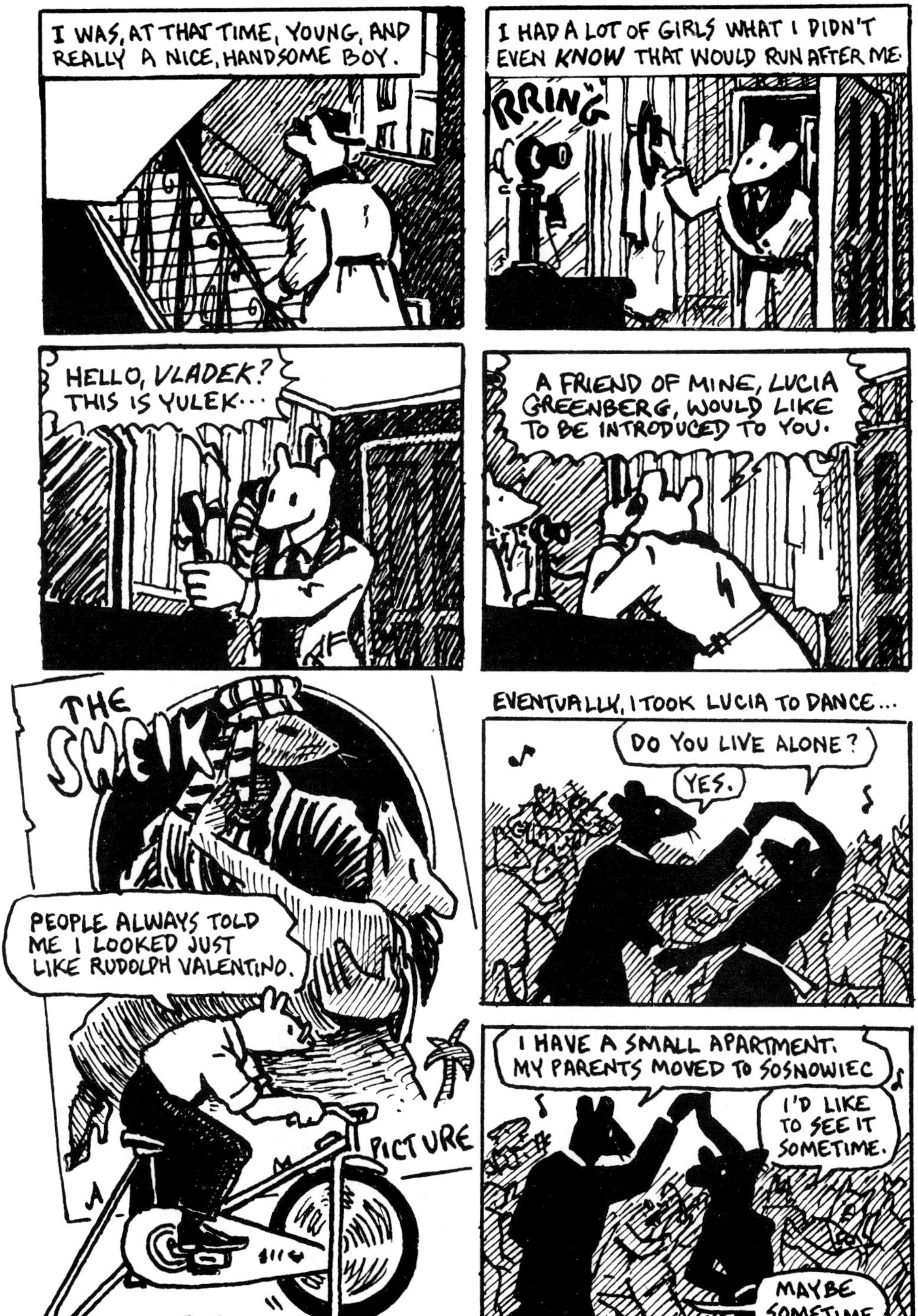
I WAS, AT THAT TIME, YOUNG, AND REALLY A NICE, HANDSOME BOY.
I HAD A LOT OF GIRLS WHAT I DIDN'T EVEN KNOW THAT WOULD RUN AFTER ME.
RRING
HELLO, VLADEK? THIS IS YULEK...
A FRIEND OF MINE, LUCIA GREENBERG, WOULD LIKE TO BE INTRODUCED TO YOU.
THE SHEIK
PICTURE
PEOPLE ALWAYS TOLD ME I LOOKED JUST LIKE RUDOLPH VALENTINO.
EVENTUALLY, I TOOK LUCIA TO DANCE...
DO YOU LIVE ALONE?
YES.
I HAVE A SMALL APARTMENT. MY PARENTS MOVED TO SOSNOWIEC
I'D LIKE TO SEE IT SOMETIME.
MAYBE SOMETIME

WHEREVER I WENT - I LOOKED AROUND - AND LUCIA GREENBERG WOULD BE ALSO THERE ...

VLADEK! - WHICH WAY ARE YOU GOING?

JUST TO THE MARKET.

ME TOO - LET'S WALK TOGETHER.

BUT, POP... MOM'S NAME WAS ANNA ZYLBERBERG! ...

ALL THIS WAS BEFORE I MET ANJA - JUST LISTEN, YES?

WHY DON'T YOU EVER INVITE ME TO YOUR HOME? ... ARE YOU ASHAMED OF IT?

SHE KEPT INSISTING ME TO SHOW HER MY APARTMENT...

- SO FINALLY, I INVITED HER ...

EVERYTHING'S SO NEAT AND CLEAN!

I LIKE TO KEEP THINGS IN ORDER.

YOU MUST HAVE ANOTHER GIRL-FRIEND WHO CLEANS FOR YOU - NO?

NO.

...I DIDN'T WANT TO BE MORE CLOSER WITH HER, BUT SHE REALLY WOULDN'T LET ME GO.

16

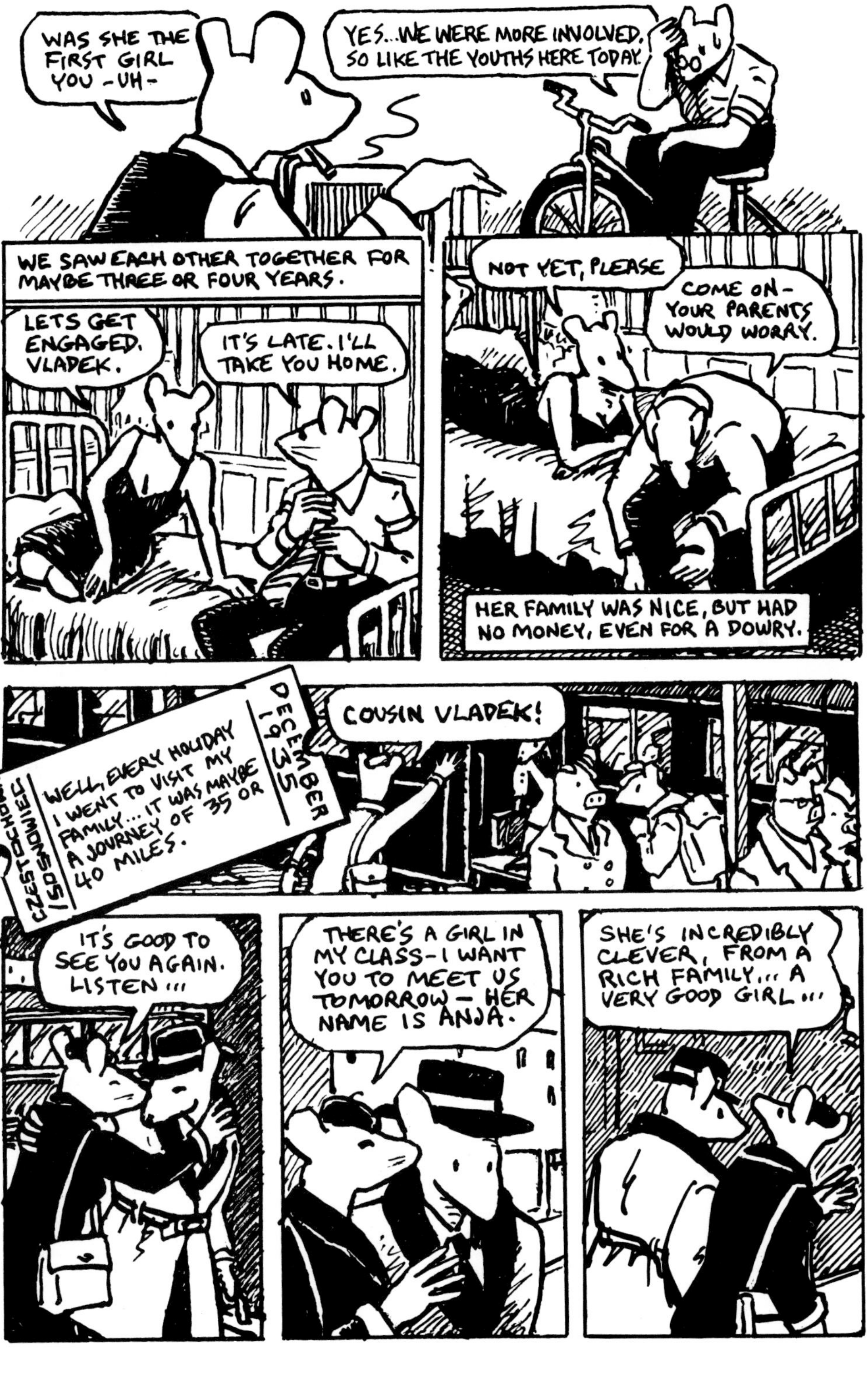

WAS SHE THE FIRST GIRL YOU -UH-
YES...WE WERE MORE INVOLVED, SO LIKE THE YOUTHS HERE TODAY.
WE SAW EACH OTHER TOGETHER FOR MAYBE THREE OR FOUR YEARS.
LETS GET ENGAGED, VLADEK.
IT'S LATE. I'LL TAKE YOU HOME.
NOT YET, PLEASE
COME ON- YOUR PARENTS WOULD WORRY.
HER FAMILY WAS NICE, BUT HAD NO MONEY, EVEN FOR A DOWRY.
CZESTOCHOWA / SOSNOWIEC
WELL, EVERY HOLIDAY I WENT TO VISIT MY FAMILY... IT WAS MAYBE A JOURNEY OF 35 OR 40 MILES.
DECEMBER 1935
COUSIN VLADEK!
IT'S GOOD TO SEE YOU AGAIN. LISTEN...
THERE'S A GIRL IN MY CLASS- I WANT YOU TO MEET US TOMORROW - HER NAME IS ANJA.
SHE'S INCREDIBLY CLEVER, FROM A RICH FAMILY... A VERY GOOD GIRL...

THE NEXT MORNING WE ALL MET TOGETHER. MY COUSIN AND ANJA SPOKE SOMETIMES IN ENGLISH

HOW YOU LIKE HIM?

HE'S A HANDSOME BOY AND SEEMS VERY NICE.

THEY COULDN'T KNOW I UNDERSTOOD.

WELL—I PROMISED TO BE HOME EARLY... I'LL LEAVE YOU TWO ALONE

YOU KNOW, YOU SHOULD BE CAREFUL SPEAKING ENGLISH—A "STRANGER" COULD UNDERSTAND.

Y-YOU KNOW ENGLISH?

DID YOU STUDY IT IN SCHOOL?

I HAD TO QUIT SCHOOL AT ABOUT 14 TO WORK.

...BUT I TOOK PRIVATE LESSONS... I ALWAYS DREAMED OF GOING TO AMERICA.

IT'S A SHAME YOU HAVE TO RETURN TO CZESTOCHOWA SO SOON.

YES—BUT I HAVE MY BUSINESS.

HAVE YOU A PHONE AT HOME?

AS SOON I CAME BACK TO CZESTOCHOWA, SHE CALLED — ONCE A DAY...TWICE... EVERY DAY WE TALKED.

AND THEN SHE STARTED WRITING TO ME SUCH BEAUTIFUL LETTERS— ALMOST NOBODY COULD WRITE POLISH LIKE SHE WROTE.

I VISITED A COUPLE TIMES TO HER. SHE SENT ME A PHOTO !!!

I BOUGHT A VERY NICE FRAME...

IT PASSED MAYBE A WEEK UNTIL LUCIA AGAIN CAME AND SAW THE PHOTO...

I'M GOING TO GET EN- GAGED TO HER, LUCIA.

PSSH! AND LOOK AT WHAT A **BEAUTY** YOU PICKED.

LOOKS AREN'T EVERYTHING, LUCIA. IT ISN'T GOOD FOR EITHER OF US THAT YOU KEEP COMING UP HERE...

... WE HAVE TO PLAN FOR OUR FUTURES, AND—

FORGET HER! LET ME MAKE YOU HAPPY!

IT WAS NOT SO EASY TO GET FREE FROM LUCIA.

19

MOM WASN'T THAT ATTRACTIVE, HUH?

NOT SO LIKE LUCIA... BUT IF YOU TALKED A LITTLE TO HER, YOU STARTED LOVING HER MORE AND MORE.

ONE TIME WE WALKED INTO THE DIRECTOR FROM HER SCHOOL...

YOU'RE VERY LUCKY, MR. SPIEGELMAN.

...YOU DON'T KNOW WHAT A GIRL YOU'RE GETTING—I'VE HAD MANY STUDENTS...

..BUT NEVER ONE AS SENSITIVE AND INTELLIGENT AS ANNA!

YES—THAT'S WHY I PICKED HER.

I WISH YOU COULD VISIT ME IN CZESTOCHOWA—I'D LIKE TO SHOW YOU OFF TO MY FRIENDS.

I'VE BEGGED MY MOTHER TO LET ME GO—BUT SHE'S SO RELIGIOUS AND OLD-FASHIONED.

...SHE WOULD NEVER ALLOW ME TO GO TO A BACHELOR'S APARTMENT!

ANJA'S PARENTS WERE ANXIOUS SHE SHOULD BE MARRIED. SHE WAS 24; I WAS THEN 30.

OH, MY PARENTS WOULD LIKE YOU TO COME TO DINNER TOMORROW NIGHT.

THE ZYLBERBERG FAMILY WAS VERY WELL OFF—MILLIONAIRES!

THE ZYLBERBERGS HAD A HOSIERY FACTORY—ONE OF THE BIGGEST IN POLAND... BUT WHEN I CAME IN TO THEIR HOUSE IT WAS SO LIKE A KING CAME...

WELCOME, WELCOME.

ANJA—VLADEK IS HERE!

MAKE YOURSELF COMFORTABLE WHILE I HELP WITH THE DINNER.

TO SEE WHAT A HOUSEKEEPER SHE WAS, I PEEKED INTO ANJA'S CLOSET.

EVERYTHING IS NEAT AND STRAIGHT JUST THE WAY I LIKE IT!

BUT WHAT'S THIS—PILLS?!

I WROTE DOWN EVERY PILL.

IF SHE WAS SICK, THEN WHAT DID I NEED IT FOR?

DINNER IS READY!

LATER, A FRIEND, A DRUGGIST, TOLD ME THE PILLS WERE ONLY BECAUSE SHE WAS SO SKINNY AND NERVOUS.

HOW ABOUT SOME MORE GEFILTE FISH, VLADEK?

SO, TO MAKE A LONG STORY SHORT, BY THE END OF 1936 WE WERE ENGAGED AND I MOVED FROM CZESTOCHOWA TO SOSNOWIEC.

ACH! HERE I FORGOT TO TELL SOMETHING FROM *BEFORE* I MOVED TO SOSNOWIEC BUT AFTER OUR ENGAGEMENT WAS MADE.

ONE EVENING THE BELL RANG...

LUCIA

WHAT ARE YOU DOING HERE? I'M ON MY WAY OUT.

I-I'LL COME WITH YOU.

NO, YOU CAN'T COME WI-

PLEASE, VLADEK!

SHE FELL ON THE FLOOR AND HELD STRONG MY LEGS.

DON'T RUN AWAY!

I SAW NOW THAT I WENT TOO FAR WITH HER.

SLAM!

I RAN OUT TO MY FRIEND WHAT INTRO-DUCED US. HE WENT TO CALM HER DOWN AND TOOK HER HOME.

I DIDN'T HEAR MORE FROM LUCIA—BUT ALSO I STOPPED HEARING FROM ANJA...

NO TELEPHONE CALLS, NO LETTERS, *NOTHING!* WHAT HAPPENED?

HELLO, MRS. ZYLBERBERG. COULD I SPEAK TO ANJA?

SHE SAYS SHE WON'T SPEAK TO YOU!

BUT WHY?

SHE GOT A LETTER FROM SOMEONE IN CZĘSTOCHOWA. MY GOD! IT SAYS THE WORST THINGS IN THE WORLD ABOUT YOU!

WELL, I CAN'T CONVINCE HER ON THE PHONE. I'LL COME DOWN BY TRAIN ON FRIDAY AFTER WORK.

IT WASN'T EVEN A HOLIDAY, BUT I WENT ANYWAY TO SOSNOWIEC.

SO, TELL ME, ANJA—WHAT HAVE I DONE THAT'S SO HORRIBLE?

YOU SHOULD KNOW—JUST READ THIS!

23

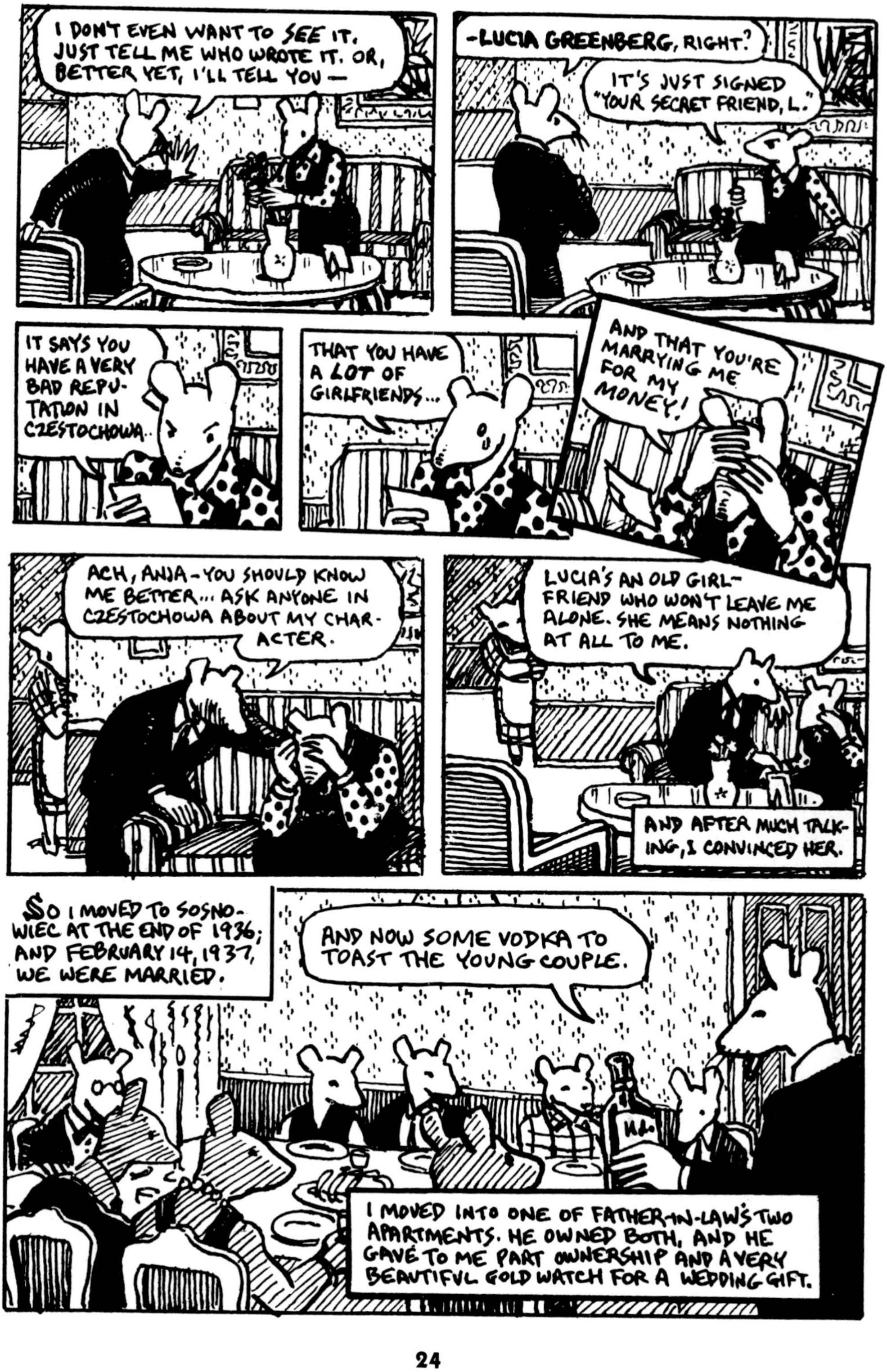

I DON'T EVEN WANT TO SEE IT. JUST TELL ME WHO WROTE IT. OR, BETTER YET, I'LL TELL YOU —
-LUCIA GREENBERG, RIGHT?
IT'S JUST SIGNED "YOUR SECRET FRIEND, L."
IT SAYS YOU HAVE A VERY BAD REPUTATION IN CZESTOCHOWA..
THAT YOU HAVE A LOT OF GIRLFRIENDS...
AND THAT YOU'RE MARRYING ME FOR MY MONEY!
ACH, ANJA - YOU SHOULD KNOW ME BETTER... ASK ANYONE IN CZESTOCHOWA ABOUT MY CHARACTER.
LUCIA'S AN OLD GIRLFRIEND WHO WON'T LEAVE ME ALONE. SHE MEANS NOTHING AT ALL TO ME.
AND AFTER MUCH TALKING, I CONVINCED HER.
SO I MOVED TO SOSNOWIEC AT THE END OF 1936; AND FEBRUARY 14, 1937, WE WERE MARRIED.
AND NOW SOME VODKA TO TOAST THE YOUNG COUPLE.
I MOVED INTO ONE OF FATHER-IN-LAW'S TWO APARTMENTS. HE OWNED BOTH, AND HE GAVE TO ME PART OWNERSHIP AND A VERY BEAUTIFUL GOLD WATCH FOR A WEDDING GIFT.

BUT THIS WHAT I JUST TOLD YOU—ABOUT LUCIA AND SO—I DON'T WANT YOU SHOULD WRITE THIS IN YOUR BOOK.

WHAT? WHY NOT?

IT HAS NOTHING TO DO WITH HITLER, WITH THE HOLOCAUST!

BUT POP— IT'S GREAT MATERIAL. IT MAKES EVERYTHING MORE *REAL*—MORE HUMAN.

I WANT TO TELL *YOUR* STORY, THE WAY IT REALLY HAPPENED.

BUT THIS ISN'T SO *PROPER*, SO RESPECTFUL.

... I CAN TELL YOU *OTHER* STORIES, BUT SUCH *PRIVATE* THINGS, I DON'T WANT YOU SHOULD MENTION.

OKAY, OKAY— I PROMISE.

CHAPTER TWO

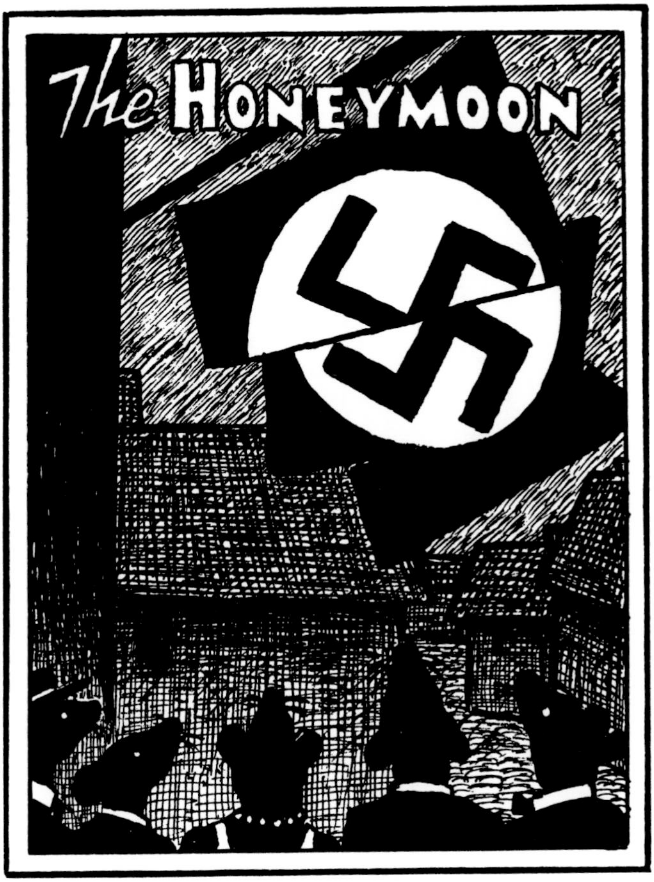
The HONEYMOON

For the next few months I went back to visit my father quite regularly, to hear his story.

ABOUT MOM....

...11...12...13...

—UH... WHAT ARE YOU DOING, POP?

I'M MAKING INTO DAILY PORTIONS MY PILLS. ...14...15...

...16...17...18...

SO MANY?

IT'S 6 PILLS FOR THE HEART, 1 FOR DIABETES... AND MAYBE 25 OR 30 VITAMINS.

FOR MY CONDITION I MUST FIGHT TO *SAVE* MYSELF. DOCTORS, THEY ONLY GIVE ME "JUNK FOOD"...

..THAT'S HOW I CALL PRESCRIPTION DRUGS NOW. I STUDY THIS IN MY **PREVENTION** MAGAZINES... MAYBE YOU WANT TO READ?

NO THANKS.

ABOUT MOM—DID SHE HAVE ANY BOYFRIENDS BEFORE SHE MET YOU?

NOT **ROMANTIC**... BUT ONE TALL BOY FROM WARSAW

HE WAS... A COMMUNIST!

EVEN AFTER THE MARRIAGE, WHEN THIS FELLOW CAME TO SOSNOWIEC, ANJA ALWAYS RAN TO SEE HIM.

I DIDN'T KNOW, OF COURSE, THAT HE WAS COMMUNIST. I **ALWAYS** KEPT FAR AWAY FROM COMMUNIST PEOPLE.

A LITTLE AFTER WE WERE MARRIED I CAME HOME FROM A SELLING TRIP...

HEY VLADEK—THEY JUST ARRESTED THE SEAMSTRESS THAT LIVES DOWN YOUR HALL!...

SHE HAD SOME SECRET COMMUNIST DOCUMENTS!

AND WHEN I WENT UPSTAIRS...

THE POLICE JUST ARRES—HUH? WHAT'S THE MATTER?

THE POLICE WERE **HERE!**

LOOKING FOR ANJA!

SHE JUST TOLD US...

THAT BOY FROM WARSAW BRINGS COMMUNIST MESSAGES.

SHE TRANSLATES THEM INTO GERMAN AND PASSES THEM ON!

ANJA WAS INVOLVED IN *CONSPIRATIONS!*

A LITTLE BEFORE THE POLICE CAME, SHE GOT FROM FRIENDS A TELEPHONE CALL ...

THEY SUSPECT YOU! HIDE THE PAPERS QUICKLY! BUT THEY'RE IMPORTANT—TRY NOT TO DESTROY THEM.

WHAT TO DO? SHE RAN TO THE SEAMSTRESS WHAT WAS ONE OF OUR TENANTS

MISS STEFANSKA—*PLEASE!* HIDE THIS PACKAGE FOR ME—DON'T TELL *ANYONE* ABOUT IT!

?

AND ANJA WAS A GOOD CUSTOMER, SO SHE AGREED.

THE POLICE WENT OVER *OUR* HOUSE TOP TO BOTTOM. IT WAS NOTHING TO FIND SO THEY SEARCHED THE NEIGHBORS.

OKAY—HOW DID YOU GET THIS PACKAGE?

I NEVER SAW IT BEFORE—ONE OF MY CUSTOMERS MUST HAVE LEFT IT!

ANJA WAS SAFE, BUT THE SEAMSTRESS THEY ARRESTED.

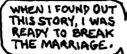

WHEN I FOUND OUT THIS STORY, I WAS READY TO BREAK THE MARRIAGE.

I TOLD HER "ANJA, IF YOU WANT ME YOU HAVE TO GO MY WAY..."

IF YOU WANT YOUR COMMUNIST FRIENDS, THEN I CAN'T STAY IN THIS HOUSE!"

AND SHE WAS A GOOD GIRL, AND OF COURSE SHE STOPPED ALL SUCH THINGS.

WHAT HAPPENED TO THE SEAMSTRESS?

MISS STEFANSKA SAT IN PRISON FOR A LONGER TIME — MAYBE 3 MONTHS.

IT WASN'T ENOUGH EVIDENCE AND FINALLY THE POLICE LEFT HER GO.

FATHER-IN-LAW PAID THE COST FROM THE LAWYERS AND GAVE TO HER SOME MONEY — IT COST MAYBE 15,000 ZLOTYS.

THAT'S A LOT, HUH?

JA, BUT NOT ONLY THIS. AT THE SAME TIME HE DID FOR US EVEN *MORE*...

YOU KNOW, VLADEK, WHEN YOU AND ANJA GIVE ME A GRANDCHILD, I WANT HIM TO BE WELL-OFF.

WELL, I ALMOST HAVE ENOUGH FROM MY SALES TRIPS TO START UP A TEXTILE SHOP...

A SHOP? PFUI! YOU OUGHT TO HAVE A TEXTILE *FACTORY!*

THAT WOULD COST A *FORTUNE!!*

PLEASE — I CAN GIVE YOU THE MONEY AND PLENTY OF CREDIT.

I STARTED A FACTORY IN *BIELSKO*, AND VISITED TO ANJA EVERY WEEK-END.

BY OCTOBER 1937, THE FACTORY WAS GOING, AND IT WAS BORN MY FIRST SON, RICHIEU.

HE'S A BIG BABY— OVER 3 KILOS.

MY GOD— ANJA ONLY WEIGHS 39!

OF COURSE, YOU NEVER KNEW HIM. HE DIDN'T COME OUT FROM THE WAR.

YES, I KNOW...

BUT WAIT— IF YOU WERE MARRIED IN FEBRUARY, AND RICHIEU WAS BORN IN OCTOBER, WAS HE PREMATURE?

YES, A LITTLE...

BUT YOU— AFTER THE WAR, WHEN YOU WERE BORN— IT WAS VERY PREMATURE. THE DOCTORS THOUGHT YOU WOULDN'T LIVE.

I FOUND A SPECIALIST WHAT SAVED YOU... HE HAD TO BREAK YOUR ARM TO TAKE YOU OUT FROM ANJA'S BELLY!

AND WHEN YOU WERE A TINY BABY YOUR ARM ALWAYS JUMPED UP, LIKE SO!

WE JOKED AND CALLED YOU "HEIL HITLER!"

ALWAYS WE PUSHED YOUR ARM DOWN, AND YOU WOULD OOPS!

LOOK NOW WHAT YOU MADE ME DO!

ME? OKAY, I'LL RE-COUNT THEM LATER.

NO! YOU DON'T KNOW COUNTING PILLS. I'LL DO IT AFTER... I'M AN EXPERT FOR THIS.

SO... ANJA STAYED WITH THE FAMILY AND I WENT TO LIVE IN BIELSKO FOR MY FACTORY BUSINESS AND TO FIND FOR US AN APARTMENT..

BUT SOON IT CAME FROM SOSNOWIEC A TELEPHONE ...

VLADEK! COME HOME RIGHT AWAY - ANJA IS SICK!

SHE WAS CRYING AS SOON I CAME IN ...

WHAT'S WRONG, DARLING?

SOB IT DOESN'T MATTER... NOTHING MATTERS.

BUT WHY ARE YOU CRYING?

I DON'T KNOW! I HAVE A GOOD FAMILY...A FINE SON.. I SHOULD BE HAPPY...

BUT I DON'T CARE. I JUST DON'T WANT TO LIVE.

HERE, BABY. DRINK THIS AND REST.

I DON'T UNDERSTAND. WHAT'S THE MATTER?

GIVING BIRTH WAS TOO MUCH OF A STRAIN. SHE'S ALWAYS HYSTERICAL OR DEPRESSED...A BREAKDOWN!

PLEASE

THE DOCTOR TOLD US ABOUT A SANITARIUM.

... BUT SOMEBODY MUST GO WITH HER...SOMEONE SHE TRUSTS.

EVERYTHING'S ARRANGED - THE CHILD CAN STAY HERE WITH A GOVERNESS.

...AND I'LL WATCH YOUR FACTORY.

SOB

33

RIGHT AWAY, WE WENT. THE SANITARIUM WAS INSIDE CZECHOSLOVAKIA, ONE OF THE MOST EXPENSIVE AND BEAUTIFUL IN THE WORLD.

I REMEMBER WHEN WE WERE ALMOST ARRIVED, WE PASSED A SMALL TOWN.

OI!

EVERYBODY-EVERY JEW FROM THE TRAIN- GOT VERY EXCITED AND FRIGHTENED.

LOOK!

IT WAS THE BEGINNING OF 1938-BEFORE THE WAR- HANGING HIGH IN THE CENTER OF TOWN, IT WAS A NAZI FLAG..

HERE WAS THE FIRST TIME I SAW, WITH MY OWN EYES, THE SWASTIKA.

I TELL YOU, THERE'S A POGROM GOING ON IN GERMANY TODAY!

ONE FELLOW TOLD US OF HIS COUSIN WHAT WAS LIVING IN GERMANY...

...HE HAD TO SELL HIS BUSINESS TO A GERMAN AND RUN OUT FROM THE COUNTRY WITHOUT EVEN THE MONEY.

I AM A FILTHY JEW

IT WAS VERY HARD THERE FOR THE JEWS—TERRIBLE!

ANOTHER FELLOW TOLD US OF A RELATIVE IN BRANDENBERG—THE POLICE CAME TO HIS HOUSE AND NO ONE HEARD AGAIN FROM HIM.

This town is Jew Free

IT WAS MANY, MANY SUCH STORIES—SYNAGOGUES BURNED, JEWS BEATEN WITH NO REASON, WHOLE TOWNS PUSHING OUT ALL JEWS—EACH STORY WORSE THAN THE OTHER.

LET'S HOPE THOSE NAZI GANGSTERS GET THROWN OUT OF POWER!

JUST PRAY THAT THEY DON'T START A WAR!!

THE SANITARIUM WAS FAR AWAY FROM EVERYTHING— SO PEACEFUL, SO QUIET.

LOOK AT HOW BEAUTIFUL THESE GARDENS ARE, ANJA.

UH HUH

PEOPLE CAME FROM ALL OVER THE WORLD WITH DIFFERENT SICKNESSES. IT WAS EVEN SHOPS HERE.... A THEATER... REALLY BEAUTIFUL...

OUR ROOM IS LIKE A LUXURY HOTEL—LOOK AT THIS VIEW.

UH HUH

EACH MORNING NURSES WOULD VISIT TO ANJA.

AND EACH FEW DAYS I TALKED TO THE BIG SPECIALIST AT THE CLINIC.

WELL, WHAT DID THE DOCTOR SAY??

HE TOLD ME YOU'RE DOING FINE... FINE.

JUST RELAX.

DR. BUL

I UNDERSTOOD MUCH OF SUCH SICKNESSES, SO I HELPED ALWAYS TO CALM HER DOWN.

LOOK—WE GOT A LETTER FROM HOME TODAY.

WITH A PHOTO OF RICHIEU—LET ME SEE.

HE'S A HANDSOME BOY... JUST LIKE HIS FATHER, YES?

YES.

IN THE EVENINGS WE WENT EITHER TO THE THEATER OR TO DANCE IN THE CAFE.

DID I TELL YOU THE TRAGEDY ABOUT THE PILLOW MY FAMILY LOST AT THE START OF THE 1914 WAR? I WAS SEVEN... WE LIVED TOO CLOSE TO THE BORDER... IT WASN'T SAFE...

I TOLD HER MANY JOKES AND STORIES TO KEEP HER BUSY...

...SO WE TOOK WHAT WE COULD ON A WAGON PULLED BY FOUR HORSES AND WENT TO MY GRANDFATHER'S HOME IN RADOMSKO.

SOMEONE RODE PAST US AND TOLD US THAT WE'D DROPPED A PILLOW A FEW MILES BACK. A GUY TRAVELING TO AMSTOW PICKED IT UP.

IMAGINE — MY FATHER NEVER RODE A HORSE BEFORE... BUT HE UNHITCHED ONE FROM THE WAGON AND RODE TOWARD AMSTOW..

WE WAITED AND WAITED.. MOTHER STARTED CRYING: "SURELY HE FELL AND GOT KILLED!" SHE HAD BEGGED HIM TO "LET THE PILLOW GO AND TAKE ALL OUR TROUBLES WITH IT!"

THE HORSE WAS BONY AND DIDN'T HAVE A SADDLE... FINALLY, LATE THAT NIGHT, FATHER RODE BACK WITH THE PILLOW ...UNDER HIS BLOODY *TUCHUS*"...

SO, FATHER GOT HIS PILLOW BACK ...BUT HE COULDN'T SIT DOWN FOR THE REST OF THE WAR!

I LOVE YOU, VLADEK.

AND SHE WAS SO LAUGHING AND SO HAPPY, SO HAPPY, THAT SHE APPROACHED EACH TIME AND KISSED ME, SO HAPPY SHE WAS.

37

WE STAYED MAYBE 3 MONTHS, AND WHEN WE CAME BACK, ANJA WAS COMPLETELY DIFFERENT FROM WHEN SHE LEFT.

YOO HOO, POPPA!

ANJA! YOU LOOK LIKE A MILLION!

LISTEN, VLADEK... I DIDN'T WANT YOU TO WORRY WHILE YOU WERE AT THE SANITARIUM, BUT—

—BRACE YOURSELF—THE BIELSKO FACTORY HAS BEEN ROBBED!

WHAT!

IT HAPPENED LAST MONTH. THEY TOOK EVERYTHING!

AI! AI! AI!

I DIDN'T EVEN HAVE TIME TO INSURE IT BEFORE WE LEFT.

WELL, AT LEAST I CAN HELP YOU BUILD IT UP AGAIN.

WERE YOU LOOTED AS PART OF SOME KIND OF ANTI-SEMITIC ACTIVITY?

I DON'T THINK THIS WAS IT. JUST A ROBBERY...

...LIKE WHEN THEY ROBBED US IN REGO PARK HERE, LAST YEAR.

WELL.... IN BIELSKO, FATHER-IN-LAW HELPED US AGAIN TO ESTABLISH OURSELVES ...

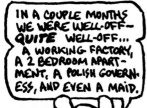 IN A COUPLE MONTHS WE WERE WELL-OFF— QUITE WELL-OFF... A WORKING FACTORY, A 2 BEDROOM APARTMENT, A POLISH GOVERN- ESS, AND EVEN A MAID.

 LOOK, RICHIEU, POPPA'S HOME!

 YOU LOOK UPSET, VLADEK. THERE WAS ANOTHER RIOT DOWNTOWN TODAY.

 ...EVERYONE YELLING, "JEWS OUT! JEWS OUT!"...EVEN TWO PEOPLE KILLED. THE POLICE JUST WATCHED!

 IT'S THOSE NAZIS STIRRING EVERYBODY UP! WHEN IT COMES TO JEWS, THE POLES DON'T NEED MUCH STIRRING UP!

 MRS. SPIEGELMAN— HOW CAN YOU SAY SUCH A THING. I THINK OF YOU AS PART OF MY OWN FAMILY! I'M SORRY, JANINA. I DIDN'T MEAN YOU! I'M JUST WORRIED!

 MAYBE WE SHOULD MOVE AWAY, LIKE SOME OTHERS HAVE. IF THINGS GET REALLY BAD WE'LL RUN BACK TO SOSNOWIEC.

 WHY WOULD SOSNOWIEC BE ANY SAFER THAN BIELSKO? WE THOUGHT THEN, THAT HITLER WANTED ONLY THE PARTS FROM POLAND, LIKE BIELSKO, WHAT USED TO BE PARTS FROM GER- MANY BEFORE THE FIRST WORLD WAR.

WE WERE VERY HAPPY, STILL, FOR OVER A YEAR—UNTIL AUGUST 24, 1939.

A LETTER—FROM THE GOVERNMENT!

A DRAFT NOTICE! I WAS IN THE POLISH RESERVES ARMY, AND SO I HAD TO GO RIGHT AWAY!

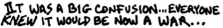

IT WAS A BIG CONFUSION... EVERYONE KNEW IT WOULD BE NOW A WAR...

QUICK! PACK EVERYTHING! YOUR FATHER WILL TAKE YOU TO SOSNOWIEC.

VLADEK, I'M AFRAID!

GRAB YOUR KNICK-KNACKS, AND THE DOLL COLLECTION!

THEY'RE NOT IMPORTANT!

YOU'LL SEE. YOU MAY ENJOY THEM.

I WAS RIGHT. WHEN THINGS WENT WORSE LATER, SHE WAS ABLE TO SELL SUCH THINGS.

SO ANJA AND RICHIEU AND THE GOVERNESS WENT IN ONE WAY—TO SOSNOWIEC...

...AND I WENT THEN IN A DIFFERENT DIRECTION... TO THE FRONTIER AGAINST GERMANY.

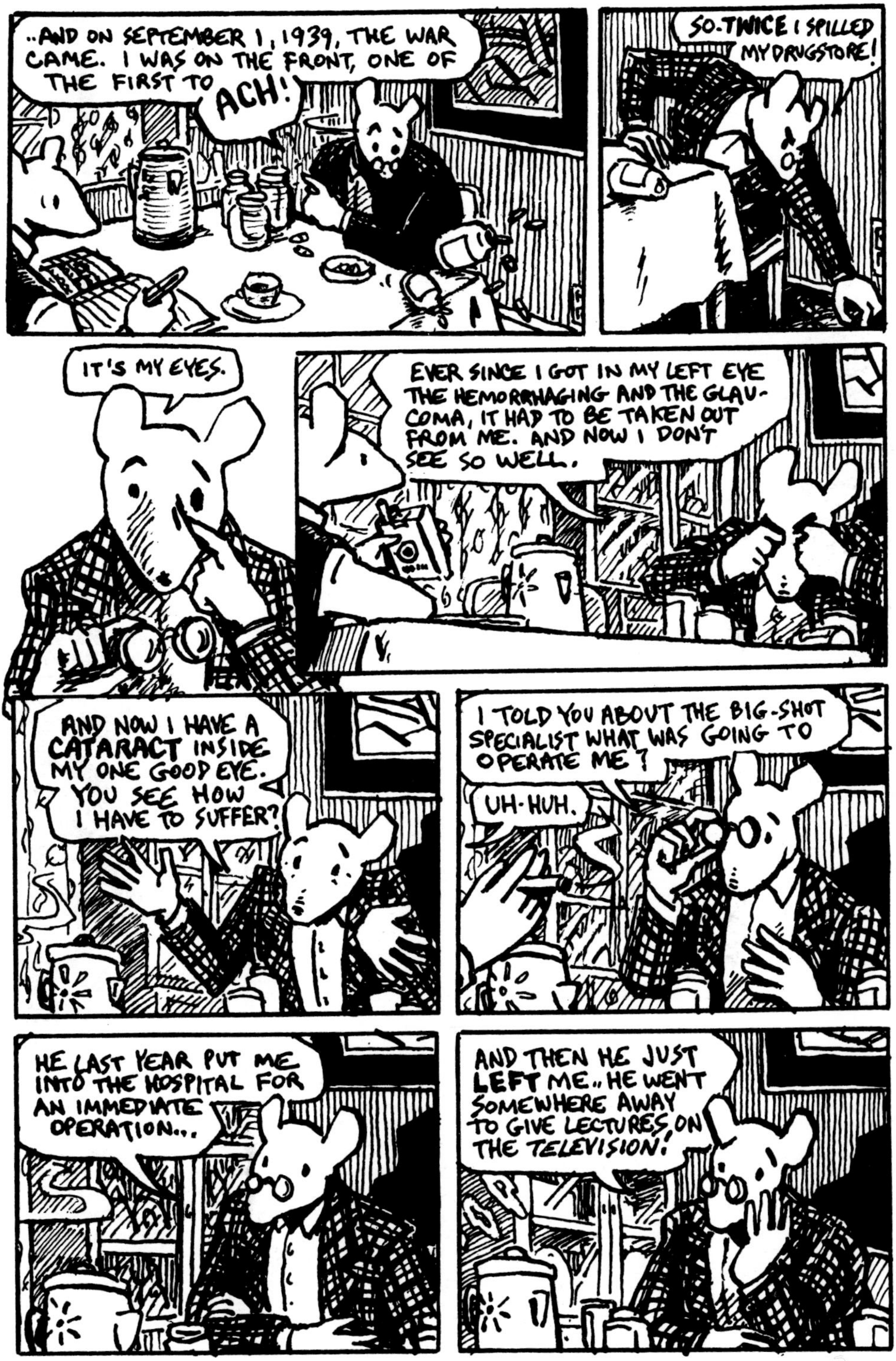
..AND ON SEPTEMBER 1, 1939, THE WAR CAME. I WAS ON THE FRONT, ONE OF THE FIRST TO
ACH!
SO-TWICE I SPILLED MY DRUGSTORE!
IT'S MY EYES.
EVER SINCE I GOT IN MY LEFT EYE THE HEMORRHAGING AND THE GLAUCOMA, IT HAD TO BE TAKEN OUT FROM ME. AND NOW I DON'T SEE SO WELL.
AND NOW I HAVE A CATARACT INSIDE MY ONE GOOD EYE. YOU SEE HOW I HAVE TO SUFFER?
I TOLD YOU ABOUT THE BIG-SHOT SPECIALIST WHAT WAS GOING TO OPERATE ME?
UH-HUH.
HE LAST YEAR PUT ME INTO THE HOSPITAL FOR AN IMMEDIATE OPERATION...
AND THEN HE JUST LEFT ME.. HE WENT SOMEWHERE AWAY TO GIVE LECTURES ON THE TELEVISION!

MY EYE STARTED SO BLEEDING, I HAD TO RUN OUT TO FIND A DOCTOR IN A DIFFERENT HOSPITAL.

THERE ANOTHER SPECIALIST OPERATED RIGHT AWAY! OTHERWISE I COULD HAVE DIED.

SO NOW ITS A GLASS EYE.

HE DID A GOOD JOB, NO? ONE TIME, EVEN, A YOUNG DOCTOR CAME TO MY BED THERE IN THE HOSPITAL....

HE LOOKED WITH A LIGHT A LONG TIME IN MY EYES AND TOLD: "MR. SPIEGELMAN YOUR LEFT EYE IS PERFECT!...

"...BUT IN YOUR RIGHT EYE IS CATARACTS."

HE DIDN'T KNOW, OF COURSE, THAT THE LEFT EYE IS GLASS...

AND I DIDN'T TELL ANYTHING TO HIM. I DIDN'T WANT TO MAKE HIM AN EMBARRASSMENT.

UH-HUH. YOU TOLD ME ABOUT THAT.

WELL, IT'S ENOUGH FOR TODAY, YES? I'M TIRED AND I MUST COUNT STILL MY PILLS.

OKAY, GOOD IDEA... MY HAND IS SORE FROM WRITING ALL THIS DOWN.

CHAPTER THREE

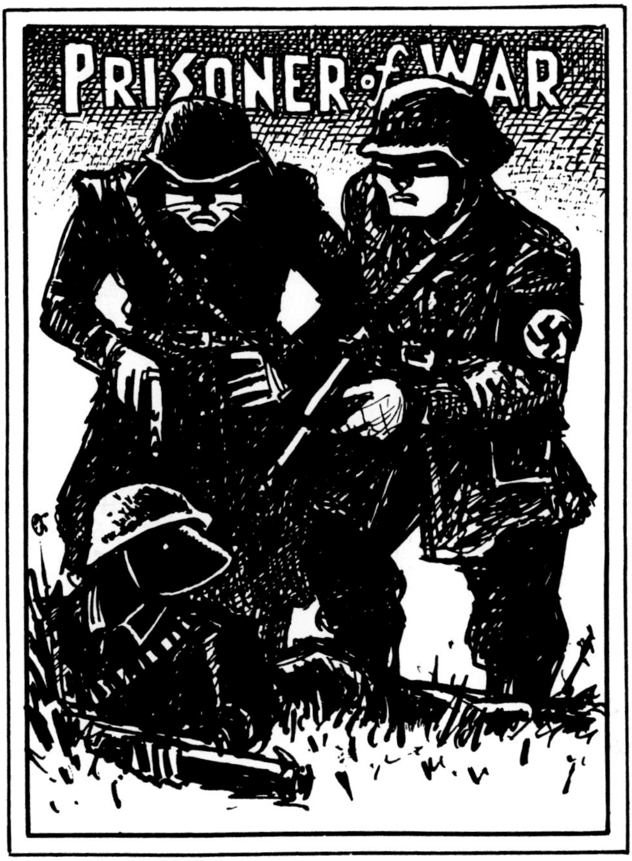
PRISONER of WAR

I visited my father more often in order to get more information about his past..

HAVE SOME MORE GREEN BEANS, ARTIE.

YES, LOOK - YOU DON'T EAT ANYTHING!

NO THANKS. I'VE HAD ENOUGH.

SO FINISH AT LEAST WHAT'S ON YOUR PLATE!

OKAY... OKAY.

Y'KNOW, MALA, WHEN I WAS LITTLE, IF I DIDN'T EAT EVERYTHING MOM SERVED, POP AND I WOULD ARGUE TIL I RAN TO MY ROOM CRYING ...

YOU SHOULD KNOW IT'S IMPOSSIBLE TO ARGUE WITH YOUR FATHER.

...MOM WOULD OFFER TO COOK SOMETHING I LIKED BETTER, BUT POP JUST WANTED TO LEAVE THE LEFTOVER FOOD AROUND UNTIL I ATE IT.

SOMETIMES HE'D EVEN SAVE IT TO SERVE AGAIN AND AGAIN UNTIL I'D EAT IT OR STARVE.

YES! SO IT HAS TO BE. ALWAYS YOU MUST EAT ALL WHAT IS ON YOUR PLATE.

ACCH, VLADEK.

FORTUNATELY FOR ME, MOM WOULD EVENTUALLY FEED ME SOMETHING I LIKED, AND THROW AWAY THE OLD FOOD WHILE YOU WEREN'T LOOKING.

YES. ANJA WAS TOO EASY WITH YOU ALWAYS.

HMMH. THANKS FOR THE DINNER, MALA. IT WAS DELICIOUS.

PFEH—THE CHICKEN WAS, I THOUGHT, TOO DRY. COME, WE'LL TALK BETTER IN THE LIVING ROOM.

OKAY—I'LL GET MY NOTEBOOK.

...I TELL YOU, WITH MALA I DON'T KNOW WHAT TO DO. SHE—

PLEASE, POP! I'D RATHER NOT HEAR ALL THAT AGAIN. TELL ME ABOUT 1939, WHEN YOU WERE DRAFTED.

1939? YES...WE WERE GIVEN ARMY TRAININGS FOR A FEW DAYS AND THEN, BY THE START OF SEPTEMBER WE WERE ON THE FRONTIER.

...WE WERE ALL DIGGED INTO TRENCHES NEAR A RIVER. ON THE OTHER SIDE IT WAS GERMANS.

46

IT WAS EVERYTHING QUIET UNTIL NEAR MORNING...

WAIT A MINUTE. THEY ONLY TRAINED YOU FOR A FEW *DAYS* BEFORE SENDING YOU INTO COMBAT?

WELL, THE *FIRST* TIME I WENT INTO THE ARMY FOR 18 MONTHS WHEN I WAS 21. THEN EVERY 4 YEARS I WENT TO LUBLIN FOR A MONTH TO TRAIN.

YOU KNOW, MY *FATHER* TRIED TO KEEP ALL HIS CHILDREN *OUT* FROM THE ARMY..

..BECAUSE WHEN *HE* WAS YOUNG, HE HAD THEN TO GO INTO THE *RUSSIAN* ARMY. ...AND THERE THEY TOOK YOU FOR 25 YEARS.

...TO SIBERIA!

MY FATHER PULLED OUT 14 OF HIS *TEETH* TO ESCAPE. IF YOU MISSED 12 TEETH THEY LEFT YOU GO.

SO WHEN MY BROTHER *MARCUS* GOT 21 YEARS, FATHER PUT HIM ON A STARVATION DIET. ALWAYS MARCUS WAS SICKLY-SO THIN.

AND WHEN HE WENT FOR THE ARMY EXAMINATION...THEY DIDN'T TAKE HIM.

A YEAR LATER WHEN IT CAME *MY* TURN, FATHER WANTED TO MAKE TO ME THE SAME THING.

IT WAS SOMETHING *TERRIBLE!*...

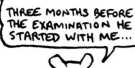 THREE MONTHS BEFORE THE EXAMINATION HE STARTED WITH ME...

WAKE UP, VLADEK! YOU'RE SLEEPING TOO MUCH!

ONLY THREE HOURS A NIGHT?

STOP, VLADEK. YOU MUSTN'T EAT SO MUCH!

BUT I'M HUNGRY!

OKAY—HAVE ONE MORE HERRING.

FOR THREE MONTHS I ATE ONLY SALTED HERRING AND NO WATER TO LOSE WEIGHT.

AND A FEW DAYS BEFORE THE EXAM, *NO* SLEEP AND *NO* FOOD...

GOOD BOY—JUST A LITTLE MORE COFFEE!

ONLY A GALLON COFFEE A DAY FOR MY HEART.

AND WHEN FINALLY I WENT FOR MY MEDICAL EXAMINATION...

HERE'S A HEALTHY ONE.

UM!...

NO...THERE SEEMS TO BE *SOMETHING* WRONG WITH HIM.

BUILD YOURSELF UP FOR A YEAR, YOUNG MAN, AND WE'LL REVIEW YOUR CASE AGAIN.

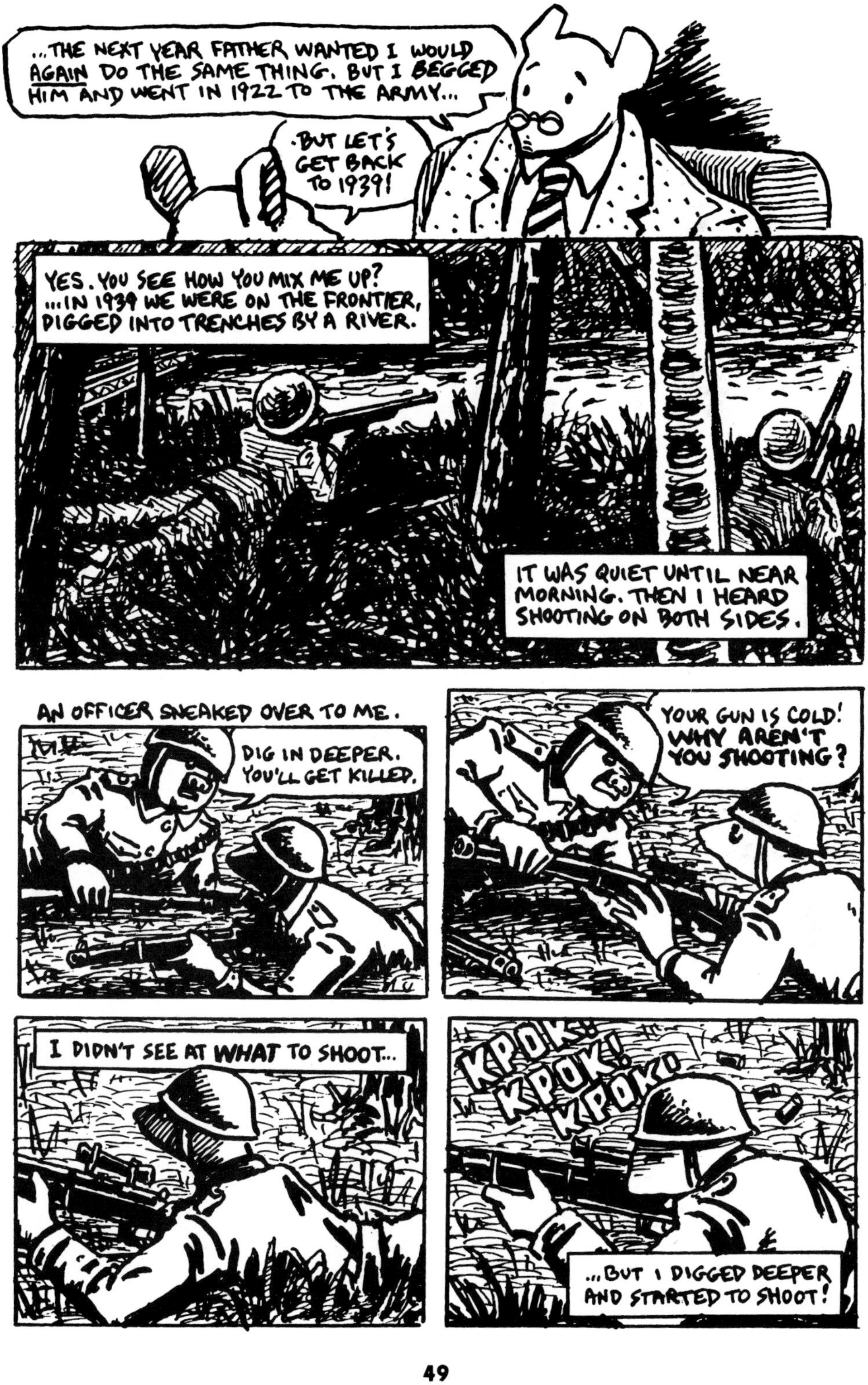
...THE NEXT YEAR FATHER WANTED I WOULD AGAIN DO THE SAME THING. BUT I BEGGED HIM AND WENT IN 1922 TO THE ARMY...
·BUT LET'S GET BACK TO 1939!
YES. YOU SEE HOW YOU MIX ME UP? ...IN 1939 WE WERE ON THE FRONTIER, DIGGED INTO TRENCHES BY A RIVER.
IT WAS QUIET UNTIL NEAR MORNING. THEN I HEARD SHOOTING ON BOTH SIDES.
AN OFFICER SNEAKED OVER TO ME.
DIG IN DEEPER. YOU'LL GET KILLED.
YOUR GUN IS COLD! WHY AREN'T YOU SHOOTING?
I DIDN'T SEE AT WHAT TO SHOOT...
KPOK! KPOK! KPOK!
...BUT I DIGGED DEEPER AND STARTED TO SHOOT!

THEN BULLETS CAME IN MY DIRECTION.

PNNNG

I DUG **DEEPER** MY TRENCH BUT I STOPPED TO SHOOT.

WHY SHOULD I KILL ANYONE?

PWNNG

BUT WHEN I LOOKED IN MY GUN, I SAW... A TREE!///

AND THE TREE WAS ACTUALLY MOVING!

I MUST BE SEEING THINGS. HOW CAN A TREE RUN?

WELL, IF IT MOVED, I HAD TO SHOOT!

AKH!

PNG

IT HELD UP A HAND TO SHOW IT WAS HURT. TO SURRENDER.

BUT I KEPT SHOOTING AND SHOOTING. UNTIL FINALLY THE TREE STOPPED MOVING. WHO KNOWS; OTHERWISE HE COULD HAVE SHOT ME!

AFTER TWO HOURS OF FIGHTING, THE NAZIS OVERCAME OUR SIDE OF THE RIVER.

GET UP!

GIVE ME YOUR GUN!

IT'S HOT! YOU WERE SHOOTING AT US!

MY COMMANDER MADE ME SHOOT. I ONLY FIRED IN THE AIR!

I ANSWERED IN GERMAN AND HIS PARTNER STOPPED HIM FROM BEATING ME.

THEY MARCHED ME TO WHERE IT WAS MORE LIKE ME. WAR PRISONERS.

AND ALL FROM US WHAT WEREN'T INJURED THEY MARCHED OVER TO THEIR SIDE OF THE RIVER TO LOOK FOR DEAD SOLDIERS.

ATTENTION! ALL PRISONERS WILL CARRY OUR DEAD AND WOUNDED TO THE WAITING RED CROSS TRUCKS.

YOU! WHERE DO YOU THINK YOU'RE GOING?

I-I THOUGHT I SAW A BODY OVER BY THE RIVER!

I KNEW WHERE THE ONE I SHOT SHOULD BE LAYING.

YES. HERE!

ER VERBLUTETE! HIS BLOOD RAN OUT! CARRY HIM OVER TO THE TRUCK WITH THE OTHERS.

HIS NAME WAS JAN...

... AND I KNEW THAT I KILLED HIM.

AND I SAID TO MYSELF: "WELL, AT LEAST I DID SOMETHING."

52

THEY TOOK US TO A PLACE NEAR NUREMBERG WHERE IT WAS **MANY** WAR PRISONERS. THE JEWS THEY MADE TO STAND SEPARATE.

IT'S ALL **YOUR** FAULT, THIS WAR!

WE SHOULD **HANG** YOU RIGHT HERE ON THIS SPOT!

OF COURSE, NOBODY OF US SAID A WORD.

PUT DOWN ALL YOUR VALUABLES!

HE CAME UP TO ME... I HAD MAYBE 300 ZLOTYS.

WHY SO MUCH MONEY, JEW?

MANY OTHERS HAD ONLY 5 OR 6 ZLOTYS.

DO YOU EXPECT TO DO SOME **BUSINESS** HERE? SHOW ME YOUR HANDS!

YOU NEVER WORKED A DAY IN YOUR LIFE!

LIKE YOU, ARTIE, MY HANDS WERE ALWAYS VERY DELICATE.

WELL, JEW, DON'T WORRY. WE'LL FIND WORK FOR YOU!

AND THEY DID.

53

ANOTHER GERMAN TOOK 4 OR 5 FROM US TO A STABLE.

SEE THIS MESS? IT BETTER BE SPOTLESSLY CLEAN IN ONE HOUR. UNDERSTAND!

IT WAS IMPOSSIBLE TO DO IT IN ONE HOUR!

WE REALLY WORKED VERY HARD. BUT, AN HOUR LATER...

SO!

NOT FINISHED YET?

THIS WILL COST YOU YOUR *SOUP,* YOU LAZY BASTARDS!

AND SOMEHOW WE *DID* MAKE THE JOB IN ONLY AN HOUR AND A *HALF.* BUT LOOK WHAT YOU DO, ARTIE!

HUH?

YOU'RE DROPPING ON THE CARPET CIGARETTE ASHES. YOU WANT IT SHOULD BE LIKE A STABLE *HERE?*

OOPS. SORRY.

CLEAN IT, YES? OTHERWISE *I* HAVE TO DO IT. MALA COULD LET IT SIT LIKE THIS FOR A *WEEK* AND NEVER TOUCH IT.

AND SHE *KNOWS* HOW WITH MY SICKNESSES IT'S HARD NOW FOR ME TO DO SUCH THINGS.

OKAY, OKAY. IT'S CLEAN.

SO WE LIVED AND WORKED A FEW WEEKS IN THE STABLE UNTIL THEY TOOK US TO AN EVEN *BIGGER* PRISONER OF WAR CAMP.

BRRR. THE POLISH PRISONERS GET *HEATED* CABINS.

YES, AND WE'RE JUST LEFT TO FREEZE IN THESE TENTS.

IT WAS TERRIBLE COLD THAT AUTUMN. ALL OVER EUROPE IT WAS SO FREEZING THAT BIRDS FELL FROM TREES.

TO KEEP WARM WE HAD ONLY OUR SUMMER UNIFORMS AND A THIN BLANKET.

AT LEAST IF THEY GAVE US ENOUGH TO EAT.

THE OTHER PRISONERS GET *TWO* MEALS A DAY. WE JEWS GET ONLY A CRUST OF BREAD AND A LITTLE SOUP.

GOOD MORNING, VLADEK.

WHERE ARE YOU GOING?

TO BATHE IN THE RIVER.

YOU'VE GONE CRAZY.

BRRR I'LL BE *CLEAN!* AND I'LL FEEL WARM ALL DAY BY COMPARISON.

MANY OTHERS GOT FROSTBITE WOUNDS. IN THE WOUNDS WAS PUS, AND IN THE PUS WAS LICE.

55

EVERY DAY I BATHED AND DID GYMNASTICS TO KEEP STRONG. ...AND EVERY DAY WE PRAYED.

מה-טבו אהליך יעקב, משבנתיך ישראל.

I WAS VERY RELIGIOUS, AND IT WASN'T ELSE TO DO.

OFTEN WE PLAYED CHESS TO KEEP OUR MINDS BUSY AND MAKE THE TIME GO.

I HAD A SET MADE FROM STONES AND BREAD CRUMBS.

AND ONE TIME A WEEK WE COULD WRITE LETTERS THROUGH THE INTERNATIONAL RED CROSS.

Dear Anja. I am fine. I miss you.

ONLY IN GERMAN. AND VERY CAREFUL.

AND THROUGH THIS IT CAME A PACKAGE...

CHOCOLATE BARS! CIGARETTES! JAM!

IT WAS SO TREASURING FOR ME THIS PACKAGE.

I HAD A SIGN MY FAMILY WAS SAFE, AND—BECAUSE I NEVER SMOKED—I HAD CIGARETTES TO TRADE FOR FOOD.

AND SO THINGS WENT FOR MAYBE SIX WEEKS, THEN...

LOOK! THERE'S AN ANNOUNCE-MENT OUTSIDE!

WORKERS NEEDED
War Prisoners may volunteer for labor assignments to replace German workers called to the front. Housing and abundant food will be supplied.

IT'S A TRICK!

NEVER VOLUNTEER!

IF WE HAVE TO DIE, LET'S DIE HERE!

NO!

I DIDN'T AGREE!

I'M NOT GOING TO DIE, AND I WON'T DIE HERE! I WANT TO BE TREATED LIKE A HUMAN BEING!

56

WHEN MY COMRADES SAW I WAS GOING, THEY TOO REGISTERED.

WE WERE RIGHT AWAY SENT TO A BIG GERMAN COMPANY.

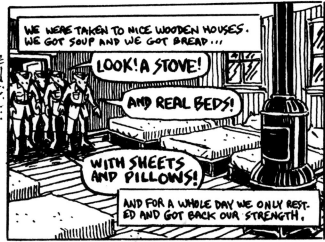

WE WERE TAKEN TO NICE WOODEN HOUSES. WE GOT SOUP AND WE GOT BREAD...

LOOK! A STOVE!

AND REAL BEDS!

WITH SHEETS AND PILLOWS!

AND FOR A WHOLE DAY WE ONLY RESTED AND GOT BACK OUR STRENGTH.

AH— IT SEEMS LIKE YEARS SINCE I'VE FELT WARM OR BEEN IN A BED!

YES—FUNNY, ISN'T IT? IT'S ONLY A LITTLE OVER 2 MONTHS SINCE WE WERE DRAFTED.

I'M WORRIED THOUGH, VLADEK—WHO KNOWS WHAT KIND OF WORK THEY'LL GIVE US.

IT DOESN'T MATTER..

..ANYTHING IS BETTER THAN ROTTING IN THOSE TENTS.

I SUPPOSE.

THE NEXT DAY WE WERE GIVEN SHOVELS AND PICKS ...

...THINGS WHAT WE NEVER HELD IN OUR HANDS BEFORE.

57

AND THE WORK WAS REALLY VERY HARD—WE HAD TO MOVE MOUNTAINS.

MOUNTAIN

VALLEY

THE HILLS WERE MAYBE 3 OR 4 YARDS HIGH. WE HAD TO MAKE IT LEVEL.

SOME COMPLAINED — THOSE WHAT WERE TOO OLD OR WEAK FOR SUCH WORK:

I-I CANT TAKE ANYMORE.

WORTHLESS JEW!

IF YOU'RE UNHAPPY—GO BACK TO THE P.O.W. CAMP.

IT'S OKAY—WE'LL HELP YOU WHEN NO ONE IS LOOKING.

WE TRIED TO HELP, BUT—WHAT YOU THINK?—SOME WENT BACK TO THE TENTS TO FREEZE AND TO STARVE.

BUT WHAT HAPPENED TO THEM, I DON'T KNOW.

STILL, EIGHTY PER CENT STAYED. THERE WAS ENOUGH TO EAT, AND A WARM BED. IT WAS BETTER TO STAY...

...ALWAYS I WENT TO SLEEP EXHAUSTED. AND ONE NIGHT I HAD A DREAM...

A VOICE WAS TALKING TO ME. IT WAS, I THINK, MY DEAD GRANDFATHER...

"DON'T WORRY...

"...DON'T WORRY, MY CHILD...

IT WAS SO REAL, THIS VOICE...

"YOU WILL COME OUT OF THIS PLACE — FREE! ...ON THE DAY OF PARSHAS TRUMA."

I WOKE UP RIGHT AWAY. AND WHEN I WENT TO SLEEP, AGAIN IT WAS: "PARSHAS TRUMA! PARSHAS TRUMA!"

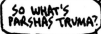

SO WHAT'S PARSHAS TRUMA?

EACH WEEK, ON SATURDAY, WE READ A SECTION FROM THE TORAH.

THIS IS SO CALLED — A PARSHA... AND ONE WEEK EACH YEAR IT IS PARSHAS TRUMA.

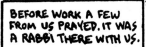

BEFORE WORK A FEW FROM US PRAYED. IT WAS A RABBI THERE WITH US.

ONE MOMENT, RABBI. WHEN WILL WE READ PARSHAS TRUMA?

PARSHAS TRUMA?...

...IN THE MIDDLE OF FEBRUARY — ALMOST THREE MONTHS FROM NOW. WHY?

THREE MONTHS — AND EVERY DAY WAS FOR US A YEAR!

I TOLD HIM MY DREAM...

LET'S HOPE IT'S TRUE. I'M AFRAID WE'LL NEVER GET OUT OF HERE.

59

SO WE WORKED, DAY AFTER DAY. WE SURVIVED. WEEK AFTER WEEK. THE SAME.

UNTIL, ONE TIME...

LOOK— SOLDIERS!

IT CAME VERY MANY GESTAPO AND WEHRMACHT.

ATTENTION! LINE UP ON THE ROAD IN TWO ROWS! IMMEDIATELY!

WE WERE NOT AT EASE. WE DIDN'T KNOW WHAT THEY COULD DO WITH US.

I STOOD ALWAYS IN THE SECOND LINE.

(PSST— VLADEK.)

I DIDN'T WANT THEY SHOULD SEE ME MUCH.

SOMEONE SNEAKED NEXT TO ME...

RABBI! DO YOU KNOW WHAT DAY IT IS?

SATURDAY, OF COURSE.

BUT DO YOU KNOW WHAT A SATURDAY?...

IT'S PARSHAS TRUMA!

60

THEY MARCHED US TO THE MAIN COURTYARD AND LINED US BY ALPHABET AT TABLES...

NAME AND RANK?

SPIEGELMAN, VLADEK. CORPORAL.

DESTINATION UPON RELEASE?

SOSNOWIEC...

THIS THE GERMANS DID VERY GOOD...

...TO MY WIFE AND CHILD.

...ALWAYS THEY DID EVERY-THING VERY SYSTEMATIC.

VERY WELL—SIGN THIS RELEASE FORM.

...AND IT WAS ALL DONE IN ONE DAY.

YOU MEAN YOUR 'PARSHAS TRUMA' DREAM ACTUALLY CAME TRUE?

YES—THIS IS FOR ME A VERY IM-PORTANT DATE...

I CHECKED LATER ON A CALENDAR. IT WAS THIS PARSHA ON THE WEEK I GOT MARRIED TO ANJA.

...AND THIS WAS THE PARSHA IN 1948, AFTER THE WAR, ON THE WEEK YOU WERE BORN!...

AND SO IT CAME OUT TO BE THIS PARSHA YOU SANG ON THE SATURDAY OF YOUR BAR MITZVAH!

THE NEXT MORNING EACH FROM US GOT A RED CROSS PACKAGE, AND THEY LOADED US ON A TRAIN TO POLAND.

DURING THE JOURNEY I SAT WITH THE RABBI.

SO, MY SON. NOW I SEE YOU ARE A "ROH-EH HANOLED," ONE WHO SEES WHAT THE FUTURE WILL BRING.

HEY! THIS TRAIN SEEMS TO BE PASSING SOSNOWIEC!

WHEN THEY DIDN'T STOP THE TRAIN I BECAME VERY WORRIED.

YOU SEE, THE NAZIS DIVIDED POLAND INTO PIECES: PROTECTORATE AND REICH, WITH A GUARDED BORDER BETWEEN.

BALTIC SEA
LITHUANIA
E. PRUSSIA
(annexed to Russia)
GERMANY
P O L A N D
WARSAW
LUBLIN
SOSNOWIEC
KRAKOW
SLOVAKIA
HUNGARY
SOVIET UNION
RUMANIA

REICH: Annexed to Germany.
PROTECTORATE: German controlled Government.

THE TRAIN WENT COMPLETELY PAST MY PART OF POLAND—THE REICH—AND STOPPED ONLY IN THE PROTECTORATE.

THOSE WITH PAPERS FOR KRAKOW—OUT!

AND, WHEN IT STOPPED IN WARSAW, THE RABBI GOT OUT.

I'LL WRITE TO YOU.

BUT I NEVER HEARD AGAIN FROM HIM. IT CAME SUCH A MISERY IN WARSAW, ALMOST NONE SURVIVED.

AND THE TRAIN WAS A LONG WAY PAST SOSNOWIEC. THEY TOOK ME UP, UP, VERY FAR—MAYBE 300 MILES—UNTIL WE CAME TO LUBLIN. THERE THEY UNLOADED ALL OF US FROM THE REICH.

IN LUBLIN, THEY TOOK US TO BIG TENTS..

AND THERE WE SAT.

EVENTUALLY CAME SOME PEOPLE TO SEE US FROM THE JEWISH AUTHORITIES...

WHY ARE WE BEING KEPT HERE?

IT'S A VERY BAD SITUA- TION... JUST BEFORE YOU ARRIVED, THERE WAS ANOTHER GROUP OF RE- LEASED WAR PRISONERS...

...TWO DAYS AGO THE NAZIS MARCHED THEM TO A FOREST,...

...AND THEY SHOT ALL OF THEM—THEY KILLED 600 PEOPLE!

WE WERE THE NEXT PARTY!

I THOUGHT YOU WERE *RELEASED* AS A PRISONER OF WAR!

EXACTLY SO..

INTERNATIONAL LAWS PROTECTED US A LITTLE AS POLISH WAR PRISONERS. BUT A JEW OF THE REICH, ANY- ONE COULD KILL IN THE STREETS!

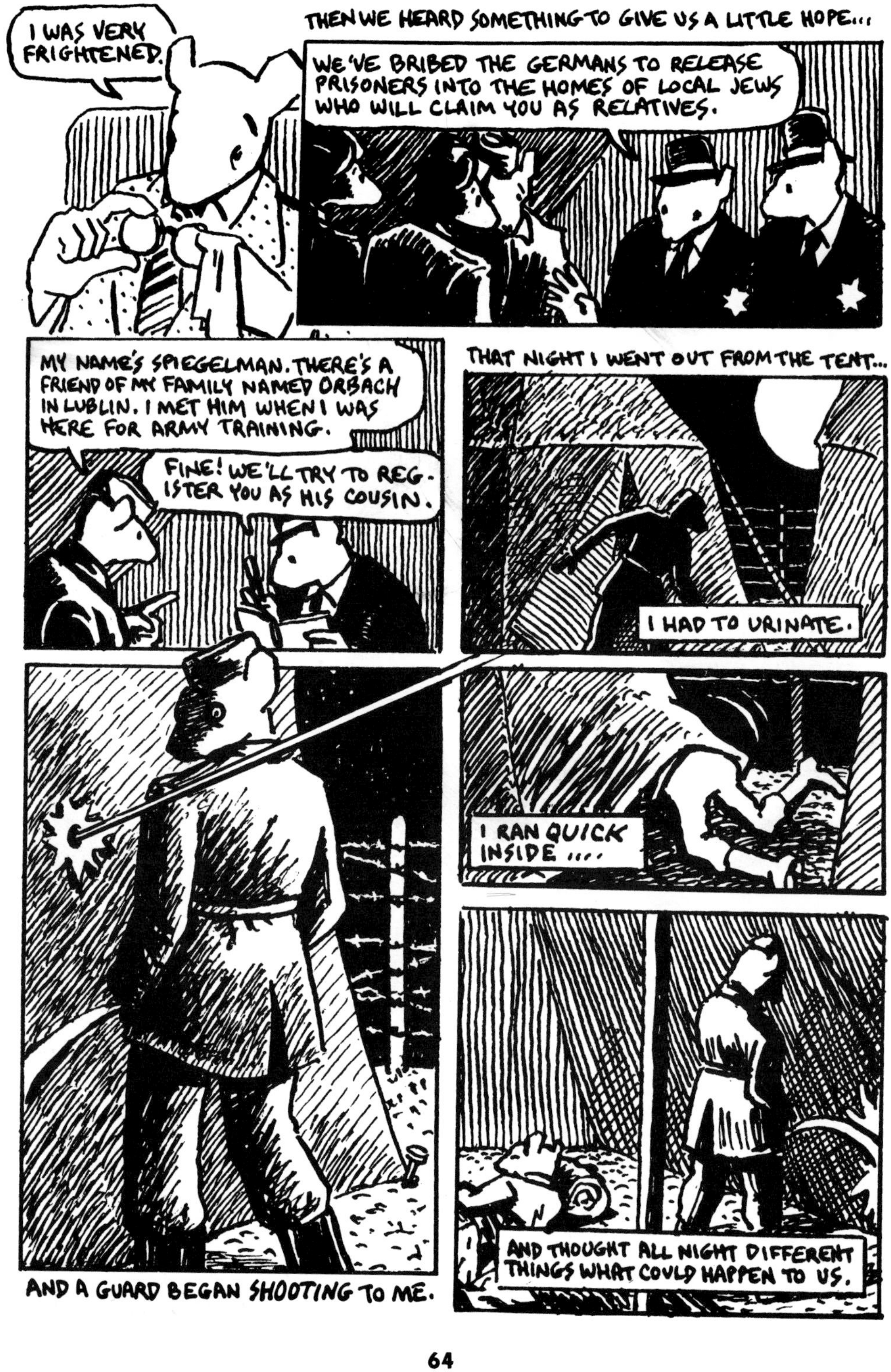
I WAS VERY FRIGHTENED.
THEN WE HEARD SOMETHING TO GIVE US A LITTLE HOPE...
WE'VE BRIBED THE GERMANS TO RELEASE PRISONERS INTO THE HOMES OF LOCAL JEWS WHO WILL CLAIM YOU AS RELATIVES.
MY NAME'S SPIEGELMAN. THERE'S A FRIEND OF MY FAMILY NAMED ORBACH IN LUBLIN. I MET HIM WHEN I WAS HERE FOR ARMY TRAINING.
FINE! WE'LL TRY TO REGISTER YOU AS HIS COUSIN.
THAT NIGHT I WENT OUT FROM THE TENT...
I HAD TO URINATE.
AND A GUARD BEGAN SHOOTING TO ME.
I RAN QUICK INSIDE ....
AND THOUGHT ALL NIGHT DIFFERENT THINGS WHAT COULD HAPPEN TO US.

THEN, AS SOON AS IT WAS LIGHT.

SPIEGELMAN!.. SPIEGELMAN!..

VLADEK!

ORBACH! AM I GLAD TO SEE YOU!

AND IN TEN MINUTES, I WAS FREE!

ORBACH WAS A FRIEND FROM MY UNCLE- HE HAD TWO BEAUTIFUL DAUGHTERS NEAR TO MY AGE.

I'M SORRY WE CAN'T OFFER YOU A BETTER MEAL, VLADEK - BUT THE JEWS OF LUBLIN GET VERY FEW FOOD COUPONS.

ONE MOMENT, GIRLS- I HAVE A GIFT FOR EACH OF YOU....

OH MY GOD! CHOCOLATE!

THESE I SAVED FROM A RED CROSS PACKAGE. ALWAYS I SAVED.... JUST IN CASE!

EVENTUALLY, WHEN I CAME AGAIN TO SOSNO-WIEC, WE SENT THEM FOOD PACKAGES...

...WE WERE FOR A WHILE A LITTLE BETTER OFF... AND THEY WROTE BACK VERY HAPPY HOW IT HELPED SURVIVE THEM...

...THEN THEY WROTE THAT THE GERMANS WERE KEEPING THE PACKAGES. AND THEN THEY STOPPED TO WRITE. FINISHED.

WITH ORBACHS' I STAYED A FEW DAYS RECUPERATING. BUT I WAS RESTLESS. HOW COULD I MANAGE TO SNEAK ACROSS THE BORDER TO MY FAMILY?

65

TRAINS WERE STILL GOING FROM PROTECTORATE TO REICH. ONLY, ONE NEEDED LEGAL PAPERS. OF COURSE, THIS I DIDN'T HAVE ...

...BUT ANYWAY I GOT ON THE TRAIN IN THE DIRECTION I WANTED.

I APPROACHED TO THE TRAIN MAN, A POLE...

MAY I TALK TO YOU FOR A MOMENT?

SURE, SOLDIER.

I STILL HAD ON MY ARMY UNIFORM, AND I DIDN'T LET KNOW I WAS A JEW.

YOU'RE A POLE LIKE ME, SO I CAN TRUST YOU...THE STINKING NAZIS HAD ME IN A WAR PRISON...I JUST ESCAPED.

THE POLES WERE VERY BITTER ON THE GERMANS, SO IT WAS GOOD TO SPEAK BAD OF THEM.

I'M TRYING TO GET TO SOSNOWIEC — BACK TO MY FAMILY.

DON'T WORRY... WHEN WE GET TO THE BORDER, HIDE IN HERE.

AND SO THE TRAIN MAN HELPED ME COME BACK TO MY SIDE OF POLAND.

I WALKED FIRST OVER TO MY PARENTS' HOUSE...

...WHAT I THOUGHT I MIGHT NEVER SEE AGAIN.

OY GEVALT! IT'S VLADEK!

MY SON! THANK GOD YOU'RE SAFE!

AND IN SPITE OF EVERYTHING, YOU LOOK HEALTHY!

I'M STRONG, MOTHER. BUT *YOU* LOOK SICK!

IT'S BECAUSE I WAS WORRIED ABOUT YOU.

BUT IT WASN'T ONLY THIS. SHE WAS SICK OF CANCER.

...AND A MONTH OR TWO LATER, SHE DIED. SHE NEVER KNEW HOW TERRIBLE EVERYTHING WOULD SOON BE!

—AND, FATHER! YOUR BEARD! WHAT HAPPENED? YOU SHAVED IT OFF?!??

IT'S GROWING BACK, NOW...

HE WAS VERY RELIGIOUS—SO LIKE A RABBI—AND, OF COURSE, HE ALWAYS HAD A BIG BEARD.

IN SEPTEMBER THE GERMAN SOLDIERS GRABBED MANY JEWS IN THE STREET...

THEY MADE US SING PRAYERS WHILE THEY LAUGHED AND BEAT US.

...AND BEFORE LETTING US GO, THEY CUT OFF OUR BEARDS.

AND NOW THE DEMONS HAVE TAKEN AWAY MY SELTZER FACTORY. THEY—

ENOUGH!

I MUST BRING VLADEK HOME TO ANJA BEFORE CURFEW.

AT 7:00 IT WAS A RULE. ALL JEWS HAD TO BE IN THEIR HOME AND ALL LIGHTS OUT.

FROM MY PARENTS' TO SOSNOWIEC WAS ONLY A SHORT RIDE.

GO IN AND SAY YOU JUST GOT A LETTER FROM ME SAYING I'D BE HOME IN A WEEK.

I STOOD AT THE DOOR, LISTENING...

DON'T JOKE! IF VLADEK WAS COMING HOME, HE'D HAVE WRITTEN TO US TOO!

SURPRISE!

OH MY GOD.

VLADEK!

I GRABBED MY SON. HE WAS 2½ YEARS.

RICHIEU!

BWAAH

HE STARTED SCREAMING.

WHY DO YOU CRY, MY BOY? I'M YOUR FATHER!

WAH

:SNF: TH' BUTTONS, YOUR METAL BUTTONS, DADDY—THEY'RE COLD!

AND I DON'T NEED TO TELL YOU HOW BIG THE JOY WAS IN OUR HOUSE.

EVEN THOUGH EVERYTHING WAS VERY TOUGH—AND IT WAS REALLY VERY TOUGH—WE WERE HAPPY ONLY TO BE TOGETHER.

..NOT SO LIKE IT IS NOW WITH ME AND MALA.

I TELL YOU, IF ANJA COULD BE ALIVE NOW, IT WOULD BE EVERYTHING DIFFERENT WITH ME!

MALA MAKES ME CRAZY. ONLY SHE TALKS ABOUT MONEY. ALWAYS ABOUT MY WILL—

PLEASE, POP! ...

YOU ALWAYS TELL ME THE SAME THINGS. THERE'S NOTHING I CAN DO.

BUT I HAVEN'T WITH WHOM ELSE TO TALK!

AND IT'S FOR YOU I WATCH OUT MY MONEY!

JEEZ—LET'S TALK ABOUT IT NEXT TIME. I'LL CALL YOU!

BESIDES, IT'S GETTING LATE. I OUGHTA GET HOME BEFORE CURFEW!

HMF.

HEY—WHERE'S MY COAT? I KNOW I PUT IT IN HERE!

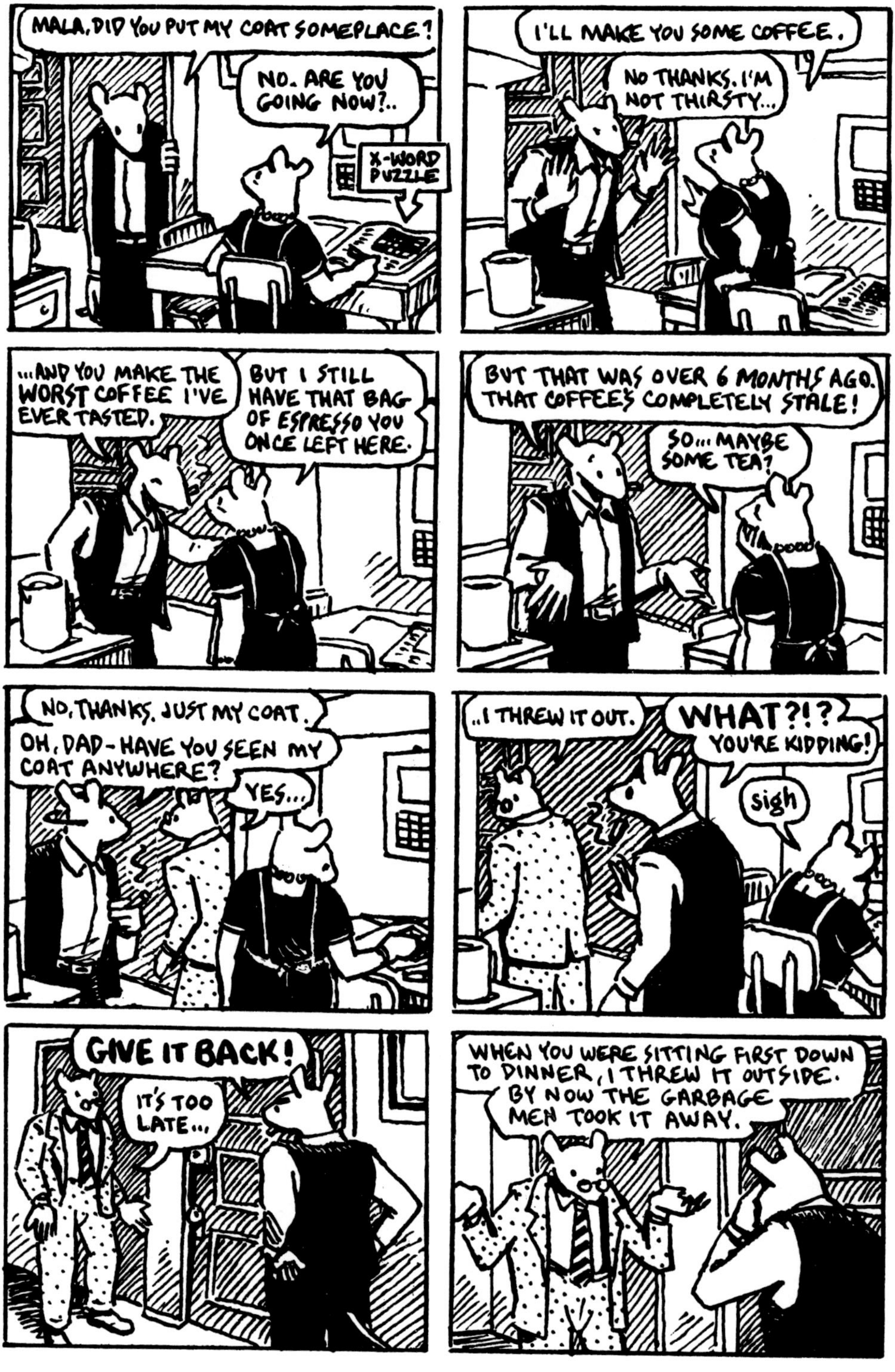
MALA, DID YOU PUT MY COAT SOMEPLACE?
NO. ARE YOU GOING NOW?..
X-WORD PUZZLE
I'LL MAKE YOU SOME COFFEE.
NO THANKS. I'M NOT THIRSTY...
...AND YOU MAKE THE WORST COFFEE I'VE EVER TASTED.
BUT I STILL HAVE THAT BAG OF ESPRESSO YOU ONCE LEFT HERE.
BUT THAT WAS OVER 6 MONTHS AGO. THAT COFFEE'S COMPLETELY STALE!
SO... MAYBE SOME TEA?
NO, THANKS. JUST MY COAT.
OH, DAD - HAVE YOU SEEN MY COAT ANYWHERE?
YES...
..I THREW IT OUT.
WHAT?!?
YOU'RE KIDDING!
sigh
GIVE IT BACK!
IT'S TOO LATE...
WHEN YOU WERE SITTING FIRST DOWN TO DINNER, I THREW IT OUTSIDE.
BY NOW THE GARBAGE MEN TOOK IT AWAY.

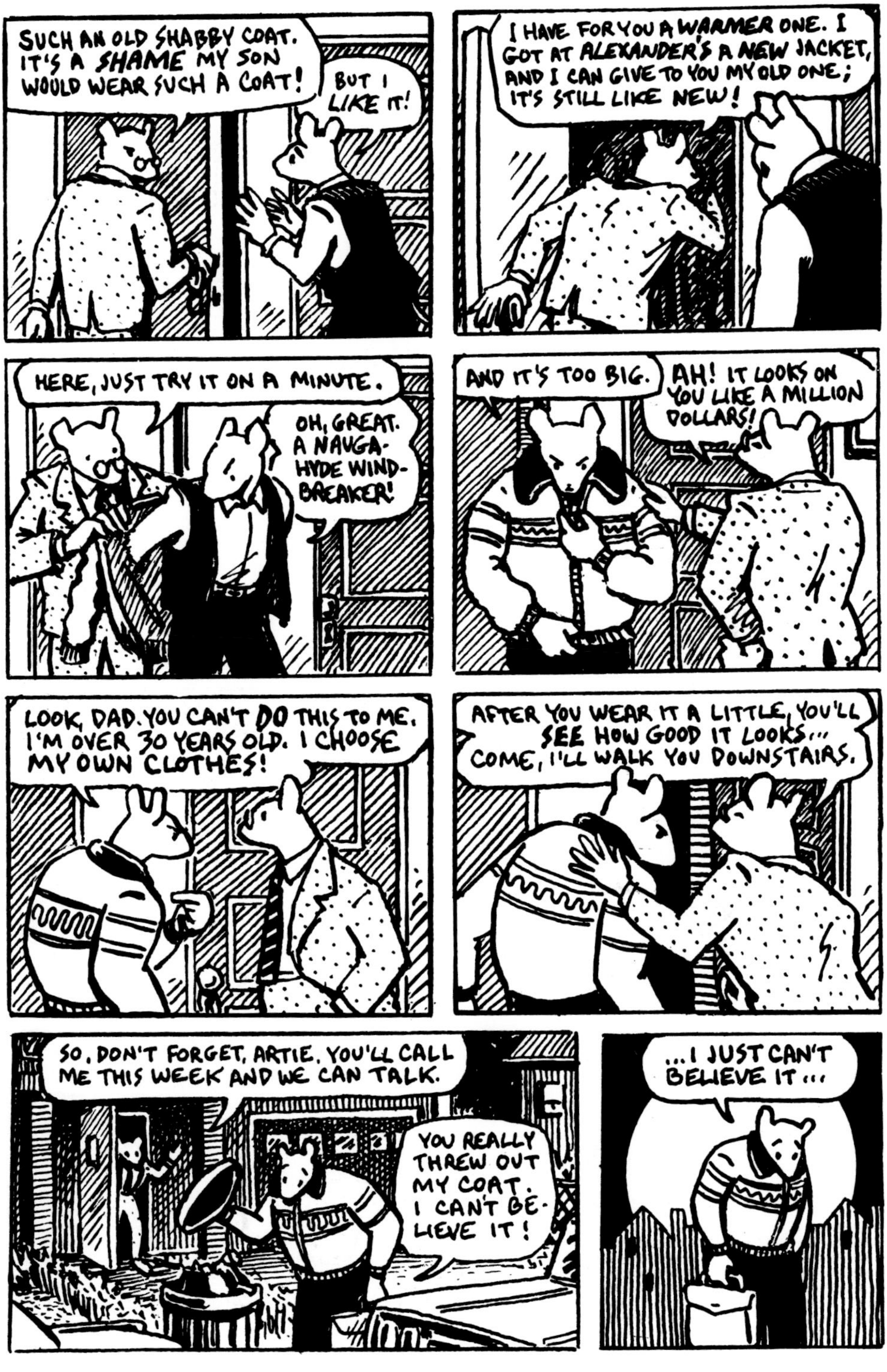
SUCH AN OLD SHABBY COAT. IT'S A SHAME MY SON WOULD WEAR SUCH A COAT!
BUT I LIKE IT!
I HAVE FOR YOU A WARMER ONE. I GOT AT ALEXANDER'S A NEW JACKET, AND I CAN GIVE TO YOU MY OLD ONE; IT'S STILL LIKE NEW!
HERE, JUST TRY IT ON A MINUTE.
OH, GREAT. A NAUGA-HYDE WIND-BREAKER!
AND IT'S TOO BIG.
AH! IT LOOKS ON YOU LIKE A MILLION DOLLARS!
LOOK, DAD. YOU CAN'T DO THIS TO ME. I'M OVER 30 YEARS OLD. I CHOOSE MY OWN CLOTHES!
AFTER YOU WEAR IT A LITTLE, YOU'LL SEE HOW GOOD IT LOOKS... COME, I'LL WALK YOU DOWNSTAIRS.
SO, DON'T FORGET, ARTIE, YOU'LL CALL ME THIS WEEK AND WE CAN TALK.
YOU REALLY THREW OUT MY COAT. I CAN'T BE-LIEVE IT!
...I JUST CAN'T BELIEVE IT...

CHAPTER FOUR

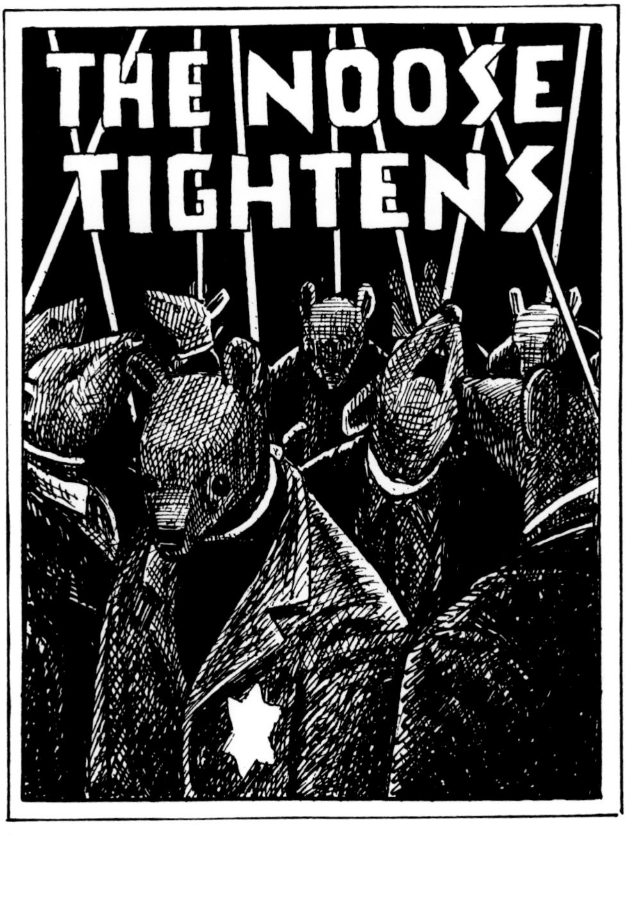
THE NOOSE
TIGHTENS

WOODEN HANGER

YOU'RE LATE!

NO I'M NOT—I *SAID* I'D BE BY AFTER DINNER.

NEW TRENCH COAT.

BUT NOW IS DARK OUT! I WANTED YOU WOULD CLIMB TO THE ROOF—IT'S A LEAK IN THE DRAIN PIPE.

HUH?

BUT I'M NO GOOD AT FIXING THAT KIND OF STUFF. WHY DON'T YOU *HIRE* SOMEBODY?

ACH!

YOU AND MALA! YOU BOTH THINK MONEY GROWS ON BUSHES. I'LL FIX IT MYSELF!

THAT'S CRAZY! YOU CAN'T CLIMB A TWO-STORY LADDER IN YOUR CONDITION ....

IF YOU WANT, I'LL PAY FOR THE HANDYMAN.

NEVER MIND—FORGET I SAID ANYTHING! .... JUST COME SIT WITH ME. I HAVE TO PEDAL ...

OTHERWISE I GET AT NIGHT A LEG CRAMP— *WHAT YOU'RE HOLDING?*

A NEW TAPE RECORDER ... WRITING THINGS DOWN IS JUST TOO HARD.

SO, HOW MUCH YOU PAID?

ONLY 75 BUCKS! IT WAS ON SALE.

PSSH, AT **KORVETTES** YOU COULD FIND IT FOR —MAXIMUM— $35.00.

BUT— SKIP IT! TELL ME ABOUT WHEN YOU GOT BACK FROM THE P.O.W. CAMP IN 1940 ...

WHEN FIRST I CAME HOME IT LOOKED EXACTLY SO AS BEFORE I WENT AWAY....

IT WAS STILL VERY LUXURIOUS. THE GERMANS COULDN'T DESTROY EVERYTHING AT ONE TIME.

IT WAS TWELVE OF US LIVING IN FATHER-IN-LAW'S HOUSEHOLD...

IT WAS ANJA AND ME, AND OUR BOY, RICHIEU...

ANJA'S OLDER SISTER, TOSHA, HER HUSBAND, WOLFÉ, AND THEIR LITTLE GIRL, BIBI...

AND IT WAS ANJA'S GRAND-PARENTS. THEY HAD MAYBE 90 YEARS, BUT VERY ALERT..

AND, OF COURSE, IT WAS MY FATHER-IN-LAW AND MY MOTHER-IN-LAW...

AND ALSO THE 2 KIDS FROM YOUR UNCLE HERMAN AND AUNT HELEN: LOLEK AND LONIA

HERMAN AND HELA WERE LUCKY. THEY WERE VISIT-ING THE N.Y. WORLD'S FAIR WHEN THE WAR CAME.

THIS SAVED THEM.

AH, GRANDMOTHER — YOUR STEW IS EVEN TASTIER THAN I REMEMBERED.

NO — IT'S NOT LIKE BEFORE THE WAR, VLADEK — I CAN'T GET THE FOODS I NEED.

EACH OF US GETS COUPONS FOR 8 OUNCES OF BREAD A DAY, AND A TINY BIT OF MARGARINE, SUGAR AND JAM PER WEEK. THAT'S ALL!

SO HOW DO WE MANAGE?

I'VE DONATED A LOT TO THE GEMEINDE — THE JEWISH COMMUNITY ORGANIZATION — AND WOLFE WORKS THERE... SO WE GET A LITTLE EXTRA.

AND THERE'S THE BLACK MARKET.

WITH MONEY YOU CAN ALWAYS GET ANYTHING!

IT'S DANGEROUS, THOUGH. THE NAZIS TAKE YOU OFF TO A WORK CAMP FOR BREAKING ANY MINOR LAW.

WORSE — EVEN IF YOU DON'T BREAK ANY LAWS!

...AND THOSE THAT ARE TAKEN AWAY — THEY'RE NEVER SEEN AGAIN!

WELL, WE SHOULD BE HAPPY WE'RE ALL TOGETHER WITH ENOUGH TO EAT.

BUT WE MUST REALLY TIGHTEN OUR BELTS UNTIL THE WAR ENDS.

COME - LET'S PLAY RUMMY WHILE THE LADIES CLEAR THE TABLE.

HAS THE FAMILY BEEN TAKING GOOD CARE OF MY BIELSKO TEXTILE FACTORY?

DON'T YOU KNOW? ...ALL JEWISH BUSINESSES HAVE BEEN TAKEN OVER BY "ARYAN MANAGERS"...

I WENT TO OUR FACTORY IN LODZ, AND THEY SAID, "BETTER GO HOME TODAY, OLD MAN...TOMORROW WE'LL CARRY YOU OUT.

WHAT?

BUT ISN'T ANY MONEY COMING IN?

NOT A SINGLE ZLOTY. AND THE FAMILY WANTS TO LIVE THE WAY IT DID BEFORE THE WAR!

OKAY, VLADEK - CUT THE CARDS.

BUT, WOLFE - WHAT KIND OF WORK ARE YOU DOING?

JUST A LITTLE OFFICE WORK FOR THE GEMEINDE ... BUT A FEW MONTHS AGO FATHER-IN-LAW TOOK ALL HIS VALUABLES HOME FROM THE BANK SAFE.

HOW LONG CAN SAVINGS LAST?

DON'T WORRY SO MUCH, VLADEK. YOU'LL SEE ... THE WAR WILL BE OVER LIKE LIGHTNING!

JA! LIKE LIGHTNING!

ACH!

WOLFE LOOKED ONLY TO PLAY CARDS.

I WENT THE NEXT DAY TO MODRZEJOWSKA STREET. HERE PEOPLE STILL MADE MONEY, FROM *SECRET* BUSINESSES... NOT SO LEGAL...

(PSST—FOOD COUPONS FOR REICHSMARKS?)

VLADEK SPIEGELMAN!

MR. ILZECKI! WHAT ARE YOU DOING IN SOSNOWIEC?

ILZECKI USED TO BE A CUSTOMER OF MINE. THE BEST TAILOR IN KATOWICE.

THE NAZIS MOVED ME TO AN APARTMENT HERE. I MAKE UNIFORMS FOR THEIR OFFICERS... AND SUITS ON THE SIDE WHEN I CAN GET THE CLOTH.

ARE YOU STILL IN BUSINESS?

I DON'T KNOW. I *JUST* GOT BACK FROM WAR PRISON.

WELL, IF YOU GET ANY CLOTH, COME SEE ME. THIS NOTE WILL GET YOU PAST THE DOORMAN.

THE NOTE TOLD THAT I WORKED WITH HIM. SUCH A PAPER COULD BE USEFUL TO HAVE.

I WENT THEN TO SHOPS WHAT STILL OWED ME MONEY FROM BEFORE THE WAR...

BUT I *CAN'T* PAY YOU! A GERMAN RUNS MY PLACE NOW. I'M LUCKY JUST TO HAVE A JOB!

THEN ADVANCE ME A FEW YARDS OF MATERIAL WITHOUT COUPONS.

OKAY, OKAY. HIDE THIS UNDER YOUR CLOTHES.

MR. ILZECKI, PLEASE.

SO I MADE A NICE FEW ZLOTYS THE VERY FIRST WEEK I CAME HOME.

I REMEMBER, FATHER-IN-LAW WAS SO HAPPY WITH ME.

YOU SEE, AT LEAST THERE'S *ONE* SMART GUY IN THE FAMILY.

OF COURSE I ONLY SAID I GOT *HALF* WHAT I REALLY MADE. OTHERWISE THEY WOULDN'T *SAVE* ANYTHING.

79

A LITTLE LATER I WAS AGAIN ON MODRZEJOWSKA, LOOKING TO BUY SOME TEXTILES WITHOUT COUPONS...

...THE S.S. CLOSED OFF THE WHOLE STREET TO INSPECT THE WORKING PAPERS FROM EVERYONE.

I DIDN'T *KNOW* BEFORE ABOUT THIS.

I MANAGED TO DISAPPEAR INTO A BUILDING.

BUT THEY TOOK MAYBE 50% OF THE PEOPLE AWAY.

I TALKED ABOUT IT TO FATHER-IN-LAW...

THEY ALMOST GOT ME! I'LL NEED MORE THAN JUST ILZECKI'S NOTE!

IT'S TRUE.

COME... WE'LL VISIT A FRIEND OF MINE WHO OWNS A TIN SHOP. I THINK HIS OVERSEER CAN BE BRIBED.

AND SO IT WENT... OKAY, VLADEK... SINCE WE MAKE THINGS FOR GERMANY WE CAN GET YOU A PRIORITY WORK CARD.

REMEMBER, IF THERE'S A ROUND-UP, RUN IN HERE AND PRETEND YOU'RE WORKING.

I LEARNED HERE TO DO THINGS WHAT WERE USEFUL TO ME WHEN I CAME TO AUSCHWITZ.

AND SO WE LIVED FOR MORE THAN A YEAR. BUT ALWAYS THINGS CAME A LITTLE WORSE, A LITTLE WORSE...

THE GERMANS LOOKED TO GRAB SUCH FURNITURE, BECAUSE IN STORES IT WASN'T ANYMORE TO GET.

WOLFE AND I SHLEPPED EVERYTHING VALUABLE DOWNSTAIRS FOR A POLISH NEIGHBOR TO HIDE.

OOF. ARE WE LEAVING THE OTHER BED UPSTAIRS?

JA. MOTHER-IN-LAW IS TOO SICK. SHE NEEDS A GOOD BED.

ANJA'S MOTHER HAD GALLSTONES. THE DAY THE GERMANS CAME SHE LAY IN THE BED.

PLEASE DON'T TAKE HER BED-LOOK AT HOW SICK SHE IS.

THE DOCTOR IS HERE EVERY DAY.

FATHER-IN-LAW HAD AN OLD FRIEND WHO CAME ALWAYS OVER TO PLAY CARDS.

...AND THEY LEFT WITHOUT TAKING ANYTHING!

YOU KNOW, I MET A GERMAN OFFICIAL WHO WOULD PAY WELL FOR A BEDROOM SET...

HIDDEN, WE HAD NO USE FROM THE FURNITURE. SO WE SHLEPPED IT AGAIN UPSTAIRS TO SELL.

YOU HAVE EXCELLENT TASTE IN FURNITURE, HERR ZYLBERBERG. THANK YOU.

MY MEN WILL BE RIGHT BACK TO GET YOUR WIFE'S BED TOO!..

YOU CHEATED US LAST TIME, JEW!

WAIT! I HAVEN'T BEEN PAID, YET.

PLEASE, IF YOU WANT TO STAY ALIVE GO BACK INSIDE.

HE WAS SO UNHAPPY AFTER. SO UNHAPPY!

81

ONE TIME I WAS GOING TO SEE ILZECKI. THIS WAS LATE IN 1941, I THINK. HIS HOUSE WAS VERY NEAR TO A TRAIN STATION...

...AND IT WAS GOING ON THERE SOMETHING TERRIBLE.

I HAD TO PASS NEAR—AND THEY WERE GRABBING JEWS, IF THEY HAD PAPERS OR NO!

WHAT HAD I TO DO?

WILL I WALK SLOWLY, THEY WILL TAKE ME...

WILL I RUN THEY CAN SHOOT ME!

THEN FROM FAR, I SAW ILZECKI WALKING, SO I WENT HASTY OVER TO HIM.

ALLO! MR. SPIEGELMAN! WHAT ARE YOU DOING HERE? DON'T YOU SEE WHAT'S GOING ON?

QUICK—COME UPSTAIRS WITH ME UNTIL THE TRAINS LEAVE!

ILZECKI LIVED IN A VERY FANCY HOUSE. HE WAS THE ONLY JEW THERE.

SO I SAT WITH HIM AND HIS WIFE A GOOD FEW HOURS. WE HEARD SHOOTING AND SCREAMS.

HE SURVIVED ME MY LIFE THAT TIME.

82

ILZECKI HAD A SON THE SAME AGE LIKE RICHIEU. IF YOU ONLY COULD SEE HOW THOSE CHILDREN PLAYED TOGETHER.

LISTEN, VLADEK...

WE CAN'T KNOW WHAT'S GOING TO HAPPEN TO **US** _ BUT WE **MUST** KEEP OUR CHILDREN SAFE.

I HAVE A GOOD FRIEND, A POLE, WHO'S WILLING TO HIDE MY SON UNTIL THE SITUATION GETS BETTER.

...I THINK HE'D TAKE YOUR BOY TOO.

YES, YOU MAY BE RIGHT! LET ME SPEAK WITH MY FAMILY.

BUT, I'M TELLING YOU, IT WAS SOMETHING **TERRIBLE** GOING ON IN OUR HOUSE WHEN I EVEN **MENTIONED** IT.

WHAT? HAVE YOU GONE **CRAZY**?

HOW CAN YOU EVEN **THINK** OF GIVING RICHIEU UP TO COMPLETE STRANGERS?!

I'LL **NEVER** GIVE UP MY BABY. NEVER!

ILZECKI AND HIS WIFE DIDN'T COME OUT FROM THE WAR.

...BUT HIS SON REMAINED ALIVE; OURS DID NOT.

...AND **ANYWAY** WE HAD TO GIVE RICHIEU TO HIDE A YEAR LATER.

WHEN WE WERE IN THE GHETTO, IN 1943, TOSHA TOOK ALL THE CHILDREN TO—

WAIT! *PLEASE, DAD, IF YOU DON'T KEEP YOUR STORY CHRONOLOGICAL, I'LL NEVER GET IT STRAIGHT... TELL ME MORE ABOUT 1941 AND 1942.*

SO?... OKAY. I'LL MAKE IT SO HOW YOU WANT IT. 1941?... AT THE END OF 1941 THE GERMANS CAME WITH SOMETHING NEW. WOLFE RAN FROM THE *GEMEINDER*...

LOOK! THEY'RE PUTTING THESE UP ALL OVER TOWN.

ORDER
All Jews of Sosnowiec must be relocated into the Stara Sosnowiec quarter by January 1, 1942. Non-Jews will be moved into vacated premises.

ALL 12 OF OUR HOUSEHOLD WERE GIVEN NOW TO LIVE IN 2½ SMALL ROOMS...

REWARD
FOR EVERY UNREGISTERED JEW YOU FIND: 1 KILO of SUGAR

MOST PEOPLE GOT EVEN *LESS* SPACE. BUT FATHER-IN-LAW AND WOLFE HAD A LITTLE *INFLUENCE*...

BUT THIS WASN'T YET A REAL GHETTO. STILL YOU COULD GO INTO OTHER PARTS OF TOWN SO LONG YOU WERE HOME AT NIGHT-TIME

HOLD THE LADDER, ANJA.

I'M PUTTING UP A CURTAIN TO GIVE US SOME PRIVACY.

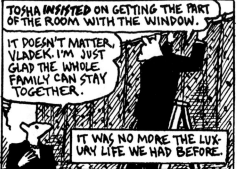

TOSHA *INSISTED* ON GETTING THE PART OF THE ROOM WITH THE WINDOW.

IT DOESN'T MATTER, VLADEK. I'M JUST GLAD THE WHOLE FAMILY CAN STAY TOGETHER.

IT WAS NO MORE THE LUXURY LIFE WE HAD BEFORE.

FOR A COUPLE MONTHS I DID HERE STILL MY BLACK MARKET BUSINESS. THEN CAME MORE BAD NEWS, VERY BAD...

WHAT'S WRONG, FATHER?

THEY JUST ARRESTED MY FRIEND, NAHUM COHN, AND HIS SON.

THEY'VE TAKEN FOUR JEWS AWAY FOR DEALING GOODS WITHOUT COUPONS.

I DID MUCH BUSINESS WITH COHN!

THE GERMANS INTEND TO MAKE AN EXAMPLE OF THEM!

THE NEXT DAY I WALKED OVER TO MODRZEJOWSKA STREET AND I SAW THEM...

THEY HANGED THERE ONE FULL WEEK.

COHN HAD A DRY GOODS STORE. HE WAS KNOWN OVER ALL SOSNOWIEC. OFTEN HE GAVE ME CLOTH WITH NO COUPONS.

I TRADED ALSO WITH PFEFER, A FINE YOUNG MAN - A ZIONIST. HE WAS JUST MARRIED. HIS WIFE RAN SCREAMING IN THE STREET.

I WAS FRIGHTENED TO GO OUTSIDE FOR A FEW DAYS... I DIDN'T WANT TO PASS WHERE THEY WERE HANGING.

AND MAYBE ONE OF THEM COULD HAVE TALKED OF ME TO THE GERMANS TO TRY TO SAVE HIMSELF.

ACH. WHEN I THINK NOW OF THEM, IT STILL MAKES ME CRY... LOOK—EVEN FROM MY DEAD EYE TEARS ARE COMING OUT!

WHAT WAS ANJA DOING AT AROUND THIS TIME?

HOUSEWORKS... AND KNITTING... READING... AND SHE WAS WRITING ALWAYS HER DIARY.

I USED TO SEE POLISH NOTEBOOKS AROUND THE HOUSE AS A KID. WERE THOSE HER DIARIES?

YES, AND ALSO NO.

HER DIARIES DIDN'T SURVIVE FROM THE WAR. WHAT YOU SAW SHE WROTE AFTER: HER WHOLE STORY FROM THE START.

OHMIGOD! WHERE ARE THEY? I NEED THOSE FOR THIS BOOK!

COFF! PLEASE, ARTIE, STOP WITH THE SMOKING. IT MAKES ME SHORT WITH BREATH.

I THINK IT'S ALL YOUR PEDALING!

DON'T BE SO SMART! "WHAT I WAS TELLING YOU? YES"... AFTER THE HANGING I LOOKED FOR ANOTHER BUSINESS ...

..."I STARTED TO TRADE GOLD AND JEWELRY...

IT WAS EASIER TO HIDE THAN CLOTHINGS. I KEPT THINGS HIDDEN IN THE CHILD'S STROLLER, AND I MADE A FEW ZLOTYS.

FOR A WHILE I HAD ALSO A FOOD BUSINESS THAT I DIDN'T YET TELL YOU...

I MET SZKLARCZYK. HE HAD A BIG GROCERY ON MODRZEJOWSKA..

YOU'RE ZYLBERBERG'S SON-IN-LAW, RIGHT? COME INSIDE AND WAIT FOR THE RAIN TO STOP.

SO, TOGETHER WE SAT AND SPOKE, AND HE HELPED, FROM TIME TO TIME, A CUSTOMER...

SORRY. YOU DON'T HAVE ENOUGH COUPONS TO BUY ½ KILO OF SUGAR.

STILL... SHE WENT OUT WITH ½ KILO. I SMELLED I COULD ARRANGE SOMETHING.

THEN A LITTLE MORE WE SPOKE AND HE MADE TO ME A PROPOSITION...

MAYBE YOU COULD SELL MY "EXTRA" ITEMS TO SMALL SHOPS IN THE AREA ...UNDER THE COUNTER.

IT WAS DANGEROUS TO CARRY THESE THINGS-BUT MAYBE I COULD BE LUCKY.

WHEN SOMEBODY IS HUNGRY HE LOOKS FOR BUSINESS....

ONE TIME I HAD 10 OR 15 KILOS SUGAR TO DELIVER...

HALT, JEW! WHAT ARE YOU CARRYING?

WHAT WAS I SUPPOSED TO SAY? FOR THIS I COULD REALLY HANG!

SUGAR.

...I'M TAKING IT OVER TO MY GROCERY STORE.

OH. YOU HAVE A SHOP?

I MADE SO THEY WOULD THINK IT WAS LEGAL.

I WENT TO THE BACK DOOR WHERE I HAD TO DELIVER...

OPEN UP, POLDEK!

..I'VE GOT OUR SUGAR.

?!

AND THEY LEFT ME GO WITHOUT EVEN CHECKING MY PAPERS!

BUT WHEN WE CAME TO STARA SOSNOWIEC, ALL MY BUSINESSES BECAME HARDER... IT WAS NOT SO EASY TO MOVE AROUND.

THE TIN SHOP FINISHED—THE OWNER WAS THE ONLY JEW THEY LET WORK THERE. I GOT THEN A JOB IN A GERMAN CARPENTRY SHOP.

FATHER-IN-LAW AND LOLEK WORKED ALREADY THERE, FOR REALLY NO MONEY. I DIDN'T NEED THIS BEFORE, BUT NOW I HAD TO HAVE THE WORK PAPER.

WOLFE COULD HAVE ARRANGED ME A JOB AT THE GEMEINDE... BUT I DIDN'T WANT TO PUT MY HANDS THERE WHERE JEWS WERE BEING TAKEN.

AND THEN IT CAME **AGAIN** SOMETHING NEW FROM THE GERMANS. WE GOT A NOTICE...

"ALL JEWS OVER 70 YEARS OLD WILL BE TRANSFERED TO THERESIENSTADT IN CZECHOSLOVAKIA ON MAY 10, 1942..."

"...A COMMUNITY BETTER PREPARED TO TAKE CARE OF THE ELDERLY THAN OURS IN SOSNOWIEC..."

IT DOESN'T **LOOK** TOO BAD!

LIKE A CONVALESCENT HOME.

NOTICE:

ANJA'S GRANDPARENTS HAD ABOUT 90 YEARS.

WE'VE BEEN TOGETHER—A **FAMILY**—FOR 70 YEARS. WE DON'T WANT TO BREAK APART NOW!

DON'T WORRY. WE WON'T LET THEM TAKE YOU.

WE DIDN'T YET **KNOW** OF AUSCHWITZ—OF THE OVENS—BUT WE WERE ANYWAY AFRAID.

...SO, IN THE YARD, WE MADE A HIDING PLACE, A BUNKER...

CUT-AWAY VIEW:

STORAGE SHEDS

FALSE WALL

GRANDPARENTS

WE SNEAKED FOOD TO THEM, AND—WHEN IT WAS SAFE—WE TOOK THEM INSIDE A LITTLE.

SEVERAL TIMES CAME THE JEWISH POLICE TO OUR HOUSE...

OUR RECORDS SHOW THAT MR. AND MRS. KARMIO LIVE HERE. THEY HAVEN'T REGISTERED FOR TRANSFER.

YES - MY WIFE'S PARENTS - THEY LEFT WITHOUT A WORD A MONTH AGO.

JEWISH POLICE?

YES - WITH BIG STICKS.

SOME JEWS THOUGHT IN THIS WAY: IF THEY GAVE TO THE GERMANS A *FEW* JEWS, THEY COULD SAVE THE REST.

AND AT LEAST THEY COULD SAVE THEMSELVES.

AND A MONTH AFTER, THEY *AGAIN* CAME TO FATHER-IN-LAW.

MR. ZYLBERBERG, YOU AND YOUR WIFE MUST COME WITH US.

IF THE KARMIOS DON'T TURN UP IN 3 DAYS YOU TWO WILL BE SENT IN THEIR PLACE!

HE HAD STILL A LITTLE "PROTECTION" FROM THE GEMEIN-DE, SO THEY TOOK ONLY *HIM* AWAY - NOT HIS WIFE.

HE SAT A FEW DAYS THERE, THEN HE SENT TO US A NOTE

HE WROTE THAT WE HAD TO GIVE OVER THE GRANDPARENTS. EVEN IF THEY TOOK ONLY HIM AWAY NOW, NEXT THEY WOULD GRAB HIS WIFE, AND THEN THE REST OF THE FAMILY.

SO, WHAT HAPPENED?

WHAT HAPPENED? WE HAD TO DELIVER THEM!

THEY THOUGHT IT WAS TO THERESIENSTADT THEY WERE GOING.

LET US KNOW IF YOU NEED ANYTHING!

BUT THEY WENT RIGHT AWAY TO AUSCHWITZ, TO THE GAS.

WHEN DID YOU FIRST HEAR ABOUT AUSCHWITZ?

RIGHT AWAY WE HEARD...

EVEN FROM THERE — FROM THAT OTHER WORLD-PEOPLE CAME BACK AND TOLD US. BUT WE DIDN'T BELIEVE.

THEN THIS SAME NEWS CAME MORE AND MORE, SO WE BELIEVED. AND LATER ON, WE SAW ... EVEN WORSE!

AFTER WHAT HAPPENED TO THE GRANDPARENTS, IT WAS A FEW MONTHS QUIET. THEN IT CAME POSTERS EVERYWHERE AND SPEECHES FROM THE GEMEINDE...

FELLOW JEWS: ON WEDNESDAY, AUGUST 12TH, EVERY ONE OF YOU, YOUNG AND OLD, MALE AND FEMALE, HEALTHY AND SICK, MUST REGISTER AT THE DIENST STADIUM...

OH NO!

NOW WHAT?

...THERE'S NO CAUSE FOR ALARM—IT'S ONLY A MATTER OF INSPECTING YOUR DOCUMENTS AND STAMPING THEM. THIS WILL PROTECT YOU AS CITIZENS OF THE REGION!...

I'M NOT GOING. IT'S A NAZI TRAP!...

EVERYBODY WAS WORRIED.

...AND OUR JEWISH COMMITTEE IS HELPING THOSE MURDERERS. GOD KNOWS WHAT WILL HAPPEN TO US AT THE STADIUM!

WELL, THEY JUST INSPECTED JEWISH DOCUMENTS IN SOME NEARBY TOWNS. IT WAS NO BIG DEAL.

ANYWAY, WE'VE GOT TO GO. WITHOUT LEGAL PAPERS, WE'RE LOST!

TO GO, IT WAS NO GOOD. BUT, NOT TO GO — IT WAS ALSO NO GOOD.

MY FATHER— HE HAD 62 YEARS—CAME BY STREETCAR TO ME FROM DABROWA, THE VILLAGE NEXT DOOR FROM SOSNOWIEC.

AFTER MY MOTHER DIED WITH CANCER, HE LIVED THERE IN THE HOUSE OF MY SISTER FELA, AND HER FOUR SMALL CHILDREN.

HERE'S A COOKIE, RICHIEU. AUNT FELA BAKED IT FOR YOU.

SAY THANK YOU TO GRANDPA.

I NEED YOUR ADVICE, VLADEK. SHOULD I GO TO THE STADIUM ON WEDNESDAY, OR HIDE AT HOME?

I DON'T KNOW. I'M NOT EVEN SURE WHAT WE'RE GOING TO DO. ...ANJA'S MOTHER SAYS SHE ISN'T GO-ING. SHE'S SICK AND AFRAID.

AT LEAST ANJA'S FATHER, LOLEK AND I ALL WORK AT THE GERMAN WOODSHOP. WE'RE A LITTLE SAFER. BUT YOU DON'T WORK. YOU HAVE NO PAPERS. YOU DON'T HAVE ANYTHING!

WELL, OUR COUSIN MORDECAI SAYS HE'LL BE AT ONE OF THE INSPECTION TABLES. I COULD BRING MY PAPERS TO HIM...

WHAT DOES FELA SAY?

SHE'S NOT SURE...BUT IF FELA DECIDES TO GO, OF COURSE I'LL GO WITH HER.

CAN I HAVE ANOTHER COOKIE?

RICHIEU!

REALLY, I DIDN'T KNOW HOW TO ADVISE HIM.

BUT FINALLY HE DID GO. PEOPLE WERE AFRAID TO NOT SHOW UP.

SO IT CAME TO THE STADIUM ALMOST ALL THE JEWS OF SOSNOWIEC, AND FROM THE OTHER VILLAGES NEAR, MAYBE 25 OR 30,000 PEOPLE.

EVERYONE CAME VERY NICE DRESSED. THEY TRIED SO THAT THEY WOULD LOOK YOUNG AND ABLE TO WORK, IN ORDER TO GET A GOOD STAMP ON THEIR PASSPORT.

WHEN WE WERE EVERYBODY INSIDE, GESTAPO WITH MACHINE GUNS SURROUNDED THE STADIUM.

LINE UP BY FAMILY AT THE TABLES TO REGISTER! QUICKLY!

THEN WAS A SELECTION, WITH PEOPLE SENT EITHER TO THE LEFT, EITHER TO THE RIGHT.

OLD PEOPLE, FAMILIES WITH LOTS OF KIDS, AND PEOPLE WITHOUT WORK CARDS ARE ALL GOING TO THE LEFT!

WE UNDERSTOOD THIS MUST BE VERY BAD.

ME AND ANJA CAME TO THE TABLE WHERE MY COUSIN WAS SITTING...

AH, YOU WORK AT THE CARPENTRY SHOP. GO TO THE RIGHT.

SO WE GOT STAMPED OUR PASSPORTS AND CAME QUICK TO THE GOOD SIDE OF THE STADIUM. THOSE THEY SENT LEFT, THEY DIDN'T GET ANY STAMP.

WE WERE SO HAPPY WE CAME THROUGH. BUT WE WORRIED NOW – WERE OUR FAMILIES SAFE?

LOOK! THERE'S POPPA, WITH LOLEK AND LONIA!

WE SAW WOLFE AND TOSHA. OUR FAMILY SEEMS TO BE OKAY.

DID YOU SEE MY FATHER?

I COULDN'T SEE ANYWHERE MY FATHER.

BUT LATER SOMEONE WHO SAW HIM TOLD ME... HE CAME THROUGH THIS SAME COUSIN OVER TO THE GOOD SIDE.

HER, THEY SENT TO THE LEFT. FOUR CHILDREN WAS TOO MANY.

SPIEGELMAN... TO THE RIGHT.

THEN CAME FELA TO REGISTER...

FELA!

MY DAUGHTER! HOW CAN SHE MANAGE ALONE – WITH FOUR CHILDREN TO TAKE CARE OF?

AND, WHAT DO YOU THINK? HE SNEAKED ON TO THE BAD SIDE!

AND THOSE ON THE BAD SIDE NEVER CAME ANYMORE HOME.

THOSE WITH A STAMP WERE LET TO GO HOME. BUT THERE WERE VERY FEW JEWS NOW LEFT IN SOSNOWIEC...

ONE FROM THREE THEY KEPT AT THE STADIUM.... MAYBE 10,000 PEOPLE – AND WITH THEM, MY FATHER.

WELL... IT'S ENOUGH FOR TODAY. YES, ARTIE?...

93

WHOO—I OVERDID A LITTLE. I'M FEELING DIZZY.

MAYBE YOU SHOULD LIE DOWN A WHILE.

ARE YOU FINISHED?

UH·HUH. MY FATHER'S WORN OUT. HE'S TAKING A NAP.

HE WAS JUST TELLING ME ABOUT THE TIME EVERYONE IN SOSNOWIEC HAD TO GET HIS PASSPORT STAMPED.

IN THE STADIUM? YES... THEY GOT MY MOTHER THEN.

SHE WAS TAKEN, WITH EVERYBODY ELSE WHO WAS GOING TO BE DEPORTED, TO FOUR APARTMENT HOUSES THAT WERE EMPTIED TO MAKE A SORT OF PRISON...

THEY PUT THOUSANDS OF PEOPLE THERE... IT WAS SO CROWDED THAT SOME OF THEM ACTUALLY SUFFOCATED... NO FOOD... NO TOILETS. IT WAS **TERRIBLE**.

PEOPLE JUMPED OUT THE WINDOWS TO END THEIR MISERY A LITTLE QUICKER.

GOD.

BUT MY MOTHER *SURVIVED* THAT. HER BROTHER WAS ON THE JEWISH COM· MITTEE, AND HE HID HER IN A COAL CELLAR 'TIL ALL THE TRANSPORTS LEFT.

THEN HE GOT ME A JOB SCRUBBING THE PEOPLE'S FILTH—VOMIT! EXCREMENT!— OUT OF SEVERAL APARTMENTS, AND I MANAGED TO SMUGGLE HER OUT.

EVENTUALLY SHE AND MY FATHER BOTH ENDED UP IN AUSCHWITZ. THEY DIED THERE.

WHERE ARE YOU GOING? YOU DIDN'T DRINK YOUR COFFEE.

I JUST THOUGHT OF SOMETHING. MY FATHER MENTIONED THAT ANJA USED TO KEEP A DIARY, AND I *VAGUELY* REMEMBER SEEING THEM ON HIS SHELVES IN THE DEN.

I DOUBT IT. I WOULD HAVE NOTICED THEM.

WELL, THERE'S SO MUCH JUNK IN THERE, IT'S WORTH A SHOT.

LOOK AT ALL THIS STUFF!...OLD MENUS HE PICKED UP ON CRUISES. ...A PILE OF STATIONERY FROM THE PINES HOTEL...

INCREDIBLE! FOUR 1965 DAY DOCK SAVINGS BANK CALENDARS...I'LL BET HE NEVER EVEN HAD AN ACCOUNT THERE.

HE DRIVES ME CRAZY! HE WON'T EVEN LET ME THROW OUT THE PLASTIC PITCHER HE TOOK FROM HIS HOSPITAL ROOM LAST YEAR!

HE'S MORE ATTACHED TO THINGS THAN TO PEOPLE!

I REALLY DON'T KNOW HOW LONG I CAN TAKE HIM. I REALLY DON'T.

I BETTER BE GETTING HOME. I'LL LOOK FOR THOSE DIARIES NEXT TIME.

WAIT! PUT EVERYTHING BACK EXACTLY LIKE IT WAS, OR I'LL NEVER HEAR THE END OF IT!

OKAY... OKAY... RELAX.

CHAPTER FIVE

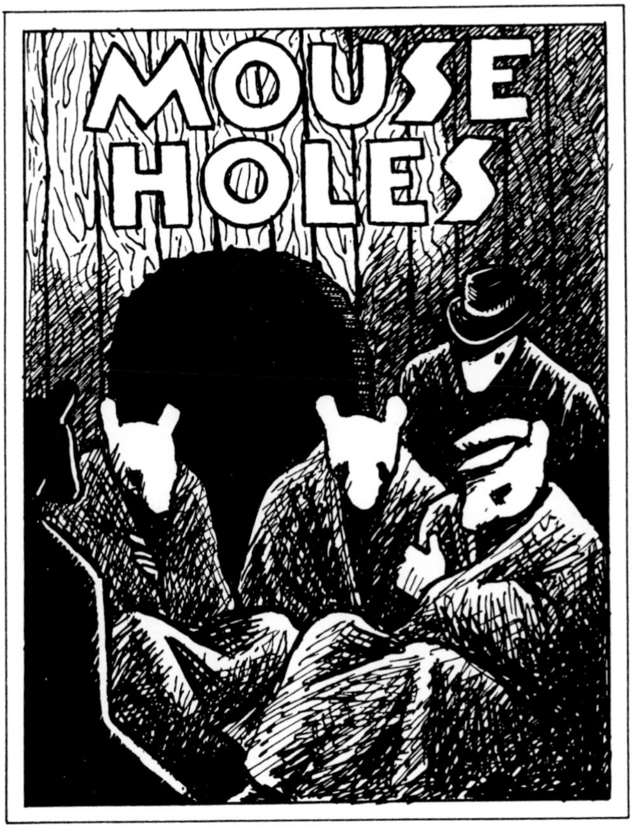
MOUSE
HOLES

MNF?

HELLO, ARTIE? I'M TELLING YOU, I DON'T KNOW WHAT TO DO WITH YOUR FATHER—HE JUST CLIMBED ONTO THE ROOF!..

UNH? MALA?

HE INSISTED ON FIXING THE DRAINPIPE AND GOT DIZZY! I DON'T KNOW HOW I EVER GOT HIM DOWN!

WHAT TIME IS IT?

NOW HE WANTS TO CLIMB BACK UP! WHAT AM I SUPPOSED TO DO?!

PLEASE DON'T SHOUT.

WHY DON'T YOU CALL A HANDYMAN? JEEZ, MALA, IT'S ONLY 7:30 AM. FRANÇOISE AND I WERE UP 'TIL 4:00! YOU KNOW WE DON'T GET UP 'TIL—

HELLO? ARTIE? IT'S POPPA HERE.

I'M TELLING YOU, MALA MAKES ME MESHUGAH! I WANT THAT MAYBE YOU COULD COME NOW TO QUEENS TO HELP ME.

WHAT? YOU'VE GOTTA BE KIDDING!

WHEN I WAS YOUNG I COULD DO BY MYSELF THESE THINGS. BUT NOW, DARLING I NEED IT YOUR HELP FOR THE DRAINPIPE!

UM—LOOK, POP. I'LL CALL YOU BACK AFTER I'VE HAD SOME COFFEE.

WHEW. MAYBE I WAS DREAMING.

WUZZIT? YOUR FATHER AGAIN?

98

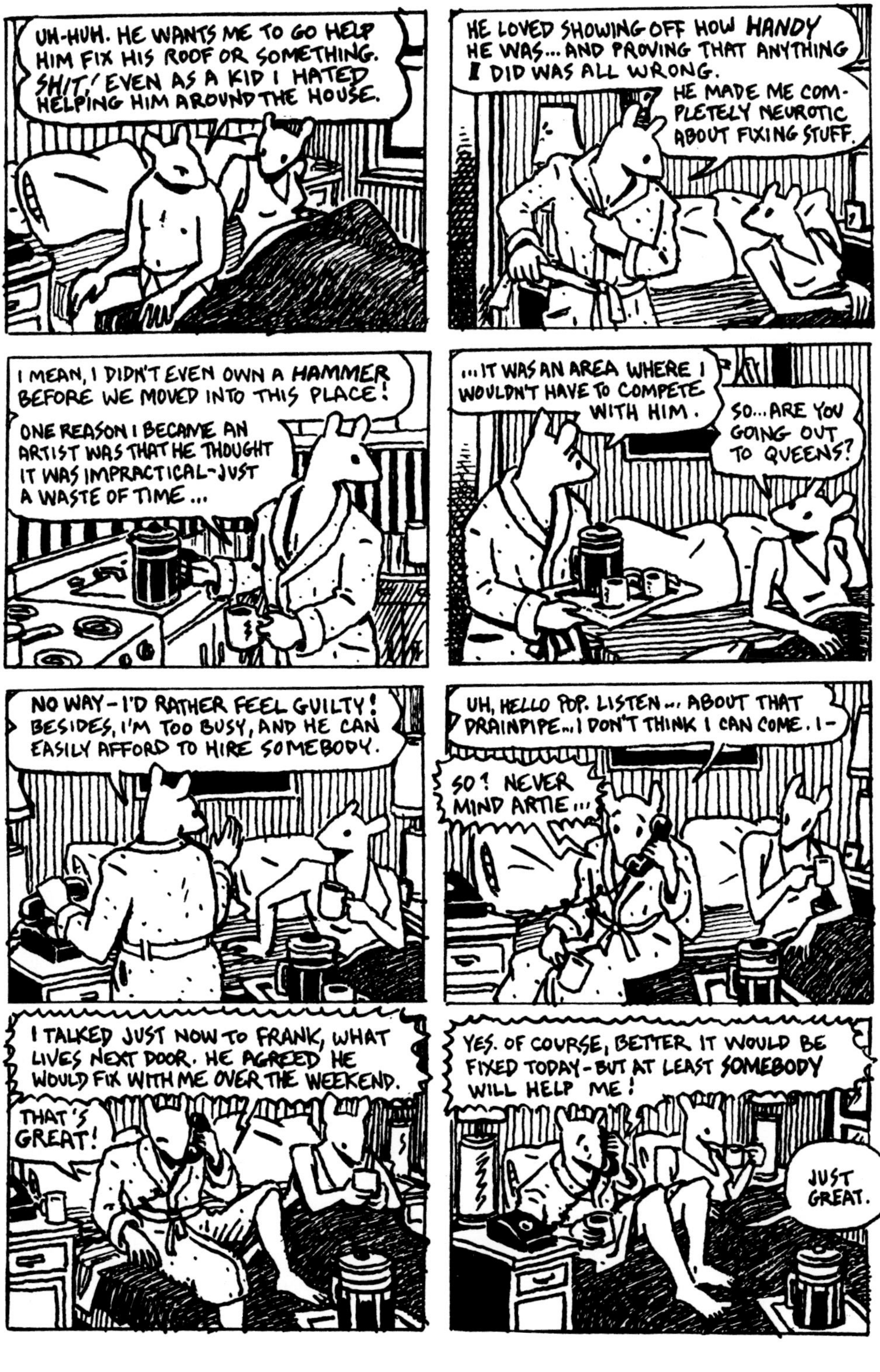
UH-HUH. HE WANTS ME TO GO HELP HIM FIX HIS ROOF OR SOMETHING. SHIT! EVEN AS A KID I HATED HELPING HIM AROUND THE HOUSE.
HE LOVED SHOWING OFF HOW HANDY HE WAS... AND PROVING THAT ANYTHING I DID WAS ALL WRONG.
HE MADE ME COMPLETELY NEUROTIC ABOUT FIXING STUFF.
I MEAN, I DIDN'T EVEN OWN A HAMMER BEFORE WE MOVED INTO THIS PLACE!
ONE REASON I BECAME AN ARTIST WAS THAT HE THOUGHT IT WAS IMPRACTICAL - JUST A WASTE OF TIME...
...IT WAS AN AREA WHERE I WOULDN'T HAVE TO COMPETE WITH HIM.
SO... ARE YOU GOING OUT TO QUEENS?
NO WAY - I'D RATHER FEEL GUILTY! BESIDES, I'M TOO BUSY, AND HE CAN EASILY AFFORD TO HIRE SOMEBODY.
UH, HELLO POP. LISTEN... ABOUT THAT DRAINPIPE... I DON'T THINK I CAN COME. I-
SO? NEVER MIND ARTIE...
I TALKED JUST NOW TO FRANK, WHAT LIVES NEXT DOOR. HE AGREED HE WOULD FIX WITH ME OVER THE WEEKEND.
THAT'S GREAT!
YES. OF COURSE, BETTER IT WOULD BE FIXED TODAY - BUT AT LEAST SOMEBODY WILL HELP ME!
JUST GREAT.

About a week later, early afternoon...

HIYA, POP. WHATCHA DOING OUT HERE IN THE GARAGE?

IT'S ALWAYS **SOMETHING** HERE I MUST DO. I'M PUTTING NOW AWAY MY OLD NAILS — THE LONG ONES SEPARATE FROM THE SHORT ONES.

PLINK

IS THE ROOF ALL FIXED UP?

YAH- FRANK FROM NEXT DOOR CAME EVENTUALLY AND TOGETHER WE FIXED.

UM... DO YOU NEED ANY HELP WITH THOSE NAILS OR ANYTHING?

NO....

SUCH JOBS I CAN DO EASY BY MYSELF.

PLUNK

UM... IS EVERY-THING OKAY?

PLINK

NU? WITH MY LIFE NOW, YOU KNOW IT **CAN'T** BE EVERYTHING OKAY!

YOU GO UPSTAIRS. I'LL FINISH HERE MY JOB, AND IN A FEW MINUTES I'LL COME UP.

OKAY.

PLINK

HI, MALA.

OY! YOU SCARED ME, ARTIE. MY NERVES ARE COMPLETELY SHOT, LIVING WITH YOUR FATHER.

HE SEEMED A LITTLE UPSET WHEN I SAW HIM DOWNSTAIRS.. DO YOU THINK HE'S ANGRY THAT I DIDN'T COME HELP HIM LAST WEEK?

I DON'T THINK SO..

BUT KEEPING THIS HOUSE FIXED UP IS TOO MUCH FOR HIM NOW. I KEEP TELLING HIM TO SELL IT AND BUY A CONDO IN MIAMI.

HE SEEMS DEPRESSED.

IT COULD BE THAT COMIC STRIP YOU ONCE MADE – THE ONE ABOUT YOUR MOTHER.

WHAT?

VLADEK SAW IT FOR THE FIRST TIME A COUPLE OF DAYS AGO.

HOW DO YOU KNOW ABOUT "PRISONER ON THE HELL PLANET"?

MY FRIEND, RUTHIE, HAS A SON IN COLLEGE. HE READS ALL THE COMICS. HE SHOWED IT TO HER, AND SHE GAVE ME A COPY.

SHIT!...

I KNEW IT WOULD UPSET YOUR FATHER, SO I KEPT IT HIDDEN. BUT, SOMEHOW HE FOUND IT.

I DREW THIS STORY YEARS AGO.

IT APPEARED IN AN OBSCURE UNDERGROUND COMIC BOOK. I NEVER THOUGHT VLADEK WOULD SEE IT.

PRISONER ON THE HELL PLANET

PRISONER ON THE HELL PLANET

A CASE HISTORY

TROJAN LAKE, N.Y. 1968

IN 1968, WHEN I WAS 20, MY MOTHER KILLED HERSELF..SHE LEFT NO NOTE!

MY FATHER FOUND HER WHEN HE GOT HOME FROM WORK... HER WRISTS SLASHED AND AN EMPTY BOTTLE OF PILLS NEARBY...

I WAS LIVING WITH MY PARENTS, AS I AGREED TO DO ON MY RELEASE FROM THE STATE MENTAL HOSPITAL 3 MONTHS BEFORE.

I'D JUST SPENT THE WEEK-END WITH MY GIRLFRIEND, ISABELLA. (MY PARENTS DIDN'T LIKE HER.) I WAS LATE GETTING HOME...

OY, GOTT!

SUBWAY

RECORDS

I SUPPOSE THAT IF I'D GOTTEN HOME WHEN EXPECTED, I WOULD HAVE FOUND HER BODY...

63-12

WHEN I SAW THE CROWD I HAD A PANG OF FEAR...I SUSPECTED THE WORST, BUT DIDN'T LET MYSELF KNOW!

A COUSIN HERDED ME AWAY FROM THE SCENE. DOCTOR ORENS LIVED NEARBY...

COME TO THE DOCTOR'S.... YOUR MOTHER IS -AH- SICK!... HE WILL EXPLAIN ......

SIT DOWN, ARTHUR... I THOUGHT I SHOULD BE THE ONE TO TELL YOU...

YOUR MOTHER KILLED HER-SELF —SHE'S DEAD!

I COULD AVOID THE TRUTH NO LONGER—THE DOCTOR'S WORDS CLATTERED INSIDE ME.... I FELT CONFUSED; I FELT ANGRY; I FELT NUMB!... I DIDN'T EXACTLY FEEL LIKE CRYING, BUT FIGURED I SHOULD!....

SHE'S DEAD! A SUICIDE!

NOW, NOW, BOY...

NO, LET HIM CRY— IT'S GOOD FOR HIM!

WE WENT HOME...MY FATHER HAD COM-PLETELY FALLEN APART!....

OY, ARTIE! WHY? WHY! SUCH A TRAGEDY! AND NOT EVEN A NOTE!!!

I WAS EXPECTED TO COMFORT *HIM*!

MOTHER... MOTHER...

SOMEHOW THE FUNERAL ARRANGE-MENTS WERE MADE...

...AND FOR $950⁰⁰ WE HAVE A BRONZE CASKET WITH BRONZE-COLORED VELVET.- OF COURSE, FOR $2,000⁰⁰ WE CAN...

PROTECT WHAT YOU HAVE

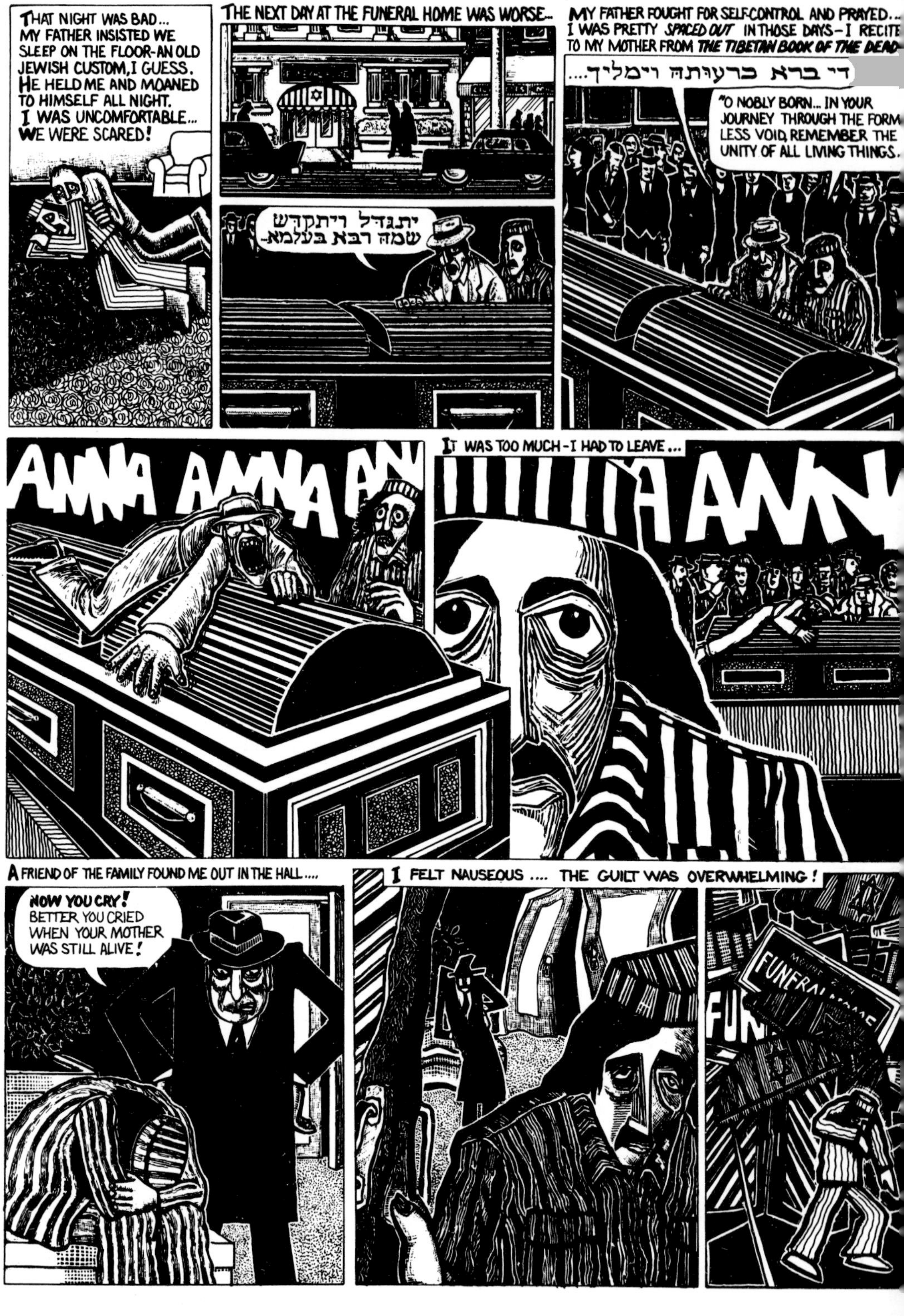

THAT NIGHT WAS BAD... MY FATHER INSISTED WE SLEEP ON THE FLOOR-AN OLD JEWISH CUSTOM, I GUESS. HE HELD ME AND MOANED TO HIMSELF ALL NIGHT. I WAS UNCOMFORTABLE... WE WERE SCARED!
THE NEXT DAY AT THE FUNERAL HOME WAS WORSE...
יתגדל ויתקדש
שמה רבא בעלמא.
MY FATHER FOUGHT FOR SELF-CONTROL AND PRAYED... I WAS PRETTY *SPACED OUT* IN THOSE DAYS-I RECITE TO MY MOTHER FROM *THE TIBETAN BOOK OF THE DEAD*
די ברא כרעותה וימליך....
"O NOBLY BORN... IN YOUR JOURNEY THROUGH THE FORM LESS VOID, REMEMBER THE UNITY OF ALL LIVING THINGS."
ANNA ANNA AN
IT WAS TOO MUCH-I HAD TO LEAVE...
IIIIIIA ANN
A FRIEND OF THE FAMILY FOUND ME OUT IN THE HALL....
NOW YOU CRY! BETTER YOU CRIED WHEN YOUR MOTHER WAS STILL ALIVE!
I FELT NAUSEOUS .... THE GUILT WAS OVERWHELMING!
FUNERAL
FUN

THE NEXT WEEK WE SPENT IN MOURNING... MY FATHER'S FRIENDS ALL OFFERED ME HOSTILITY MIXED IN WITH THEIR CONDOLENCES...

ARTHUR—WE'RE *SO* SORRY...

IT'S HIS FAULT— THE PUNK!

THEY THINK IT'S MY FAULT?!

...BUT, FOR THE MOST PART, I WAS LEFT ALONE WITH MY THOUGHTS...

MENOPAUSAL DEPRESSION

HITLER DID IT!

MOMMY!

BITCH

I REMEMBERED THE LAST TIME I SAW HER...

...ARTIE...

SHE CAME INTO MY ROOM... IT WAS LATE AT NIGHT....

...ARTIE ... YOU... STILL... LOVE... ME .... DON'T YOU? ....

...I TURNED AWAY, RESENTFUL OF THE WAY SHE TIGHTENED THE UMBILICAL CORD...

SURE, MA!

...SHE WALKED OUT AND CLOSED THE DOOR!

CLIK!

AGH!

WELL, MOM, IF YOU'RE LISTENING...

CONGRATULATIONS!... YOU'VE COMMITTED THE PERFECT CRIME ....

...YOU PUT ME HERE .... SHORTED ALL MY CIRCUITS...CUT MY NERVE ENDINGS ... AND CROSSED MY WIRES!....

...YOU *MURDERED* ME, MOMMY, AND YOU LEFT ME HERE TO TAKE THE RAP!!!

PIPE DOWN, MAC! SOME OF US ARE TRYING TO SLEEP!

© art spiegelman, 1972

GEE, I'M SURPRISED THAT VLADEK **READ** THIS WHEN HE FOUND IT. HE **NEVER** READS COMICS...

HE DOESN'T EVEN LOOK AT MY WORK WHEN I STICK IT UNDER HIS NOSE.

BUT THIS ISN'T **LIKE** OTHER COMICS...

I TELL YOU, WHEN RUTHIE SHOWED IT TO ME I THOUGHT I'D **FAINT**, I WAS SO SHOCKED.

IT WAS SO... SO PERSONAL!

...BUT VERY ACCURATE... OBJECTIVE. I SPENT A LOT OF TIME HELPING OUT HERE AFTER ANJA'S FUNERAL. IT WAS JUST AS YOU SAID.

SO, ARTIE. I'M READY.

LET'S WALK NOW TO THE BANK TOGETHER.

MALA JUST TOLD ME THAT YOU SAW MY COMIC...THE ONE ABOUT MOM.

YES. I FOUND IT WHEN I LOOKED FOR THE THINGS YOU ASKED ME LAST TIME. HOO! I SAW THE PICTURE THERE OF MOM, SO I READ IT... AND I CRIED.

I-I'M SORRY.

IT'S GOOD YOU GOT IT OUTSIDE YOUR SYSTEM.

BUT FOR ME IT BROUGHT IN MY MIND SO MUCH **MEMORIES** OF ANJA.

...OF COURSE I'M THINKING ALWAYS ABOUT HER **ANYWAY.**

YES. YOU KEEP PHOTOS OF HER ALL AROUND YOUR DESK—LIKE A SHRINE!

WHAT HAVE I TO DO, MALA? IN THE GARBAGE PUT THEM? OF YOU **ALSO** I HAVE A PHOTO ON THE DESK!

ACH! DON'T DO ME ANY FAVORS!

YOU SEE WHAT I HAVE WITH HER? ALWAYS, WHATEVER I DO IS NO GOOD.

DID YOU FIND MOM'S DIARY?

SO FAR THIS DIDN'T SHOW UP. I LOOKED, BUT I CAN'T FIND. I'VE **GOT** TO HAVE THAT!

ANOTHER TIME I'LL AGAIN LOOK. BUT NOW BETTER WE GO TO THE BANK.

OKAY.

..EVERY DAY I WALK, OTHERWISE IN MY LEGS THE CIRCULATION MAKES ME A CRAMP. IT'S SOMETHING TERRIBLE AND I CAN'T SLEEP.

BUT FOR MY HEART, I MUST WALK SLOW.

WHAT HAPPENED TO YOU AND ANJA AFTER THE BIG SELECTION AT THE STADIUM?

WELL, FOR A TIME IT WAS EVERYTHING QUIET. THEN IN 1943 CAME AN ORDER: ALL JEWS WHAT ARE LEFT IN SOSNOWIEC MUST GO TO LIVE IN AN OLD VILLAGE NEARBY CALLED SRODULA.

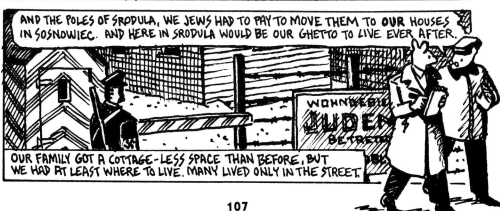

AND THE POLES OF SRODULA, WE JEWS HAD TO PAY TO MOVE THEM TO **OUR** HOUSES IN SOSNOWIEC. AND HERE IN SRODULA WOULD BE OUR GHETTO TO LIVE EVER AFTER.

WOHNGEBIE **JUDEN** BETRE

OUR FAMILY GOT A COTTAGE - LESS SPACE THAN BEFORE, BUT WE HAD AT LEAST WHERE TO LIVE. MANY LIVED ONLY IN THE STREET.

EACH DAY WE WERE TAKEN TO SOSNOWIEC, TO WORK IN GERMAN "SHOPS"...

ANJA, WITH HER SISTER, TOSHA, THEY WORKED IN A CLOTHINGS FACTORY...

AND I WENT, TOGETHER WITH MY NEPHEW, LOLEK, TO A WOODWORK SHOP.

EVERY DAY THE GUARDS MARCHED US ABOUT AN HOUR AND A HALF TO WORK.

THE GUARDS, IT WAS JEWS WITH BIG STICKS. THEY ACTED SO, JUST LIKE THE GERMANS.

...AND EVERY NIGHT THEY MARCHED US BACK, COUNTED US, AND LOCKED US IN.

VLADEK! LOLEK! HURRY HOME!

ANJA! WHAT IS IT?

WOLFE'S UNCLE PERSIS IS AT OUR HOUSE!

FROM ZAWIERCIE?

YES. HE'S A BIG SHOT THERE...THE HEAD OF THEIR JEWISH COUNCIL. HE WANTS WOLFE, TOSHA AND BIBI TO GO LIVE WITH HIM IN ZAWIERCIE.

...YOU'VE ALL HEARD THE STORIES ABOUT AUSCHWITZ. HORRIBLE UNBELIEVABLE STORIES.

THEY CAN'T BE TRUE!

ONE THING IS CERTAIN— AS BAD AS THINGS ARE IN THE GHETTO, BEING DEPORTED IS EVEN WORSE.

PLEASE! IT'S BAD LUCK TO EVEN SPEAK OF IT!

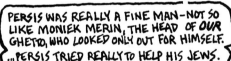

LOOK. YOU DON'T HAVE MUCH INFLUENCE HERE. IN ZAWIERCIE I HAVE SOME INFLUENCE WITH THE GERMANS... I CAN BRIBE THEM.

MY 90-YEAR-OLD FATHER STILL LIVES WITH ME...WHENEVER THERE'S A ROUND-UP, AN S.S. MAN GUARDS HIM TO KEEP HIM SAFE!

NINETY! THIS WAS 1943! IT WASN'T **LEFT** ANY OTHER JEWS WHAT HAD NINETY YEARS!

PERSIS WAS REALLY A FINE MAN—NOT SO LIKE MONIEK MERIN, THE HEAD OF **OUR** GHETTO, WHO LOOKED ONLY OUT FOR HIMSELF. ...PERSIS TRIED REALLY TO HELP HIS JEWS.

I CAN MANAGE PAPERS TO TAKE WOLFE, TOSHA AND BIBI—AND MAYBE LITTLE LONIA AND RICHIEU IF YOU'LL LET ME.

YES. THEY'D BE BETTER OFF.

YOU SEE? I WANTED TO SEND RICHIEU SOMEPLACE SAFE A **YEAR** AGO— WITH ILZECKI'S CHILD!

THINGS ARE EVEN WORSE NOW, VLADEK. WE HAVE NO CHOICE!

NO! WE MUST ALL STAY TOGETHER! WE'VE MADE IT THIS FAR. GOD WILL STILL HELP US!

MATKA! BE REALISTIC!

ANJA'S MOTHER DIDN'T LIKE TO LOOK AT THE FACTS. BUT FINALLY EVEN SHE AGREED,

SO PERSIS ARRANGED, AND HE CAME AGAIN TO SRODULA.

IT WENT WITH HIM WOLFE, TOSHA AND BIBI

LOLEK'S LITTLE SISTER, LONIA

AND OUR BOY, RICHIEU.

WE WATCHED UNTIL THEY DISAPPEARED FROM OUR EYES...

IT WAS THE LAST TIME EVER WE SAW THEM; BUT THAT WE COULDN'T KNOW.

WHEN THINGS CAME WORSE IN OUR GHETTO WE SAID ALWAYS: "THANK GOD THE KIDS ARE WITH PERSIS, SAFE."

THAT SPRING, ON ONE DAY, THE GERMANS TOOK FROM SRODULA TO AUSCHWITZ OVER 1,000 PEOPLE.

MOST THEY TOOK WERE KIDS — SOME ONLY 2 OR 3 YEARS.

SOME KIDS WERE SCREAMING AND SCREAMING. THEY COULDN'T STOP.

SO THE GERMANS SWINGED THEM BY THE LEGS AGAINST A WALL...

AND THEY NEVER ANYMORE SCREAMED.

IN THIS WAY THE GERMANS TREATED THE LITTLE ONES WHAT STILL HAD SURVIVED A LITTLE.

THIS I DIDN'T SEE WITH MY OWN EYES, BUT SOMEBODY THE NEXT DAY TOLD ME. AND I SAID, "THANK GOD WITH PERSIS OUR CHILDREN ARE SAFE!"

110

SO..WHAT HAPPENED TO RICHIEU?

ACH! OUR BEAUTIFUL BOY. WE ONLY FOUND OUT MUCH LATER.

A FEW MONTHS AFTER WE SENT RICHIEU TO ZAWIERCIE, THE GERMANS DECIDED THEY WOULD FINISH OUT THAT GHETTO.

BANG BANG

MORE GUNSHOTS! WHAT'S GOING ON?

IT'S HORRIBLE, TOSHA!...

ALL THE GESTAPO IN THE GHETTO HAVE BEEN REPLACED BY OTHERS FROM OPOLE. THEY JUST SHOT PERSIS AND THE REST OF THE JEWISH COUNCIL!...

WHAT?

THEY'RE EVACUATING ZAWIERCIE. WE'RE ALL SUPPOSED TO GO TO THE SQUARE WITH OUR BAGGAGE RIGHT AWAY. THEY'RE SENDING ALL OF US OUT — TO AUSCHWITZ!

OH MY GOD.

NO!

I WON'T GO TO THEIR GAS CHAMBERS!...

AND MY **CHILDREN** WON'T GO TO THEIR GAS CHAMBERS.

BIBI! LONIA! RICHIEU! COME HERE QUICKLY!

ALWAYS TOSHA CARRIED AROUND HER NECK SOME POISON...SHE KILLED NOT ONLY HERSELF, BUT ALSO THE 3 CHILDREN.

I'M TELLING YOU, IT WAS A TRAGEDY AMONG TRAGEDIES. HE WAS SUCH A HAPPY, BEAUTIFUL BOY!

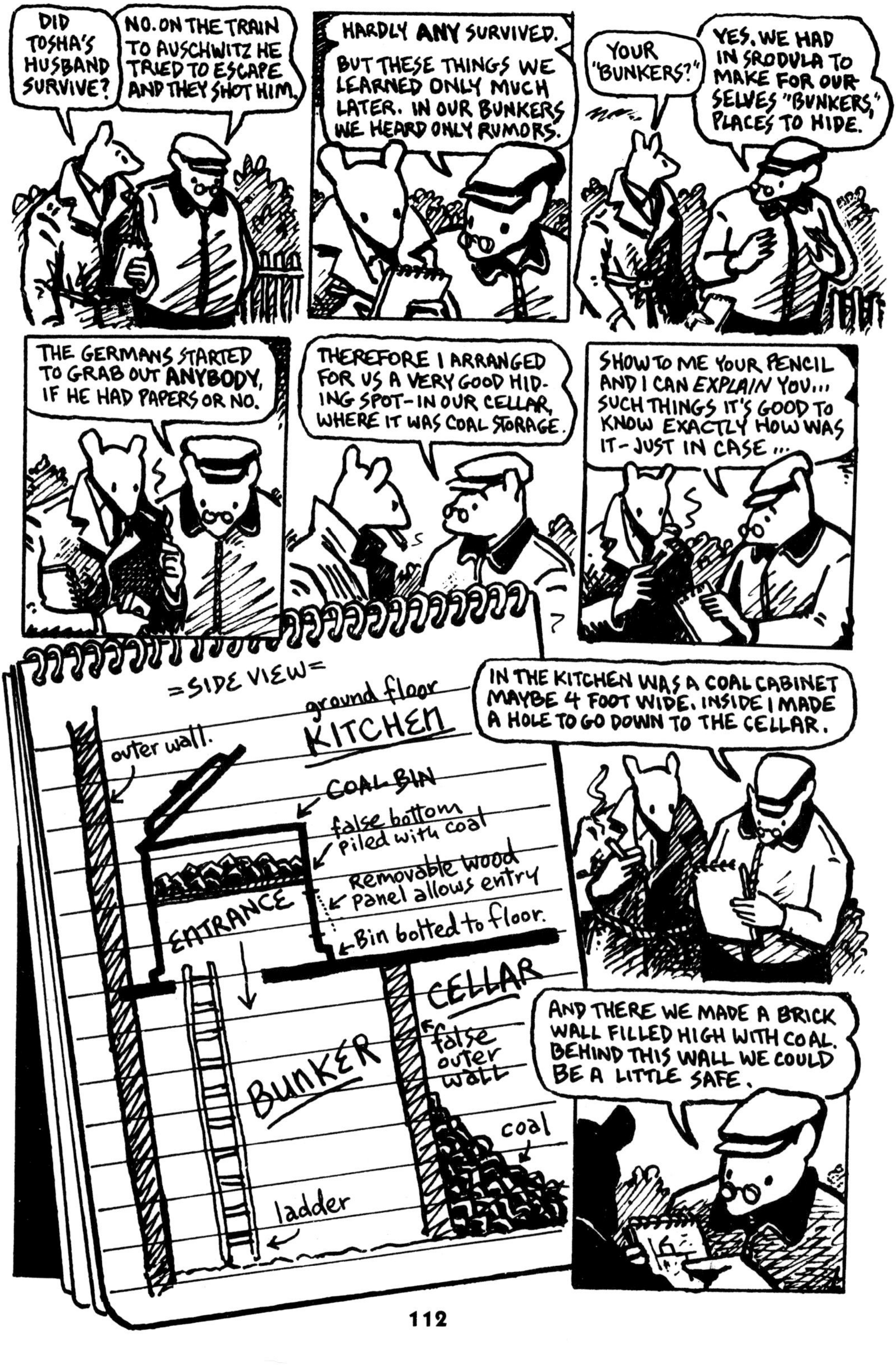
DID TOSHA'S HUSBAND SURVIVE?
NO. ON THE TRAIN TO AUSCHWITZ HE TRIED TO ESCAPE AND THEY SHOT HIM.
HARDLY ANY SURVIVED.
BUT THESE THINGS WE LEARNED ONLY MUCH LATER. IN OUR BUNKERS WE HEARD ONLY RUMORS.
YOUR "BUNKERS?"
YES. WE HAD IN SRODULA TO MAKE FOR OUR SELVES "BUNKERS," PLACES TO HIDE.
THE GERMANS STARTED TO GRAB OUT ANYBODY, IF HE HAD PAPERS OR NO.
THEREFORE I ARRANGED FOR US A VERY GOOD HIDING SPOT - IN OUR CELLAR, WHERE IT WAS COAL STORAGE.
SHOW TO ME YOUR PENCIL AND I CAN EXPLAIN YOU... SUCH THINGS IT'S GOOD TO KNOW EXACTLY HOW WAS IT - JUST IN CASE...
=SIDE VIEW=
ground floor
KITCHEN
outer wall.
COAL BIN
false bottom piled with coal
removable wood panel allows entry
Bin bolted to floor.
ENTRANCE
CELLAR
false outer wall
BUNKER
coal
ladder
IN THE KITCHEN WAS A COAL CABINET MAYBE 4 FOOT WIDE. INSIDE I MADE A HOLE TO GO DOWN TO THE CELLAR.
AND THERE WE MADE A BRICK WALL FILLED HIGH WITH COAL. BEHIND THIS WALL WE COULD BE A LITTLE SAFE.

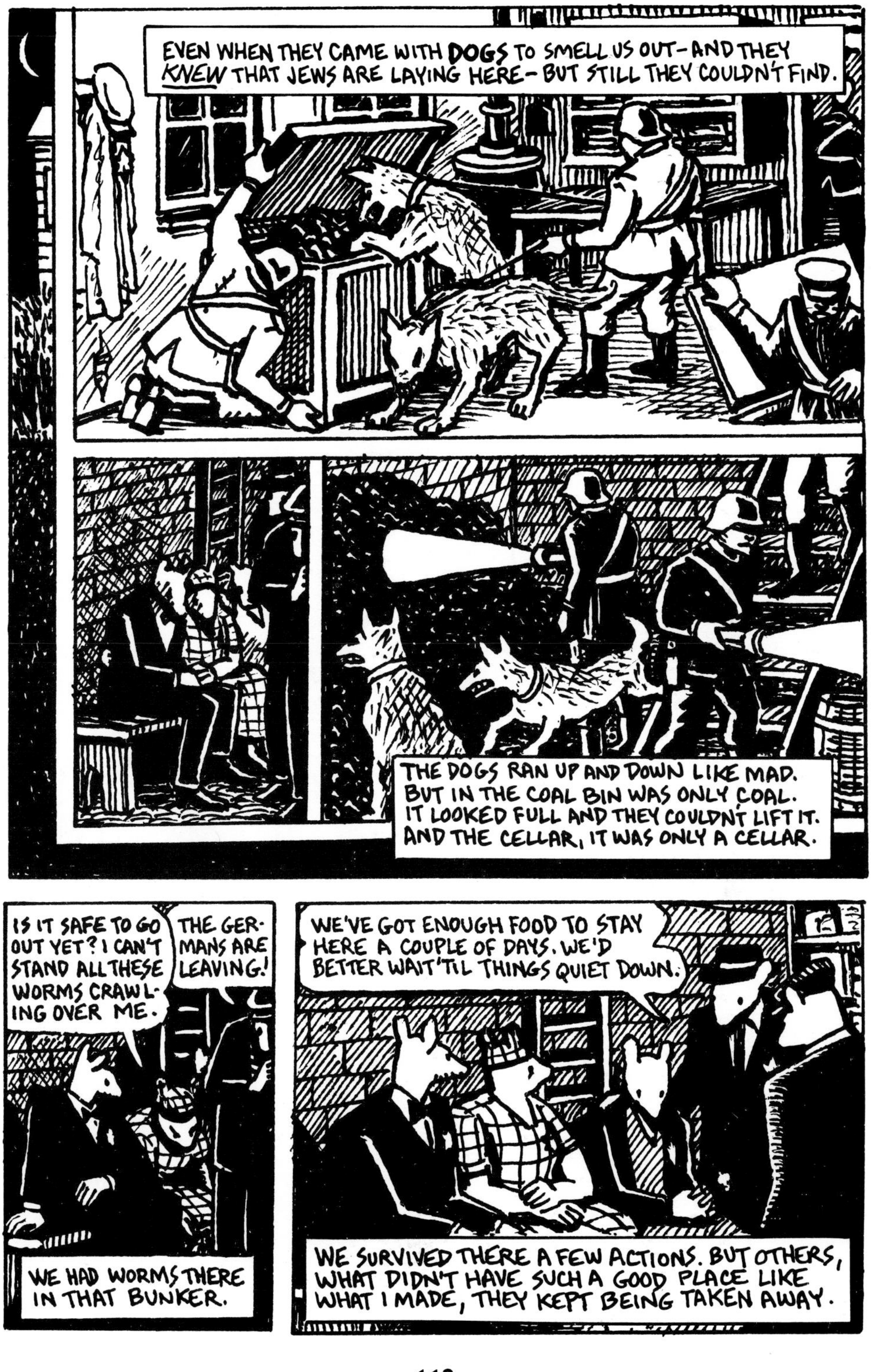
EVEN WHEN THEY CAME WITH DOGS TO SMELL US OUT- AND THEY KNEW THAT JEWS ARE LAYING HERE- BUT STILL THEY COULDN'T FIND.
THE DOGS RAN UP AND DOWN LIKE MAD. BUT IN THE COAL BIN WAS ONLY COAL. IT LOOKED FULL AND THEY COULDN'T LIFT IT. AND THE CELLAR, IT WAS ONLY A CELLAR.
IS IT SAFE TO GO OUT YET? I CAN'T STAND ALL THESE WORMS CRAWLING OVER ME.
THE GERMANS ARE LEAVING!
WE HAD WORMS THERE IN THAT BUNKER.
WE'VE GOT ENOUGH FOOD TO STAY HERE A COUPLE OF DAYS. WE'D BETTER WAIT 'TIL THINGS QUIET DOWN.
WE SURVIVED THERE A FEW ACTIONS. BUT OTHERS, WHAT DIDN'T HAVE SUCH A GOOD PLACE LIKE WHAT I MADE, THEY KEPT BEING TAKEN AWAY.

THEN, IN JUNE, THEY ARRESTED MONIEK MERIN AND ALL THE OTHER HIGHEST BIG SHOTS OF THE *JUDENRAT*, THE JEWISH COUNCIL.

false wall

BUNKER

ATTIC

Entrance hidden by chandelier

UPSTAIRS BEDROOM

AROUND THIS TIME WE WERE PUT INTO A DIFFERENT HOUSE. HERE ALSO WE MADE A BUNKER.

BY THE END OF JULY THE NAZIS MADE TO LIQUIDATE COMPLETELY OUR GHETTO—IT WAS 10,000 JEWS TAKEN AWAY IN ONE WEEK.

EXCEPT TO SNEAK FOR FOOD, WE STAYED MOSTLY IN THE BUNKER.

LOLEK! THANK GOD YOU'RE SAFE!

IT'S LIKE A BATTLEFIELD OUTSIDE!

THERE'S HARDLY ANYONE LEFT IN SRODULA. EVERYONE HAS BEEN DEPORTED OR SHOT.

FROM ALL THE JEWS OF ALL SOSNOWIEC IT WAS LEFT MAYBE 1,000 IN THE GHETTO.

AT LEAST YOUR BAG IS FULL... YOU FOUND A LOT OF FOOD, YES?

JUST A FEW OLD TURNIPS... AND SOME BOOKS.

BOOKS!? WHAT'S THE MATTER WITH YOU? WE CAN'T EAT BOOKS!

SHH

ALL THE TIME WE WERE HUNGRY. WE JUST DIDN'T HAVE WHAT TO EAT.

ONE NIGHT WE WENT TO SNEAK FOR FOOD...

WE DRAGGED HIM UP TO OUR BUNKER

MY WIFE AND I HAVE A STARVING BABY. I WAS OUT HUNTING FOR SCRAPS!

HE'S LYING!

HE MAY BE AN INFORMER. THE SAFEST THING WOULD BE TO KILL HIM!

WHAT HAD WE TO DO? WE TOOK ON HIM PITY.

IN THE MORNING WE GAVE A LITTLE FOOD TO HIM AND LEFT HIM GO TO HIS FAMILY...

JUDEN RAUS!

...THE GESTAPO CAME THAT AFTERNOON.

THEY TOOK US TO A BUILDING IN A PART OF SRODULA SEPARATED BY WIRES— A GHETTO INSIDE THE GHETTO — AND THERE WE HAD TO SIT AND TO WAIT.

115

WE WERE MAYBE 200 PEOPLE TOGETHER WAITING... EACH WEDNESDAY WENT VANS TO AUSCHWITZ. WHEN WE WERE CAUGHT, IT WAS THEN MAYBE A THURSDAY.

LOOK, ANJA! THAT'S MY COUSIN, JAKOV SPIEGELMAN, IN THE COURTYARD.

HEY! JAKOV! HELP! JAKOV-HELP US!

VLADEK?! THERE'S NOTHING I CAN DO!

I MADE SIGNS TO SHOW I COULD PAY.

SOME GOLD I HID IN THE CHIMNEY OF OUR BUNKER WHEN THEY TOOK US. BUT A FEW VALUABLES I HAD STILL WITH ME.

OKAY. DON'T WORRY! HASKEL WILL COME HELP YOU!

HASKEL SPIEGELMAN WAS ANOTHER COUSIN.

WOULDN'T THEY HAVE HELPED YOU EVEN IF YOU COULDN'T PAY? I MEAN, YOU WERE FROM THE SAME FAMILY..

HAH! YOU DON'T UNDERSTAND...

AT THAT TIME IT WASN'T ANYMORE FAMILIES. IT WAS EVERYBODY TO TAKE CARE FOR HIMSELF!

THE NEXT DAY CAME IN TWO GIRLS CARRYING FOOD. WITH THEM CAME HASKEL, A CHIEF OF THE JEWISH POLICE.

LOOK, VLADEK. I CAN GET YOU AND YOUR WIFE OUT—EVEN YOUR NEPHEW. BUT YOUR IN-LAWS ARE TOO OLD. THEY'LL NEVER GET PAST THE GUARDS.

PLEASE! WE'LL MAKE IT WORTH YOUR WHILE.

THE TWO GIRLS HE SENT BACK TO THE KITCHEN.

QUICK, BOY. GRAB THIS EMPTY PAIL AND CARRY IT OUT WITH ME.

FROM THE WINDOW WE SAW LOLEK GO.

MY GOD, VLADEK...

YOU MUST GET MATKA AND ME OUT TOO. GIVE YOUR COUSIN THIS GOLD WATCH, THIS DIAMOND—ANYTHING!

OF COURSE I-I'LL DO EVERY-THING I CAN.

THE DAY AFTER, ANJA AND I CARRIED PAST THE GUARDS THE EMPTY PAILS.

HASKEL TOOK FROM ME FATHER-IN-LAW'S JEWELS. BUT, FINALLY, HE DIDN'T HELP THEM.

ON WEDNESDAY THE VANS CAME. ANJA AND I SAW HER FATHER AT THE WINDOW. HE WAS TEARING HIS HAIR AND CRYING.

HE WAS A MILLIONAIRE, BUT EVEN THIS DIDN'T SAVE HIM HIS LIFE.

117

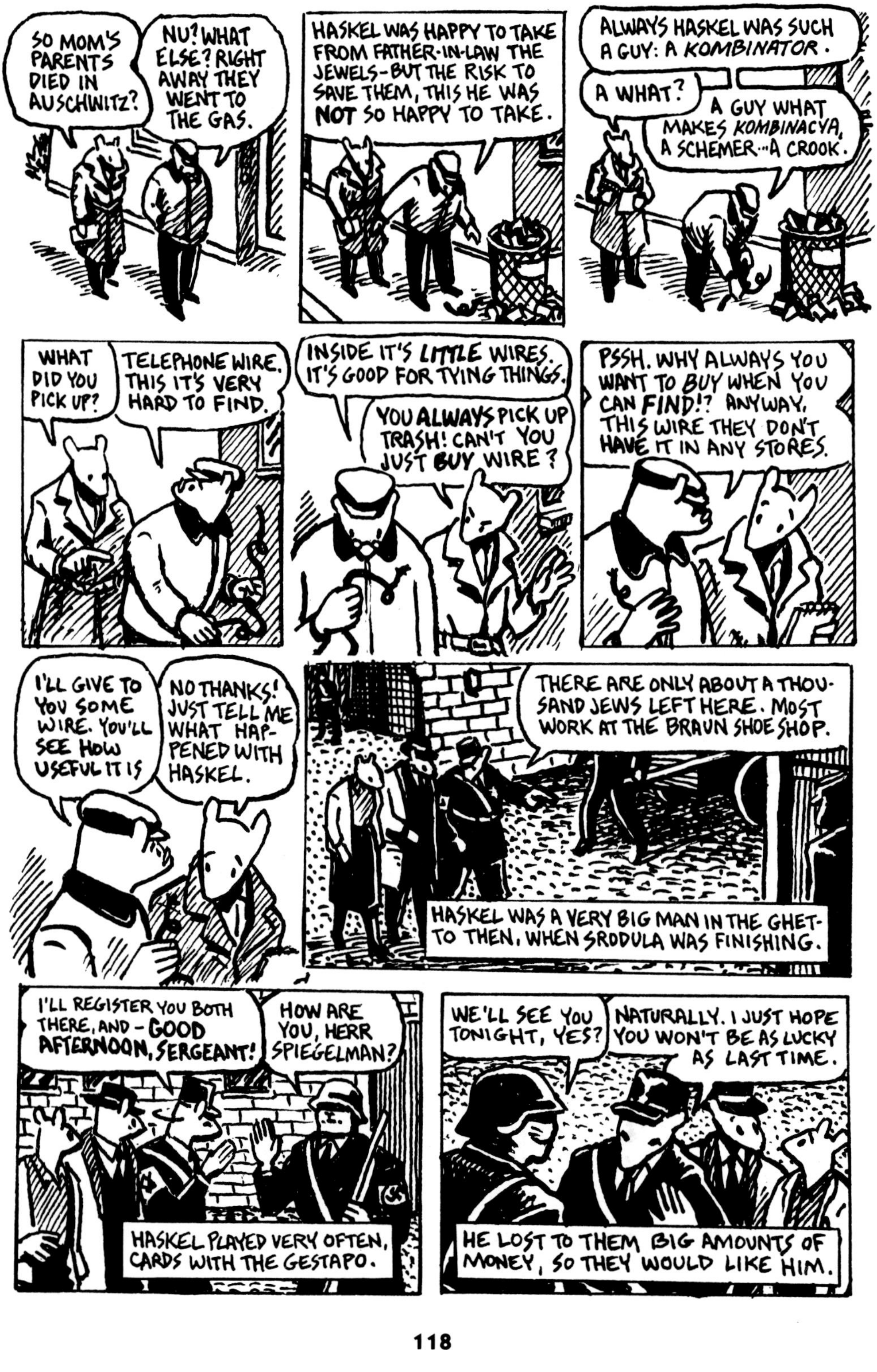
SO MOM'S PARENTS DIED IN AUSCHWITZ?
NU? WHAT ELSE? RIGHT AWAY THEY WENT TO THE GAS.
HASKEL WAS HAPPY TO TAKE FROM FATHER-IN-LAW THE JEWELS—BUT THE RISK TO SAVE THEM, THIS HE WAS **NOT** SO HAPPY TO TAKE.
ALWAYS HASKEL WAS SUCH A GUY: A *KOMBINATOR*.
A WHAT?
A GUY WHAT MAKES *KOMBINACYA*, A SCHEMER...A CROOK.
WHAT DID YOU PICK UP?
TELEPHONE WIRE. THIS IT'S VERY HARD TO FIND.
INSIDE IT'S **LITTLE** WIRES. IT'S GOOD FOR TYING THINGS.
YOU **ALWAYS** PICK UP TRASH! CAN'T YOU JUST **BUY** WIRE?
PSSH. WHY ALWAYS YOU WANT TO *BUY* WHEN YOU CAN **FIND**!? ANYWAY, THIS WIRE THEY DON'T HAVE IT IN ANY STORES.
I'LL GIVE TO YOU SOME WIRE. YOU'LL SEE HOW USEFUL IT IS
NO THANKS! JUST TELL ME WHAT HAPPENED WITH HASKEL.
THERE ARE ONLY ABOUT A THOUSAND JEWS LEFT HERE. MOST WORK AT THE BRAUN SHOE SHOP.
HASKEL WAS A VERY BIG MAN IN THE GHETTO THEN, WHEN SRODULA WAS FINISHING.
I'LL REGISTER YOU BOTH THERE, AND—**GOOD AFTERNOON, SERGEANT!**
HOW ARE YOU, HERR SPIEGELMAN?
HASKEL PLAYED VERY OFTEN, CARDS WITH THE GESTAPO.
WE'LL SEE YOU TONIGHT, YES?
NATURALLY. I JUST HOPE YOU WON'T BE AS LUCKY AS LAST TIME.
HE LOST TO THEM BIG AMOUNTS OF MONEY, SO THEY WOULD LIKE HIM.

MILOCH-TAKE CARE OF COUSIN VLADEK.

GLADLY

BEN HERE CAN SHOW YOU HOW TO RESOLE THE GERMAN BOOTS.

HASKEL HAD 2 BROTHERS, PESACH AND MILOCH. PESACH WAS ALSO A *KOMBINATOR*. BUT MILOCH, HE WAS A FINE FELLOW.

WE'LL RESERVE THIS WORKBENCH FOR YOU...

YOU DON'T HAVE TO SIT HERE ALL THE TIME, BUT WHENEVER THE GERMAN COMMISSION COMES TO INSPECT, JUST SIT THERE AND LOOK BUSY...

FROM TIME TO TIME I HAD OTHER JOBS ALSO TO DO AROUND THE GHETTO...

YES! THIS REMINDS ME SOMETHING NOW...

REMEMBER THIS GUY WHAT I TOLD YOU GAVE US OUT OF OUR BUNKER?...

WELL, YOU KNOW, I BURIED HIM...

HEY! THIS IS THE RAT THAT TURNED MY FAMILY OVER TO THE GESTAPO.

HE WAS SHOT!

HASKEL HAD ARRANGED HE WOULD BE KILLED.

BUT IF HE'S DEAD WHY ARE HIS EYES STILL WIDE OPEN?

HE WAS STRUGGLING TO SURVIVE.

IT HAPPENED I WAS ON THE WORK DETAIL, SO... I BURIED HIM.

119

HASKEL IS ALIVE STILL IN PO-LAND, WITH A POLISH WOMAN, A JUDGE, WHAT KEPT HIM HIDDEN WHEN **HYAAK!**

MMY HEART-ARTIE! QUICK! TAKE FROM MY POCKET A NITROSTAT PILL.

H-HERE... YOU OKAY?

HOOSH

I-I'LL BE FINE NOW. I HAVE ONLY TO CATCH MY BREATH STILL FOR A MINUTE.

LET'S SIT ON THAT STOOP.

JUST RELAX. DON'T TALK FOR A WHILE.

HOOH! I MADE TOO FAST, OUR WALKING!

THANK GOD, WITH THE NITROSTAT IT'S COMPLETE-LY OVER RIGHT AWAY! WHAT WAS I TELLING YOU?

YOU SURE YOU'RE OKAY?

WELL... YOU WERE SAYING THAT HASKEL SURVIVED THE WAR.

YES. EVEN A FEW YEARS AGO I SENT HIM PACKAGES.

GIFTS? WHY? HE SOUNDS LIKE A ROTTEN GUY!

YES. I DON'T KNOW WHY. I KNOW ONLY THAT I SENT.

YOU KNOW, ONE TIME I WAS IN THE GHETTO WALKING AROUND...

HALT, JEW!

GIVE ME YOUR I.D. PA-PERS- I'M GOING TO BLOW YOUR BRAINS OUT.

AH. I SEE YOU'RE A MEMBER OF THE ILLUS-TRIOUS SPIEGELMAN FAMILY... GO ON YOUR WAY THEN, AND GIVE HASKEL MY REGARDS.

..... *SUCH* FRIENDS HASKEL HAD.

I TOLD HASKEL AND MILOCH LATER ABOUT THIS.

YOU WERE VERY LUCKY, VLADEK...

THEY CALL HIM "THE SHOOTER". EVERY DAY HE KILLS SOME POOR JEW, JUST FOR FUN.

HEY! AREN'T YOU GOING OVER TO PESACH'S TO BUY SOME CAKE?

CAKE?

FOR YEARS WE DIDN'T SEE ANY CAKE. HARDLY EVEN BREAD WE SAW!

IT'S IM-POSSIBLE!

HE'S JOKING!

CAKE!

BUT COUSIN PESACH WAS REALLY SELLING CAKE! EVERYONE WHAT COULD AFFORD IT STOOD ON LINE TO BUY A PIECE...

IT LOOKS DELICIOUS.

HOW DID YOU MAN-AGE IT, PESACH?

WHEN PEOPLE ARE SENT TO AUSCHWITZ, MY MEN SEARCH THEIR HOUSES.

PESACH WAS LIKE HASKEL. PART OF THE JEWISH POLICE.

THEY FIND A LITTLE FLOUR HERE, A FEW GRAMS OF SUGAR THERE....I SAVED IT!

HE WAS YOUNGER FROM HAS-KEL, BUT ALSO A "KOMBINATOR."

YOU KNOW WHAT A COOK MY RIFKA IS... TRY IT! ONLY 75 ZLOTYS A SLICE.

I HAD STILL SAVINGS, SO I GOT FOR ANJA AND ME SOME CAKE.

BUT, THE WHOLE GHETTO, WE WERE SO SICK LATER, YOU CAN'T IMAGINE...

SOME OF THE FLOUR PESACH FOUND—IT WASN'T REALLY FLOUR, ONLY LAUNDRY SOAP, WHAT HE PUT IN THE CAKE BY MISTAKE.

OW!

GROAN

OY!

OUCH!

...WE WERE, ALL OF US, SICK LIKE DOGS.

BEFORE THE WAR PESACH HAD A RESORT HOTEL IN ZAKOPANE...

IN THOSE DAYS ALSO HE FOUND ALWAYS SCHEMES.

ALL GUESTS HAD TO PAY BIG POLISH TAXES... SO PESACH TOOK BRIBES TO NOT REGISTER THEM. BUT IF AN INSPECTOR CAME, THE GUESTS HAD TO HIDE THEMSELVES AWAY.

ONE TIME HIS WIFE MADE NOT ENOUGH DESSERTS TO GIVE TO EVERYBODY...
SO PESACH RAN INTO THE DINING ROOM AND YELLED, "INSPECTORS ARE COMING!"

IT WAS NO INSPECTOR, OF COURSE. BUT 40% OF THE GUESTS RAN FAST FROM THE ROOM. ... PESACH HAD ENOUGH DESSERTS LEFT OVER EVEN FOR THE NEXT DAY!

COME.

ARE YOU READY TO WALK AGAIN?

YES, IT'S TOO DIRTY TO SIT!
...BUT, REALLY, IF I DIDN'T HAVE MY NITROSTAT, IT COULD HAVE BEEN JUST NOW SOMETHING TERRIBLE.

MILOCH SPIEGELMAN—HE SURVIVED THE WAR WITH HIS WIFE AND CHILD AND THEY MOVED TO AUSTRALIA. ABOUT FIVE YEARS AGO HE GOT A BIG HEART ATTACK...

AND LAST YEAR, HE GOT ON THE STREET A SEIZURE—LIKE WHAT I HAD JUST NOW... BUT HE DIDN'T HAVE WITH HIM HIS PILLS. HIS WIFE RAN TO FIND A DRUG STORE.

WHEN SHE CAME BACK MILOCH WAS DEAD!

NU? SO LIFE GOES.

BUT I MUST FINISH QUICK TO TELL YOU THE REST ABOUT SRODULA, BECAUSE WE WILL COME SOON OVER TO THE BANK.

SALE

BY THE END OF 1943 THE VANS WENT EVERY WEDNESDAY WITH MORE AND MORE AND MORE PEOPLE FROM SRODULA TO AUSCHWITZ. UNTIL IT WAS VERY FEW LEFT.

IT COULD BE OUR TURN SOON, EH VLADEK?

LET'S HOPE NOT, MILOCH.

HASKEL HEARD THAT ANY DAY NOW THEY INTEND TO DEPORT EVERYONE THAT'S STILL LEFT HERE.

MILOCH TOOK ME TO THE SHOE SHOP

IT WAS EARLY AND NOBODY WAS THERE...

HASKEL MADE PLANS TO SMUGGLE HIMSELF OUT OF THE GHETTO.

PESACH AND I HAVE A PLAN ALSO...

HE MOVED A FEW SHOES FROM A PILE HIGH TO THE CEILING...

...AND TOOK ME INSIDE A TUNNEL...

DON'T TELL ANYONE ABOUT THIS EXCEPT ANJA AND YOUR NEPHEW.

...A TUNNEL MADE FROM SHOES!

WE CAME OUT TO A BUNKER...

BE PREPARED TO BRING THEM ON A MOMENT'S NOTICE!

INCREDIBLE!

EVERYTHING WAS READY HERE SO 15 OR 16 PEOPLE COULD HIDE.

...BUT WHEN ANJA AND I APPROACHED TO DISCUSS THIS BUNKER WITH LOLEK...

NO THANKS, FORGET IT!

BUT MILOCH ORGANIZED EVERYTHING!

I'M SICK OF HIDING!

OUR NEPHEW WAS THEN ONLY 15. HE WAS WORKING AS AN ELECTRICIAN.

ALWAYS LOLEK WAS A LITTLE MESHUGA...

I'M A SKILLED WORKER. WHEREVER THEY TAKE ME, I'LL BE OKAY.

YOU'RE CRAZY! YOU'RE GOING STRAIGHT TO THE OVENS!

AND HE DID GET PUT INTO ONE OF THE NEXT TRANSPORTS TO AUSCHWITZ.

ANJA BECAME COMPLETELY HYSTERICAL.

THE WHOLE FAMILY IS GONE! GRANDMA AND GRANDPA! POPPA! MOMMA! TOSHA! BIBI! MY RICHIEU!! NOW THEY'LL TAKE LOLEK!

IT WAS ALSO AROUND THIS TIME THAT WE HEARD FIRST THE BAD NEWS FROM ZAWIERCIE-ABOUT TOSHA AND RICHIEU.

OH GOD. LET ME DIE TOO!

COME, ANJA. GET UP!

WHY ARE YOU PULLING ME, VLADEK? LET ME ALONE! I DON'T WANT TO LIVE!

NO, DARLING! TO DIE, IT'S EASY...

BUT YOU HAVE TO STRUGGLE FOR LIFE!

UNTIL THE LAST MOMENT WE MUST STRUGGLE TOGETHER! I NEED YOU!

AND YOU'LL SEE THAT TOGETHER WE'LL SURVIVE.

THIS ALWAYS I TOLD TO HER.

THE GHETTO FINISHED OUT SO LIKE MILOCH SAID. ABOUT TWELVE FROM US RAN INTO HIS BUNKER WITH HIM, HIS WIFE AND HIS THREE-YEARS-OLD BABY BOY.

GUTCHA, YOU'VE GOT TO KEEP THE BABY QUIET!

WAAH! I'M HUNGRY!

WE'LL HAVE TO KEEP HIM UNDER BLANKETS UNTIL HE CALMS DOWN.

HUSH.

IN A BUNKER IN ANOTHER PART FROM THE SHOE SHOP LAY PESACH AND SOME OTHERS.

IT WAS NOTHING TO DO ALL DAY BUT TO LIE AND TO STARVE.

THE WHOLE DAY AND NIGHT ANJA SAT WRITING INTO HER NOTEBOOK.

THERE! I'VE MANAGED TO DIG A SMALL HOLE IN THE STONE WALL.

I CAN SEE SOLDIERS.

ALL AROUND WERE GUARDS TO FIND ANY WHO REMAINED HIDING.

WHAT LITTLE FOOD WE HAD, SOON IT WAS GONE.

OHH... I WISH I HAD SOME BREAD... I WISH I HAD SOME BREAD... I WISH—

QUIET! WE'RE ALL STARVING!

AT NIGHT WE SNEAKED OUT TO LOOK FOR WHAT TO EAT... BUT IT WAS NOTHING TO FIND.

HERE, ANJA— CHEW ON THIS.

YOU FOUND FOOD?

NEVER ANY OF US HAD BEEN SO HUNGRY LIKE THEN.

NO, IT'S ONLY WOOD. BUT CHEWING IT FEELS A LITTLE LIKE EATING FOOD.

AFTER A TIME PESACH CAME OVER TO US FROM HIS BUNKER...

MAYBE YOU FOOLS ARE WILLING TO LIE HERE UNTIL YOU STARVE TO DEATH—BUT NOT ME!...

I'VE CONTACTED ONE OF THE GUARDS.

IT'LL COST A FORTUNE, BUT HE'S AGREED TO LOOK THE OTHER WAY.

OUR GROUP WILL MIX IN WITH THE POLES WHEN THEY WALK PAST SRODULA ON THE WAY TO WORK TOMORROW... IF YOU WANT TO CHIP IN YOU CAN COME WITH US.

MANY FROM OUR BUNKER SAID YES.

MILOCH AND I, WE SAID NO TO THIS IDEA. WE DIDN'T TRUST TO THE GERMANS.

ONE GUY FROM OUR BUNKER, AVRAM, CAME TO ME.

HE SAID, "TELL ME WHEN *YOU* WILL GO OUT, VLADEK. *THEN* I'LL KNOW IT'S SAFE."

HE AND HIS GIRLFRIEND WANTED TO PAY ME TO ADVISE.

THEY HAD STILL 2 WATCHES AND SOME DIAMOND RINGS. I DIDN'T WANT TO TAKE. THEY *NEEDED* THESE TO LIVE.

SO I TOOK ONLY THE SMALL WATCH.

THE NEXT MORNING, VERY EARLY, THE GROUP WALKED OUT.

I STOOD, SECRET, BEHIND A CORNER. I HEARD LOUD SHOOTING, AND I DIDN'T GO TO SEE WHAT HAPPENED...

THEY GAVE OVER THE MONEY AND WENT PAST THE GUARD.

TAKKA TAKKA TAKKA

I ONLY RAN VERY FAST BACK TO OUR BUNKER.

ONLY A FEW OF US REMAINED.

THERE HAVEN'T BEEN ANY LIGHTS ON IN THE GUARD-HOUSE FOR TWO NIGHTS... I THINK IT'S SAFE.

A LITTLE BEFORE DAWN WE WENT OUT FROM SRODULA...

THEY'RE ALL GONE!

THE GHETTO IS EMPTY!

WHEW

AHEAD OF TIME WE ORGANIZED OUR-SELVES GOOD CLOTHES AND I.D. PAPERS.

WE MIXED WITH THE POLES GOING TO WORK.

WE'LL BE HIDING AT THIS AD-DRESS. WHEN YOU FIND A SAFE PLACE, TRY TO CONTACT US, VLADEK.

GOOD LUCK, MILOCH.

WE WENT ALL IN DIF-FERENT DIRECTIONS.

THAT GUY, AVRAM, HIS WOMAN HAD FRIENDS TO KEEP THEM.

AND THE FRIENDS KEPT THEM... UNTIL AVRAM'S MONEY FINISHED. THEN THEY WERE REPORTED.

ANJA AND I DIDN'T HAVE WHERE TO GO.

WE WALKED IN THE DIRECTION OF SOSNOWIEC - BUT *WHERE TO GO?!*

IT WAS *NOWHERE* WE HAD TO HIDE.

CAN I HELP YOU, MR. SPIEGELMAN?

YES, I HAVE HERE MY SON, ARTIE. I WANT TO SIGN HIM A KEY. SO HE CAN GO ALSO TO MY SAFETY BOX.

IN CASE ANYTHING BAD HAPPENS TO ME YOU MUST RUN *RIGHT AWAY* OVER HERE.

THEREFORE I ARRANGED FOR YOU THIS KEY.

TAKE EVERYTHING OUT FROM THE SAFE. OTHERWISE IT CAN GO ONLY TO TAXES. OR *MALA* WILL GRAB IT.

PLEASE, POP....

TALKING ABOUT YOUR ESTATE JUST MAKES ME UNCOMFORTABLE.

YOU'RE NOW OLD ENOUGH SO WE *MUST* THINK OF THESE THINGS.

WHY DON'T YOU JUST ENJOY YOUR SAVINGS WHILE YOU STILL CAN?

I'LL KEEP IN MY DESK YOUR COPY OF THE KEY. YOU ONLY WOULD LOSE IT!

LOOK, YOU SEE WHAT I HAVE HERE? THIS CIGARETTE CASE AND THE LADY'S POWDER CASE—IT'S 14 KARATS GOLD.

UH HUH

ANK

THESE THINGS I HAD WITH ME *THEN*—IN SRODULA, IN THE CHANDELIER BUNKER.

REALLY? HOW CAN YOU POSSIBLY STILL HAVE THEM?

BAN

WHEN THE GESTAPO FOUND US I DROPPED *QUICK* A FEW THINGS INTO THE CHIMNEY.... IF THEY FOUND THE REST OF MY JEWELS, AT LEAST *THESE* MIGHT REMAIN.

AFTER I CAME OUT FROM THE CAMPS IN 1945 I SNEAKED BACK TO SRODULA AND—AT NIGHT, WHILE THE PEOPLE INSIDE SLEPT—I DIGGED THESE THINGS OUT FROM THE BOTTOM OF THE CHIMNEY.

BM

GOSH.

 YOU SEE THIS DIAMOND? THIS I GAVE TO ANJA WHEN FIRST WE CAME TO THE U.S.

 EVEN WHEN YOU WERE A LITTLE BOY, ANJA WANTED THAT THIS RING SHOULD BE FOR YOUR WIFE.

 BUT IF I GIVE IT TO YOU, MALA WILL DRIVE ME CRAZY. SHE WANTS EVERYTHING ONLY FOR HER.

 SHE WANTS THAT I GIVE NOTHING FOR MY BROTHER IN ISRAEL, AND NOTHING FOR YOU — THREE TIMES ALREADY SHE MADE ME CHANGE OVER MY WILL.

C'MON — MALA'S OKAY!

 YOU ONLY CAN'T KNOW! EVEN RIGHT AFTER MY LAST HEART ATTACK, WHEN STILL I WAS IN BED, SHE STARTED AGAIN ABOUT CHANGING THE WILL!

 I SAID, "MALA, YOU SEE HOW SICK I AM. LET ME A LITTLE BIT HAVE SOME PEACE. WHAT YOU WANT FROM ME?"

 AND SHE SCREAMED, "I WANT THE MONEY! THE MONEY, THE MONEY!"

 WHY, ARTIE? WHY I EVER REMARRIED?

 OY, ANJA! ANJA! ANJA!

EASY, POP... LET'S GO HOME.

C H A P T E R   S I X

MOUSE
TRAP

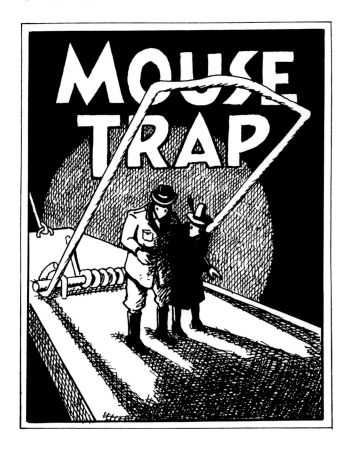

Another visit...

ANYBODY HOME? THE DOOR WASN'T LOCKED, SO I ...

HUH? MALA? WERE YOU CRYING?

NO. SNK I DON'T KNOW.

I TELL YOU, I'M AT MY WITS' END!

WHAT NOW?

YOUR FATHER! HE TREATS ME AS IF I WERE JUST A MAID OR HIS NURSE... **WORSE**!

AT LEAST A MAID HAS SOME DAYS OFF AND GETS PAID!

HE ONLY GIVES ME $50⁰⁰ A MONTH. WHEN I NEED A PAIR OF STOCKINGS I HAVE TO USE MY OWN SAVINGS!

WELL... HE HASN'T CHANGED...

WHENEVER I NEEDED SCHOOL SUPPLIES OR NEW CLOTHES MOM WOULD HAVE TO PLEAD AND ARGUE FOR **WEEKS** BEFORE HE'D COUGH UP ANY DOUGH!

WHEN I TRY TO ARGUE WITH HIM HE MOANS LIKE HE'S GOING TO HAVE ANOTHER HEART ATTACK.

I CAN'T BE SURE IF HE'S FAKING, SO I HAVE TO STOP!

I FEEL LIKE I'M IN PRISON!

I FEEL LIKE I'M GOING TO **BURST**!

132

I'M GONNA GET SOME JUICE. WANT SOME?

NO. I'LL TELL YOU SOME- THING—WHEN WE FIRST GOT MARRIED, I NEEDED CLOTHES...

IT WAS A YEAR AND A HALF AFTER ANJA DIED. HE TOOK ME TO HER CLOSET, AND SAID: "ALL THESE ARE FOR YOU!"

I SAID I WOULDN'T *TOUCH* HER THINGS!

..MY GOD, HOW THAT MAN CARRIED ON! I SWEAR, SOMETIMES I THINK HE MARRIED ME BECAUSE I'M THE SAME SIZE AS ANJA!

HE'S ALWAYS BEEN -UH- PRAGMATIC.

PRAGMATIC? **CHEAP!!** IT CAUSES HIM PHYSICAL PAIN TO PART WITH EVEN A NICKEL!

UH-HUH

I USED TO THINK THE **WAR** MADE HIM THAT WAY...

FAH! I WENT THROUGH THE CAMPS...

ALL OUR FRIENDS WENT THROUGH THE CAMPS. **NOBODY** IS LIKE HIM!

MM..

...IT'S SOMETHING THAT WORRIES ME ABOUT THE BOOK I'M DOING ABOUT HIM...

IN SOME WAYS HE'S JUST LIKE THE RACIST CARICATURE OF THE MISERLY OLD JEW.

HAH! YOU CAN SAY *THAT* AGAIN!

I MEAN, I'M JUST TRYING TO PORTRAY MY FATHER ACCURATELY!...

EVEN FOR HIMSELF HE WON'T SPEND ANY MONEY...

HE HAS HUNDREDS OF THOUSANDS OF DOLLARS IN THE BANK, AND HE LIVES LIKE A PAUPER!...

LOOK! HE GRABS PAPER TOWELS FROM REST ROOMS SO HE WON'T HAVE TO BUY NAPKINS OR TISSUES!

I WISH I GOT MOM'S STORY WHILE SHE WAS ALIVE. SHE WAS MORE SENSITIVE... IT WOULD GIVE THE BOOK SOME BALANCE.

YOUR MOTHER!...

...I JUST DON'T KNOW HOW SHE COULD STAND LIVING WITH HIM...

...I DON'T KNOW HOW I CAN STAND IT!

SO..HI, "KIDS."...

I DIDN'T KNOW YOU ARE UPSTAIRS HERE. I WAS WATERING DOWNSTAIRS THE GARDEN.

MALA AND I WERE JUST TALKING ABOUT MY BOOK...

I'VE ALREADY STARTED TO SKETCH OUT SOME PARTS.

I'LL SHOW YOU...

...SEE, HERE ARE THE BLACK MARKET JEWS THEY HANGED IN SOSNOWIEC...

ACH.

AND HERE'S **YOU**, SAYING: "ACH. WHEN I THINK OF THEM, IT STILL MAKES ME CRY!"

YES. **STILL** IT MAKES ME CRY!

IT'S AN IMPORTANT BOOK. PEOPLE WHO DON'T USUALLY READ SUCH STORIES WILL BE INTERESTED.

YES. I DON'T READ **EVER** SUCH COMICS, AND EVEN **I** AM INTERESTED.

OF COURSE **YOU** ARE INTERESTED. IT'S YOUR STORY!

YES. I KNOW ALREADY MY STORY BY **HEART**, AND EVEN **I** AM INTERESTED!

IT SHOULD BE VERY SUCCESSFUL.

YAH. SOMEDAY YOU'LL BE **FAMOUS**, LIKE ...WHAT'S-HIS-NAME?

HUH? "FAMOUS LIKE WHAT'S-HIS-NAME?!"

YOU KNOW... THE BIG-SHOT CARTOONIST...

WHAT CARTOONIST COULD **YOU** KNOW? ...WALT DISNEY??

YAH! WALT DISNEY!

WAIT! WHERE DO YOU GO, ARTIE?

...TO GET A PENCIL... I'VE JUST **GOTTA** WRITE THIS CONVERSATION DOWN BEFORE I FORGET IT!

COME. WE'LL ALL OF US GO TO THE GARDEN...YOU'LL SEE HOW NICE IT LOOKS, THE BUSHES.

YOU GO! I'VE GOT TO GET READY...

...I HAVE AN APPOINTMENT AT THE HAIRDRESSER'S.

AGAIN TO THE HAIRDRESSER? ONLY A WEEK AGO YOU WENT!

SHE SEES MORE OFTEN THE HAIRDRESSER THAN SHE SEES ME!

YOU **SEE** HOW IT IS? ANY TIME I WANT TO GO OUT FOR A FEW MINUTES HE TRIES TO MAKE ME FEEL **GUILTY**! I'M SUPPOSED TO BE AT HIS CONSTANT BECK AND CALL!

WHAT I SAID THAT'S SO TERRIBLE? BELIEVE ME, YOU'D HAVE MORE FRESH AIR FROM THE GARDEN THAN FROM A **HUNDRED** HAIRDRESSERS!

OI, VLADEK. STOP IT!

YOU SEE HOW SHE IS? WHAT HAVE I TO DO WITH HER?

C'MON, POP. LET'S GO SIT IN THE GARDEN.

IF I SAY ONLY ONE WORD TO HER, SHE MAKES RIGHT AWAY AN ARGUMENT!

SHE SAYS SHE WANTS TO **LEAVE** ME! I TELL TO HER: "SO? HERE IS THE DOOR. BUT, REMEMBER, IT'S ONLY ONE WAY... IF YOU GO OUT, YOU CAN'T COME BACK!"

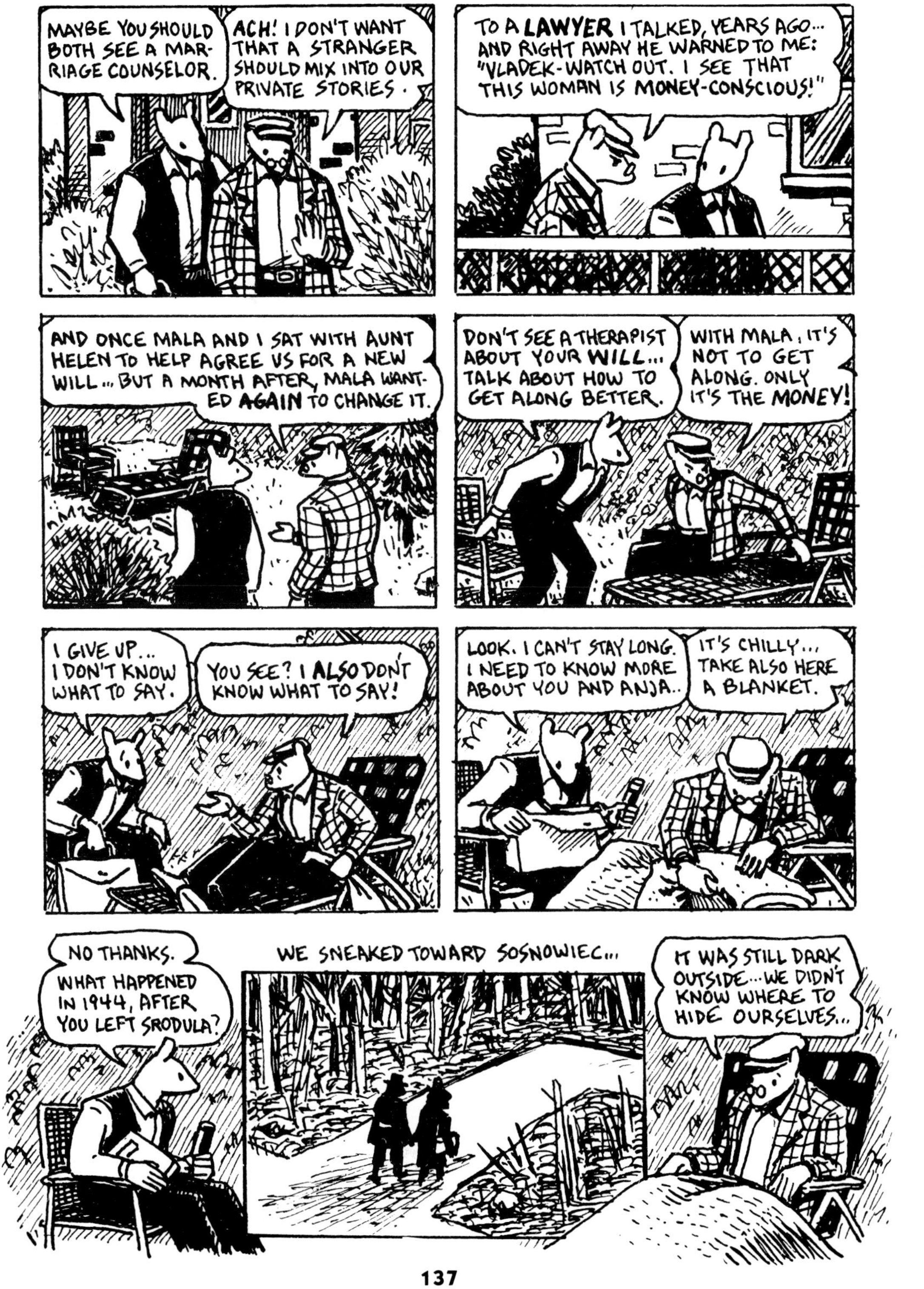
MAYBE YOU SHOULD BOTH SEE A MARRIAGE COUNSELOR.
ACH! I DON'T WANT THAT A STRANGER SHOULD MIX INTO OUR PRIVATE STORIES.
TO A LAWYER I TALKED, YEARS AGO... AND RIGHT AWAY HE WARNED TO ME: "VLADEK-WATCH OUT. I SEE THAT THIS WOMAN IS MONEY-CONSCIOUS!"
AND ONCE MALA AND I SAT WITH AUNT HELEN TO HELP AGREE US FOR A NEW WILL... BUT A MONTH AFTER, MALA WANTED AGAIN TO CHANGE IT.
DON'T SEE A THERAPIST ABOUT YOUR WILL... TALK ABOUT HOW TO GET ALONG BETTER.
WITH MALA, IT'S NOT TO GET ALONG. ONLY IT'S THE MONEY!
I GIVE UP... I DON'T KNOW WHAT TO SAY.
YOU SEE? I ALSO DON'T KNOW WHAT TO SAY!
LOOK. I CAN'T STAY LONG. I NEED TO KNOW MORE ABOUT YOU AND ANJA..
IT'S CHILLY... TAKE ALSO HERE A BLANKET.
NO THANKS.
WHAT HAPPENED IN 1944, AFTER YOU LEFT SRODULA?
WE SNEAKED TOWARD SOSNOWIEC...
IT WAS STILL DARK OUTSIDE... WE DIDN'T KNOW WHERE TO HIDE OURSELVES...

JANINA LIVES OVER THERE.

RICHIEU'S GOVERNESS ALWAYS OFFERED SHE WOULD HELP US.

WE CAME TO HER HOUSE NEAR TOWN...

OPEN UP, JANINA! QUICK!

W-WHO'S THERE?

MY GOD! IT'S THE SPIEGELMANS!

YOU'LL BRING TROUBLE! GO AWAY! QUICKLY!

SLAM

I'M FRIGHTENED, VLADEK.

MAYBE WE SHOULD TRY MY FATHER'S OLD HOUSE. THE JANITOR HAS KNOWN OUR FAMILY FOR YEARS.

LET'S TRY. WE'VE GOT TO GET OFF THE STREETS BEFORE DAWN!

I WAS A LITTLE SAFE. I HAD A COAT AND BOOTS, SO LIKE A GESTAPO WORE WHEN HE WAS NOT IN SERVICE. BUT ANJA-HER APPEARANCE-YOU COULD SEE MORE EASY SHE WAS JEWISH. I WAS AFRAID FOR HER.

WAKE UP, MR. LUKOWSKI. LET US IN. PLEASE!!

HUH? W-WHO IS IT?

ANJA! ANJA ZYLBERBERG!

WHAT ARE YOU DOING HERE, CHILD? IT ISN'T SAFE! WAIT- I'LL UNLOCK THE GATE.

GO THROUGH THE COURTYARD TO THE SHED IN THE BACK. I'LL BRING YOU SOME FOOD.

THANK GOD THERE ARE STILL SOME KIND PEOPLE LEFT. I THOUGHT—

A JEWESS!

THERE'S A JEWESS IN THE COURTYARD! POLICE!

HURRY!

AN OLD WITCH RECOGNIZED ANJA FROM HER WINDOW.

WE RAN FAST TO THE SHED AND HID IN THE STRAW.

IT'S OKAY FOR NOW...

I DON'T THINK ANYONE HEARD HER... SHE'S A LITTLE SENILE ANYWAY.

BUT YOU MUST LOOK FOR A BETTER PLACE TO STAY. SOMEONE HERE IS BOUND TO RECOGNIZE YOU!

IT'S ALMOST MORNING. WAIT HERE. I'M GOING OUT TO SCOUT AROUND.

B-BE CAREFUL.

I WALKED, BUT I DIDN'T KNOW WHERE TO GO.

CLIK CLIK

AND I HEARD SOON IT WAS SOME-BODY FOLLOWING BEHIND ME.

I WALKED SLOW...

BEHIND ME ALSO WALKED SLOW.

IF I WALKED *FAST*...

BEHIND ME ALSO WALKED FAST.

WE WERE ALONE. HE SPOKE...

AMCHA?

IN HEBREW HE SAID TO ME, "OUR NATION?"

HAD I TO ANSWER HIM, OR NO?

A-AMCHA.

I *THOUGHT* YOU WERE A JEW..

... I'M JEWISH TOO! THERE ARE VERY FEW OF US LEFT...

..MY WIFE AND I HAVE BEEN HIDING IN SOSNOWIEC FOR OVER A YEAR.

I'M WITH MY WIFE TOO. WE'RE HUNGRY AND WE NEED A PLACE TO HIDE!

GO TO THE BLACK MARKET ON DE-KERTA STREET, NUMBER 8.

SO I LEFT HIM AND WENT RIGHT AWAY TO DEKERTA 8. THERE IT WAS A BIG COURTYARD...

?

ALL AROUND I LOOKED, BUT IT WAS NOBODY.

PSSST!

!

WANNA BUY SOME FOOD WITHOUT COUPONS, MISTER?

SHE SHOWED TO ME SAUSAGES, EGGS, CHEESE ...THINGS I ONLY WAS ABLE TO *DREAM* ABOUT.

I BOUGHT AND WENT QUICK BACK TO ANJA.

GOOD MORNING.

VLADEK! YOU WERE GONE SO LONG.

I HAD TO GET BREAKFAST.'... WANT SOME SAUSAGES? ...OR EGGS?..OR WOULD YOU PREFER CHOCOLATE?

WHAT?

IT'S A **MIRACLE!** HOW DID YOU MANAGE IT?

I'M A MAGICIAN! HAVE SOME MILK.

I WENT AGAIN BACK TO DEKERTA. THERE I COULD CHANGE JEWELRY FOR MARKS-AND MARKS FOR FOOD, OR A PLACE TO STAY.

THIS TIME IT WAS MORE PEOPLE ...THERE EVEN, I SAW SOME JEWISH BOYS I KNEW FROM BEFORE THE WAR.

VLADEK SPIEGELMAN?! I HARDLY RECOGNIZED YOU. SO YOU'RE STILL ALIVE, EH?

LEO? YES. I'M WITH ANJA.

WE NEED A HIDING PLACE..

HOW ABOUT MRS. KAWKA?

SHE HAS A SMALL FARM ON THE OUTSKIRTS OF TOWN...

SHE MIGHT TAKE YOU IN, IF YOU CAN PAY.

IT WAS NOT SO FAR TO GO TO KAWKA'S FARM...

ALRIGHT THEN, MR. SPIEGELMAN. YOU AND YOUR WIFE CAN STAY IN MY BARN.

WE'LL COME LATE TONIGHT.

BUT, REMEMBER-IF YOU'RE FOUND THERE, I DON'T KNOW YOU! ... YOU MUST SAY THAT THE BARN DOOR WAS OPEN AND YOU JUST SNEAKED IN.

DON'T WORRY...WE WON'T BETRAY YOU!

AND SO WE CAME THERE. TO LIVE WITH KAWKA'S COW.

IT'S ALMOST DAWN - WHEN MRS. KAWKA COMES TO MILK HER COW, SHE'LL BRING YOU SOME COFFEE.

WHERE ARE YOU GOING?

TO DEKERTA.

DON'T LEAVE ME ALONE AGAIN. I'M **TERRIFIED** WHILE YOU'RE GONE.

DON'T WORRY, ANJA. I'LL BE SAFE. IF I DIDN'T GO OUT WE WOULDN'T HAVE **FOOD**...WE WOULDN'T HAVE **THIS PLACE!**...

AND WE'VE **GOT** TO FIND A WARMER PLACE FOR THE WINTER...AWAY FROM SOSNOWIEC IF POSSIBLE...

I-I'LL BE OKAY. COME BACK QUICK.

I TRAVELED OFTEN WITH THE STREETCAR TO TOWN.

IT WAS TWO CARS. ONE WAS ONLY GERMANS AND OFFICIALS. THE SECOND, IT WAS ONLY THE POLES.

ALWAYS I WENT STRAIGHT IN THE **OFFICIAL** CAR...

HEIL HITLER.

THE GERMANS PAID NO ATTENTION OF ME....IN THE **PO-LISH** CAR THEY COULD **SMELL** IF A POLISH JEW CAME IN.

142

AT THE BLACK MARKET I SAW SEVERAL TIMES A NICE WOMAN, WHAT I MADE A LITTLE FRIENDS WITH HER...

HOW ABOUT A LOAF OF FRESH BREAD?

FINE, FINE.

GOOD MORNING, MR. SPIEGELMAN.

HOW DO YOU DO, MRS. MOTONOWA! WHAT DO YOU HAVE IN YOUR BASKET TODAY?

OH. I'M SORRY. I DON'T HAVE ANY CHANGE.

IT'S OKAY... KEEP IT FOR YOUR LITTLE BOY.

ARE YOU AND YOUR WIFE STILL LIVING IN A BARN?

WE HAVEN'T FOUND ANYTHING BETTER.

I'VE BEEN THINKING ABOUT IT... WHY DON'T YOU BOTH MOVE IN WITH MY SON AND ME?

WHAT ABOUT YOUR HUSBAND?

HE WORKS IN GERMANY, AND ONLY COMES HOME FOR 10 DAYS EVERY 3 MONTHS... I'LL KEEP YOU HIDDEN IN THE CELLAR WHEN HE'S AROUND.

IT SOUNDS GOOD TO ME, BUT IT'S OVER 20 KILOMETERS TO YOUR HOUSE IN SZOPIENICE. MY WIFE WILL BE AFRAID TO GO!

DON'T WORRY. I'LL ESCORT YOU!

THE NEXT EVENING SHE CAME WITH HER 7-YEARS-OLD BOY TO KAWKA'S FARMHOUSE...

I WALKED WITH MOTONOWA AS IF *SHE* WAS MY WIFE.

AND ANJA, LIKE A GOVERNESS, WENT WITH THE LITTLE BOY BEHIND. AND NOBODY EVEN *LOOKED* ON US.

REMEMBER, LITTLE ONE – NEVER TELL **ANYBODY** THERE ARE JEWS HERE. THEY'LL SHOOT US ALL!

YES, AUNT ANJA.

THE LITTLE BOY WAS VERY SMART AND HE LOVED VERY MUCH ANJA.

YOU HAD TO **PAY** MRS. MOTONOWA TO KEEP YOU, RIGHT?

OF COURSE I PAID... AND **WELL** I PAID.

...WHAT YOU THINK? SOMEONE WILL RISK THEIR LIFE FOR NOTHING?

...I PAID ALSO FOR THE **FOOD** WHAT SHE GAVE TO US FROM HER SMUGGLING BUSINESS.

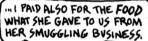

BUT, ONE TIME I MISSED A FEW COINS TO THE BREAD...

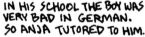

I'LL PAY YOU THE REST TOMORROW, AFTER I GO OUT AND CASH SOME VALUABLES.

SORRY... I WASN'T ABLE TO **FIND** ANY BREAD TODAY.

ALWAYS SHE GOT BREAD, SO I DIDN'T BELIEVE... BUT, STILL, SHE WAS A GOOD WOMAN.

IN HIS SCHOOL THE BOY WAS VERY BAD IN GERMAN. SO ANJA TUTORED TO HIM.

ICH BIN... DU BIST... ER IST...

SHE KNEW GERMAN LIKE AN EXPERT.

AND SOON HE CAME OUT WITH **VERY** GOOD GRADES.

MY TEACHER ASKED ME HOW I IMPROVED SO MUCH...

SO I TOLD HIM MY **MOTHER** WAS HELPING ME.

WHEW

HE WAS REALLY A CLEVER BOY.

BUT IT WAS A FEW THINGS HERE NOT SO GOOD... HER HOME WAS VERY SMALL AND IT WAS ON THE GROUND FLOOR...

BE SURE TO KEEP AWAY FROM THE WINDOW — YOU MIGHT BE SEEN!

NOK NOK

ONE MINUTE! (QUICK — GET IN THE CLOSET!)

IF SOMEBODY CAME, WE HAD FAST TO HIDE,

A LETTER FROM YOUR HUSBAND, MRS. MOTONOWA.

THANKS.

BUT I HAD SOMETHING ALLERGIC IN THE CLOSET...

AAH·

OR MAYBE IT WAS A COLD — I CAN'T REMEMBER...

·CHMF

BUT ALWAYS I HAD TO SNEEZE.

STILL, EVERYTHING HERE WAS FINE, UNTIL ONE SATURDAY MOTONOWA RAN VERY EARLY BACK FROM HER BLACK MARKET WORK...

THIS IS TERRIBLE!

THE GESTAPO JUST SEARCHED ME...THEY TOOK MY GOODS!

THEY MAY COME SEARCH HERE ANY MINUTE! YOU'VE GOT TO LEAVE!

WHAT?

BUT WHERE CAN WE GO?

I DON'T KNOW. BUT YOU MUST GET OUT NOW!

OH MY GOD...THIS IS THE END!

ANJA STARTED TO CRY... BUT WE HAD NOT A CHOICE.

WE'LL WALK TOWARD SOS-NOWIEC – AT LEAST WE'LL KNOW OUR WAY AROUND.

ANJA WAS SO AFRAID SHE WAS SHAKING.

STAY CALM – WALK AS IF WE'RE JUST STROLLING... AND SPEAK GERMAN.

FOR HOURS WE WALKED.

B-BESUCHEN WIR DOCH FRAU KAWKA.

GUTE IDEE.

VLADEK · WE'RE BEING FOLLOWED.

RELAX

BUT IF WE TURNED A CORNER, THEY ALSO TURNED.

ES IST KALT.

JA. JA.

OF COURSE I WAS RIGHT – THEY DIDN'T MEAN ANYTHING ON US.

WOOSH

THEY JUST WERE WALKING.

STAYING ON THE STREET ALL NIGHT IS TOO DANGEROUS... MAYBE WE CAN HIDE IN THAT CONSTRUCTION SITE.

GOOD – I'M EXHAUSTED.

HERE WAS A FOUNDATION MADE VERY DEEP DOWN IN THE GROUND..

BE CAREFUL!

I JUMPED FIRST IN, AND I PULLED OVER BRICKS FOR ANJA TO STEP DOWN.

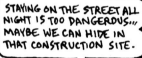

AND HERE WE WAITED A COLD FEW HOURS FOR THE DAY.

IT STARTED TO BE LIGHT...

COME. WE WON'T BE NOTICED IF WE MIX WITH PEOPLE OUT ON THE STREET.

I'M SO TIRED AND COLD...

WE CAN REST NOW.

WE CAME FINALLY AGAIN TO THIS PLACE WITH THE COW AND WENT INSIDE.

LATER, KAWKA CAME IN...

W-WHO'S IN HERE?

THE SPIEGEL- MANS... WE HAD NOWHERE ELSE TO GO.

WELL... I GUESS YOU CAN STAY. BUT, REMEMBER: I DON'T KNOW YOU'RE HERE!

WHY, MRS. SPIEGELMAN, YOU'RE SHIVERING!

YOU CAN COME INTO MY HOUSE FOR AN HOUR OR SO, 'TIL YOU WARM UP.

SHE TOOK ANJA INSIDE AND BROUGHT TO ME SOME FOOD...IN THOSE DAYS I WAS SO STRONG I COULD SIT EVEN IN THE SNOW ALL NIGHT...

THINGS CAN'T BE THIS BAD EVERYWHERE! I'D GIVE ANYTHING TO GET OUT OF POLAND!

YOU KNOW, BEFORE I TOOK YOU IN, I HAD A YOUNG MAN AND HIS SON HERE...

TWO PEOPLE I KNOW SMUG- GLED THEM INTO HUNGARY. I HEARD HE AND HIS BOY WERE DOING WELL THERE.

HUNGARY! REALLY?! I'D LIKE TO MEET THOSE SMUGGLERS!

SHE TOLD ME THESE TWO ACQUAINTANCES VISITED OFTEN TO HER ON THURSDAY EVENINGS... TODAY WAS MAYBE A MONDAY...

I DON'T GET IT... WASN'T HUNGARY AS DANGEROUS AS POLAND?

NO. FOR A LONGER TIME IT WAS *BETTER* THERE IN HUNGARY FOR THE JEWS... BUT THEN, NEAR THE VERY FINISH OF THE WAR, THEY ALL GOT PUT *ALSO* TO AUSCHWITZ.

I WAS THERE, AND I SAW IT. THOUSANDS-HUNDREDS OF THOUSANDS OF JEWS FROM HUNGARY...

SO MANY, IT WASN'T EVEN ROOM ENOUGH TO BURY THEM ALL IN THE OVENS.

BUT AT THAT TIME, WHEN I WAS THERE WITH KAWKA, WE COULDN'T *KNOW* THEN.

SO... I WENT NEXT DAY TO DEKERTA STREET TO BUY FOOD...

OH GOD! OH GOD! MR. SPIEGELMAN, YOU'RE ALIVE! I'M SO GLAD TO SEE YOU!

MRS. MOTONOWA!

I WANTED TO FIND A NEW CONNECTION TO HIDE US. BUT *REALLY* I DIDN'T THINK TO FIND AGAIN *HER*.

PRAISE MARY, YOU'RE SAFE! I COULDN'T *SLEEP*, I FELT SO GUILTY ABOUT CHASING YOU AND YOUR WIFE OUT.

THE GESTAPO NEVER EVEN CAME TO MY HOUSE. I JUST PANICKED FOR NOTHING.

PLEASE COME BACK AGAIN.

ANJA WAS GLAD OF GOING BACK. AND MOTONOWA ALSO... ALWAYS I PAID HER NICELY.

AND THAT SAME NIGHT WE SAID GOODBYE TO KAWKA AND WENT AGAIN TO SZOPIENICE.

AFTER WE WERE BACK ONLY A SHORT TIME...

WELL, MY HUSBAND WRITES THAT HE'S COMING HOME FOR HIS 10-DAY VACATION.

IF HE KNEW YOU WERE HERE HE'D THROW US **ALL** OUT. BUT, DON'T WORRY... YOU'LL BE ALL RIGHT IN MY CELLAR.

...I SET UP A MATTRESS... I'LL COME DOWN WHEN- EVER I CAN.

SO EACH DAY AND NIGHT WE SAT IN SUCH A STORAGE LOCKER...

IN THE DAYS WE WERE AFRAID TO BREATHE – PEOPLE CAME DOWN OFTEN TO **THEIR** LOCKERS.

AT NIGHT WE COULD MOVE AROUND A LITTLE, BUT IT WAS SOMETHING ELSE DOWN THERE...

AIEEE!

WH-WHAT IS IT?

TH-THERE ARE **RATS** DOWN HERE!

SHH- CALM DOWN, STOP SCREAMING!

THOSE AREN'T RATS. THEY'RE VERY SMALL. ONE RAN OVER MY HAND BEFORE. THEY'RE JUST **MICE!**

OF COURSE, IT **WAS** REALLY RATS. BUT I WANTED ANJA TO FEEL MORE EASY.

BUT, THEN, MOTONOWA STOPPED TO COME DOWN.

IT'S BEEN 3 DAYS SINCE SHE BROUGHT ANY FOOD.

HERE... HAVE AN- OTHER CANDY...

I HAD STILL CANDIES I ORGANIZED ON DEKERTA. ONLY *THIS* WE HAD TO EAT.

ALSO, HERE WE HAD NO PLACE WHERE TO WASH, SO ANJA GOT ON ALL HER SKIN A TERRIBLE RASH.

I DON'T KNOW WHAT'S WORSE- THE HUNGER OR THE ITCHING.

DON'T SCRATCH! IT ONLY- SHH!

KLIK

THE DOOR.

I'M SORRY I COULDN'T GET DOWN BEFORE...MY HUSBAND IS GETTING SUSPICIOUS.

HE ASKED WHY I GO TO THE CELLAR SO OFTEN. HE EVEN ASKED IF I WAS HIDING JEWS HERE! ...HE WAS *JOKING*, BUT STILL...

ARE YOU ALL RIGHT HERE?

THERE ARE *RATS*, GIANT RATS! THEY'RE *HORRIBLE!*

WELL- YOU'RE BETTER OFF WITH THE RATS THAN WITH THE GESTAPO... AT LEAST THE RATS WON'T *KILL* YOU!

MMM..

AND SHE WAS RIGHT. WE WERE HAPPY EVEN TO HAVE *THESE* CONDITIONS.

AFTER THE TEN DAYS HER HUSBAND LEFT, AND SHE TOOK US BACK.

IT'S GOOD TO BE "HOME," EH, VLADEK!

IT'S A LOT NICER THAN THAT CELLAR.

BUT I DIDN'T FEEL SAFE HERE. IT WAS TOO MANY WAYS SOME- BODY COULD FIND US OUT. I WANT- ED TO GO BETTER TO HUNGARY.

SO, WHEN IT CAME THURSDAY, I WENT IN THE DIRECTION TO TAKE A STREETCAR TO SEE KAWKA IN SOSNOWIEC.

LOOK!

I HAD TO PASS WHERE SOME CHILDREN WERE PLAYING.

A JEW! A JEW!

THEY RAN SCREAMING HOME.

HELP! MOMMY! A JEW!!

A JEW!

QUICK, THE MOTHERS CAME OUTSIDE TO SEE WHAT WAS!

THE MOTHERS ALWAYS TOLD SO: "BE CARE-FUL! A JEW WILL CATCH YOU TO A BAG AND EAT YOU!" '" SO THEY TAUGHT TO THEIR CHILDREN.

I APPROACHED OVER TO THEM...

HEIL HITLER.

IF I RAN AWAY THEY, WOULD SEE: "YES, IT *IS* A JEW HERE."

DON'T BE AFRAID, LITTLE ONES. I'M NOT A JEW. I WON'T HURT YOU.

SORRY, MISTER. YOU KNOW HOW KIDS ARE... HEIL HITLER.

SO I CAME OUT WELL FROM THIS...

BUT THE EXPERIENCE COST ME REALLY A LOT OF HAIRS.

WHEN I ARRIVED TO KAWKA, THE TWO SMUGGLERS WERE THERE TOGETHER SITTING IN THE KITCHEN..

PLEASE WAIT IN THE OTHER ROOM. THEY'LL SEE YOU SOON.

MR. MANDELBAUM!

VLADEK SPIEGELMAN!

MANDELBAUM, BEFORE THE WAR OWNED A SWEETS SHOP.

ANJA AND I BOUGHT ALWAYS PASTRIES THERE. HE USED TO BE A VERY RICH MAN IN SOSNOWIEC.

THIS IS MY WIFE....AND YOU KNOW MY NEPHEW.

HELLO, ABRAHAM. WHAT ARE YOU ALL DOING HERE?

BACK WHEN IT WAS THE GHETTO, ABRAHAM WAS A BIG MEMBER OF THE JEWISH COUNCIL.

WE'RE TRYING TO GET OUT OF POLAND—

—TO HUNGARY?! YES. ANJA AND I ARE TRYING TO ARRANGE THAT TOO!

THE SMUGGLERS PROPOSED US HOW THEY WOULD DO.

"...AND AT THE BORDER OUR PARTNERS WILL TAKE YOU THROUGH THE MOUNTAINS.

WHEW- IT'S RISKY AND VERY EXPENSIVE!

WE SPOKE YIDDISH SO THE POLES DON'T UNDERSTAND.

NIE, VAS DENKST DIE?

YECH KENN DIE FRAU KAWKA, UBER YECH BIN NISH ZICHER VEGEN DIE ZWEI.

So, what do you think?

I know Mrs. Kawka, but I'm not sure about these two.

HERR MECH TSE! YECH GEI KOIDEM MIT ZEI. AZ ALLES VET ZEIN BESEDER, YECH VIL SCHREIBEN TSE DEYER.

Listen! I'll go first. If everything is okay, I'll write back to you.

THE OTHERS WANT TO THINK ABOUT IT A LITTLE LONGER, BUT I'M READY TO GO NOW.

FINE, FINE.

I AGREED WITH MANDELBAUM TO MEET AGAIN HERE. IF IT CAME A GOOD LETTER, WE'LL GO.

BUT IF EVER I TALKED OF THIS PLAN TO ANJA...

NO, VLADEK! YOU'RE CRAZY! IT'S TOO DANGEROUS!

BUT IF WE HEAR FROM ABRAHAM—

WE'RE SAFE HERE- FORGET ABOUT HUNGARY!

BUT WHAT DO WE DO IF THE GESTAPO COMES TO SEARCH FOR ILLEGAL GOODS? ...WHAT IF A NEIGHBOR NOTICES US THROUGH THE KITCHEN WINDOW?...

I'M NOT GOING!

WHAT IF HER HUSBAND FINDS OUT ABOUT US? EVEN THE BOY COULD LET SOMETHING SLIP! ...THIS WAR COULD LAST ANOTHER 4 OR 5 YEARS. WHAT DO WE DO WHEN OUR MONEY RUNS OUT?

PLEASE!

IN HUNGARY WE COULD BE FREE TO WALK THE STREETS AGAIN, LIKE HUMAN BEINGS... I'VE ALWAYS TAKEN CARE OF YOU- TRUST ME.

I'M SO SCARED. >SOB<

DON'T DO IT, MR. SPIEGELMAN— IT'S JUST NOT SAFE! YOU DON'T KNOW ANYTHING ABOUT THESE SMUGGLERS.

SNF. IT'S LIKE TALKING TO A WALL.

WE WON'T GO UNLESS WE HEAR THAT OUR FRIEND GOT THROUGH.

I'VE HAD AWFUL NIGHTMARES ABOUT YOUR TRIP- PLEASE STAY WITH ME!

SNF

WAIT- NOW WHERE ARE YOU GOING?

-TO VISIT MY COUSIN AND SEE WHERE HE'S HIDING. IF WE DO GO TO HUNGARY, HE MAY BE BETTER OFF HERE WITH YOU!

MILOCH HELPED ME IN SRODULA. MAYBE NOW, IF HE NEEDED, I COULD HELP HIM.

153

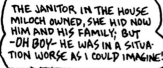

THE JANITOR IN THE HOUSE MILOCH OWNED, SHE HID NOW HIM AND HIS FAMILY; BUT —OH BOY— HE WAS IN A SITUATION WORSE AS I COULD IMAGINE!

I WENT TO THE JANITOR BY TROLLEY

HELLO—I'M MILOCH'S COUSIN, VLADEK.

YES, HE TOLD ME YOU MIGHT COME.

I HAVE SOME COMPANY UPSTAIRS. I CAN'T TAKE YOU TO MILOCH UNTIL THEY LEAVE.

GENTLEMEN. THIS IS MY COUSIN, VLADEK.

HI "CUZ," HAVE A DRINK.

SO WE TALKED, AND THEY BELIEVED I AM *HER* COUSIN.

WE'RE ALMOST OUT OF VODKA. BRING SOME MORE, MEINKA.

THERE ISN'T ANY.

BAH! SHE'S HIDING HER VODKA!

JUST LIKE SHE'S HIDING JEWS IN HER YARD!

THE JANITOR AND I FROZE OUR BLOOD FROM FEAR...

IF YOU DON'T PUT ANOTHER BOTTLE ON THE TABLE *RIGHT AWAY*, WE'LL TELL THE GESTAPO ABOUT THE JEWS YOU'RE KEEPING!!

R-RELAX FELLOWS.

HERE'S A FEW MARKS, MEINKA. RUN DOWNSTAIRS AND GET ANOTHER BOTTLE FOR OUR FRIENDS.

'ATTA BOY. HIC.

IN 15 MINUTES SHE CAME WITH A BOTTLE AND THEY WERE HAPPY.

YOU SEE? YOUR COUSIN KNOWS HOW TO ENTERTAIN GUESTS! TO YOUR HEALTH.

WE DRANK AND WE DRANK— ONLY NEAR MIDNIGHT FINALLY THEY WENT HOME.

I THINK IT'S SAFE TO GO DOWN.

ARE YOU -SNF- CARRYING FOOD FOR MILOCH?

I FED THEM EARLIER. THIS IS JUST TRASH.

THE CONDITIONS HOW MILOCH WAS LIVING - YOU COULDN'T BELIEVE.

...I ALWAYS BRING GARBAGE SO THE NEIGHBORS DON'T GET SUSPICIOUS.

PSST-MILOCH. YOUR COUSIN IS HERE.

?

IN EACH COURTYARD WAS A VERY DEEP HOLE TO THROW IN ALL THE GARBAGE.

INSIDE THIS GARBAGE HOLE WAS HERE SEPARATED A TINY SPACE — MAYBE ONLY 5 FEET BY 6 FEET.

VLADEK! I'M GLAD YOU'RE STILL ALIVE!

MY GOD!

I LOOKED DOWN ONLY FOR A SECOND. BUT IN THERE WAS LIVING MILOCH, HIS WIFE AND THEIR 3-YEARS-OLD BOY.

HOW CAN YOU LIVE THERE? YOU MUST BE FREEZING!

WE HAVE NO CHOICE. AT LEAST OUR BUNKER IS UNDERGROUND..

AND THE DECOMPOSING GARBAGE GIVES SOME HEAT.

BUT PEOPLE KNOW YOU'RE IN THERE...

I TOLD HIM MY STORY WITH THESE POLES UPSTAIRS.

WHAT CAN WE DO?

LISTEN-ANJA AND I MAY BE GOING TO HUNGARY!..

I EXPLAINED OUR HIDING PLACE WAS NOT PERFECT, BUT BETTER THAN HIS.

I'LL COME AGAIN WHEN I HAVE MORE NEWS, BUT IT'S VERY LATE NOW – I MUST GET BACK HOME.

AND I WAS LUCKY. NOBODY MADE ME ANY QUESTIONS GOING BACK TO SZOPIENICE.

155

A FEW DAYS AFTER, I CAME AGAIN TO THE SMUGGLERS. AND MANDELBAUM WAS ALSO THERE.

LOOK, VLADEK—MY NEPHEW IS SAFE! THEY BROUGHT ME A LETTER FROM HIM.

IT WAS IN YIDDISH AND IT WAS SIGNED REALLY BY ABRAHAM SO WE AGREED RIGHT AWAY TO GO AHEAD.

BUT ANJA JUST DIDN'T WANT WE WOULD GO...

PLEASE, VLADEK, CALL IT OFF!

BUT IT'S ALL AR- RANGED. I'VE EVEN GIVEN THEM HALF THEIR MONEY!

NO! NO! NO! IT'S SOME KIND OF TRICK!

BE REASONABLE. I SAW ABRAHAM'S LETTER WITH MY OWN EYES!

WH-WHAT DID IT SAY?

"DEAR AUNT AND UNCLE, EVERYTHING IS WON- DERFUL HERE. I AR- RIVED SAFELY. I'M FREE AND HAPPY. DON'T LOSE A MINUTE. JOIN ME AS SOON AS YOU CAN. YOUR LOVING NEPHEW, ABRAHAM."

I-I DON'T KNOW...

WE LEAVE THE DAY AFTER TOMORROW FROM THE KA- TOWICE TRAIN STATION.

AND FINALLY I CONVINCED HER.

SO, I WENT ONE MORE TIME OVER TO MILOCH IN HIS GAR- BAGE BUNKER AND DIRECTED HIM HOW HE MUST GO TO SZOPIENICE AND HIDE...

AND, YOU KNOW, MILOCH AND HIS WIFE AND BOY, THEY ALL SURVIVED THEMSELVES THE WHOLE WAR... SITTING THERE ... WITH MOTONOWA...

BUT, FOR ANJA AND I, IT WAS FOR US WAITING ANOTHER DESTINY...

WE CAME WITH NO PROBLEM BY TROLLEY CAR TO OUR MEET- ING POINT WITH THE MANDEL- BAUMS AND THE SMUGGLERS.

EVERYTHING IS ARRANGED. HERE ARE YOUR TICKETS.

DO YOU HAVE THE REST OF OUR PAYMENT?

YES. OF COURSE.

HERE.

WH-WHERE IS YOUR PARTNER GOING?

HE'S PHONING AHEAD TO THE MEN WHO WILL MEET YOU AT THE BORDER. HE'LL JOIN US ON THE TRAIN-DON'T WORRY!

BUT, OF COURSE, WE *DID* WORRY...

SO, ALL OF US TOGETHER STARTED ON OUR JOURNEY...

WE TRAVELED LESS THAN AN HOUR 'TIL WE CAME TO BIELSKO-BIALA. HERE I USED TO HAVE MY FACTORY AND HERE THE SMUGGLERS DISAPPEARED.

IT WAS A BIG COMMOTION... GESTAPO CAME ON EVERY SIDE

JUDEN RAUS!

HERE THEY ARE!

IN KATOWICE, IT WAS ONLY TO *THEM* THE SMUGGLER PHONED.

THEY MARCHED US THROUGH THE CITY OF BIELSKO. WE PASSED BY THE FACTORY WHAT ONCE I OWNED...

WE PASSED THE MARKET WHERE ALWAYS WE BOUGHT TO EAT, AND PASSED EVEN THE STREET WHERE WE USED TO LIVE, AND WE CAME 'TIL THE PRISON, AND THERE THEY PUT US.

157

I HAD A SMALL BAG TO TRAVEL. WHEN THEY REGISTERED ME IN, THEY LOOKED OVER EVERYTHING.

WITH A SPOON HE TOOK OUT, LITTLE BY LITTLE, ALL THE POLISH.

IT WAS THIS WATCH I GOT FROM FATHER-IN-LAW WHEN FIRST I MARRIED TO ANJA.

WHAT'S THIS? SHOE POLISH??

YES. I LIKE TO KEEP MYSELF NEAT.

WELL, WELL... A GOLD WATCH. YOU JEWS ALWAYS HAVE GOLD!

WRAPPED IN FOIL, I KEPT IT HIDDEN THERE... IT WAS MY LAST TREASURE.

WELL, NEVER MIND... THEY TOOK IT AND THREW ME WITH MANDELBAUM INTO A CELL...

WAIT A MINUTE! WHAT EVER HAPPENED TO ABRAHAM?

WHO?

AH, MANDELBAUM'S NEPHEW! YES. HE FINISHED THE SAME AS US TO CONCENTRATION CAMP.

-BUT

YES. I'LL TELL YOU HOW IT WAS WITH HIM- BUT NOW I'M TELLING HERE IN THE PRISON...

HERE WE GOT VERY LITTLE TO EAT—MAYBE SOUP ONE TIME A DAY—AND WE SAT WITH NOTHING TO DO.

WHY DON'T THEY PUT US TO WORK LIKE THE REST OF YOU?

IT MEANS YOU WON'T BE HERE VERY LONG...

...EVERY WEEK OR SO A TRUCK TAKES SOME OF THE PRISONERS AWAY.

EXCUSE ME... DO ANY OF YOU KNOW GERMAN?

MY FAMILY JUST SENT ME A FOOD PARCEL. IF I WRITE BACK THEY'LL SEND ANOTHER, BUT WE'RE ONLY ALLOWED TO WRITE GERMAN.

I KNEW **WELL** TO WRITE GERMAN... SO I WROTE....

IN A SHORT TIME HE GOT AGAIN A PACKAGE...

YOU DID A GREAT JOB! TAKE ANYTHING YOU WANT FOR YOU AND YOUR FRIEND!

IT WAS EGGS THERE... IT WAS EVEN CHOCOLATES. ...I WAS VERY LUCKY TO GET SUCH GOODIES!

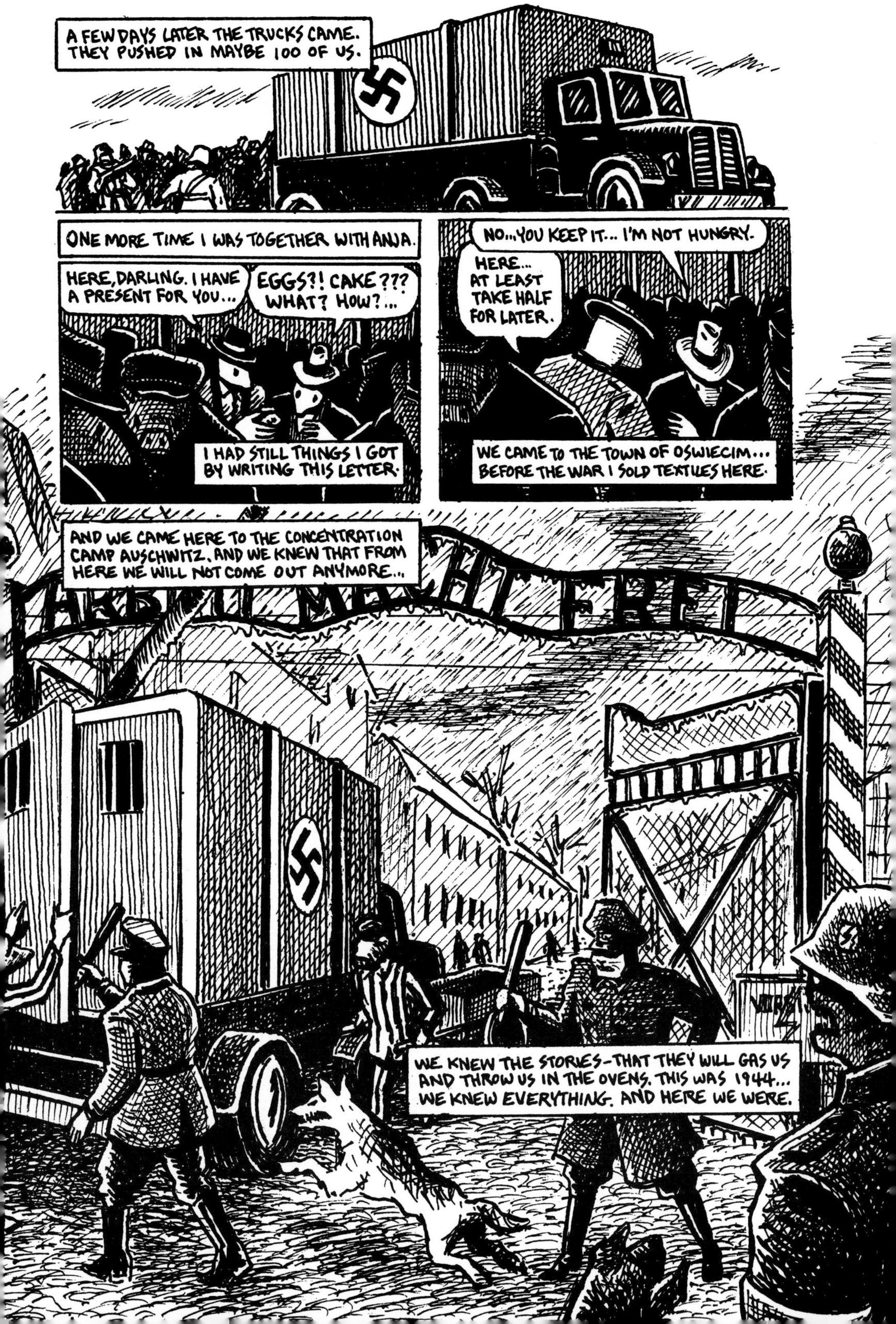
A FEW DAYS LATER THE TRUCKS CAME. THEY PUSHED IN MAYBE 100 OF US.
ONE MORE TIME I WAS TOGETHER WITH ANJA.
HERE, DARLING. I HAVE A PRESENT FOR YOU...
EGGS?! CAKE??? WHAT? HOW?...
I HAD STILL THINGS I GOT BY WRITING THIS LETTER.
NO... YOU KEEP IT... I'M NOT HUNGRY.
HERE... AT LEAST TAKE HALF FOR LATER.
WE CAME TO THE TOWN OF OSWIECIM... BEFORE THE WAR I SOLD TEXTILES HERE.
AND WE CAME HERE TO THE CONCENTRATION CAMP AUSCHWITZ, AND WE KNEW THAT FROM HERE WE WILL NOT COME OUT ANYMORE...
WE KNEW THE STORIES–THAT THEY WILL GAS US AND THROW US IN THE OVENS. THIS WAS 1944... WE KNEW EVERYTHING. AND HERE WE WERE.

MY GOD.

YES. SO IT WAS...

...AND WHEN THEY OPENED THE TRUCK, THEY PUSHED MEN ONE WAY, WOMEN TO THE OTHER WAY...

ANJA AND I WENT EACH IN A DIFFERENT DIRECTION, AND WE COULDN'T KNOW IF EVER WE'LL SEE EACH OTHER ALIVE AGAIN.

THIS IS WHERE MOM'S DIARIES WILL BE **ESPECIALLY** USEFUL. THEY'LL GIVE ME SOME IDEA OF WHAT SHE WENT THROUGH WHILE YOU WERE APART.

I CAN TELL YOU ... SHE WENT THROUGH THE SAME WHAT ME: TERRIBLE!

IT'S GETTING COLD. WHY DON'T WE GO UPSTAIRS AND SEE IF WE CAN FIND HER NOTEBOOKS...

NO... I **LOOKED** ALREADY...

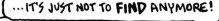

...IT'S JUST NOT TO **FIND** ANYMORE!

WELL... LET'S CHECK OUT THE GARAGE. YOU'VE GOT LOADS OF STUFF IN THERE.

NO. YOU'LL NOT FIND IT. BECAUSE I **REMIND** TO MYSELF WHAT HAPPENED...

THESE NOTEBOOKS, AND OTHER REALLY NICE THINGS OF MOTHER... ONE TIME I HAD A VERY BAD DAY... AND ALL OF THESE THINGS I **DESTROYED.**

YOU **WHAT?**

AFTER ANJA DIED I HAD TO MAKE AN ORDER WITH EVERYTHING... THESE PAPERS HAD TOO MANY MEMORIES. SO I BURNED THEM.

YOU BURNED THEM?

CHRIST! YOU SAVE TONS OF WORTHLESS SHIT, AND YOU...

YES, IT'S A SHAME! FOR YEARS THEY WERE LAYING THERE AND NOBODY EVEN LOOKED IN.

DID YOU EVER READ ANY OF THEM?... CAN YOU REMEMBER WHAT SHE WROTE?

NO. I LOOKED IN, BUT I DON'T REMEMBER...ONLY I KNOW THAT SHE SAID, "I WISH MY SON, WHEN HE GROWS UP, HE WILL BE INTERESTED BY THIS."

GOD DAMN YOU! YOU—YOU MURDERER! HOW THE HELL COULD YOU DO SUCH A THING!!

ACH

TO YOUR FATHER YOU YELL IN THIS WAY?... EVEN TO YOUR FRIENDS YOU SHOULD NEVER YELL THIS WAY!

BUT, I'M TELLING YOU, AFTER THE TRAGEDY WITH MOTHER, I WAS SO DEPRESSED THEN, I DIDN'T KNOW IF I'M COMING OR I'M GOING!

I'M SORRY. LOOK, POP. IT'S GETTING LATE. I'D BETTER GET HOME...

COME FIRST UP-STAIRS FOR A LITTLE COFFEE.

NO...REALLY. I'D BETTER GET GOING RIGHT AWAY...

SO...TELEPHONE TO ME... YOU SHOULD VISIT HERE MORE OFTEN—DON'T BE SUCH A STRANGER!

SURE... YOU BET! SO LONG.

...MURDERER.

MAUS II

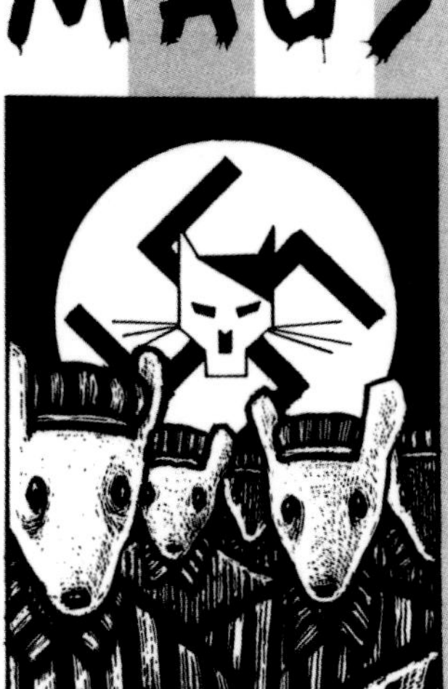

"Mickey Mouse is the most miserable ideal ever revealed. . . . Healthy emotions tell every independent young man and every honorable youth that the dirty and filth-covered vermin, the greatest bacteria carrier in the animal kingdom, cannot be the ideal type of animal. . . . Away with Jewish brutalization of the people! Down with Mickey Mouse! Wear the Swastika Cross!"

—newspaper article, Pomerania, Germany, mid-1930s

FOR RICHIEU

AND FOR NADJA
AND DASHIELL

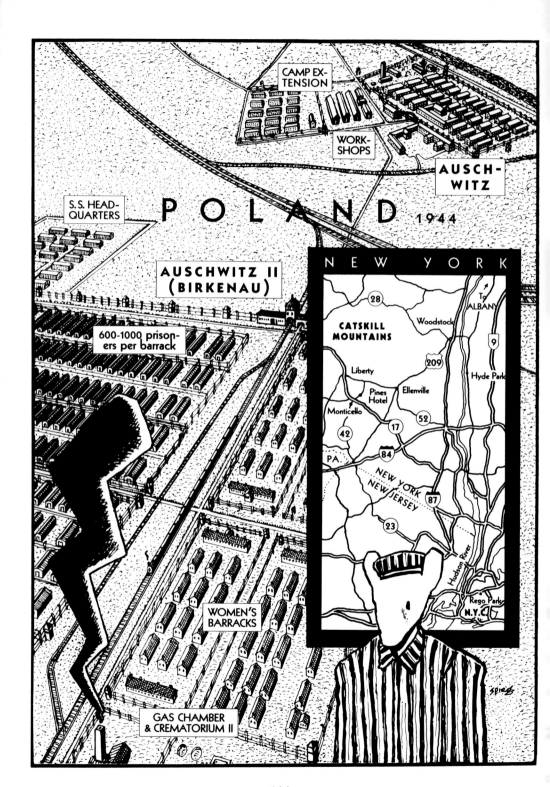

CAMP EX-
TENSION

WORK-
SHOPS

AUSCH-
WITZ

S.S. HEAD-
QUARTERS

P O L A N D 1944

AUSCHWITZ II
(BIRKENAU)

600-1000 prison-
ers per barrack

N E W Y O R K

CATSKILL
MOUNTAINS

28

Woodstock

To
ALBANY

9

Liberty

209

Hyde Park

Pines
Hotel

Ellenville

Monticello

52

42

17

PA.

84

NEW YORK
NEW JERSEY

87

23

Hudson River

WOMEN'S
BARRACKS

Rego Park
N.Y.C.

GAS CHAMBER
& CREMATORIUM II

166

AND HERE MY TROUBLES BEGAN

(FROM MAUSCHWITZ TO THE CATSKILLS AND BEYOND)

CONTENTS

HALT!

CHAPTER ONE

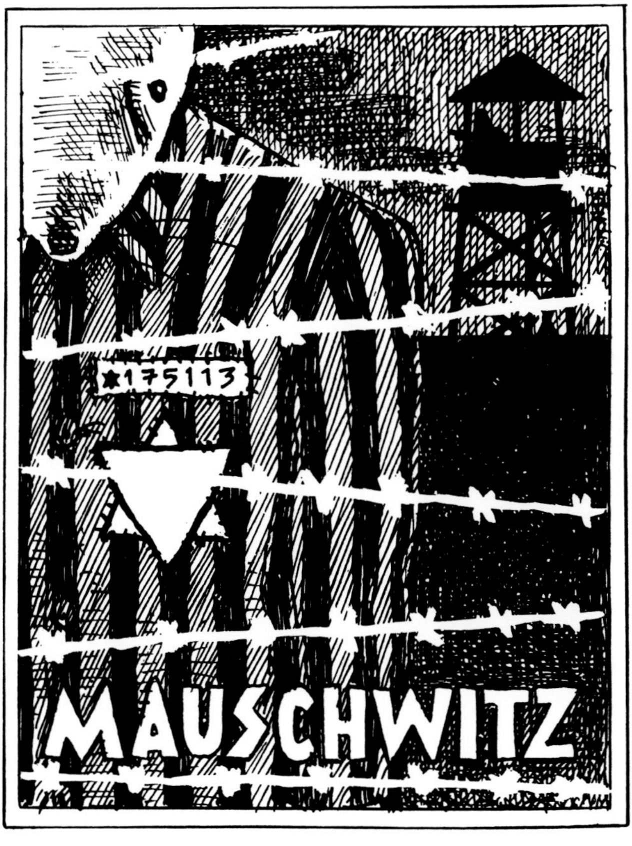

175113
MAUSCHWITZ

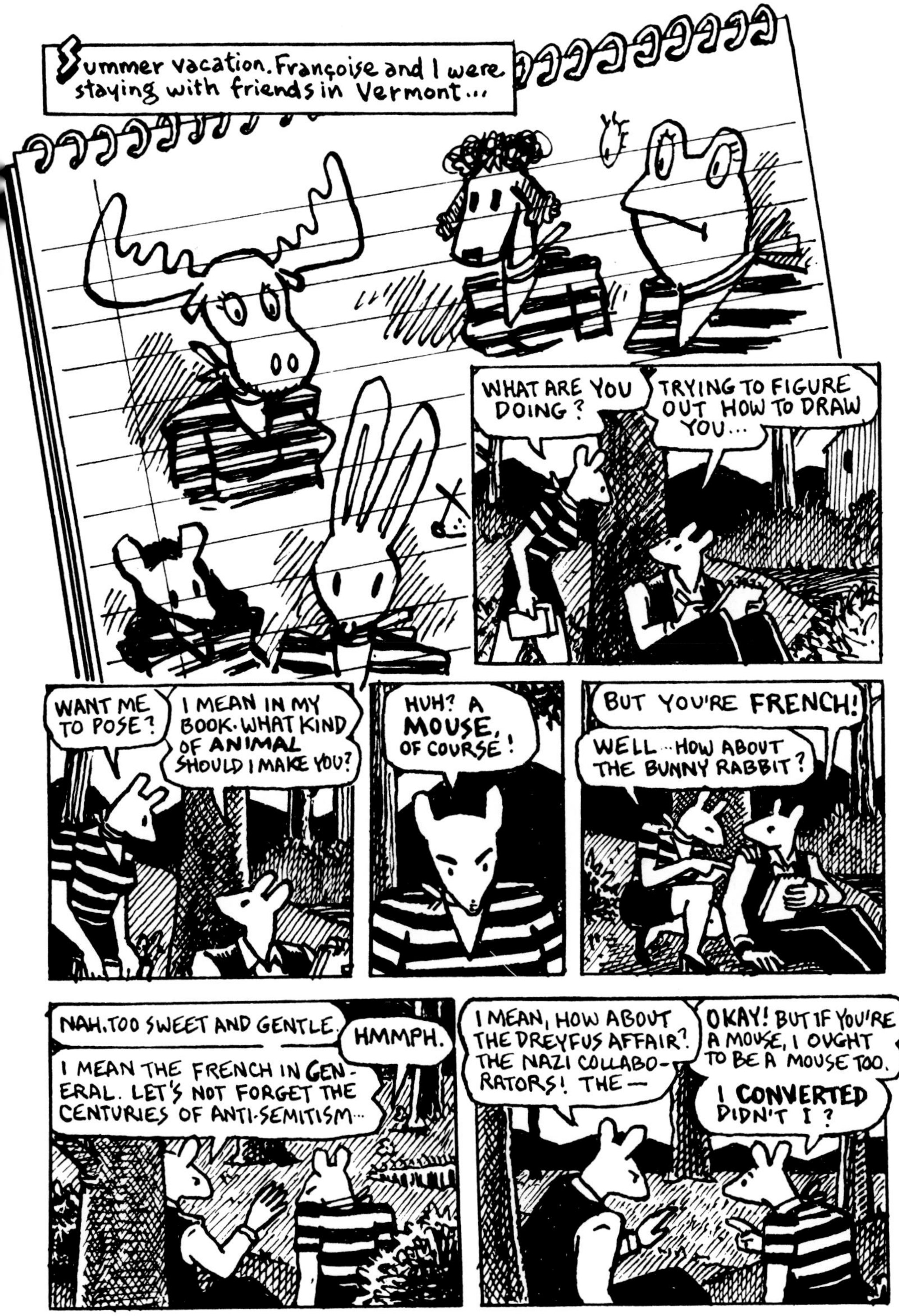
Summer vacation. Françoise and I were staying with friends in Vermont...
WHAT ARE YOU DOING?
TRYING TO FIGURE OUT HOW TO DRAW YOU...
WANT ME TO POSE?
I MEAN IN MY BOOK. WHAT KIND OF ANIMAL SHOULD I MAKE YOU?
HUH? A MOUSE, OF COURSE!
BUT YOU'RE FRENCH!
WELL... HOW ABOUT THE BUNNY RABBIT?
NAH. TOO SWEET AND GENTLE.
HMMPH.
I MEAN THE FRENCH IN GENERAL. LET'S NOT FORGET THE CENTURIES OF ANTI-SEMITISM...
I MEAN, HOW ABOUT THE DREYFUS AFFAIR? THE NAZI COLLABORATORS! THE —
OKAY! BUT IF YOU'RE A MOUSE, I OUGHT TO BE A MOUSE TOO.
I CONVERTED DIDN'T I?

I'VE GOT IT!...PANEL ONE: MY FATHER IS ON HIS EXERCYCLE...

I TELL HIM I JUST MARRIED A FROG...

PANEL TWO: HE FALLS OFF HIS CYCLE IN SHOCK.

SO, YOU AND I GO TO A MOUSE RABBI. HE SAYS A FEW MAGIC WORDS AND ZAP! ...

BY THE END OF THE PAGE THE FROG HAS TURNED INTO A BEAUTIFUL MOUSE!

HMPH

I ONLY CONVERTED TO MAKE VLADEK HAPPY.

YEAH. BUT NOTHING CAN MAKE HIM HAPPY.

YOU KNOW, YOU SHOULD HAVE MARRIED WHAT'S-HER-NAME? THE GIRL YOU WERE SEEING WHEN WE FIRST MET?...

SANDRA?

YES. THEN YOU COULD JUST DRAW MICE. NO PROBLEM.

C'MON. I JUST DATED HER TO GET OVER MY PREJUDICE AGAINST MIDDLE-CLASS, NEW YORK, JEWISH WOMEN.

THEY REMIND ME TOO MUCH OF MY RELATIVES TO BE EROTIC, SO I JUST—

ART! FRANÇOISE!!

HURRY—YOUR FATHER JUST PHONED US! HE HAD A HEART ATTACK!

WHAT?

OH NO!

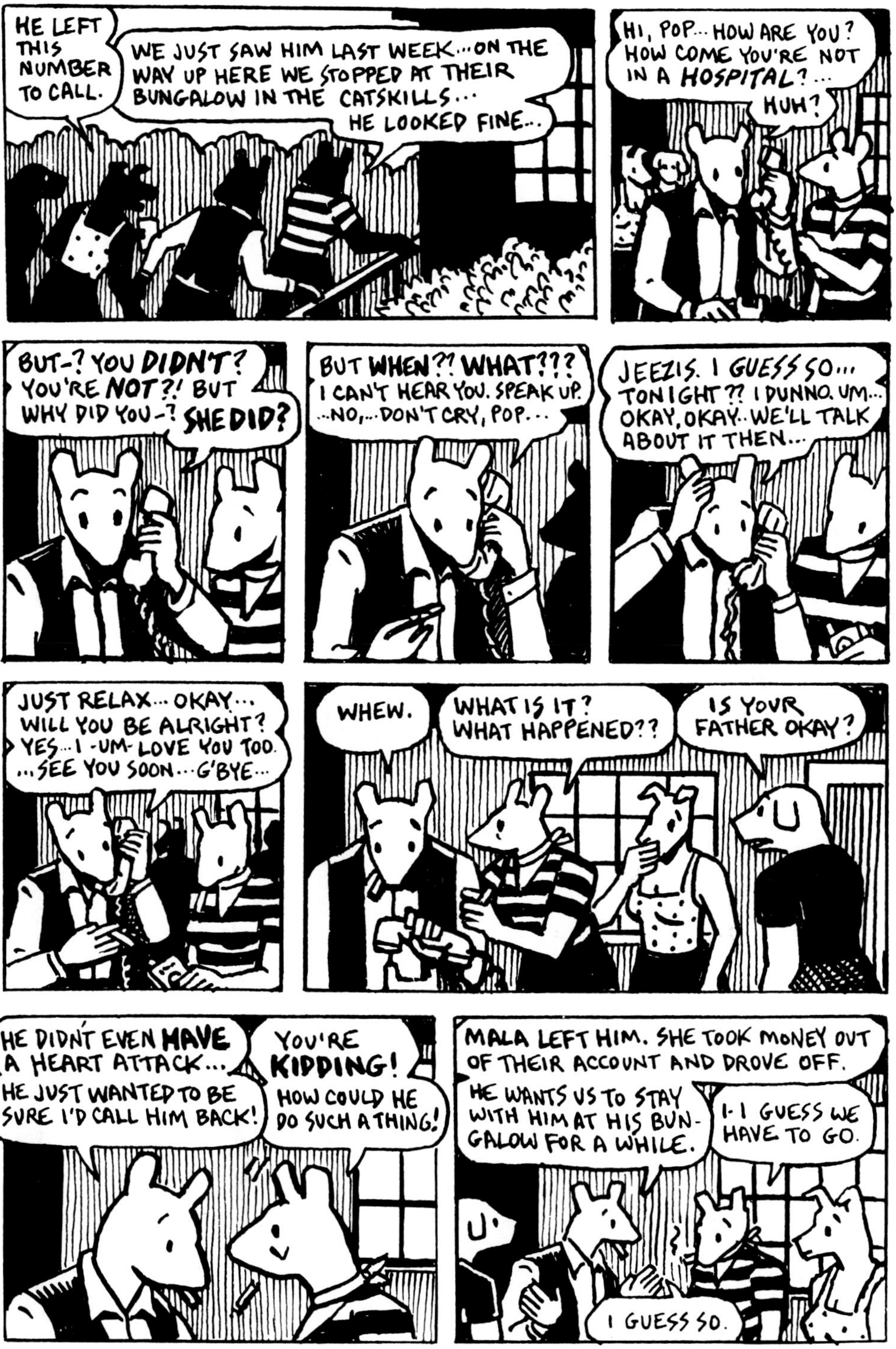
HE LEFT THIS NUMBER TO CALL.
WE JUST SAW HIM LAST WEEK...ON THE WAY UP HERE WE STOPPED AT THEIR BUNGALOW IN THE CATSKILLS...
HE LOOKED FINE...
HI, POP... HOW ARE YOU? HOW COME YOU'RE NOT IN A HOSPITAL?...
HUH?
BUT-? YOU DIDN'T? YOU'RE NOT?! BUT WHY DID YOU-?
SHE DID?
BUT WHEN?? WHAT??? I CAN'T HEAR YOU. SPEAK UP. ...NO,...DON'T CRY, POP...
JEEZIS. I GUESS SO... TONIGHT?? I DUNNO. UM... OKAY, OKAY.. WE'LL TALK ABOUT IT THEN...
JUST RELAX... OKAY... WILL YOU BE ALRIGHT? YES...I -UM- LOVE YOU TOO. ...SEE YOU SOON... G'BYE...
WHEW.
WHAT IS IT? WHAT HAPPENED??
IS YOUR FATHER OKAY?
HE DIDN'T EVEN HAVE A HEART ATTACK...
HE JUST WANTED TO BE SURE I'D CALL HIM BACK!
YOU'RE KIDDING!
HOW COULD HE DO SUCH A THING!
MALA LEFT HIM. SHE TOOK MONEY OUT OF THEIR ACCOUNT AND DROVE OFF.
HE WANTS US TO STAY WITH HIM AT HIS BUN-GALOW FOR A WHILE.
I-I GUESS WE HAVE TO GO.
I GUESS SO.

WHAT A PITY. YOU JUST **GOT** UP HERE...

WE'LL BE BACK.

WE'RE NOT TAKING MUCH LUGGAGE, SO WE HAVE AN EXCUSE NOT TO STAY LONG.

VLADEK SOUNDED HALF-HYSTERICAL ON THE PHONE.

POOR GUY... I FEEL SO SORRY FOR HIM.

YEAH, ME TOO... 'TIL I HAVE TO SPEND ANY TIME WITH HIM— THEN HE DRIVES ME **CRAZY!**

MM.

SIGH.

DEPRESSED AGAIN?

JUST THINKING ABOUT MY BOOK... IT'S SO **PRESUMPTUOUS** OF ME.

I MEAN, I CAN'T EVEN MAKE ANY SENSE OUT OF MY RELATIONSHIP WITH MY FATHER... HOW AM I SUPPOSED TO MAKE ANY SENSE OUT OF AUSCHWITZ?... OF THE HOLOCAUST?...

WHEN I WAS A KID I USED TO THINK ABOUT WHICH OF MY PARENTS I'D LET THE NAZIS TAKE TO THE OVENS IF I COULD ONLY SAVE ONE OF THEM...

USUALLY I SAVED MY MOTHER. DO YOU THINK THAT'S NORMAL?

NOBODY'S NORMAL.

I WONDER IF RICHIEU AND I WOULD GET ALONG IF HE WAS STILL ALIVE.

YOUR BROTHER?

MY *GHOST*-BROTHER, SINCE HE GOT KILLED BEFORE I WAS BORN. HE WAS ONLY FIVE OR SIX.

AFTER THE WAR MY PARENTS TRACED DOWN THE VAGUEST RUMORS, AND WENT TO ORPHANAGES ALL OVER EUROPE. THEY COULDN'T BELIEVE HE WAS DEAD.

I DIDN'T THINK ABOUT HIM MUCH WHEN I WAS GROWING UP... HE WAS MAINLY A LARGE, BLURRY PHOTOGRAPH HANGING IN MY PARENTS' BEDROOM.

UH-HUH. I THOUGHT THAT WAS A PICTURE OF YOU, THOUGH IT DIDN'T *LOOK* LIKE YOU.

THAT'S THE POINT. THEY DIDN'T *NEED* PHOTOS OF ME IN THEIR ROOM... I WAS *ALIVE!*...

THE PHOTO NEVER THREW TANTRUMS OR GOT IN ANY KIND OF TROUBLE.... IT WAS AN IDEAL KID, AND I WAS A PAIN IN THE ASS. I COULDN'T COMPETE.

THEY DIDN'T *TALK* ABOUT RICHIEU, BUT THAT PHOTO WAS A KIND OF REPROACH. HE'D HAVE BECOME A *DOCTOR*, AND MARRIED A WEALTHY JEWISH GIRL...THE CREEP.

BUT AT LEAST WE COULD'VE MADE *HIM* GO DEAL WITH VLADEK. ...IT'S *SPOOKY*, HAVING SIBLING RIVALRY WITH A SNAPSHOT!

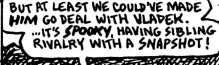

175

I NEVER FELT *GUILTY* ABOUT RICHIEU. BUT I DID HAVE NIGHTMARES ABOUT S.S. MEN COMING INTO MY CLASS AND DRAGGING ALL US JEWISH KIDS AWAY.

DON'T GET ME WRONG. I WASN'T *OBSESSED* WITH THIS STUFF ... IT'S JUST THAT SOMETIMES I'D FANTASIZE ZYKLON B COMING OUT OF OUR SHOWER INSTEAD OF WATER.

I KNOW THIS IS INSANE, BUT I SOMEHOW WISH I HAD BEEN IN AUSCHWITZ *WITH* MY PARENTS SO I COULD REALLY KNOW WHAT THEY LIVED THROUGH!

...I GUESS IT'S *SOME* KIND OF GUILT ABOUT HAVING HAD AN EASIER LIFE THAN THEY DID.

SIGH. I FEEL SO INADEQUATE TRYING TO RECONSTRUCT A REALITY THAT WAS WORSE THAN MY DARKEST DREAMS.

AND TRYING TO DO IT AS A *COMIC STRIP!* I GUESS I BIT OFF MORE THAN I CAN CHEW. MAYBE I OUGHT TO FORGET THE WHOLE THING.

THERE'S SO MUCH I'LL NEVER BE ABLE TO UNDERSTAND OR VISUALIZE. I MEAN, REALITY IS TOO *COMPLEX* FOR COMICS... SO MUCH HAS TO BE LEFT OUT OR DISTORTED.

JUST KEEP IT HONEST, HONEY.

SEE WHAT I MEAN... IN REAL LIFE YOU'D *NEVER* HAVE LET ME TALK THIS *LONG* WITHOUT INTERRUPTING.

HMMPH. LIGHT ME A CIGARETTE.

And so, the Catskills...

HE SAID HE'D LEAVE THE KEY ABOVE THE-AH. THERE IT IS!

ARTIE?

YAWN. SO, DARLINGS... YOU **CAME** FINALLY. I WAITED AND I WAITED AND I COULDN'T SLEEP.

EMERGENCY OXYGEN UNIT.

YOU SEE HOW IT IS NOW, ARTIE. SHE TOOK MY MONEY AND SHE RAN AWAY. **OY!** HOW COULD SHE DO IT, TO LEAVE SUCH A SICK MAN LIKE ME ALONE??

BUT NOW, AT LEAST, I'M HAPPY I HAVE HERE YOU "KIDS" TO STAY TOGETHER WITH ME...

LOOK HOW NICE I MADE FOR YOU A BED. FOR THE WHOLE **SUMMER** YOU CAN BE COMFORTABLE HERE!

HEY! WE'RE JUST STAYING FOR A FEW DAYS, POP. WE-

WELL! IN THE MORNING WE CAN SPEAK MORE- BUT NOW YOU CAN MAKE YOUR-SELF AT HOME, SO AS LIKE IT'S YOUR OWN.

G'NIGHT, POP.

(MY GOD-DOES HE EXPECT US TO STAY HERE ALL SUMMER?)

(I GUESS SO. IF HE HAD HIS WAY WE'D MOVE TO **QUEENS** WITH HIM TOO. HE-)

PLEASE! I'M SO TIRED FROM WAITING 'TIL YOU CAME. **TOMORROW** YOU CAN TALK!

SUCH A SUNNY DAY AND **STILL** YOU'RE BOTH SLEEPING?!

WHU? WHATIME IZZIT?

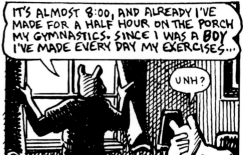

IT'S ALMOST 8:00, AND ALREADY I'VE MADE FOR A HALF HOUR ON THE PORCH MY GYMNASTICS. SINCE I WAS A **BOY** I'VE MADE EVERY DAY MY EXERCISES...

UNH?

AT FIRST THE NEIGHBORS TRIED TO MAKE EXERCISES **WITH** ME, BUT THEY COULDN'T KEEP UP... SO NOW ONLY THEY WATCH!

IS THERE ANY COFFEE?

MALA HAD HERE SOME **INSTANT** COFFEE... TOMORROW WE'LL EXERCISE **TOGETHER**.

WHA? **MY** ONLY EXERCISE IS WALKING OUT FOR CIGARETTES! ...INSTANT COFFEE'LL HAVE TO DO.

YOU HAVE TO HURRY NOW TO GET READY... TODAY I NEED YOU'LL HELP ME TO PREPARE MY BANK AND TAX PAPERS— MALA LEFT THEM IN A MESS, YOU CAN'T IMAGINE!

?

YAH—HERE I HAVE IT. IT'S THE CAFFEINE-FREE KIND OF COFFEE.

GROAN.

UM. HAVE YOU SEEN MY **PANTS**?

ALL YOUR THINGS I PUT ALREADY IN ORDER IN THE BUREAU, THERE.

WELL... THANKS FOR NOT THROWING THEM OUT.

WAKE UP, HONEY. I'VE GOT BAD NEWS. THE ONLY COFFEE HERE IS **SANKA**!

UNF? I BROUGHT **OUR** COFFEE AND OUR POT. LOOK IN MY BAG.

ACH!

NOW WHAT?

I'M MAKING FOR YOU *BREAKFAST,* AND I SEE HERE THE *SALT!* JUST *LOOK* WHAT MALA DID...

THE SALT HERE, IT'S HALF *FULL,* AND SHE OPENED *ANYWAY* A NEW ONE!

I CAN'T EAT ON MY DIET *ANY* SODIUM. I DON'T NEED EVEN *ONE* CONTAINER SALT, AND HERE IT'S *TWO* OPEN SALTS!

SO...WHAT HAPPENED? WHY DID MALA LEAVE?

SHE WANTS THAT ALL MY MONEY, WHAT I WORKED SO HARD ALL MY LIFE, IT WILL ONLY BE FOR HER.

I HAD A DOCTOR'S APPOINT-MENT IN REGO PARK AND WE WENT AFTER TO THE BANK TO RENEW SOME BONDS.

ONE I WANTED IN TRUST OF MALA, ONE FOR MY BROTHER IN ISRAEL, AND ONE I WANTED FOR *YOU*...

BUT SHE DIDN'T LIKE I'LL PUT FOR YOU AND PINEK *ANYTHING*—SHE SCREAMED LIKE A *CRAZY PERSON!*

SHE DROVE AWAY AND LEFT ME BY THE BANK, AND WHEN I WALKED HOME SHE WAS GONE ALREADY.

THE LAWYER SAYS I MUST MAKE *DRASTIC* STEPS. SHE STOLE AWAY THE JEWELRY, THE CAR AND THE CASH OUT FROM OUR JOINT ACCOUNT—I CAN MAKE *CHARGES!*

OH, C'MON...

179

WHERE'S MALA NOW?

TO FLORIDA SHE DROVE. WE'RE BUYING THERE A CONDO. SHE WANTS TO SELL AND TO GRAB OUT THE DEPOSIT MONEY.

BUT THIS SHE **CAN'T** DO. SHE NEEDS MY SIG-**ARTIE! WHAT DO YOU DO?!!**

HUH? I'M JUST LIGHTING MY CIGARETTE...

BETTER YOU **SHOULDN'T** SMOKE: FOR **YOU** IT'S TERRIBLE, AND FOR **ME**, WITH MY SHORTNESS OF BREATH, IT'S ALSO NO GOOD TO **BE NEAR**...

BUT IF **ANYWAY** YOU'RE SMOKING, PLEASE DON'T USE FROM ME MY **WOODEN** MATCHES. I DON'T HAVE LEFT SO MANY, AND ALREADY TO MAKE **COFFEE** YOU USED ONE.

ONLY TO LIGHT **THE OVEN** I USE THEM. THESE **WOOD** MATCHES I HAVE TO **BUY!** THE PAPER MATCHES I CAN HAVE **FREE** FROM THE LOBBY OF THE PINES HOTEL.

JEEZ! I'LL BUY YOU A WHOLE **BOX** OF WOODEN MATCHES!

IT ISN'T NECESSARY... AT HOME OUR OVEN IS AUTOMATIC, AND HERE I'M STAYING ONLY 15 MORE DAYS.

AND I HAVE STILL 50 MATCHES LEFT. HOW MANY MATCH-ES CAN I USE?...

WHAT A **MISER!** I CAN'T TAKE ANY MORE. I'M GOING OUT FOR AIR!

ALWAYS ARTIE IS **NERVOUS**-SO LIKE HIS MOTHER-SHE ALSO WAS NERVOUS.

BAH.

PSST.

YOU MUST BE ARTIE. I'M MRS. KARP. WE'RE NEIGHBORS.

YES. MY DAD MENTIONED THAT YOU'VE LOOKED AFTER HIM WHILE MALA'S GONE.

HE SAID *THAT*? WELL...EDGAR *DID* GIVE HIM A RIDE BACK HERE A FEW DAYS AGO. MALA HAS THEIR CAR NOW, BUT - **COME**, VISIT A MINUTE!

HUH? I CANT! I - UH -

LOOK, EDDIE. LOOK WHAT I FOUND: VLADEK'S BOY, ARTIE!

SO! YOU CAME TO TAKE YOUR FATHER TO LIVE BY YOU?

WHAT? NO, WE'RE JUST HELPING HIM GET HIS BEARINGS FOR A FEW DAYS. HE'LL STAY UP HERE 'TIL LABOR DAY.

WHAT? ALONE? HOW CAN HE MANAGE?

HE CAN GET BY. BUT IT'D BE NICE IF YOU GAVE HIM RIDES TO TOWN...LOOKED IN ON HIM SOMETIMES..

MAYBE SOMETIMES, BUT HE'S A SICK OLD MAN. HE CAN'T BE ALL ALONE....

AND **AFTER** THE SUMMER? THEN HE'LL GO LIVE BY YOU, OR WHAT?

NO! I DUNNO WHAT HE'LL DO. MAYBE HE'LL NEED A NURSE OR SOMETHING.

A NURSE, IT COSTS **MONEY.** YOU THINK YOUR FATHER SPENDS MONEY SO EASY?

POOR MALA. ONE TIME I WENT TO THE *SUPERMARKET* WITH HER...

SHE HAD TO ERASE A **HAIRBRUSH** FROM THE BILL BECAUSE HE WOULDN'T PAY FOR HER *PERSONAL* ITEMS—HOW COULD A COUPLE LIVE LIKE THAT?

ART? HELLO? WHERE ARE YOU HONEY?

MY WIFE IS CALLING ME...

YOUR WIFE, SHE'S **JEWISH**?

(HUSH ED-GAR!) INVITE HER IN FOR LEMONADE.

MAYBE SOME OTHER TIME. I'D BETTER GO NOW...

WHEW.

SO THERE YOU ARE!...

WHERE **WERE** YOU?

A COUPLE OF VLADEK'S FRIENDS, THE KARPS, JUST HIJACKED ME... Y'KNOW EVEN **THEY** CAN'T STAND HIM.

IT'S SO **CLAUSTROPHOBIC** BEING AROUND VLADEK. HE STRAIGHTENS EVERYTHING YOU TOUCH—HE'S SO **ANXIOUS.**

HE NEVER LEARNED **HOW** TO RELAX.

MAYBE AUSCHWITZ MADE HIM LIKE THAT.

MAYBE. BUT LOTS OF THE PEOPLE UP HERE ARE SURVIVORS—LIKE THOSE KARPS—IF THEY'RE WHACKED UP IT'S IN A **DIFFERENT** WAY FROM VLADEK.

OH, ABOUT VLADEK'S MATCHES—IT'S EVEN CRAZIER THAN YOU THOUGHT...

SINCE GAS IS INCLUDED IN THE RENT, HE LEAVES A BURNER LIT ALL DAY TO SAVE ON MATCHES.

GOD. IF IT WASN'T SO PATHETIC, IT'D BE KINDA **FUNNY.**

SO! YOU'VE BEEN ENJOYING YOURSELF, KIDS? COME—WE'LL SIT TOGETHER AND YOU CAN HELP ME TO PREPARE MY BANK PAPERS.

A few tense hours later...

ACCH, ARTIE. **AGAIN** YOU MADE THE WRONG ADDITION.

BUT LOOK- WE'VE CHECKED IT **TWICE**. IT'S **CORRECT**!

PFAH. IT DOESN'T COME OUT SO AS ON THE STATEMENT. WE'LL HAVE NOW EVERYTHING TO DO AGAIN.

WHA? THAT WOULD TAKE 2 OR 3 HOURS... IT'S OFF BY LESS THAN A BUCK. LET'S JUST FORGET IT.

ALWAYS YOU'RE SO **LAZY**! EVERY JOB WE SHOULD MAKE SO AS TO DO IT THE RIGHT WAY.

LAZY?! DAMN IT, YOU'RE DRIVING ME **NUTS**!

WAIT! WHY DON'T YOU TAKE A BREAK? I'LL FIND THE MISTAKE.

YES! WITH FRANÇOISE I CAN DO IT!

UM... I CAN HANDLE IT ALONE. WHY DON'T YOU **BOTH** GO OUT FOR A WALK?

THANKS A LOT.

WELL... DON'T MIX TOGETHER FOR ME ANY OF THE PAPERS. I'LL **REVIEW** WITH YOU WHEN I COME BACK...

...BUT FOR MY LEGS I COULD **USE** NOW THAT WE WALK A LITTLE.

SIGH. OKAY... I'LL GET MY TAPE RE- CORDER, SO TODAY ISN'T A **TOTAL LOSS**.

183

WHAT ARE YOUR PLANS NOW, POP?

WE'LL WALK OVER TO THE PINES HOTEL AND THEN BACK

I MEAN, IN **GENERAL**, NOW THAT MALA IS GONE.

MAYBE WE'LL **TOGETHER** STAY TO THE END OF THE SUMMER HERE ... IT'S SO BEAUTIFUL...

I **TOLD** YOU—FRANÇOISE AND I CAN ONLY STAY THROUGH THE WEEKEND.

SO? THEN WHEN **YOU** GO BACK, I ALSO WILL GO. WHAT HAVE I HERE TO STAY ALL ALONE?

AND **THEN?**

NU? MAYBE YOU'LL WANT WITH ME IN **QUEENS** TO STAY?.

TO HAVE YOU WITH ME, IT'S ALWAYS A PLEASURE. ...REMEMBER, MY HOUSE IT'S ALSO YOUR HOUSE TOO.

I'M SORRY, POP. I DON'T THINK IT WOULD WORK OUT. I MEAN, WE'VE GOT OUR **OWN** PLACE TO LIVE, AND—

YES. YOU DON'T HAVE TO ANSWER NOW ... ONLY TO **THINK** OF IT...

UM—CAN I ASK YOU MORE ABOUT YOUR PAST... ABOUT AUSCHWITZ?

OF COURSE, DARLING. TO ME YOU CAN ASK **ANYTHING!**

WELL...WHAT HAPPENED WHEN YOU AND MOM ARRIVED THERE AND WERE SEPARATED?

WHEN WE CAME, THEY PUSHED IN ONE WAY THE MEN, AND SOMEWHERE ELSE THE WOMEN.

OUT!

I WAVED VERY FAST GOODBYE TO ANJA.

BUT YOU UNDERSTAND, **NEVER** ANJA AND I WERE SEPARATED!

NO??

NO! THE WAR PUT US APART. BUT ALWAYS, BEFORE AND AFTER, WE WERE TOGETHER.

NOT SO LIKE MALA, WHAT GRABS OUT MY MONEY!-

AUSCHWITZ, POP. TELL ME ABOUT AUSCHWITZ.

AUSCHWITZ WAS IN A TOWN CALLED OSWIECIM. BEFORE THE WAR I CAME OFTEN HERE TO SELL MY TEXTILES.

...AND NOW, I CAME AGAIN.

WE CAME TO A BIG HALL AND THEY SHOUTED ON US.

GET UNDRESSED! LEAVE YOUR VALUABLES! LINE UP! SCHNELL!

I WAS, AT THAT TIME, STILL WITH MY FRIEND MANDELBAUM.

THEY TOOK FROM US OUR PAPERS, OUR CLOTHES AND OUR HAIR..

(PSST- WH-WHAT'S GOING TO HAPPEN TO US?)

(DON'T WORRY..)

WE WERE COLD, AND WE WERE AFRAID.

(IF THEY BROUGHT YOU HERE, THEY'LL PUT YOU TO WORK. THEY'RE NOT READY TO KILL YOU **YET.**)

(WHAT ABOUT OUR WIVES AND OUR -)

SHUT UP, YIDS! TO THE BATH HOUSE. QUICK!

EVERYWHERE WE HAD TO RUN - SO LIKE *JOGGERS* - AND THEY RAN US TO THE SAUNA...

IT'S FREEZING!

JUST THANK GOD IT'S NOT GAS!

HERE IT WAS THE **LIVE** SHOWERS, NOT THE DEAD GAS SHOWERS WHAT WE HEARD SOMETIMES RUMORS.

IN THE SNOW THEY THREW TO US PRISONERS CLOTHINGS.

ONE GUY TRIED TO EXCHANGE.

SCHNELL! SCHNELL! SCHNELL!

THEY NEVER EVEN **LOOKED** ON WHAT SIZE THEY THREW.

E-EXCUSE ME. THESE SHOES ARE TOO SMALL.

MAYBE **NOW** THEY'LL FIT!

CRAK

THE SHOES WERE **WOOD** SHOES!

I WAS A LUCKY ONE. EVERYTHING FITTED ME A LITTLE. ONLY THE SHIRT WAS TORN AND TOO BIG FOR ME ...

THEY REGISTERED US IN... THEY TOOK FROM US OUR NAMES. AND HERE THEY PUT ME MY NUMBER.

175113

ALL AROUND WAS A SMELL SO TERRIBLE, I CAN'T EXPLAIN...
SWEETISH... SO LIKE RUBBER BURNING. AND **FAT**.

HERE WAS **ABRAHAM**—
MANDELBAUM'S NEPHEW!

UNCLE! UNCLE!

WHEN WE CAME INSIDE THE GATES SOMEONE RAN TO US FROM FAR AWAY.

SO, UNCLE... YOU'VE ENDED UP HERE TOO.

YOU **TOLD** US TO COME!

YOU WROTE US ABOUT HOW **HAPPY** YOU ARE IN HUNGARY—THAT WE SHOULD JOIN YOU RIGHT AWAY! WELL ... HERE WE ARE.

HUN-GARY. HAH!

THE POLES WHO ARRANGED OUR "ESCAPE" UNDERSTOOD **YIDDISH**. SO THEY KNEW YOU WERE WAITING TO HEAR IF I WAS SAFE.

IN BIELSKO THE POLES DICTATED THAT LETTER WHILE THE GESTAPO HELD A PISTOL UP TO MY HEAD.

WHAT COULD I DO? THEY'D HAVE SHOT ME THEN AND THERE.

WELL... SO HERE'S OUR HUNGARY...

AND THERE'S ONLY ONE WAY OUT OF HERE FOR ALL OF US ... THROUGH THOSE CHIMNEYS.

ABRAHAM I DIDN'T SEE AGAIN.... I THINK HE CAME OUT THE CHIMNEY.

BUT I SAW AGAIN ONCE THE POLES WHO BETRAYED US.

THE GERMANS DIDN'T NEED THEM. SO THEY FINISHED ALSO IN AUSCHWITZ.

WE NEWCOMERS WERE PUT INSIDE A ROOM. OLD-TIMERS PASSED AND SAID ALL THE SAME.

YOU SEE THOSE CHIMNEYS?...

OKAY. SO I WAS **MORE** SAD.

I WAS WORN AND SHIVERING AND CRYING A LITTLE.

NOBODY EVEN **LOOKED.**

BUT FROM ANOTHER ROOM SOMEONE APPROACHED OVER

WHY ARE YOU CRYING, MY SON?

SHOULD I BE **HAPPY?** AM I AT A CARNIVAL?

LET ME SEE YOUR ARM...

HE WAS A PRIEST...

HMM...YOUR NUMBER STARTS WITH 17. IN HEBREW THAT'S "K'MINYAN TOV." SEVENTEEN IS A VERY GOOD OMEN...

HE WASN'T JEWISH - BUT VERY INTELLIGENT!

IT ENDS WITH 13, THE AGE A JEWISH BOY BECOMES A MAN...

AND **LOOK!** ADDED TOGETHER IT TOTALS 18. THAT'S "CHAI," THE HEBREW NUMBER OF LIFE.

I CAN'T KNOW IF **I'LL** SURVIVE THIS HELL, BUT I'M CERTAIN **YOU'LL** COME THROUGH ALL THIS ALIVE!

I STARTED TO BELIEVE. I TELL YOU, HE PUT ANOTHER LIFE IN ME.

AND WHENEVER IT WAS VERY BAD I LOOKED AND SAID: "YES. THE PRIEST WAS **RIGHT!** IT TOTALS EIGHTEEN.

WHEW. THAT GUY WAS A **SAINT!**

YES... I NEVER SAW HIM AGAIN.

FOR ME IT WAS HARD HERE, BUT FOR MY FRIEND MANDEL-BAUM IT WAS MORE HARD.

IN SOSNOWIEC, EVERYONE KNEW MANDELBAUM. HE WAS OLDER AS ME... NICE...A VERY RICH MAN...

...BUT NOW, IN AUSCHWITZ, MANDELBAUM WAS A MESS.

HIS PANTS WERE BIG LIKE FOR 2 PEOPLE, AND HE HAD NOT EVEN A PIECE OF STRING TO MAKE A BELT. HE HAD ALL DAY TO HOLD THEM WITH ONE HAND...

ONE SHOE, HIS FOOT WAS TOO BIG TO GO IN. THIS ALSO HE HAD TO HOLD SO HE COULD FIND MAYBE WITH WHOM TO EXCHANGE IT.

ONE SHOE WAS BIG LIKE A BOAT, BUT THIS AT LEAST HE COULD WEAR.

IT WAS WIN-TER, AND EVERYWHERE HE HAD TO GO AROUND WITH ONE FOOT ONTO THE SNOW.

CAN I USE YOUR SPOON, VLADEK?

OF COURSE, BUT WHERE'S YOURS?

I DROPPED IT, AND BY THE TIME I BENT DOWN, SOME-ONE STOLE IT.

FOR A SPOON YOU COULD GET A HALF DAY'S BREAD.

I SPILLED MOST OF MY SOUP, TOO. WHEN I ASKED FOR MORE, THEY BEAT ME!

I HOLD ONTO MY BOWL AND MY SHOE FALLS DOWN, I PICK UP THE SHOE AND MY PANTS FALL DOWN....

BUT WHAT CAN I DO? I ONLY HAVE TWO HANDS!

MY GOD. PLEASE GOD... HELP ME FIND A PIECE OF STRING AND A SHOE THAT FITS!

BUT HERE GOD DIDN'T COME. WE WERE ALL ON OUR OWN.

So, Mandelbaum and I were two in a bed. We didn't know why, since it was spaces left.

But a day after, they pushed in a shipment of maybe 400 more Jews there.

It was room hardly to move. Only to go down to the toilet was 15 minutes walking on the unlucky ones sleeping on the floor.

And coming back I couldn't find again where is my bed.

In the barrack was a KAPO—a supervisor—he was screaming and kicking, whatever he could.

Line up in rows of five, you shits! Stand straight!

He was also a prisoner, a peasant from the German part of Poland.

Now lie on your bellies. Quick!

Stand up! Lie down!

Stand up! Faster!

LIE DOWN!

We did such "sport" all day—kicking, hitting, yelling—'til some dropped dead. Then more.

ONE TIME THIS BLOCK SUPERVISOR STARTED SCREAMING ON US:

WHO KNOWS ENGLISH? RAISE YOUR HAND!

(YOU SHOULD RAISE YOUR HAND, VLADEK.)

(NO...)

(I DON'T WANT TO GET TOO CLOSE TO HIS STICK. BESIDES, LOOK AT ALL THE HANDS UP ALREADY...)

MANY FRENCH JEWS HERE KNEW TO SPEAK ENGLISH.

HE TOOK THEM APART - BUT SENT THEM SOON BACK.

IT WAS 8 OR 9 OF US. EACH HAD TO SPEAK A FEW WORDS.

WHO KNOWS ENGLISH AND POLISH?

NOW IT WAS VERY FEW HANDS, SO I APPROACHED.

VHERE... IST... DER PEN?... DER PEN IST... IN... DER TABLE...

NEXT.

WHAT I HEARD THE OTHERS SPEAK I SAW I HAD A CHANCE.

I SPOKE ONLY ENGLISH TO HIM: FOR POLISH, I HAD A **GOOD** ENGLISH

YES. I GAVE PRIVATE LESSONS OF ENGLISH WHEN I LIVED THEN IN CZESTOCHOWA.

HE WANTED TO LEARN HERE **ENGLISH**!

YOU MANAGED TO GET THE BERLITZ BOOKS HERE! YOU STUDIED ALREADY TO CONJUGATE VERBS?

?

AND HE KEPT ME ASIDE THE REST.

LISTEN. THERE ARE TOO MANY PRISONERS HERE. THE S.S. WILL LINE YOU ALL UP TOMORROW. ...BE SURE TO STAND ON THE FAR LEFT.

IN THE MORNING, THE S.S. CHOSE WHO TO TAKE FOR THE DAY TO WORK. WEAK ONES THEY PUT ON THE SIDE TO TAKE AWAY FOREVER. BEFORE THEY CAME TO ME, THEY TOOK ENOUGH.

I KEPT CLOSE TO ME MANDELBAUM. AND WE WENT BACK SAFE INSIDE.

THE KAPO PUSHED THOSE REMAINING TO CLEAN UP IN THE BLOCK.

WAIT! SPIEGELMAN- YOU COME WITH ME!

EVERYONE THEY CALLED BY NUMBER BUT ME, HE CALLED BY NAME.

SIT HERE... I'LL BE BACK SOON.

HERE I SAW ROLLS! I SAW EGGS! MEAT! COFFEE! ALL THE TABLE **FULL**! YOU KNOW WHAT IT WAS TO SEE SUCH THINGS?

IT MUST BE IT'S HIS BREAKFAST. SEE HOW HAPPY HE HAS IT HERE!

I WAS AFRAID TO **LOOK**. I WAS SO HUNGRY, I COULD GRAB ALL OF IT!

WHAT ARE YOU WAITING FOR? SIT DOWN AND **EAT**!

THIS FOOD, IT WAS FOR ME.

I ATE, ATE, ATE AS HE WATCHED. THEN I TAUGHT HIM A COUPLE HOURS AND WE SPOKE A LITTLE.

BUT **WHY** ARE YOU STUDYING ENGLISH?

I SPEAK GERMAN AS WELL AS POLISH—THAT'S WHY I'M A **KAPO**. OTHERWISE I'D BE A **NOTHING** LIKE YOU...

NOW THE ALLIES ARE BOMBING THE REICH. IF THEY **WIN** THIS WAR, IT WILL BE **WORTH** SOMETHING TO KNOW ENGLISH!

WELL, THAT'S ENOUGH FOR TODAY. COME WITH ME.

TAKE OFF ALL YOUR CLOTHES. CHOOSE THINGS THAT FIT.

SO I TOOK MYSELF CLOTHES LIKE TAILORED.

I GOT ALSO A PAIR REAL SHOES— NOT WOOD BUT LEATHER

ALWAYS I WAS HANDSOME... BUT WITH EVERYTHING FITTED, I LOOKED LIKE A MILLION!

SO. ARE YOU ALL SET?

YES SIR. BUT I HAVE ONE MORE FAVOR TO ASK...

...COULD I ALSO TAKE THIS EXTRA PAIR OF SHOES, A BELT AND A SPOON FOR—

WHAT?!

YOU JEW! YOU'VE ONLY BEEN HERE A FEW DAYS AND YOU'RE READY TO DO BUSINESS?!

I HAVE TO ACCOUNT FOR EVERY PAIR OF SHOES IN HERE!

I-I DON'T WANT TO MAKE TROUBLE. YOU'VE BEEN SO KIND TO ME... IT WAS FOR MY FRIEND...

I EXPLAINED HIM EVERYTHING ABOUT MANDELBAUM.

WELL... I COULD "LOSE" THE BELT AND SPOON— BUT BRING ME YOUR FRIEND'S OLD SHOES TOMORROW— OR ELSE!

I'M TELLING YOU— I WAS AMAZING WELL-OFF!

I RAN TO FIND MANDELBAUM...

VLADEK?!! YOU LOOK LIKE A...A GENERAL!

HAH! NOT QUITE. BUT I'VE BEEN LUCKY, AND I DIDN'T FORGET YOU...

LOOK. I GOT YOU YOUR OWN SPOON.

A SPOON! THANK YOU, VLADEK, THANK YOU.

AND HERE'S A BELT—NOT JUST STRING—A REAL BELT!

OH MY GOD!

AND ONE MORE THING: A PAIR OF WOODEN SHOES THAT WILL FIT YOU!

∶gasp∶

SOB

MY GOD. MY GOD. MY GOD... IT'S A MIRACLE, VLADEK.

GOD SENT SHOES THROUGH YOU.

...HE WAS SO HAPPY, HE WAS CRYING... AND I STARTED ALSO CRYING WITH HIM.

HE WAS SO HAPPY WITH THIS. ...AND THE KAPO KNEW MANDELBAUM WAS MY FRIEND SO HE LEFT HIM ALSO ALONE.

HOW LONG I COULD, I KEPT HIM. BUT A FEW DAYS LATER THE GERMANS CHOSE HIM TO TAKE AWAY TO WORK...

NOBODY COULD HELP THIS. SO. IT WAS FINISHED WITH MANDEL-BAUM. I NEVER SAW HIM MORE AGAIN.

SO YOU DON'T KNOW WHAT HAPPENED TO MANDELBAUM?

HE GOT KILLED. OR HE DIED. I KNOW THEY FINISHED HIM.

MAYBE ON THE WALK TO WORK, A GUARD GRABBED HIS CAP AWAY.

GO GET YOUR CAP-QUICK!

SO WHAT COULD HE DO? HE RAN TO PICK IT UP. AND THE GUARD SHOT ON HIM FOR TRYING TO ESCAPE.

THE GUARD GOT A CONGRATULATIONS AND A FEW DAYS VACATION FOR STOPPING THE ESCAPE.

I DONT **KNOW** IF THIS WAS HOW IT WAS WITH MANDELBAUM—ONLY THAT VERY OFTEN THEY DID SO...

THEY WANTED ONLY TO FINISH EVERYONE OUT. IT WAS VERY HARD WORK AND VERY LITTLE FOOD.

...MAYBE THEY KICKED AND HIT HIM IN HIS HEAD BECAUSE HE COULDN'T WORK FAST ENOUGH.

...OR MAYBE HE GOT SICK. SO THEY PUT HIM FIRST IN THE "HOSPITAL" AND THEN IN THE OVEN...

YOU SEE HOW THEY DID? AND I HAD IT STILL HAPPY THERE. FOR **ME** IT WAS NOT YET THE END.

NEWCOMERS WERE AFRAID FROM ME. I LOOKED LIKE A **BIG SHOT** AND THE KAPO KEPT ME CLOSE.

THEY'LL WANT 200 WORKERS TOMORROW. I'VE ONLY GOT 180 STILL **REGISTERED** HERE. ...YOU'D BETTER HIDE IN MY ROOM...

FOR OVER TWO MONTHS I STAYED HERE SAFE AND TAUGHT TO HIM ENGLISH.

VLADEK, WHAT WAS YOUR PROFESSION BEFORE YOU WERE BROUGHT HERE?

I WORKED IN A *LOT* OF DIFFERENT BUSINESSES. WHY?

I'VE KEPT YOU HERE IN THE "QUARANTINE BLOCK" AS LONG AS I CAN. YOU'LL HAVE TO BE ASSIGNED OUT TO A WORK CREW... SKILLED WORKERS GET BETTER TREATMENT.

I CAN DO *ANYTHING* ONCE I'M SHOWN HOW. IN THE GHETTO I WORKED IN A WOOD SHOP... IN SOSNOWIEC I WAS A TINSMITH.

A TIN-SMITH! I'LL SEE WHAT I CAN DO!

I WAS NOT *REALLY* A TINMAN. BUT I KNEW A LITTLE. IN SOSNOWIEC I WAS IN A TIN SHOP REGISTERED TO GET A SAFE WORK PASSPORT, AND I WATCHED HOW THEY WORKED.

THE Pines
GUESTS ONLY
No Trespassing

ALWAYS AROUND AUSCHWITZ THEY WERE BUILDING. TO THE ROOFS THEY NEEDED GOOD TINMEN.

UH-HUH. YOU TOLD ME. WHAT I WANTED TO ASK YOU ABOUT THOUGH, IS WHAT HAPPENED TO MOM WHILE YOU

STOP!...

Pi
GUE
No Tr

WE MUST TURN *QUICK* AND GO BY *THIS* ROAD TO COME TO THE PINES!

HUH?

ERVICE
TRANCE

IN THIS WAY THE HOTEL GUARD CAN'T SEE US, AND WE CAN SIT ON THEIR PATIO. IT'S *PRETTY* THERE TO SIT. I COME ALMOST EVERY DAY IN THIS WAY.

SOMETIMES I GET HERE FREE DANCING LESSONS, OR THEY HAVE FOR THE GUESTS FREE BINGO GAMES AND PRIZES.

DOWNSTAIRS IS A GYM WITH A STEAM ROOM AND A WHIRLPOOL... MAYBE I CAN TAKE YOU IN THERE TOMORROW.

NO THANKS. AREN'T YOU AFRAID YOU'LL GET CAUGHT TRESPASSING?

FEH. FROM OUR BUNGALOWS EVERYBODY COMES HERE ALWAYS, OR TO BRICKMAN'S HOTEL UP THE ROAD.

...I LIKE BETTER THE PINES. ONLY IT'S THAT IN THE GYM HERE YOU CAN'T HAVE A LOCKER WITHOUT GIVING A ROOM KEY.

LOOK. THEY'RE GIVING NOW CARDS FOR BINGO. YOU WANT WE'LL PLAY?

UH-UH. I'LL PUT IN A NEW TAPE AND WE CAN CONTINUE.

I WON HERE A BINGO GAME ONE TIME. THE WINNER GOT A PRIZE OVER TO HIS ROOM. ...ONLY IT WAS, I HAD NO ROOM.

BEHIND ME SAT A YOUNG LADY WHAT GOT SO DISAPPOINTED THAT SHE LOST— SHE HAD JUST ONE NUMBER AWAY...

...SO I GAVE TO HER MY CARD AND SAID: "I DON'T CARE FOR SUCH PRIZES—YOU GO UP TO BE THE WINNER."...WAS SHE HAPPY.

DID YOU TELL HER YOU WEREN'T A GUEST HERE?

WHY TO TELL?? THIS WASN'T HER BUSINESS.

YOU KNOW, IN TOWN IS A BINGO PLACE—50¢ A CARD. MALA LIKED SOMETIMES TO GO.... AND I SAID TO HER, "FOR WHAT? FOR THE COFFEE THEY GIVE AFTER? BINGO WE CAN PLAY AT THE PINES, AND BETTER COFFEE WE HAVE AT HOME!"

..B-5 G-22...

BINGO!

197

C H A P T E R   T W O

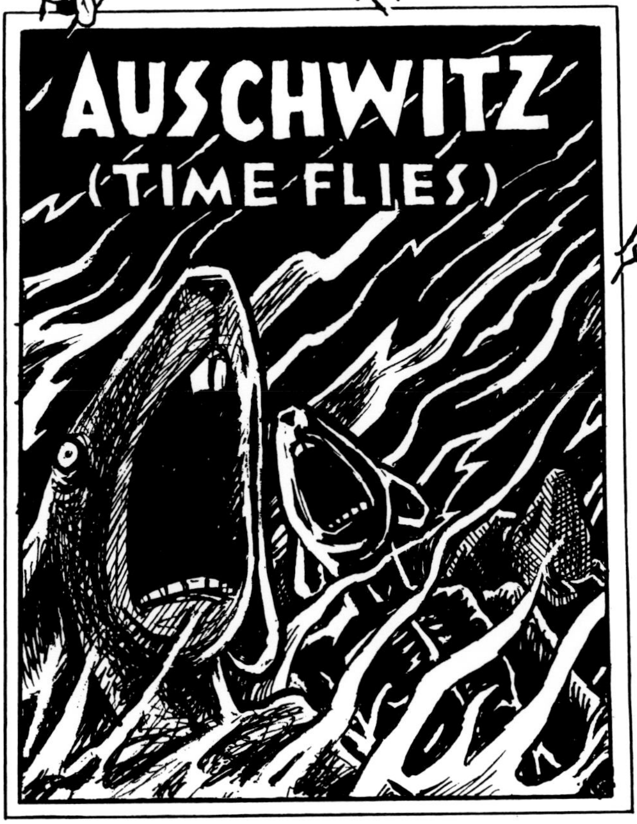
AUSCHWITZ
(TIME FLIES)

Time flies...

Vladek died of congestive heart failure on August 18, 1982...

Françoise and I stayed with him in the Catskills back in August 1979.

Vladek started working as a tinman in Auschwitz in the spring of 1944...

I started working on this page at the very end of February 1987.

In May 1987 Françoise and I are expecting a baby...

Between May 16, 1944, and May 24, 1944 over 100,000 Hungarian Jews were gassed in Auschwitz...

In September 1986, after 8 years of work, the first part of MAUS was published. It was a critical and commercial success.

At least fifteen foreign editions are coming out. I've gotten 4 serious offers to turn my book into a T.V. special or movie. (I don't wanna.)

In May 1968 my mother killed herself. (She left no note.)

Lately I've been feeling depressed.

Alright Mr. Spiegelman... We're ready to shoot!...

201

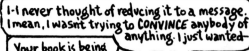

Panel 1: Tell our viewers what message you want them to get from your book?

a message? I dunno...

Panel 2: I-I never thought of reducing it to a message. I mean, I wasn't trying to CONVINCE anybody of anything. I just wanted—

Your book is being translated into German...

Panel 3: Many younger Germans have had it up to HERE with Holocaust stories. These things happened before they were even born. Why should THEY feel guilty?

Who am I to say?...

Panel 4: But a lot of the corporations that flourished in Nazi Germany are richer than ever. I dunno... Maybe EVERYONE has to feel guilty. EVERYONE! FOREVER!

Okay... Let's talk about Israel...

Panel 5: If your book was about ISRAELI Jews, what kind of animal would you draw?

I have no idea. ...porcupines?

Excuse me...

Panel 6: Artie, baby. Check out this licensing deal. You get 50% of the profits. We'll make a million. Your dad would be proud!

HUH?

MAUS
YOU'VE READ THE BOOK
NOW BUY THE VEST!

Panel 7: So, whaddya WANT— a bigger percentage? Hey, we can talk.

I want... ABSOLUTION. No...No... I want...I want... my MOMMY!

Panel 8: Could you tell our audience if drawing MAUS was cathartic? Do you feel better now?

WAH!

≡ whew. ≡ they're gone. Sometimes I just don't feel like a functioning adult.

I can't believe I'm gonna be a father in a couple of months.* My father's ghost still hangs over me.

*NADJA MOULY SPIEGELMAN. BORN 5/13/87

It's 9:30 p.m. already. I've gotta head uptown for my appointment with Pavel.

Pavel is my shrink. He sees patients at night.

He's a Czech Jew, a survivor of Terezin and Auschwitz. I see him once a week.

His place is overrun with stray dogs and cats.

Hi Art. Come on in.

Can I mention this, or does it completely louse up my metaphor?

So, how are you feeling?

Completely messed up. I mean, things couldn't be going better with my "career," or at home, but mostly I feel like crying.

I can't work. My time is being sucked up by interviews and business propositions I can't deal with.

But even when I'm left alone I'm totally BLOCKED. Instead of working on my book I just lie on my couch for hours and stare at a small grease spot on the upholstery.

FRAMED PHOTO OF PET CAT. REALLY!

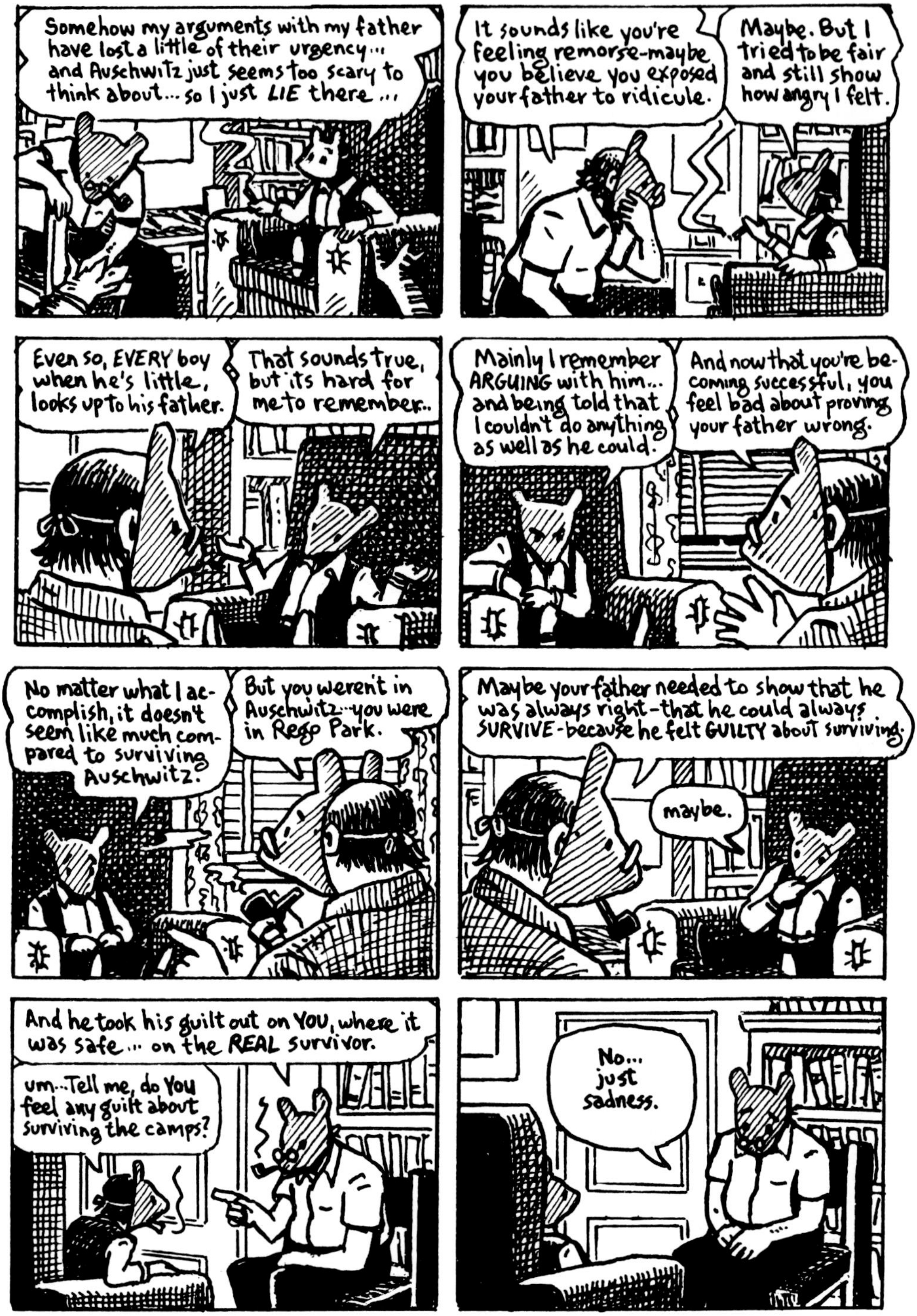
Somehow my arguments with my father have lost a little of their urgency... and Auschwitz just seems too scary to think about... so I just LIE there...
It sounds like you're feeling remorse-maybe you believe you exposed your father to ridicule.
Maybe. But I tried to be fair and still show how angry I felt.
Even so, EVERY boy when he's little, looks up to his father.
That sounds true, but its hard for me to remember..
Mainly I remember ARGUING with him... and being told that I couldn't do anything as well as he could.
And now that you're becoming successful, you feel bad about proving your father wrong.
No matter what I accomplish, it doesn't seem like much compared to surviving Auschwitz.
But you weren't in Auschwitz... you were in Rego Park.
Maybe your father needed to show that he was always right-that he could always SURVIVE-because he felt GUILTY about surviving.
maybe.
And he took his guilt out on YOU, where it was safe... on the REAL survivor.
um...Tell me, do YOU feel any guilt about surviving the camps?
No... just sadness.

So, do you ADMIRE your father for surviving?

Well... sure. I know there was a lot of LUCK involved, but he WAS amazingly present-minded and resourceful...

Then you think it's admirable to survive. Does that mean it's NOT admirable to NOT survive?

whoosh.

I-I think I see what you mean. It's as if life equals winning, so death equals losing.

Yes. Life always takes the side of life, and somehow the victims are blamed. But it wasn't the BEST people who survived, nor did the best ones die. It was RANDOM!

Sigh. I'm not talking about YOUR book now, but look at how many books have already been written about the Holocaust. What's the point? People haven't changed...

Maybe they need a newer, bigger Holocaust.

Anyway, the victims who died can never tell THEIR side of the story, so maybe it's better not to have any more stories.

Uh-huh. Samuel Beckett once said: "Every word is like an unnecessary stain on silence and nothingness."

Yes.

On the other hand, he SAID it.

He was right. Maybe you can include it in your book.

My book? Hah! What book?? Some part of me doesn't want to draw or think about Auschwitz. I can't visualize it clearly, and I can't BEGIN to imagine what it felt like.

What Auschwitz felt like? Hmm... How can I explain?...

BOO!

Yiii!

It felt a little like *that*. But ALWAYS! From the moment you got to the gate until the very end.

So, what part of your book are you trying to visualize?

My father worked in a tin shop near the camp. I have no idea what kind of tools and stuff to draw. There's no documentation.

Let's see. There would be a cutter—like a giant paper cutter—and maybe an electric drill press or two.

How do you KNOW that?

Oh, I worked in a tool and die shop in Czechoslovakia when I was a kid.

But it's getting late now, and I still have to walk my dogs.

Okay, I'll see you in a week...

Gee. I don't understand exactly why...

but these sessions with Pavel somehow make me feel better...

Maybe I could show the tin shop and not draw the drill press. I hate to draw machinery.

And so...

CLIK ...THEN, WHEN I CAME OUT FROM THE HOS-PITAL, RIGHT AWAY SHE STARTED AGAIN THAT I CHANGE MY WILL!

PLEASE POP. THE TAPE'S ON. LET'S CONTINUE...

I WAS STILL SO SICK AND TIRED. AND TO HAVE PEACE ONLY, I AGREED. TO MAKE IT LEGAL SHE BROUGHT RIGHT TO MY BED A NOTARY.

LET'S GET BACK TO AUSCHWITZ.

FIFTEEN DOLLARS HE CHARGED TO COME! IF SHE WAITED ONLY A WEEK UNTIL I WAS STRONGER, I'D GO TO THE BANK AND TAKE A NOTARY FOR ONLY A QUARTER!

ENOUGH! TELL ME ABOUT AUSCHWITZ!

sigh

YOU WERE TELLING ME HOW YOUR KAPO TRIED TO GET YOU WORK AS A TINSMITH...

YAH. EVERY DAY I WORKED THERE RIGHT OUTSIDE. FROM THE CAMP...

THE CHIEF OF THE TINMEN IT WAS A RUSSIAN JEW NAMED YIDL.

BAH! YOU'RE NO TINSMITH. YOU CAN'T EVEN CUT IT RIGHT.

BUT THIS IS HOW I'VE ALWAYS DONE IT!...

I'VE ONLY BEEN A TINSMITH FOR A FEW YEARS. IF YOU SHOW ME HOW YOU WANT IT CUT I CAN LEARN QUICKLY.

HAH! YOU NEVER DID AN HONEST DAY'S WORK IN YOUR WHOLE LIFE, SPIEGELMAN! I KNOW ALL ABOUT YOU...

I DON'T KNOW WHERE FROM HE HEARD STORIES ABOUT ME.

YOU OWNED BIG FACTORIES AND EXPLOITED YOUR WORK-ERS, YOU DIRTY CAPITALIST!

HE WAS A COMMU-NIST, THIS YIDL.

PFUI! THEY SEND DREK LIKE YOU HERE WHILE THEY SEND REAL TINMEN UP THE CHIMNEY. WATCH OUT. I'VE GOT MY EYE ON YOU!

I WAS AFRAID. HE COULD REALLY DO ME SOMETHING.

WITH THE OTHER BOYS THERE, I GOT ALONG FINE.

DON'T WORRY...YOU JUST HAVE TO KNOW HOW TO HANDLE YIDL...

BRING HIM A FEW EGGS, SOME BUTTER OR CHEESE...

YOU'LL SEE. HE'LL SING A DIFFERENT TUNE.

HA! AND WHERE DO I GET ALL THIS FOOD?

JUST KEEP YOUR EYES OPEN. YOU CAN ORGANIZE THINGS WITH THE POLES HERE.

POLES FROM NEARBY THEY HIRED TO WORK ALSO HERE— NOT PRISONERS, BUT SPECIALIST BUILDING WORKERS ...

(PSST-I CAN GET YOU A FINE GOLD WATCH FOR A POUND OF SAUSAGE AND SIX EGGS.)

(AGREED.)

THEY HAD **NOTHING**, ONLY FOOD FROM THEIR FARMS. THEY WERE HAPPY TO MAKE EXCHANGES.

THE HEAD GUY FROM THE AUSCHWITZ LAUNDRY WAS A FINE FELLOW WHAT KNEW WELL MY FAMILY BEFORE THE WAR...

FROM HIM I GOT CIVILIAN **CLOTHINGS** TO SMUGGLE OUT BELOW MY UNIFORM. I WAS SO THIN THE GUARDS DIDN'T SEE IF I WORE EXTRA.

HERE YIDL. I'VE GOT A BIG PIECE OF CHEESE FOR YOU.

A GIFT? VERY NICE, SPIEGELMAN.

AND WHAT ELSE DO YOU HAVE THERE? A LOAF OF BREAD? YOU'RE A RICH MAN!

WAIT! I NEED THAT TO PAY OFF THE GUY WHO HELPED ME ORGANIZE THE CHEESE!

HMPH.

HE WAS SO GREEDY, YIDL, HE WANTED I RISK ONLY FOR HIM EVERYTHING. I TOO HAD TO EAT.

EVERYBODY WAS SO HUNGRY ALWAYS, WE DIDN'T KNOW EVEN WHAT WE ARE DOING...

IN THE MORNING FOR BREAKFAST WE GOT ONLY A BITTER DRINK MADE FROM ROOTS.

I WOKE BEFORE EVERYBODY TO HAVE TIME TO THE TOILET AND FIND STILL SOME TEA LEFT.

ONE TIME A DAY THEY GAVE A SOUP FROM TURNIPS. TO STAND NEAR THE FIRST OF THE LINE WAS NO GOOD. YOU GOT ONLY WATER.

MIX IT! MIX IT!

NEAR THE END WAS BETTER - SOLID THINGS TO THE BOTTOM FLOATED.

BUT TOO FAR TO THE END IT WAS ALSO NO GOOD

..BECAUSE MANY TIMES IT COULD BE NO SOUP ANYMORE.

AND ONE TIME EACH DAY THEY GAVE TO US A SMALL BREAD, CRUNCHY LIKE GLASS.

THE FLOUR THEY MIXED WITH SAWDUST TOGETHER - WE GOT ONE LITTLE BRICK OF THIS WHAT HAD TO LAST THE FULL DAY.

MOST GOBBLED IT RIGHT AWAY, BUT ALWAYS I SAVED A HALF FOR LATER.

AND IN THE EVENING WE GOT A SPOILED CHEESE OR JAM. IF WE WERE LUCKY A COUPLE TIMES A WEEK WE GOT A SAUSAGE BIG LIKE TWO OF MY FINGERS. ONLY THIS MUCH WE GOT

IF YOU ATE HOW THEY GAVE YOU, IT WAS JUST ENOUGH TO DIE MORE SLOWLY.

EACH MORNING AND EVENING THEY MADE AN *APPEL*. THEY COUNTED THE LIVE ONES AND DEAD ONES TO SEE IT WASN'T ANY MISSING ...

WE STOOD SOMETIMES THE WHOLE NIGHT WHILE THEY COUNTED AGAIN AND AGAIN.

ON OUR APPELS IT WAS ONE OLD GUY THERE, ALWAYS HE WAS COMPLAINING ...

I DON'T BELONG HERE WITH ALL THESE YIDS AND POLACKS!

I'M A **GERMAN** LIKE YOU!

I HAVE MEDALS FROM THE KAISER. MY SON IS A GERMAN SOLDIER!

ONLY THEY HIT HIM AND THEY LAUGHED.

WAS HE REALLY A GERMAN?

WHO KNOWS_IT WAS GERMAN PRISONERS ALSO... BUT FOR THE GERMANS THIS GUY WAS JEWISH!

ON ONE APPEL HE DIDN'T STAND SO STRAIGHT AND A GUARD DRAGGED HIM AWAY. I HEARD HE PUSHED HIM DOWN AND JUMPED HARD ON HIS NECK ...

OR THEY SENT HIM TO THE GAS, I DON'T REMEMBER, BUT THEY FINISHED HIM AND HE NEVER ANYMORE COMPLAINED.

210

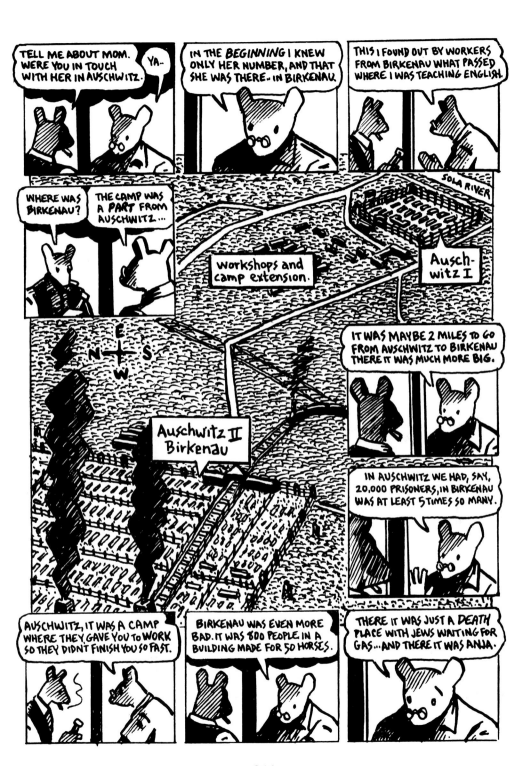

TELL ME ABOUT MOM. WERE YOU IN TOUCH WITH HER IN AUSCHWITZ.

YA-

IN THE *BEGINNING* I KNEW ONLY HER NUMBER, AND THAT SHE WAS THERE.. IN BIRKENAU.

THIS I FOUND OUT BY WORKERS FROM BIRKENAU WHAT PASSED WHERE I WAS TEACHING ENGLISH.

WHERE WAS BIRKENAU?

THE CAMP WAS A *PART* FROM AUSCHWITZ ...

SOLA RIVER

workshops and camp extension.

Auschwitz I

Auschwitz II Birkenau

IT WAS MAYBE 2 MILES TO GO FROM AUSCHWITZ TO BIRKENAU THERE IT WAS MUCH MORE BIG.

IN AUSCHWITZ WE HAD, SAY, 20,000 PRISONERS, IN BIRKENAU WAS AT LEAST 5 TIMES SO MANY.

AUSCHWITZ, IT WAS A CAMP WHERE THEY GAVE YOU TO WORK SO THEY DIDN'T FINISH YOU SO FAST.

BIRKENAU WAS EVEN MORE BAD. IT WAS 800 PEOPLE IN A BUILDING MADE FOR 50 HORSES.

THERE IT WAS JUST A *DEATH* PLACE WITH JEWS WAITING FOR GAS... AND THERE IT WAS ANJA.

COME...IT'S TIME NOW WE'LL HURRY FOR LUNCH HOME TO THE BUNGALOW.

SO YOU WERE ACTUALLY IN *TOUCH* WITH ANJA IN BIRKENAU?

YAH. FROM MANCIE I HAD A REAL CONTACT WITH MOTHER, UNTIL LATER I COULD BRING ANJA TO—

WAIT! WHO'S MANCIE?

SHE WAS A HUNGARIAN, MANCIE, WHO WORKED SOMETIMES THERE. BEAUTIFUL. A TALL BLONDE GIRL. AND CLEVER.

REST BEHIND THAT STACK OF WOOD. I'LL WARN YOU IF A GUARD COMES CLOSE.

SHE HAD A LOVER, I HEARD LATER AN S.S. MAN. HE GOT FOR HER A GOOD POSITION OVER 10 OR 12 OTHER GIRLS FROM BIRKENAU.

(PSST, MISS—UP HERE! I SEE HOW KIND YOU ARE. HELP ME. PLEASE!)

HUH? (WHAT DO YOU WANT?)

(NOTHING FOR ME, BUT I'M AFRAID FOR MY WIFE IN BIRKENAU. CAN YOU FIND OUT IF SHE'S STILL ALIVE?)

I TOLD TO HER ANJA'S NAME AND NUMBER.

(I'VE SAVED SOME FOOD, I CAN PAY FOR YOUR HELP.)

(KEEP YOUR FOOD. WE'LL BE WORKING HERE AGAIN IN A FEW DAYS. I'LL SEE WHAT I CAN FIND OUT.)

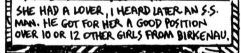
EACH DAY I LOOKED. FOUR DAYS AFTER, I SAW HER.

I MET A WOMAN NAMED ANJA FROM SOSNOWIEC. SHE'S VERY FRAIL...

SHE SPOKE OVER TO ONE OF HER WORKERS; I SPOKE ONLY TO MY TIN SO NOBODY WILL NOTICE.

SOMEONE TOLD HER THAT HER HUSBAND IS STILL ALIVE AND SHE STARTED SOBBING WITH JOY.

I HEARD THIS, AND I STARTED ALSO CRYING A LITTLE. AND MANCIE, SHE TOO STARTED CRYING.

A FEW DAYS AFTER, MANCIE AGAIN CAME THERE.

I PUT SOME "GARBAGE" UNDER A ROCK NEAR THE DOORWAY.

SHE BROUGHT TO ME A LETTER—A REAL LETTER!—FROM ANJA.

"I MISS YOU," SHE WROTE TO ME. "EACH DAY I THINK TO RUN INTO THE ELECTRIC WIRES AND FINISH EVERYTHING. BUT TO KNOW YOU ARE ALIVE IT GIVES ME STILL TO HOPE...,"

SHE TOLD ME HER KAPO WAS VERY MEAN ON HER AND GAVE WORK ANJA REALLY COULDN'T DO.

LIKE TO RUN FROM THE KITCHEN WITH THE BIG CANS OF SOUP.

EVEN FOR ME SUCH CANS WERE HEAVY, AND FOR ANJA—SHE WAS SO SMALL—IT WAS IMPOSSIBLE.

SHE COULDN'T HOLD WELL HER END. ALWAYS SHE *SPILLED*.

THE KAPO BEAT ANJA VERY HARD BUT *KEPT* HER TO THIS JOB.

AND IF ANJA SPILLED OVER ALL FROM THE SOUP, THEN NOBODY GOT WHAT TO EAT, ESPECIALLY ANJA.

I WROTE TO HER: "I THINK OF YOU ALWAYS," AND SENT WITH MANCIE TWO PIECES OF BREAD.

IF THE S.S. WOULD SEE SHE IS TAKING FOOD INTO THE CAMP, RIGHT AWAY THEY WILL KILL HER.

BUT ALWAYS SHE TOOK.

SO SHE SAID: "IF A COUPLE IS LOVING EACH OTHER SO MUCH, I MUST HELP HOWEVER I CAN."

213

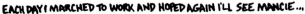

SHE COULD HAVE MORE NEWS OF ANJA.

I JUST READ ABOUT THE CAMP ORCHESTRA THAT PLAYED AS YOU MARCHED OUT THE GATE...

AN ORCHESTRA?...

NO. I REMEMBER ONLY *MARCHING,* NOT ANY ORCHESTRAS...

FROM THE GATE GUARDS TOOK US OVER TO THE WORKSHOP. HOW COULD IT BE THERE AN ORCHESTRA?

I DUNNO, BUT IT'S VERY WELL DOCUMENTED...

NO. AT THE GATE I HEARD ONLY GUARDS SHOUTING.

DID YOU EVER *TALK* WITH ANY OF THE GUARDS?

ACH! WE WERE BELOW THEIR DIGNITY. WE WERE NOT EVEN MEN. BUT IT WAS ONE GUY...

IF HE SPOKE OF COURSE I ANSWERED. HE HAD EVEN A LITTLE HEART.

AAH. GUTEN MORGEN. THIS SPRING AIR REMINDS ME OF HOME... OF NUREMBURG...

YES. I WAS THERE ONCE. IT'S A BEAUTIFUL CITY.

AND IF HE LIKED ME, MAYBE SOMEDAY HE WON'T SHOOT ME

ONE TIME HE WAS MISSING A FEW DAYS...

YOU LOOK PALE. WERE YOU SICK HERR SOLDAT?

NO...I WAS... WORKING... IN BIRKENAU.

YES... I'VE HEARD ABOUT WHAT GOES ON THERE...

SHUT UP!

AND HE WAS AFRAID ANYMORE TO SPEAK.

WHEN I VISITED TO ANJA THERE, I SAW WITH MY OWN EYES HOW IT WAS...

YOU *SAW* ANJA?

YA. EVERY FEW DAYS IT CAME AN S.S. COMMISSION TO THE TIN SHOP...

YOU HAVE MORE WORKERS THAN YOU NEED HERE...

GIVE US 10 PRISONERS TO TAKE BACK TO THE MAIN CAMP FOR OTHER WORK.

WELL ...TAKE *THAT* ONE ... AND THAT ONE--

AND - WAIT! DON'T TAKE *HIM!* HE'S ONE OF MY BEST ROOFERS... TAKE THAT ONE ... AND *THAT* ONE--

THE UNLUCKY ONES WENT OVER FOR *BAD* JOBS, BUT ME YIDL KEPT PROTECTED.

...SEND A CREW TO SECTOR B1b IN BIRKENAU. SOME OF THE ROOFS IN THE WOMEN'S CAMP HAVE COLLAPSED.

LET ME GO TO BIRKENAU. I'VE NEVER SEEN IT.

GO, SPIEGELMAN, AND DON'T COME BACK FOR ALL I CARE. BAH! I GIVE UP MY BEST TINMEN, AND YOU I SAVE.

WHY?!

SO I MARCHED WITH A FEW TIN-MEN OVER TO BIRKENAU. I CAME THE FIRST TIME IN SUMMER 1944.

THOUSANDS-HUNDREDS OF THOUSANDS OF HUN-GARIANS WERE ARRIV-ING THERE AT THIS TIME.

INSIDE THE CAMP WE CALLED OUT. MAYBE SOME-BODY KNEW IF OUR LOVED ONES ARE HERE ALIVE.

EVA. EVA GOLD-BERG FROM LODZ!

ANJA ZYLBERBERG! FROM SOSNOWIEC!

MY GOD. THAT'S VLADEK! I'LL GO FIND ANJA!

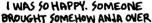
I WAS SO HAPPY. SOMEONE BROUGHT SOMEHOW ANJA OVER

DON'T LOOK UP, DARLING. A GUARD MAY SPOT US.

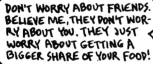

SHE LOOKED SO LIKE A SKELETON.

DID MAN-CIE BRING YOU MY LETTERS?

YES. AND WHEN SHE CAN, SHE GETS ME JOBS IN THE KITCHEN!

MY FRIENDS WAIT OUTSIDE AND I BRING THEM SCRAPS.

NO! SAVE YOUR SCRAPS! WHAT IF YOU LOSE THAT JOB? WHAT IF SOMETHING HAP-PENS TO MANCIE?

DON'T WORRY ABOUT FRIENDS. BELIEVE ME, THEY DON'T WOR-RY ABOUT YOU. THEY JUST WORRY ABOUT GETTING A BIGGER SHARE OF YOUR FOOD!

BUT MY FRIENDS ARE ALWAYS HUNGRY, AND I-I DON'T HAVE MUCH OF AN APPETITE.

I BEG YOU, ANJA-KEEP YOURSELF STRONG. FOR MY SAKE.

JUST SEEING YOU AGAIN GIVES ME STRENGTH.

I HAVE TO GO BEFORE ANY-ONE NOTICES I'M MISSING.

I... I THINK ABOUT YOU ... ALWAYS.

I WAS A *FEW* TIMES IN BIRKENAU, AND ONCE I HAD *REALLY* TROUBLES. I WAS GOING FROM WORK AND PASSED BY ANJA...

VLADEK! VLADEK! VLADEK!

ANJA! DARLING! DID YOU GET THE FOOD I SENT YOU!

YES. YOU ALWAYS ARRANGE MIRACLES.

I THINK ABOUT YOU ...ALWAYS.

WE SPOKE A MINUTE ONLY AND I WENT ON MY WAY.

A GUARD SCREAMED TO ME:

HALT!

WHO WERE YOU TALKING TO?

N-NOBODY...

A STRANGER ASKED IF I KNEW HER BROTHERS IN AUSCHWITZ. I DIDN'T KNOW ANYTHING, SO I HARDLY ANSWERED.

GET INSIDE!

WHEN I'M FINISHED WITH YOU, YOU'LL KNOW *SOMETHING*, JEWISH PIMP! YOU'RE NOT HERE TO FLIRT AND GOSSIP.

COUNT THE BLOWS. IF YOU LOSE COUNT — I'LL START AGAIN!

EINS!

ZWEI!

DREI!

SO HE BEAT ME, WHAT CAN I TELL YOU? ONLY, THANK GOD, ANJA DIDN'T GET ALSO SUCH A BEATING. SHE WOULDN'T LIVE.

THE NEXT DAYS IT WAS HARD TO GO WORK, BUT TO GO TO THE HOSPITAL, I COULD EASY NOT COME AGAIN OUT.

IT WASN'T A PLACE WITH MEDICINES, ONLY A PLACE FULL WITH PRISONERS TOO SICK TO GO WORK.

EACH DAY IT WAS SELEKTIONS. THE DOCTORS CHOSE OUT THE WEAKER ONES TO GO AND DIE.

IN THE WHOLE CAMP WAS SELEKTIONS. I WENT TWO TIMES IN FRONT OF DR. MENGELE.

WE STOOD WITHOUT ANYTHING, STRAIGHT LIKE A SOLDIER. HE GLANCED AND SAID: "FACE LEFT!"

THEY LOOKED TO SEE IF IT WAS SORES OR PIMPLES ON THE BODY. THEN AGAIN: "FACE LEFT!"

THEY LOOKED TO SEE IF EATING NO FOOD MADE YOU TOO SKINNY...

FACE LEFT!

IF YOU HAD STILL A HEALTHY BODY TO WORK, THEY PASSED YOU THROUGH AND GAVE YOU ANOTHER UNIFORM UNTIL IT CAME THE NEXT SELEKTION...

WHEN FIRST I CAME I WAS VERY STRONG THEN, AND CAME WELL TO THE GOOD SIDE.

THE ONES THAT HAD NOT SO LUCKY THE S.S. WROTE DOWN THEIR NUMBER AND SENT TO THE OTHER SIDE.

THE SECOND SELEKTION I WAS IN THE BARRACK, IN THE BED UP FROM ME WAS A FINE BOY, A BELGIAN.

I DREAMED MY WIFE WAS ALIVE. SHE WAS COOKING A GIANT ROAST WITH THICK GRAVY AND FRIED—

STOP, FELIX! DON'T THINK ABOUT FOOD!

WE WERE EXPECTING DINNER GUESTS. WE WAITED AND WAITED... THEN THE GONG RANG. I WOKE UP WITHOUT EVEN TASTING THE—

BLOCKSPERRE!

A "BLOCKSPERRE," THIS MEANT YOU MUST NOT STEP OUT FROM THE ROOM.

THEY TOOK THEN THE JEWS TO A SELEKTION. I CAME AGAIN TO THE GOOD SIDE, BUT THIS BELGIAN, HE HAD MAYBE A RASH, AND THEY WROTE HIS NUMBER...

ANY TIME THEY COULD TAKE HIM. ALL NIGHT HE CRIED AND SCREAMED.

AAWOOWWAH!

HERE FELIX. HAVE A PIECE OF BREAD...

SOB

LOOK. THEY'RE GOING TO KILL ALL OF US HERE EVENTUALLY... YOU THIS WEEK, ME THE NEXT...

...NONE OF US CAN ESCAPE IT. YOU MUST BE BRAVE... AND, WHO KNOWS, MAYBE IT'S NOT EVEN YOUR TURN YET...

SO HE CALMED A LITTLE...

BUT LATER HE AGAIN STARTED...

AWOOOWAA!

WHAT COULD I DO? I COULDN'T TELL TO THE GERMANS THEY WON'T TAKE HIM... AND THE NEXT DAY, THEY TOOK.

SO... IN THE TINSHOP I HAD STILL THE SAME STORY WITH YIDL.

ONLY ONE APPLE FOR ME TODAY? IS BUSINESS BAD, MR. CAPITALIST?

WHAT HAPPENED TO THE SHOEMAKER WHO WORKED IN THERE?

A LOT OF THE POLISH PRISONERS WERE SENT TO CAMPS INSIDE THE REICH. THEY TOOK SOME OF MY BOYS TOO.

I RAN TO THE KAPO IN CHARGE FROM ALL THE SHOP.

DO YOU NEED A NEW SHOEMAKER?

SURE. THE S.S. TOOK THE OLD ONE AWAY, BUT THEY'RE STILL BRINGING SHOES IN!

YOU KNOW, I'VE BEEN A SHOEMAKER SINCE CHILDHOOD.

YOU DON'T LOOK LIKE A SHOEMAKER TO ME... YOU'RE A TINMAN!

DO I HAVE TO HAVE IT WRITTEN ON MY FOREHEAD?

ALRIGHT, THEN... FIX THIS!

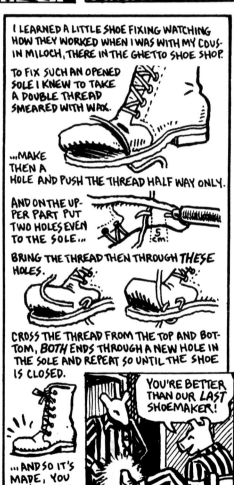

I LEARNED A LITTLE SHOE FIXING WATCHING HOW THEY WORKED WHEN I WAS WITH MY COUSIN MILOCH, THERE IN THE GHETTO SHOE SHOP.

TO FIX SUCH AN OPENED SOLE I KNEW TO TAKE A DOUBLE THREAD SMEARED WITH WAX.

...MAKE THEN A HOLE AND PUSH THE THREAD HALF WAY ONLY.

AND ON THE UPPER PART PUT TWO HOLES EVEN TO THE SOLE...

5 cm

BRING THE THREAD THEN THROUGH THESE HOLES.

CROSS THE THREAD FROM THE TOP AND BOTTOM, BOTH ENDS THROUGH A NEW HOLE IN THE SOLE AND REPEAT SO UNTIL THE SHOE IS CLOSED.

...AND SO IT'S MADE, YOU CAN'T EVEN SEE IT HAS STITCHES!

YOU'RE BETTER THAN OUR LAST SHOEMAKER!

YOU SEE? IT'S GOOD TO KNOW HOW TO DO EVERYTHING!

SO, NOW I WAS A SHOEMAKER. I HAD HERE A WARM AND PRIVATE ROOM WHERE TO SIT...

OFFICIALS LIKED BETTER IF I FIX THEIR SHOES THAN TO SEND TO THE BIG SHOP INSIDE CAMP.

HA! I KNEW YOU WERE AN EXPERT TINMAN, BUT I NEVER KNEW YOU HAD SO MANY OTHER TALENTS!

AND HERE I DIDN'T HAVE ANYMORE TO WORRY WILL YIDL GIVE ME OUT.

THIS IS A NEW BOOT. I DON'T WANT YOUR REPAIR TO SHOW.

IT'S A BAD RIP...I'LL DO MY BEST.

IF IT DOESN'T LOOK BRAND NEW BY TOMORROW YOU WON'T BE HERE ANYMORE. UNDERSTAND ME?

I KNEW TO FIX SOLES AND HEELS, BUT WHAT THIS GESTAPO WANTED, IT NEEDED A SPECIALIST.

SO, GOING FROM WORK, I HID THIS BOOT TO SNEAK IT TO A REAL SHOEMAKER IN AUSCHWITZ.

CAN YOU FIX THIS? I'LL GIVE YOU A DAY'S RATION OF BREAD.

FOR A DAY'S RATION OF BREAD I CAN FIX ANYTHING!

I WATCHED CAREFUL HOW HE DID, SO NEXT TIME I CAN SAVE MYSELF SUCH A BREAD.

NEXT DAY I HAD THE BOOT READY FOR THIS GESTAPO.

HE LEFT THE BOOT AND WENT WITHOUT ONE WORD.

AND HE CAME BACK WITH A WHOLE SAUSAGE.

HMM

YOU DID A GOOD JOB.

YOU KNOW WHAT THIS WAS, A WHOLE SAUSAGE? YOU CAN'T IMAGINE! I CUT WITH A SHOE KNIFE AND ATE SO FAST I WAS A LITTLE SICK AFTER.

I COULDN'T ANYMORE MAKE A BUSINESS SMUGGLING WITH POLISH WORKERS FROM HERE AS A SHOEMAKER, BUT STILL I WAS WELL-OFF...

THE GESTAPO WHAT I FIXED HIS BOOT RECOMMENDED ME, SO HIS FRIENDS WANTED I'LL FIX ALSO THEIR SHOES AND PAID ME FOOD.

I SHARED SOMETIMES TO THE KAPO IN CHARGE.

I JUST ORGANIZED SOME EGGS-WANT ONE?

WHAT A FRIENDLY JEW! SURE-WE CAN COOK THEM ON MY HEATER.

IF YOU WANT TO LIVE, IT'S GOOD TO BE FRIENDLY.

AND HERE'S A LITTLE BREAD FOR OUR MEAL.

GREAT! SAY, WHAT ARE ALL THOSE NEW BUILDINGS THEY'RE PUTTING UP THERE?

JUST SOME NEW WORKSHOPS. THEY'RE EXPANDING THE UNION WERKE MUNITIONS FACTORY...

AND THEY'RE PUTTING UP SOME BARRACKS TO MOVE SOME WOMEN WORKERS FROM BIRKENAU OVER HERE.

M-MY WIFE IS IN BIRKENAU. MAYBE I COULD GET HER INTO ONE OF THOSE BARRACKS!

HAH! IMPOSSIBLE! IT WOULD COST A FORTUNE IN BRIBES!

HE UNWRAPPED SOME CHEESE AND ATE HIMSELF A PIECE.

PLEASE. COULD I HAVE THAT PIECE OF PAPER?

WELL, SURE. I CAN LET YOU HAVE THE PAPER — BUT NOT THE CHEESE!

I NEEDED TO WRITE OVER TO ANJA!

EVEN PAPER WAS HARD TO HAVE THERE. MY FRIENDS CAME ALWAYS TO ME WHEN THEY NEEDED.

I FOUND AND SAVED. FOR THE TOILET MOST USED A PIECE FROM THEIR CLOTHES OR THEIR HAND.

WHY DIDN'T OTHER PEOPLE SAVE PAPER?

ACH! YOU KNOW HOW MOST PEOPLE ARE!

SO... I WROTE OVER TO ANJA THAT NOW I AM A SHOEMAKER, AND I HEARD HERE ABOUT THESE NEW BARRACKS...

AND MANCIE TOOK IT, SHE WAS SO GOOD, ALWAYS SHE TOOK.

ON THE BACK FROM MY LETTER ANJA WROTE HOW MUCH SHE WANTED ONLY TO COME TO SUCH A BARRACK NEAR TO ME.

ANJA'S BARRACK WAS MAYBE 1000 GIRLS WITH A BAD KAPO WHAT HIT ANYBODY WHAT CAME NEAR.

SNEAK! I SAW YOU TAKE A SECOND PIECE OF BREAD!

NO.1—

SHE HAD LEATHER BOOTS-NOT WOOD. THEY WERE IN A VERY BAD SHAPE, BUT REALLY LEATHER.

N-NICE BOOTS—IT'S A PITY THE SOLES ARE COMING APART.

SO? WHAT DO YOU CARE?

YOU COULD SEND THEM TO MY HUSBAND, HE'S A SHOEMAKER IN AUSCHWITZ....

OH, REALLY

SO, SHE ARRANGED THE BOOTS OVER TO ME.

OF COURSE I FIXED VERY NICE THE SHOES, AND THE KAPO THEN WAS VERY DIFFERENT WITH ANJA.

THAT SOUP CAN IS TOO HEAVY FOR YOU. COME REST IN MY ROOM UNTIL THE APPEL.

...VERY DIFFERENT.

I THOUGHT ONLY HOW HAPPY IT WOULD BE TO HAVE ANJA SO NEAR TO ME IN THESE NEW BARRACKS.

IT COULD BE "ARRANGED" FOR 100 CIGARETTES AND A BOTTLE VODKA, BUT THIS WAS A FORTUNE.

one day's bread. = 3 cigarettes

200 cigarettes = 1 bottle of vodka

HOW COULD YOU GET CIGARETTES?

EACH WEEK TO THE WORKERS, THEY GAVE US THREE.

THEY ISSUED A LUXURY LIKE THAT!

YA. AND IF YOU DON'T SMOKE YOU CAN EXCHANGE FOR BREAD.

I STARVED A LITTLE TO PAY TO BRING ANJA OVER.

ALL WHAT I ORGANIZED I KEPT IN A BOX UNDER MY MATTRESS.

BUT, WHEN I CAME BACK ONE TIME FROM WORK...

IT—IT'S GONE!

I'M TELLING YOU I WANTED TO CRY.

YOU LEFT THE BOX IN THE BARRACK? HOW COULD IT NOT BE TAKEN?

I DIDN'T THINK ON IT...

BUT EVERYONE WAS STARVING TO DEATH! SIGH—I GUESS I JUST DON'T UNDERSTAND.

YES...ABOUT AUSCHWITZ, NOBODY CAN UNDERSTAND.

SO... I SAVED A SECOND TIME A FORTUNE, AND GAVE OVER BRIBES TO BRING ANJA CLOSE TO ME. AND IN THE START OF OCTOBER, 1944, I SAW A FEW THOUSAND WOMEN IN THESE NEW BARRACKS...

AND WITH THEM WAS ANJA. THIS I ARRANGED. IT WAS THE ONLY TIME I WAS HAPPY IN AUSCHWITZ.

WHEN NOBODY SAW I WENT BACK AND FORTH UNTIL I SAW HER FROM FAR GOING TO MAKE MUNITIONS...

SHE WENT ALSO BACK AND FORTH UNTIL IT WAS SAFE TO APPROACH OVER TO MY FOOD PACKAGES...

BUT ONE TIME, IT WAS VERY BAD.

HEY, YOU! STOP!

DROP THAT PACKAGE AND STOP RIGHT THERE!

STOP!

SHE RAN—SHE DIDN'T KNOW WHERE—INTO HER OWN BLOCK.

ONLY A FRIEND FROM ANJA WAS THERE AS A ROOM CLEANER...

H-HIDE ME, LONIA, QUICK!

GET UNDER ONE OF THE BLANKETS!

I KNOW YOU'RE IN HERE SOMEPLACE, AND WHEN I FIND YOU, I'LL KILL YOU RIGHT HERE ON THE SPOT!

IT WAS SEVERAL ROOMS THERE, AND HUNDREDS OF BEDS. IN ONE, ANJA LAY SHAKING, AFRAID TO BREATHE EVEN.

225

I'LL KILL YOU! KILL YOU!

FOR MAYBE AN HOUR, LIKE CRAZY SHE RAN FROM ROOM TO ROOM, THROWING UPSIDE DOWN THE BEDS.

BAH! GET ALL THE BEDS IN ORDER BEFORE THE APPEL.

OKAY, ANJA. IT'S SAFE TO COME OUT NOW.

BUT THIS WASN'T YET OVER.

ON THE EVENING APPEL SHE CAME AGAIN THIS KAPO.

THE PRISONER I CHASED THIS AFTER-NOON WILL NOW STEP FORWARD!

BUT MOTHER DIDN'T STEP OUT.

IT WILL BE BETTER FOR YOU IF YOU STEP OUT THAN IF I FIND YOU!

SHE CAME BACK AND FORTH, LOOKING IN EACH FACE, BUT WITH THE STRIPES EVERYONE LOOKED ALL THE SAME.

IF YOU KNOW WHO SHE IS PUSH HER FORWARD OR YOU'LL ALL SUFFER!

SHE MADE THEM TO RUN, TO JUMP, TO BEND UNTIL THEY COULDN'T ANYMORE. THEN MORE, THE SAME.

FOR A FEW APPELS IT WENT SO, BUT NOBODY OF ANJA'S FRIENDS GAVE HER OUT. YOU CAN IMA-GINE WHAT SHE WENT THROUGH.

I HAD TO STOP SENDING OVER SUCH PACKAGES MORE TO ANJA.

I LOST ANYWAY MY JOB NEAR TO HER SOON AFTER. MY WHOLE WORKSHOP THEY CLOSED OUT...

THEY PUT US BACK TO THE MAIN CAMP AND TOOK ME FOR *BLACK WORK.*

BLACK WORK?

CARRYING BACK AND FORTH BIG STONES, DIGGING OUT HOLES, EACH DAY DIFFERENT, BUT ALWAYS THE SAME. VERY HARD...

AND GOD FORBID, IF YOU STOPPED ONLY A MINUTE TO *BREATHE.*

YOU GOT A HIT TO THE HEAD, OR WORSE.

TO ME THEY NEVER HIT, BECAUSE I WORKED ALL MY MUSCLES AWAY.

I LIKED BETTER *INDOORS* WORK. I SOMETIMES WAS A "BETTNACH-ZIEHER"... A BED-AFTER-PULLER...

AFTER EVERYBODY FIXED THEIR BED, WE CAME TO FIX BETTER, SO THE STRAW LOOKED SQUARE.

WHAT A CRAZY JOB!

NO. THEY WANTED EVERYTHING NEAT AND IN GOOD ORDER.

BUT THESE DAYS I GOT TOO SKINNY AND IT CAME AGAIN A *SELEKTION.*

RIGHT AWAY I RAN INSIDE THE TOILETS. AND IF SOMEBODY LOOKED, I'LL TELL I HAD A BAD STOMACH. WHAT HAD I TO LOSE?

BLOCKSPERRE!

NOW IT COULD BE MY TURN.

NOBODY LOOKED, SO I SAT LUCKY THE WHOLE SELEKTION.

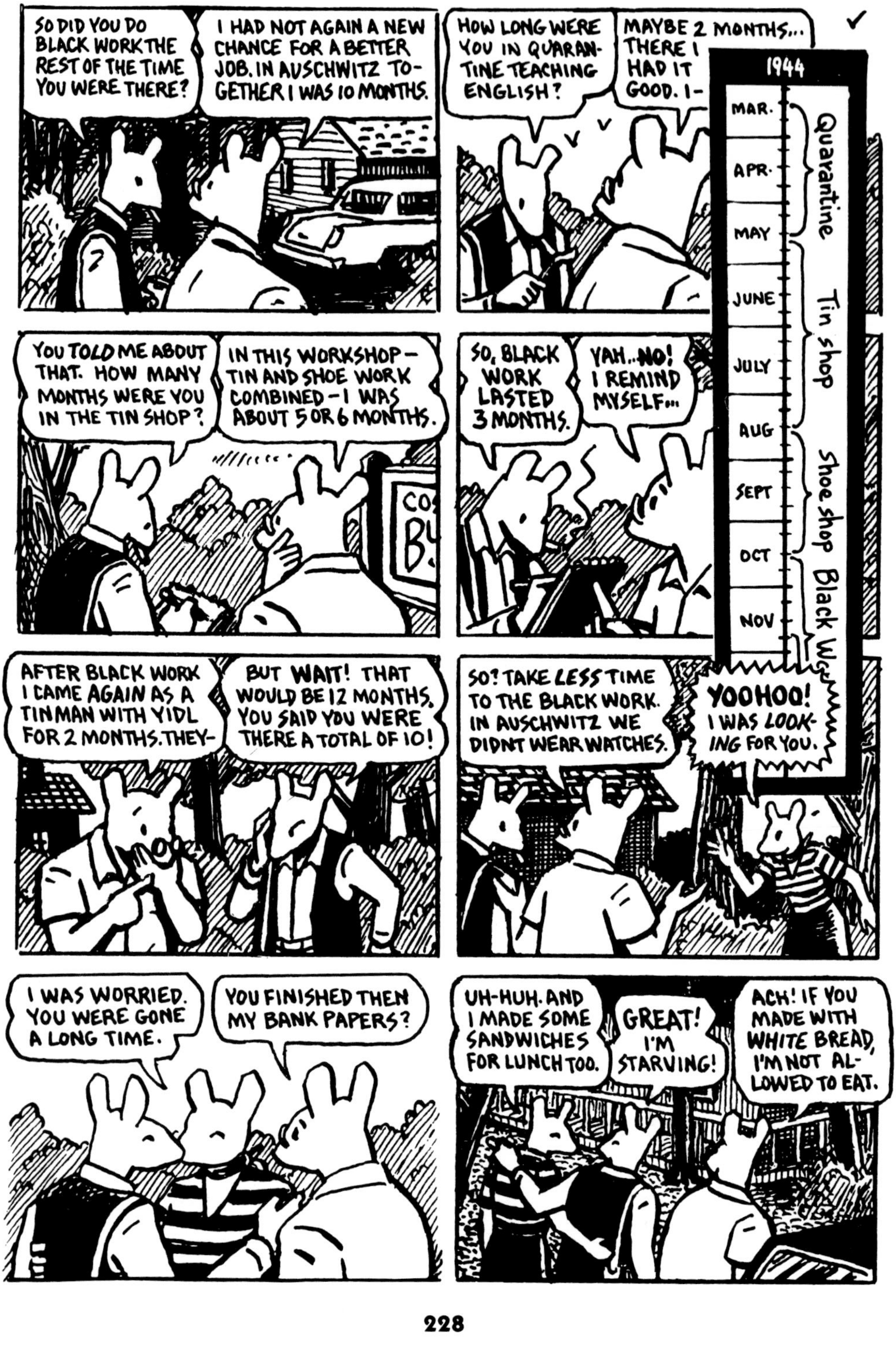
SO DID YOU DO BLACK WORK THE REST OF THE TIME YOU WERE THERE?
I HAD NOT AGAIN A NEW CHANCE FOR A BETTER JOB. IN AUSCHWITZ TOGETHER I WAS 10 MONTHS.
HOW LONG WERE YOU IN QUARANTINE TEACHING ENGLISH?
MAYBE 2 MONTHS... THERE I HAD IT GOOD. I-
1944
MAR.
APR.
MAY
JUNE
JULY
AUG
SEPT
OCT
NOV
Quarantine
Tin shop
Shoe shop
Black Wo
YOU TOLD ME ABOUT THAT. HOW MANY MONTHS WERE YOU IN THE TIN SHOP?
IN THIS WORKSHOP – TIN AND SHOE WORK COMBINED – I WAS ABOUT 5 OR 6 MONTHS.
SO, BLACK WORK LASTED 3 MONTHS.
YAH...NO! I REMIND MYSELF...
AFTER BLACK WORK I CAME AGAIN AS A TINMAN WITH YIDL FOR 2 MONTHS. THEY-
BUT WAIT! THAT WOULD BE 12 MONTHS. YOU SAID YOU WERE THERE A TOTAL OF 10!
SO? TAKE LESS TIME TO THE BLACK WORK. IN AUSCHWITZ WE DIDNT WEAR WATCHES.
YOOHOO! I WAS LOOKING FOR YOU.
I WAS WORRIED. YOU WERE GONE A LONG TIME.
YOU FINISHED THEN MY BANK PAPERS?
UH-HUH. AND I MADE SOME SANDWICHES FOR LUNCH TOO.
GREAT! I'M STARVING!
ACH! IF YOU MADE WITH WHITE BREAD, I'M NOT ALLOWED TO EAT.

SUCH A GOOD GIRL—WITH MY *SPECIAL* BREAD SHE KNEW TO MAKE.... MALA WOULDN'T HAVE DONE SUCH A GOOD SANDWICH.

IT WAS THE ONLY BREAD IN THE HOUSE.

WANT SOME TEA OR COFFEE?

I CAN MAKE. I HAVE A TEA BAG NEAR TO THE SINK DRYING FROM BREAKFAST.

HOW DID YOU BE-COME A TINMAN AGAIN?

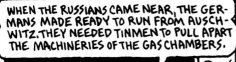

MALA COULD GO FOR A WHOLE EVENING OUT WITH HER FRIENDS AND LEAVE FOR ME NOTHING COOKED TO EAT OR DRINK.

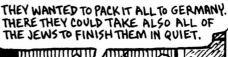

SIGH. YOU SEE HOW IT IS? I HAVE NOW ONE MORE TIME AN UNNECESSARY SUFFERING IN MY LIFE.

SO HOW DID YOU GET BACK INTO THE TIN SHOP?

WHEN THE RUSSIANS CAME NEAR, THE GER-MANS MADE READY TO RUN FROM AUSCH-WITZ. THEY NEEDED TINMEN TO PULL APART THE MACHINERIES OF THE GAS CHAMBERS.

THEY WANTED TO PACK IT ALL TO GERMANY. THERE THEY COULD TAKE ALSO ALL OF THE JEWS TO FINISH THEM IN QUIET.

THE GERMANS DIDN'T WANT TO LEAVE ANYWHERE A *SIGN* OF ALL WHAT THEY DID.

YOU *HEARD* ABOUT THE GAS, BUT I'M TELLING NOT *RUMORS,* BUT ONLY WHAT REALLY I SAW.

FOR THIS I WAS AN *EYEWITNESS.*

I CAME TO ONE OF THE FOUR CREMO BUILDINGS. IT LOOKED SO LIKE A BIG BAKERY...

EXE-CUTION ROOM

UNDRESS-ING ROOM

RM. FOR MELTING GOLD FILLINGS

CORPSE LIFT

GAS CHAMBER

INCINERATION RM. & OVENS

CHIMNEY

TOILET

COAL STORAGE

CREMATORIUM II.

FROM BELOW GROUND, IN THE GAS ROOM, WE TINMEN HAD TO TAKE OUT THE PIPES AND FANS FOR VENTILATING.

THIS WAS A FACTORY TO MAKE —ONE, TWO, THREE— ASHES AND SMOKE FROM ALL WHAT CAME HERE.

underground undressing room

underground gas chamber

ovens

SPECIAL PRISONERS WORKED HERE SEPARATE. THEY GOT BETTER BREAD, BUT EACH FEW MONTHS THEY ALSO WERE SENT UP THE CHIMNEY. ONE FROM THEM SHOWED ME EVERYTHING HOW IT WAS.

DISINFEKTION
DEZYNFEKCIE
DISINFECTION

PEOPLE BELIEVED *REALLY* IT WAS HERE A PLACE FOR SHOWERS. SO THEY WERE TOLD.

THEY CAME TO A BIG ROOM TO UNDRESS THEIR CLOTHES WHAT LOOKS SO, YES-HERE IS A PLACE SO LIKE THEY SAY.

Sauber ...ein Ges ...eit

IMPORTANT REMEMBER YOUR HOOK NUMBER

PLEASE TIE YOUR SHOES TO-GETH-ER

IF I SAW A COUPLE MONTHS BEFORE HOW IT WAS ALL ARRANGED HERE, ONLY *ONE* TIME I COULD SEE IT!'

AND EVERYBODY CROWDED INSIDE INTO THE SHOWER ROOM, THE DOOR CLOSED HERMETIC, AND THE LIGHTS TURNED DARK.

Zyklon B, a pesticide, dropped into hollow columns.

IT WAS BETWEEN 3 AND 30 MINUTES—IT DEPENDED HOW MUCH GAS THEY PUT—BUT SOON WAS NOBODY ANYMORE ALIVE.

THE BIGGEST PILE OF BODIES LAY RIGHT NEXT TO THE DOOR WHERE THEY TRIED TO GET OUT.

THIS GUY WHO WORKED THERE, HE TOLD ME....

WE PULLED THE BODIES APART WITH HOOKS. BIG PILES, WITH THE STRONGEST ON TOP, OLDER ONES AND BABIES CRUSHED BELOW... OFTEN THE SKULLS WERE SMASHED ...

THEIR FINGERS WERE BROKEN FROM TRYING TO CLIMB UP THE WALLS,... AND SOMETIMES THEIR ARMS WERE AS LONG AS THEIR BODIES, PULLED FROM THE SOCKETS.

ENOUGH!

I DIDN'T WANT MORE TO HEAR, BUT ANYWAY HE TOLD ME.

THEY PULLED THE BODIES WITH AN ELEVATOR UP TO THE OVENS—MANY OVENS—AND TO EACH ONE THEY BURNED 2 OR 3 AT A TIME.

TO SUCH A PLACE FINISHED MY FATHER, MY SISTERS, MY BROTHERS, SO MANY

WHAT ARE THEY DOING OVER THERE—DIGGING TRENCHES IN CASE THE RUSSIANS ATTACK?

TRENCHES..HAH! THOSE ARE GIANT **GRAVES** THEY'RE FILLING IN!...

IT STARTED IN MAY AND WENT ON ALL SUMMER. THEY BROUGHT JEWS FROM HUNGARY—TOO MANY FOR THEIR OVENS, SO THEY DUG THOSE BIG CREMATION PITS.

THE HOLES WERE BIG, SO LIKE THE SWIMMING POOL OF THE PINES HOTEL HERE.

AND TRAIN AFTER TRAIN OF HUNGARIANS CAME.

AND THOSE WHAT FINISHED IN THE GAS CHAMBERS BEFORE THEY GOT PUSHED IN THESE GRAVES, IT WAS THE **LUCKY** ONES.

THE OTHERS HAD TO JUMP IN THE GRAVES WHILE STILL THEY WERE ALIVE...

PRISONERS WHAT WORKED THERE POURED GASOLINE OVER THE LIVE ONES AND THE DEAD ONES.

AND THE FAT FROM THE BURNING BODIES THEY SCOOPED AND POURED AGAIN SO EVERYONE COULD BURN BETTER.

JESUS.

ACH! IT'S 2:30. LOOK HOW THE TIME IS FLYING. AND IT'S STILL SO MUCH TO DO TODAY...

IT'S DISHES TO CLEAN, DINNER TO DEFROST, AND MY *PILLS* I HAVEN'T YET COUNTED.

I DON'T GET IT... WHY DIDN'T THE JEWS AT LEAST *TRY* TO RESIST?

IT WASN'T SO EASY LIKE YOU THINK. EVERYONE WAS SO STARVING AND FRIGHTENED, AND TIRED THEY COULDN'T *BELIEVE* EVEN WHAT'S IN FRONT OF THEIR EYES.

..AND THE JEWS LIVED ALWAYS WITH HOPE. THEY HOPED THE RUSSIANS CAN COME BEFORE THE GERMAN BULLET ARRIVED FROM THE GUN INTO THEIR HEAD AND—

OOPS!

CRASH!

OI! YOU SEE HOW MY HEAD IS? IT'S MY FAVORITE DISH NOW BROKEN!

IT'S ONLY A *DISH!*... BUT WHY DIDN'T THEY TRY TO TAKE JUST ONE NAZI WITH THEM?

IN SOME SPOTS PEOPLE *DID* FIGHT... BUT YOU CAN KILL MAYBE ONE GERMAN BEFORE THEY KILL FAST A HUNDRED FROM YOU. THEN IT'S *EVERYONE* DEAD.

...AND THIS WAY IT WAS *ALSO* EVERYONE DEAD. NU?

DON'T THROW AWAY! I CAN GLUE STILL TOGETHER THAT PLATE.

I GUESS I'LL DO THE DISHES NOW.

NO. YOU CAN DEFROST OUT THE TURKEY LEGS... YOU ONLY WOULD BREAK ME THE *REST* OF MY PLATES.

That night...

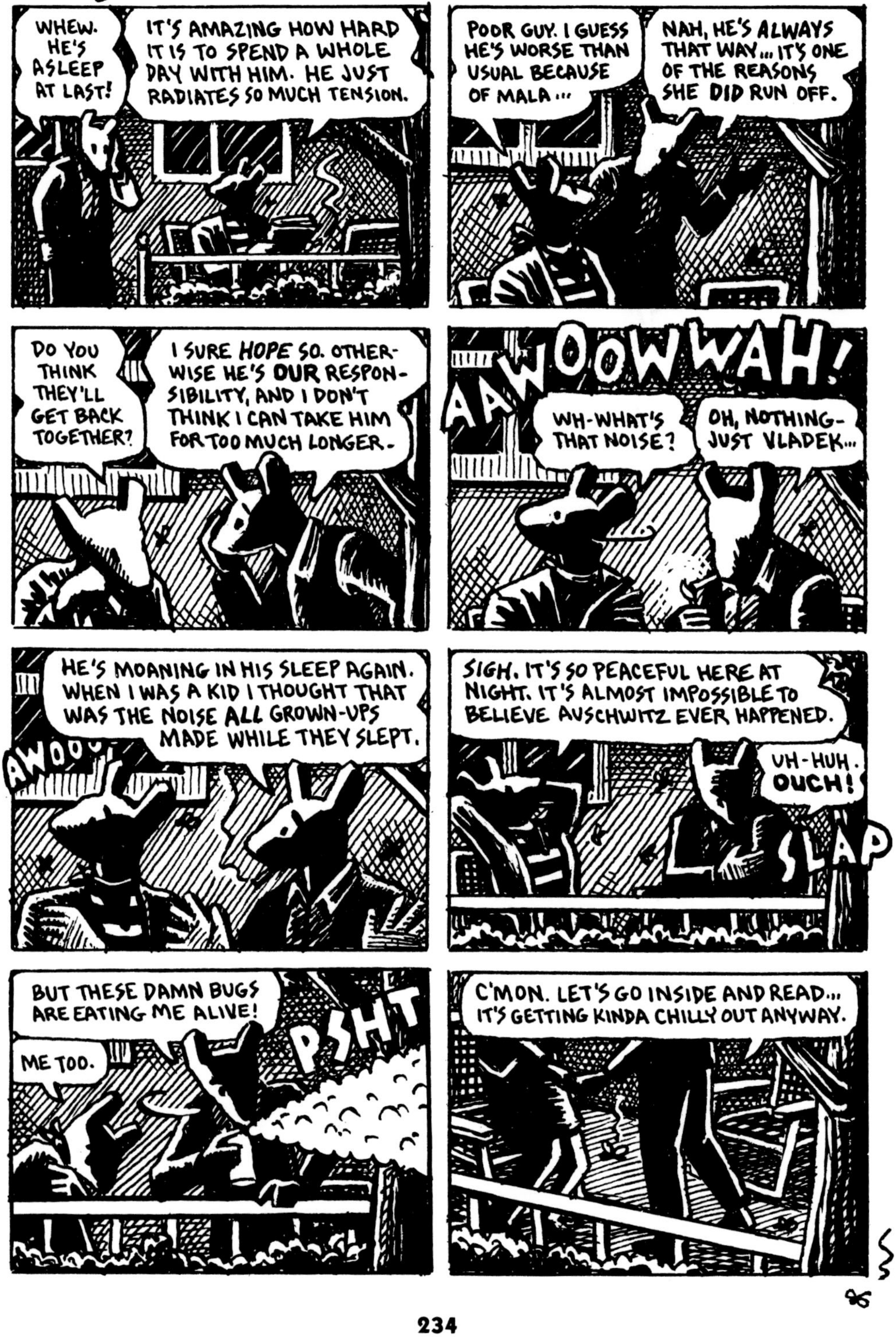
WHEW. HE'S ASLEEP AT LAST!
IT'S AMAZING HOW HARD IT IS TO SPEND A WHOLE DAY WITH HIM. HE JUST RADIATES SO MUCH TENSION.
POOR GUY. I GUESS HE'S WORSE THAN USUAL BECAUSE OF MALA...
NAH, HE'S ALWAYS THAT WAY... IT'S ONE OF THE REASONS SHE DID RUN OFF.
DO YOU THINK THEY'LL GET BACK TOGETHER?
I SURE HOPE SO. OTHERWISE HE'S OUR RESPONSIBILITY, AND I DON'T THINK I CAN TAKE HIM FOR TOO MUCH LONGER.
AAWOOOWWAH!
WH-WHAT'S THAT NOISE?
OH, NOTHING-JUST VLADEK...
HE'S MOANING IN HIS SLEEP AGAIN. WHEN I WAS A KID I THOUGHT THAT WAS THE NOISE ALL GROWN-UPS MADE WHILE THEY SLEPT.
AWOOO
SIGH. IT'S SO PEACEFUL HERE AT NIGHT. IT'S ALMOST IMPOSSIBLE TO BELIEVE AUSCHWITZ EVER HAPPENED.
UH-HUH. OUCH!
SLAP
BUT THESE DAMN BUGS ARE EATING ME ALIVE!
ME TOO.
PSHT
C'MON. LET'S GO INSIDE AND READ... IT'S GETTING KINDA CHILLY OUT ANYWAY.

CHAPTER THREE

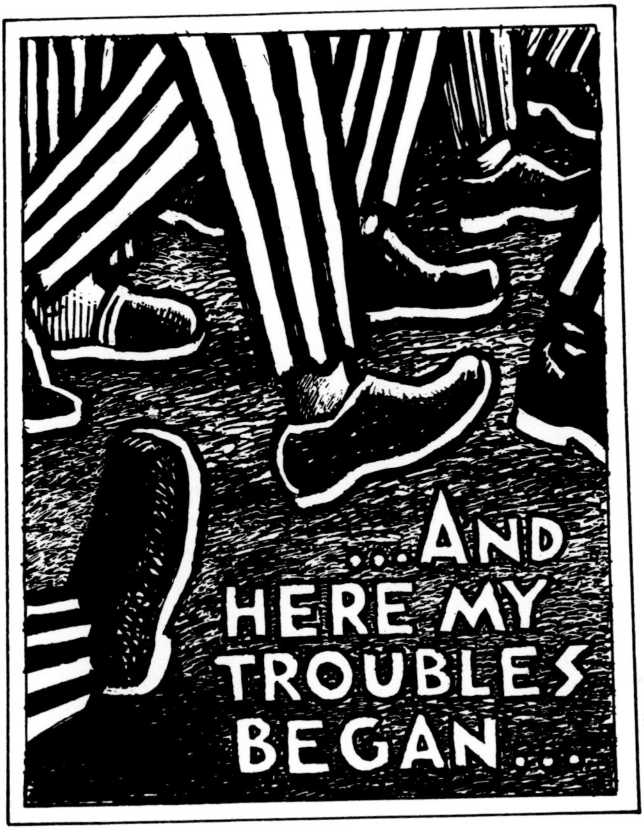
...AND
HERE MY
TROUBLES
BEGAN...

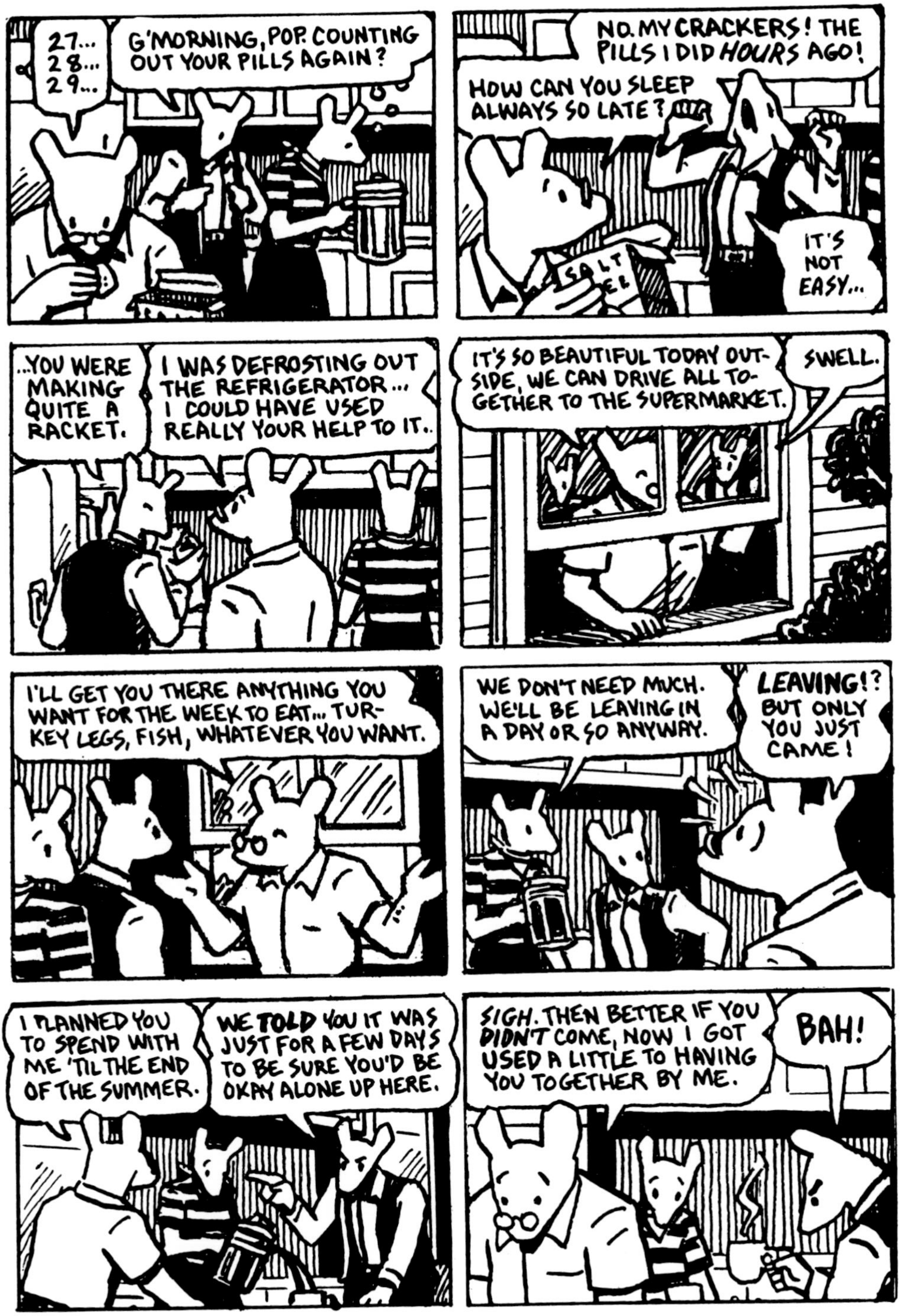
27... 28... 29...
G'MORNING, POP. COUNTING OUT YOUR PILLS AGAIN?
NO. MY CRACKERS! THE PILLS I DID HOURS AGO!
HOW CAN YOU SLEEP ALWAYS SO LATE?
IT'S NOT EASY...
...YOU WERE MAKING QUITE A RACKET.
I WAS DEFROSTING OUT THE REFRIGERATOR... I COULD HAVE USED REALLY YOUR HELP TO IT..
IT'S SO BEAUTIFUL TODAY OUTSIDE, WE CAN DRIVE ALL TOGETHER TO THE SUPERMARKET.
SWELL.
I'LL GET YOU THERE ANYTHING YOU WANT FOR THE WEEK TO EAT... TURKEY LEGS, FISH, WHATEVER YOU WANT.
WE DON'T NEED MUCH. WE'LL BE LEAVING IN A DAY OR SO ANYWAY.
LEAVING!? BUT ONLY YOU JUST CAME!
I PLANNED YOU TO SPEND WITH ME 'TIL THE END OF THE SUMMER.
WE TOLD YOU IT WAS JUST FOR A FEW DAYS TO BE SURE YOU'D BE OKAY ALONE UP HERE.
SIGH. THEN BETTER IF YOU DIDN'T COME, NOW I GOT USED A LITTLE TO HAVING YOU TOGETHER BY ME.
BAH!

I'LL PACK THE FOODS WHAT MALA LEFT TO RETURN IT OVER TO THE *SHOP-RITE*. HELP YOURSELF FOR A LITTLE CEREAL...

NO THANKS. I'LL STICK TO COFFEE.

PLEASE. JUST TASTE AND YOU'LL SEE HOW GOOD IT IS.

NO THANKS. I DON'T LIKE SPECIAL K.

BUT IT HAS *SALT* AND ALSO *SUGAR*. FOR ME IT'S *POISON*—I'LL GIVE FOR YOU A LITTLE, YES FRANÇOISE?

NO THANKS.

IT'S A SHAME TO WASTE. I'LL PACK AND YOU CAN TAKE IT HOME WITH YOU.

THE BOX IS ALMOST EMPTY. JUST *LEAVE* IT HERE.

OKAY, IF NOT, IS NOT. ONLY JUST TRY THEN A PIECE FROM THIS FRUIT CAKE.

I'M NOT HUNGRY!

SO, FINE. I CAN PACK THE FRUITCAKE IN WITH THE CEREAL FOR YOU TO TAKE HOME.

LOOK. WE DON'T WANT ANY, OK? JUST FORGET IT!

I CANNOT FORGET IT... EVER SINCE HITLER I DON'T LIKE TO THROW OUT EVEN A CRUMB.

THEN JUST *SAVE* THE DAMN SPECIAL K IN CASE HITLER EVER COMES BACK!

I CAN GLUE TOGETHER THE BOX, BUT *STILL* I DON'T THINK THE SHOP-RITE WILL EXCHANGE IT!

And so...

LOOK, I'M SORRY I SNAPPED AT YOU BEFORE...

YES, THE WALLS ARE SO THIN, THE NEIGHBORS CAN HEAR EVERYTHING

I MEAN, FRANÇOISE AND I ARE BOTH WORRIED ABOUT YOU NOW THAT MALA IS GONE, BUT YOU CAN'T EXPECT US TO MOVE IN WITH YOU PERMANENTLY...

WHAT PERMANENTLY? I WANT ONLY YOU'LL ENJOY HERE THE SUMMER WITH ME... IT'S PAID ALREADY IN FULL, WITH NO REFUND.

HOW WILL YOU MANAGE, LIVING IN REGO PARK ALL ALONE?

ALONE I CAN MANAGE MORE EASY THAN WITH MALA, BELIEVE ME.

COME, WE'LL SIT ALL THREE TOGETHER IN THE FRONT.

Y'KNOW... LAST NIGHT I WAS READING ABOUT AUSCHWITZ...

SOME PRISONERS WORKING IN THE GAS CHAMBERS REVOLTED. THEY KILLED 3 S.S. MEN AND BLEW UP A CREMATORIUM.

YAH. FOR THIS THEY ALL GOT KILLED.

AND THE FOUR YOUNG GIRLS WHAT SNEAKED OVER THE AMMUNITIONS FOR THIS, THEY HANGED THEM NEAR TO MY WORKSHOP.

THEY WERE GOOD FRIENDS OF ANJA, FROM SOSNOWIEC. THEY HANGED A LONG, LONG TIME. SIGH.

A COUPLE WEEKS MORE AND THEY *WOULDN'T* HANG.... IT WAS VERY NEAR TO THE END, THERE IN AUSCHWITZ.

YOU HEAR THAT, VLADEK? THE FRONT IS NO MORE THAN 25 MILES AWAY...

IF WE CAN JUST STAY ALIVE A LITTLE BIT LONGER, THE RUSSIANS WILL BE HERE.

THIS BOY WORKED IN THE OFFICE AND KNEW RUMORS.

THE GERMANS ARE GETTING WORRIED. THE BIG SHOTS HERE ARE ALREADY RUNNING BACK INTO THE REICH.

THEY'RE PLANNING TO TAKE EVERYBODY HERE BACK TO CAMPS INSIDE GERMANY. EVERYBODY!

BUT A FEW OF US HAVE A PLAN.... WE'RE NOT GOING!

!

YOU HAVE A FRIEND IN THE CAMP LAUNDRY. HELP US GET CIVILIAN CLOTHES AND JOIN US.

HE TOOK ME QUICK TO AN ATTIC IN ONE OF THE BLOCKS.

THIS ROOM ISN'T BEING USED ANYMORE. WHEN THE EVACUATION STARTS, THE SEVEN OF US WILL COME UP HERE TO HIDE.

WE ARRANGED THERE CLOTHING AND EVEN IDENTITY PAPERS, AND HALF EACH DAY'S BREAD WE PUT OVER HERE.

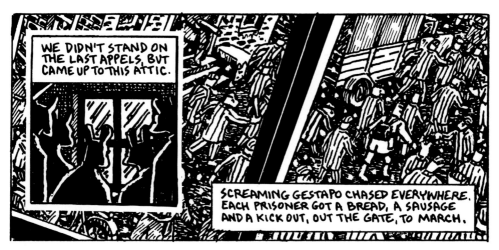

WE DIDN'T STAND ON THE LAST APPELS, BUT CAME UP TO THIS ATTIC.

SCREAMING GESTAPO CHASED EVERYWHERE. EACH PRISONER GOT A BREAD, A SAUSAGE AND A KICK OUT, OUT THE GATE, TO MARCH.

THEN THIS GUY FROM THE OFFICE RAN IN...

TERRIBLE NEWS! WE HAVE TO LEAVE!

THEY'RE GOING TO SET FIRE TO THE CAMP AND BOMB ALL THE BLOCKS! HURRY!

FINALLY THEY *DIDN'T* BOMB, BUT THIS WE COULDN'T KNOW. WE LEFT BEHIND EVERY-THING, WE WERE SO AFRAID, EVEN THE CIVILIAN CLOTHES WE ORGANIZED. AND RAN OUT!

IT WAS ALREADY NIGHT. THEY GAVE TO EACH OF US A BLANKET AND A LITTLE BIT FOOD TO CARRY, AND WE WENT OUT FROM AUSCHWITZ, MAYBE THE LAST ONE.

ALL NIGHT I HEARD SHOOTING HE WHO GOT TIRED, WHO CAN'T WALK SO FAST, THEY SHOT.

THE MORE WE WALKED, THE MORE I HEARD SHOOTING...

AND IN THE DAYLIGHT, FAR AHEAD, I SAW IT.

SOMEBODY IS JUMPING, TURNING, ROLLING 25 OR 35 TIMES AROUND. AND STOPS.

"OH," I SAID. "THEY MAYBE KILLED THERE A DOG."

WHEN I WAS A BOY OUR NEIGHBOR HAD A DOG WHAT GOT MAD AND WAS BITING.

THE NEIGHBOR CAME OUT WITH A RIFLE AND SHOT.

THE DOG WAS ROLLING SO, AROUND AND AROUND, KICKING, BEFORE HE LAY QUIET.

AND NOW I THOUGHT: "HOW AMAZING IT IS THAT A HUMAN BEING REACTS THE SAME LIKE THIS NEIGHBOR'S DOG."

ONE OF THE BOYS WHAT WE WERE IN THE ATTIC TOGETHER, TALKED OVER TO THE GUARD...

PSST— LOOK. THE WAR IS ALMOST OVER. SOME OF US WANT TO ESCAPE INTO THE WOODS. WE CAN PAY...

?

SHARE THIS GOLD WITH THE GUARDS IN FRONT AND BEHIND. JUST DON'T SHOOT WHEN WE RUN...

WE'LL GIVE YOU THE SIGNAL LATE TO-NIGHT, AND SHOOT OVER YOUR HEADS.

ALL DAY LONG THEY WERE ARRANGING...

IT'S ALL SET, VLADEK. HELP PAY OFF THE GUARDS AND JOIN US.

ACH. HOW CAN YOU TRUST THE GERMANS?!

AT NIGHT WAS A COMMOTION. 8 OR 9 RAN OFF...

BANG

AND OF COURSE YOU COULDN'T TRUST...

SO THE MARCH WAS GOING AND GOING. FOREVER WE MARCHED. AND THE ONES WHAT DIDN'T FALL DOWN, WE MARCHED.

AND SO WE CAME OVER TO GROSS-ROSEN. HERE WAS A SMALL CAMP, WITH NO GAS.

POLAND
1 INCH=90 MILES

Breslau
GROSS-ROSEN
GERMANY
SUDETEN-LAND
CZECHOSLOVAKIA
Czestochowa
Krakow
AUSCHWITZ

IT WAS THOUSANDS OF PRISONERS FROM ALL AROUND BEING PULLED BACK INTO GERMANY.

EVERYWHERE WAS CONFUSION AND HITTING. TERRIBLE!

YOU SHITS OVER THERE! GO HAUL THE SOUP FROM THE KITCHEN—TWO TO EACH PAIL.

THEY CAUGHT 20 OF US TO CARRY.

YOU SEE WHAT'S GOING ON HERE. STAY WITH ME!

I GRABBED FAST A GUY WHAT WAS STILL STRONG LIKE ME.

MOST COULDN'T EVEN LIFT THEY WERE WEAK FROM MARCHING AND NO FOOD.

QUICK! QUICK!

BEHIND I HEARD YELLING AND SHOUTING. I DIDN'T LOOK.

LAZY BASTARDS! LOOK AT HOW THOSE TWO RUN!

WE GOT AN EXTRA PORTION SOUP FOR THIS. MOST WERE NOT LUCKY TO BE STILL STRONG.

IN THE MORNING THEY CHASED US TO MARCH AGAIN OUT, WHO KNOWS WHERE...

THROUGH THE TOWN WE WERE GOING. IT WAS EMPTY, WITH NO PRIVATE PEOPLE. AND WE SAW, FROM FAR, A TRAIN.

IT WAS SUCH A TRAIN FOR HORSES, FOR COWS.

INSIDE! MOVE! MOVE!

THEY PUSHED UNTIL IT WAS NO ROOM LEFT.

WE LAY ONE ON TOP THE OTHER, LIKE MATCHES, LIKE HERRINGS.

I PUSHED TO A CORNER NOT TO GET CRUSHED...

HIGH UP I SAW A FEW HOOKS TO CHAIN UP MAYBE THE ANIMALS.

I HAD STILL THE THIN BLANKET THEY GAVE ME.

I CLIMBED TO SOME-BODY'S SHOULDER AND HOOKED IT STRONG.

IN THIS WAY I CAN REST AND BREATHE A LITTLE.

THIS SAVED ME. MAY-BE 25 PEOPLE CAME OUT FROM THIS CAR OF 200.

SO, THE TRAIN WAS GOING, WE DIDN'T KNOW WHERE. FOR DAYS AND NIGHTS, NOTHING

AND THEN IT **STOPPED.**

NO FOOD AND NO WATER, ONLY SCREAMS INSIDE.

YOU SEE, PEOPLE BEGAN TO DIE, TO FAINT...

AI! MY LEGS! I'M BEING STABBED!

AII!

IT WASN'T **ROOM** TO FALL ...AND IF HE FELL, THEY STOOD ON HIM.

SO HE JABBED TO THEIR LEGS WITH A KNIFE, BUT USUALLY HE ANYWAY DIED.

IF SOMEONE HAD TO MAKE A VRINE OR A BOWEL MOVEMENT, HE DID WHERE HE STOOD.

IF HE HAD STILL FOOD, HE ATE IT.

I ATE MOSTLY SNOW FROM UP ON THE ROOF.

SOME HAD SUGAR SOMEHOW, BUT IT BURNED.

MY THROAT! I NEED WATER! WATER! GIVE ME SOME SNOW!

I CAN ONLY REACH A LITTLE FOR MYSELF!

PLEASE! PLEASE!! I BEG YOU!

OKAY. GIVE ME SOME SUGAR, I'LL GET YOU SOME SNOW...,

SO I ATE ALSO SUGAR AND SAVED THEIR LIFE.

THE TRAIN STAYED SO, WITHOUT MOVING, I DON'T KNOW HOW LONG, UP TO A WEEK...

THEN, ONE DAY THEY OPENED...

THROW OUT THE DEAD, AND CLEAN UP YOUR FILTH!

IF THE DEAD HAD BREAD LEFT, OR BETTER SHOES, WE KEPT...

OUTSIDE WERE MANY TRAINS STANDING FOR WEEKS, WHAT THEY *NEVER* OPENED, AND IT WAS EVERYONE DEAD INSIDE...

...THEY DIDN'T NEED ANYMORE.

THEY CLOSED US AGAIN. WE WERE VERY HAPPY WE HAD NOW ROOM WHERE TO STAND.

NEAR TO THE DOOR WE PILED NEW DEAD ONES. EACH DAY THE GERMANS OPENED: "HOW MANY DEAD?" AND WE THREW OUT, AND SOON WE HAD ROOM EVEN TO SIT.

247

THEN THE TRAIN STARTED AGAIN GOING AND GOING...
INSIDE WE WERE MORE DYING AND SOME GOT CRAZY.

WE'VE GOTTA GET OUT!
LET US OUT! OUT! OUT!

THEN AGAIN IT STOPPED.

THEY OPENED THAT WE WILL
THROW OUT THE DEAD...

ALL OF
YOU-GET
DOWN!

WE COULD NOT
BELIEVE WHAT
WE ARE SEEING!

THERE IS THE
RED CROSS!...

YES! AND THE GIRLS ARE GIVING TO EVERYBODY A
SNACK-A LITTLE COFFEE AND A PIECE OF BREAD...

WE DIDN'T REMEMBER EVEN HOW
BREAD LOOKS. WE WERE VERY HAPPY.

THEN THEY CHASED US BACK IN THE TRAIN AGAIN
TO DIE, AND SO THE TRAVEL CONTINUED MORE...

IN THE MIDDLE WE FOUND OUT
THAT WE ARE COMING TO DACHAU.

FROM ALL THE CAMPS
OF EUROPE THEY NOW
BROUGHT BACK ALL OF
US INSIDE GERMANY.

248

THIS WAS EARLY FEBRUARY, IN 1945. IT WAS NO FOOD AND SO CROWDED—

LOOK WHERE YOU GO!

ACH! THE SHOP-RITE IS *THERE*, AND YOU DIDN'T TURN TO IT!

WHOOSH

SO, COME. WE'LL GO NOW IN TO GIVE BACK OUR GROCERIES.

NO WAY! I'M NOT GOING IN TO RETURN A LOAD OF OPEN BOXES AND PARTIALLY EATEN FOOD.

WHAT'S TO BE SO ASHAMED? IT'S FOODS I CAN'T EAT. YOU WAIT THEN IN THE CAR WHILE *I* ARRANGE IT.

Y'KNOW... I'LL BET YOU THAT ANJA'S NOTEBOOKS WERE WRITTEN ON BOTH SIDES OF THE PAGE...

HUH? I CAN'T REMEMBER. WHY D'YOU SAY THAT?

WELL...IF THERE WERE ANY *BLANK* PAGES VLADEK WOULD NEVER HAVE BURNED THEM.

UH HUH... HEY! YOU CAN SEE HIM IN THE WINDOW!

JEEZ. VLADEK AND THE MANAGER ARE SHOUTING AT EACH OTHER...

NOW THE MANAGER IS JUST WALKING AWAY FROM HIM...

AND NOW VLADEK IS TRAILING AFTER HIM...

HOW EMBARRASSING.

249

SIGH. I'D RATHER KILL MYSELF THAN LIVE THROUGH ALL THAT...

WHAT? RETURNING GROCERIES?

NO. EVERYTHING VLADEK WENT THROUGH. IT'S A MIRACLE HE SURVIVED.

UH-HUH. BUT IN SOME WAYS HE DIDN'T SURVIVE.

MAYBE WE SHOULD STAY WITH HIM A FEW DAYS LONGER. HE NEEDS HELP.

ARE YOU KIDDING?

...I DON'T THINK WE'D SURVIVE.

YOO-HOO!

YOU SEE? I EXCHANGED AND GOT SIX DOLLARS WORTH OF NEW GROCERIES FOR ONLY ONE DOLLAR!

INCRED-IBLE!...

...WE WERE SURE YOU'D GET KICKED OUT OF THE STORE!

WHAT ARE YOU TALKING? THE MANAGER IS A VERY FINE GENTLEMAN...

HE HELPED ME AS SOON I EXPLAINED TO HIM MY HEALTH, HOW MALA LEFT ME, AND HOW IT WAS IN THE CAMPS.

OY! GET IN... WE CAN'T EVER SHOW OUR FACES HERE AGAIN.

NOW WE'LL DRIVE BACK SO I CAN PHONE TO MY LAWYER ON MALA.

DACHAU... YOU WERE SAYING IT WAS VERY CROWDED IN THAT CAMP...

YAH-THIS WAS A CAMP-*TERRIBLE!* I HAD A MISERY, I CAN'T TELL YOU... HERE, IN DACHAU, MY TROUBLES BEGAN.

WE WERE CLOSED IN BARRACKS, SITTING ON STRAW, WAITING ONLY TO DIE.

IN THE STRAW, IT WAS LICE...

FROM THE LICE WAS TYPHUS.

TO EAT WE GOT ONLY BREAD AND SOUP, BUT YOU HAD TO SHOW FIRST YOUR SHIRT....

IF IT WAS ANY LICE, YOU GOT NO SOUP. THIS WAS IMPOSSIBLE. EVERYWHERE WAS LICE!

AND, GOD FORBID, IF SOMEONE GOT SOUP AND SOMEONE *SPILLED* HIM A DROP....

LIKE WILD ANIMALS THEY WOULD FIGHT UNTIL THERE WAS BLOOD.

YOU CAN'T KNOW WHAT IT IS, TO BE HUNGRY.

THERE, IN DACHAU, I GOT AN INFECTION IN MY HAND...

I TRIED TO MAKE WORSE AND WORSE MY INFECTION...

I WANTED THEY TAKE ME TO THE INFIRMARY.

EACH FEW DAYS SOMEONE CAME TO SEE WHO IS SICK...

GO WITH THEM...

YOU SEE, THE INFIRMARY, I HEARD IT WAS A PARADISE.

PUT THIS OINTMENT ON HIS HAND AND KEEP IT BANDAGED. IT WILL CLEAR UP QUICKLY.

HERE I HAD THREE TIMES A DAY SOMETHING TO EAT, AND IT WAS ONLY TWO PATIENTS FOR EACH BED.

I WORKED HOW I COULD WITH ONE HAND, SO THEY WILL LIKE ME.

THAT'S STRANGE, IT SHOULD HAVE HEALED BY NOW!

I IRRITATED EACH DAY MY HAND, TO STAY LONGER.

AII!

THERE! I OPENED IT UP AGAIN!

THIS HURT ME REALLY VERY VERY MUCH...

I GOT AFRAID FOR MY HAND AND LET IT HEAL.

...I HAVE STILL TODAY A SCAR ON THIS PLACE.

252

FROM THE INFIRMARY I HAD TO GO BACK TO A BAD BARRACK, WHERE WE WERE ALL DAY STANDING OUTSIDE.

PARLEZ-VOUS FRANÇAIS?

WHA? NO...

IT WAS NOTHING TO EAT, AND NOTHING TO DO, ONLY TO WAIT AND TO DIE.

I CAN SPEAK GERMAN, YIDDISH, POLISH AND ENGLISH.

ANGLAIS?!

DIEU MERCI! I TALK ENGLISH ALSO A LITTLE. I WAS BECOMING CRAZY!...

THERE IS NO OTHER FRENCH HERE AND I DO NOT KNOW TO TALK GERMAN. I HAD NOBODY TO WHO TO TALK.

YOU ARE A POLE-JEW, YES? HOW YOU KNOW ENGLISH?

ACCH... I DREAMED ALWAYS TO GO ONE DAY TO AMERICA.

SO, WE TALKED, AND IT MADE THE TIME LIGHTER.

EACH DAY HE FOUND ME, THE FRENCH MAN...

BRR. GOOD MORNING. IT IS AGAIN VERY COLD TODAY.

LOOK TO THIS, MY FRIEND. I HAVE A BOX!

HE WAS NOT A JEW, SO BY THE RED CROSS THEY LET PACKAGES COME TO HIM.

MY FAMILY SENDS. I WANT THAT YOU ALSO EAT SOMETHING.

MY GOD. SARDINES! BISCUITS! CHOCOLATE!

HE INSISTED TO SHARE WITH ME, AND IT SAVED ME MY LIFE.

WITH MY NEW FOOD I CAME TO AN IDEA...

PSST- DO YOU WANT TO BUY A BAR OF CHOCOLATE?

CHOCOLATE?! DO I LOOK LIKE A MILLIONAIRE?

I'LL TRADE IT FOR YOUR SHIRT.

MY SHIRT?! YOU'RE CRAZY- I'D FREEZE!

UM- GIVE ME YOUR DAY'S RATION OF BREAD TOO.

IN AUSCHWITZ A SHIRT WAS NOT SO EXPENSIVE, BUT HERE NO GOODS CAME IN.

I CLEANED THE SHIRT VERY, VERY CAREFUL.

AND OUTSIDE, I DRIED IT.

I WAS LUCKY TO FIND A PIECE OF PAPER...

SO, CAREFUL I WRAPPED IT.

I UNWRAPPED ONLY WHEN THEY CALLED TO SOUP...

HERE WAS A SHIRT WITH REALLY NO LICE!

MY OLD SHIRT I HID TO MY PANTS. I SHOWED THE NEW ONE.

OKAY.

RIGHT AWAY THEY GAVE ME TO EAT.

YOU ARE A GENIUS, VLADEK. A GENIUS!

I HELPED THE FRENCHMAN TO ALSO ORGANIZE A SHIRT, SO WE BOTH GOT ALWAYS SOUP.

BUT AFTER A FEW WEEKS I GOT TOO SICK EVEN TO EAT...

TYPHUS!

I GOT VERY HOT FEVER AND I COULDN'T SLEEP. *TYPHUS!*

EVERY NIGHT PEOPLE DIED OF THIS.

AT NIGHT I HAD TO GO TO THE TOILET DOWN. IT WAS ALWAYS FULL, THE WHOLE CORRIDOR, WITH THE DEAD PEOPLE PILED THERE. YOU COULDN'T GO THROUGH...

YOU HAD TO GO ON THEIR HEADS, AND THIS WAS TERRIBLE, BECAUSE IT WAS SO SLIPPERY, THE SKIN, YOU THOUGHT YOU ARE FALLING. AND THIS WAS EVERY NIGHT.

SO NOW I HAD TYPHUS, AND I HAD TO GO TO THE TOILET DOWN, AND I SAID, "NOW IT'S MY TIME. NOW I WILL BE LAYING LIKE THIS ONES AND SOMEBODY WILL STEP ON ME!"

I WAS ALIVE STILL THE NEXT TIME IT CAME A GUY FROM THE INFIRMARY...

MANY DIDN'T LIVE LONG ENOUGH TO GO TO DIE IN THE INFIRMARY.

THERE I LAY TOO WEAK EVEN TO MOVE OR TO GO TO THE TOILET OUT FROM BED.

I ASKED HELP FROM THE FELLOWS NEXT TO ME, BUT IN A FEW HOURS THEY WERE DEAD AND OTHERS CAME.

THEY GAVE BREAD AND SOUP, BUT I WAS TOO WEAK TO EAT...

SO I PUT MY PORTION BELOW MY PILLOW.

HEY! THERE'S STALE BREAD ALL OVER THIS ONE'S BED!

WELL, TAKE IT AWAY..., HE'LL NEVER NEED IT.

I SCREAMED. BUT I COULDN'T SCREAM.

MMUH MMNH.

I WAS TOO WEAK TO SCREAM...

SO I TOOK MY SHOE AND KNOCKED LOUD.

KLAKK KLAKK KLAKK

STOP THAT RACKET!

BAH! KEEP YOUR DAMN BREAD!

I COULDN'T EAT, BUT I CUT PIECES TO PAY FOR HELP TO GO DOWN TO THE TOILET.

SO... MY FEVER FELL DOWN, AND SOMETHING NEW CAME.

ATTENTION!...

EVERYONE STRONG ENOUGH TO TRAVEL, LINE UP OUTSIDE...

YOU WILL BE EXCHANGED AS WAR PRISONERS AT THE SWISS BORDER.

WAS I DREAMING ONLY?!

THEY LIKED TO SEND OUT THE SICK ONES, BUT NOT SO SICK THAT WE ARRIVE DEAD.

I WAS VERY WEAK, BUT, FOR MY BREAD I HAD TWO FRIENDS WHAT HELPED ME.

WHEN THEY LEFT ME GO FOR EVEN A SECOND, MY LEGS DIDN'T HOLD ME.

BUT I CAME SOMEHOW OUTSIDE THE GATE...

GASP! A TRAIN!

HERE WAS A TRAIN NOT FOR COWS AND HORSES, BUT A REAL TRAIN TO TAKE PASSENGERS - A TRAIN FOR PEOPLE!

I THOUGHT THIS TRAIN, IT MUST BE FOR THE *GESTAPO*, BUT NO!

IT TOOK US OUT FROM DACHAU, IN THE DIREC-TION TO SWITZERLAND.

WHATEVER HAPPENED TO THAT FRENCH GUY WHO HELPED YOU?

YAH. HE WAS A FINE FELLOW....

I CAN'T REMEMBER EVEN HIS NAME, BUT IN PARIS HE IS LIVING.... FOR YEARS WE EXCHANGED LETTERS IN THE ENGLISH I TAUGHT TO HIM.

WELL..DID YOU SAVE ANY OF HIS LETTERS?

OF COURSE I SAVED. BUT ALL THIS I THREW AWAY TOGETHER WITH ANJA'S NOTEBOOKS.

ALL SUCH THINGS OF THE WAR, I TRIED TO PUT OUT FROM MY MIND ONCE FOR ALL..., UNTIL YOU *REBUILD* ME ALL THIS FROM YOUR QUESTIONS.

?!

HAH?! WHAT FOR DO YOU STOP, FRANÇOISE? WE'RE NOT YET TO THE BUNGALOW?

THERE'S A HITCH-HIKER....

S K R E E E E E K!

A HITCH-HIKER? AND -OY- IT'S A COLORED GUY, A SHVARTSER!

HIYA.

PUSH QUICK ON THE GAS!

THANKS. IT'S A HOT DAY FO' WALKIN'.
MÓZ BOŻE! CO SIĘ STAŁO JEGO ŻONIE? CZY ONA ZGŁUPIAŁA?*
*(POLISH:) Oh my God! What's happened to his wife? She's lost her head!!
MAH COUSIN'S PLACE IS JUS' UP TH' ROAD.
PSIA KREW! CHOLERA! TO NIE MOŻLIWE. A SHVARTSER SIEDZI TU ZE MNĄ! *
*(POLISH:) @!★!! I just can't believe it! There's a SHVARTSER sitting in here!
Y'ALL TAKE CARE NOW, AN' BE GOOD.
WHAT HAPPENED ON YOU, FRANÇOISE? YOU WENT CRAZY, OR WHAT?!
I HAD THE WHOLE TIME TO WATCH OUT THAT THIS SHVARTSER DOESN'T STEAL US THE GROCERIES FROM THE BACK SEAT!
WHAT?!
THAT'S OUTRAGEOUS! HOW CAN YOU, OF ALL PEOPLE, BE SUCH A RACIST! YOU TALK ABOUT BLACKS THE WAY THE NAZIS TALKED ABOUT THE JEWS!
ACH!...
I THOUGHT REALLY YOU ARE MORE SMART THAN THIS, FRANÇOISE...
IT'S NOT EVEN TO COMPARE, THE SHVARTSERS AND THE JEWS!

BUT HOW *DARE* YOU GENERALIZE AND SAY ALL BLACKS STEAL! IT'S—

JUST STOP, YES? YOU ONLY DON'T *KNOW* THEM....

WHEN FIRST I CAME TO NEW YORK I WORKED IN THE GARMENT CENTER. BEFORE THIS I DIDN'T *SEE* COLOREDS...

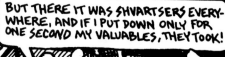

BUT THERE IT WAS SHVARTSERS EVERY-WHERE, AND IF I PUT DOWN ONLY FOR ONE SECOND MY VALUABLES, THEY TOOK!

BUT, YOU—

FORGET IT, HONEY.... HE'S HOPELESS!

YAH!...

BETTER WE'LL JUST *FORGET* IT.

AH!... YOU SEE, KIDS... WE'RE HOME SWEET HOME ALREADY...

...NOW WE CAN MAKE A VERY HAPPY LUNCH FROM ALL MY NEW GROCERIES.

ONLY THANK GOD THAT YOUR *SHVARTSER* DIDN'T TAKE THEM.

CHAPTER FOUR

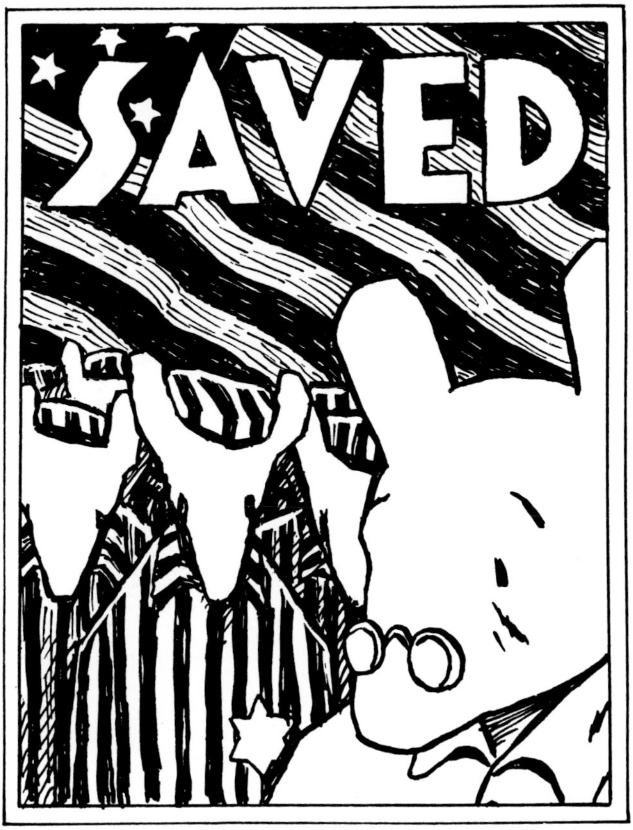
SAVED

ALWAYS I SAVED…

I SAVED ONLY SO I CAN HAVE A LITTLE SOMETHING FOR MY OLD AGE.

SO, NOW I HAVE MY OLD AGE, AND *LOOK* WHAT I HAVE …

I HAVE A TANK WITH OXYGEN AND I'M SO WEAK WITH MY HEART, AND MY DIABETES, I CAN'T LIVE ANYMORE ALONE

I HAVE SO MUCH *ROOM.* YOU AND FRANÇOISE CAN COME AND, FOR NO RENT, LIVE HERE BY ME …

NO! THAT'S TOTALLY OUT OF THE QUESTION.

SO, HOW HAVE I TO LIVE, ARTIE… TELL ME! TO GO TO A *RETIRING* HOME, IT'S NOT FOR ME.

WELL, WHY NOT GET A LIVE-IN NURSE? YOU CAN AFFORD IT.

AND WHAT WILL MY NEIGHBORS SAY TO IT IF THEY SEE A WOMAN IS LIVING BY ME!

WHA?? SO HIRE A *MALE* NURSE!

YAH! YOU AND MALA, YOU DON'T KNOW TO *MAKE* MONEY, ONLY TO MAKE IT *DISAPPEAR!*

IF I GIVE ON MALA $100,000 OVER TO HER NAME, *THEN* SHE'LL LIVE AGAIN HERE. *THIS* YOU ADVISE ME?

IT'S UP TO YOU.

I ONLY DON'T KNOW HOW TO ARRANGE MYSELF... MAYBE TO YOUR ROOM I CAN FIND A TENANT TO TAKE CARE ON ME.

UH-HUH. MAY-BE...

WELL... COME! WE HAVE NOW TO CARRY UP MY STORM WINDOWS TO PUT IN.

SHIT. I WAS HOPING YOU'D TELL ME MORE OF YOUR STORY...

THIS WE CAN TALK MAYBE AFTER, BUT ALREADY I'M COLD. I LOSE MONEY TO HEAT WITH NO STORM WINDOWS.

SIGH.

IN OTHER YEARS I PUT BY NOW THE WINDOWS, THAT I DIDN'T NEED HELP.

LOOK... I'LL DO IT, BUT FIRST, JUST TELL ME MORE ABOUT ANJA.

ANJA? WHAT IS TO TELL? EVERYWHERE I LOOK I'M SEEING ANJA...

FROM MY GOOD EYE, FROM MY GLASS EYE, IF THEY'RE OPEN OR THEY'RE CLOSED, ALWAYS I'M THINKING ON ANJA.

UH, I MEANT WHEN YOU WERE IN DACHAU. WHERE WAS ANJA?

KLIK

I DON'T KNOW-TO DIFFERENT CAMPS... SHE MARCHED FROM AUSCHWITZ EARLIER AS ME, AND CAME ALSO THROUGH GROSS-ROSEN, AND THEN - I DON'T REMEMBER--

BUT HOW DID ANJA SURVIVE?

MANCIE - THE HUNGARIAN GIRL WHAT I KNEW THERE IN AUSCHWITZ - SHE KEPT ANJA CLOSE BY TO HER.

AFTER THE WAR I LOOKED ALWAYS FOR MANCIE, TO GIVE A NICE REWARD, BUT I DIDN'T KNOW EVEN HER FULL NAME, AND I NEVER FOUND!

MOM USED TO MENTION RAVENSBRÜCK. WAS MANCIE WITH HER THERE?

YAH... MAYBE IT WAS THERE...

I KNOW ONLY THAT ANJA CAME OUT FREE BY THE RUSSIAN SIDE AND SHE CAME BACK TO SOSNOWIEC BEFORE ME. MY LIBERATION, IT TOOK LONGER...

IT WAS THE LAST MINUTES OF THE WAR, I LEFT DACHAU...

I WENT TO BE EXCHANGED FOR GERMAN PRISONERS ON THE SWISS BORDER BUT WE NEVER CAME.

I REMEMBER WE GOT EACH A TREASURE BOX FROM THE SWISS RED CROSS: SARDINES! BISCUITS! CHOCOLATE!

SOME ATE RIGHT AWAY EVERYTHING. I KEPT, OF COURSE, TO HAVE LATER.

SO, AT NIGHT, SOME TRIED TO STEAL FROM ME...

HEY!

WITH MY TYPHUS I NEEDED STILL MUCH TO REST, BUT THIS TREASURE WAS MORE TO ME THAN SLEEPING.

264

EVERYBODY OUT! LINE UP IN FIVES!

HERE WAS THE END OF OUR RIDE.

WE HAD FROM HERE TO GO BY FOOT TO THE FRONTIER...

AND I SAW, IT'S NOT EVERYWHERE, MY HELL. IT'S STILL LIFE THINGS GOING ON.

WE MARCH. WE STOP. FOR *HOURS* WE STOOD.

(WHAT'S GOING ON?)

(THEY'RE TAKING US BACK TO DACHAU!)

(NO, NO. THE AMERICANS ARE COMING.)

IT WAS COMMOTIONS AND RUMORS, THEN SHOUTS:

THE WAR IS OVER!

IT WAS OVER.

MARCH BACK TO THE TRACKS! *SCHNELL!*

THEY DIDN'T LEAVE US GO, BUT PUT US TO A FREIGHT TRAIN.

THE AMERICANS WILL BE IN THE NEXT TOWN. THEY CAN HAVE YOU.

ON THIS TRAIN NO GUARDS CAME. SO REALLY WE SAW, IT IS OVER NOW.

IN A HALF HOUR THIS TRAIN STOPPED

HEY! THE AMERICANS AREN'T HERE!

WHY WAIT? LET'S GO!

SOME WENT ONE WAY, SOME ANOTHER...

WE DIDN'T KNOW *WHERE* WE WENT.

HALT OR WE'LL SHOOT!

ALL OF A SUDDEN, IT WAS A WEHRMACHT PATROL!

LITTLE BY LITTLE THEY GOT ALL OF US WHAT WERE GOING TO BE FREE, MAYBE 150 OR 200 PEOPLE, OVER IN THE WOODS, BY A BIG LAKE !!!

I DIDN'T UNDERSTAND WHAT IS GOING ON, BUT I WAS AGAIN HERE IN GERMAN HANDS.

THEY GUARDED SO WE COULDN'T GO AWAY.

THERE ARE MACHINE GUNS SET UP ALL AROUND US!

WE OVERHEARD. THEY INTEND TO MURDER EVERY ONE OF US TONIGHT, RIGHT ON THIS SPOT!

IN THE LATER AFTERNOON I WENT OVER CLOSE TO THE EDGE OF THE WATER ...

VLADEK SPIEGELMAN! IS THAT YOU?!

SHIVEK?! YOU'RE ALIVE?

SHIVEK WAS FROM BEFORE THE WAR. A FRIEND FROM BEDZIN, NEAR SOSNOWIEC.

WE SURVIVED EVERYTHING JUST TO GET SHOT WHILE THE WAR ENDS!

I STILL HAVE A LITTLE COFFEE I ORGANIZED. LET'S MAKE A LAST CUP.

LOOK! GET HIM!

SPLASH

ONE OLDER GUY, HE WAS MAYBE 50, JUMPED TO THE LAKE. IT WAS A FAR SWIM.

KBANG! KBANG!

HE MADE IT! DO YOU HAVE THE STRENGTH TO TRY?

JUST STAY NEAR THE WATER. WE CAN ALWAYS TRY IT WHEN THE REAL SHOOTING STARTS.

SO IT CAME NIGHT. WE WERE TERRIBLE FRIGHTENED. WE SAT AND WAITED.

IT WAS CRYING AND PRAYING. SO LONG WE SURVIVED, AND NOW WE WAITED ONLY THAT THEY SHOOT, BECAUSE WE HAD NOT ELSE TO DO.

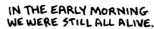

IN THE EARLY MORNING WE WERE STILL ALL ALIVE.

THEY'RE GONE!

IT'S A MIRACLE! THERE'S NOT ONE GERMAN LEFT— JUST THEIR GUNS!

WHAT HAP-PENED?

I WAS LYING NEAR THE HEAD OFFICER'S TENT— HIS GIRLFRIEND WAS ARGUING WITH HIM...

SHE BEGGED HIM TO LET US GO. SHE WARNED HIM HE'D BE PUNISHED.

"THE WAR IS OVER," SHE CRIED. "LET'S RUN AWAY!" SHE SAVED US!

SOME, WE WENT ONE WAY, SOME ANOTHER.

MAYBE WE CAN GET FOOD AT ONE OF THESE FARMS.

HALT!

ON THE ROAD WAS ANOTHER PATROL, ALSO CATCHING JEWS.

SO WE HAD AGAIN THE SAME STORY. THEY FOUND 40 OR 50 OF US, AND CLOSED US TO A BIG BARN.

WE HEARD ALL NIGHT SHOOTING IN THE MOUNTAINS AROUND...

KPOK KPOK KPOK

OUR GUARDS— THEY ALL RAN AWAY!

SO THIS NEXT MORNING WE WERE *STILL* AGAIN ALIVE!

COME, SHIVEK. LET'S FIND A BUNKER UNTIL THINGS QUIET DOWN.

WE CAME BY A GARAGE. SO I WENT OVER...

PLEASE, SIR. WE NEED A PLACE TO HIDE 'TIL THE AMERICANS GET HERE.

GO AWAY! I DON'T WANT TO GET IN-VOLVED!

HAVE PITY. IT'S JUST FOR A DAY OR TWO!...

WELL ...THERE'S A *PIT* IN THE BACK. IT'S NONE OF MY BUSINESS IF YOU WANT TO LIE IN IT!

OVER A DAY WE LAY THERE. THEN TWO WEHRMACHT CAME.

HEY! WHICH WAY IS INNSBRUCK?

THAT WAY, OFFICER.

BUT WAIT-TWO JEWS ARE BACK THERE, HIDING IN A PIT!

THEY WERE IN SO BIG A HURRY TO *RUN*, THEY DIDN'T EVEN *LOOK* TO US.

LET'S GO, SHIVEK. WE'LL FIND A SAFER SPOT.

WE PASSED TO A FEW HOUSES AND PEEKED INSIDE...

LOOK. NOBODY SEEMS TO BE HOME HERE.

A PART OF THIS HOUSE, IT WAS A BARN.

WE CAN HIDE UP HERE UN-DER THE HAY.

FROM THE WALLS WE HEARD SHOUTING:

SCHNELL, ELSA! PACK WHAT YOU CAN.

HURRY! THIS MAY BECOME A BATTLEFIELD ANY MINUTE!

THE VILLAGERS ARE RUNNING AWAY!

FINE. THE FARTHER THE BETTER!

KABOOM

THE FAR SIDE FROM OUR BARN FELL DOWN A LITTLE...

MY GOD! WH-WHAT HAPPENED?!

THE WEHRMACHT IS RETREATING AND BLEW UP THE BRIDGE TO SEAL THEIR TRAIL. IT MEANS WE'RE FREE!

LET'S LOOK AROUND. IT'S SAFE NOW!

UH-UH. I'M NOT GOING ANYWHERE!

I WENT MYSELF TO THE EMPTY HOUSE.

GASP. MILK!

I DRANK SO LONG, I DON'T KNOW WHEN I STOPPED!

I TOLD YOU IT'S SAFE NOW. I GOT YOU SOME MILK!

MILK!

SO, WE BOTH DRANK TOO MUCH MILK AND LOOKED AROUND.

AAH! CHICKENS!

HE WAS A FARM BOY, SHIVEK. HE KILLED EACH DAY A CHICKEN, AND MILKED US A COW.

I USED TO DREAM ABOUT CHICKENS!

LOOK! I FOUND CLOTHES UPSTAIRS. WE CAN THROW AWAY OUR STRIPES.

SKRAAAK!

THERE! I'M STARTING TO FEEL HUMAN AGAIN!

ME TOO. EXCEPT I'M -ULP GETTING N-NAUSEOUS...

WE LAY A FEW DAYS IN BAD SHAPE UNTIL THE AMERICANS CAME...

HANDS UP! IDENTIFY YOURSELVES!

OUR STOMACH GOT A SHOCK TO EAT MILK AND CHICKENS. WE GOT VERY SICK OF DIARRHEA.

271

I TOLD EVERYTHING HOW WE SURVIVED TO HERE...

...AND FROM DACHAU WE CAME OVER BY TRAIN TO—

AII!

BANG! BANG!

THAT'S JUST MY MEN SIGNALING THAT THEY FOUND A CACHE OF GERMAN AMMO...

THOSE KRAUTS CAN'T HURT YOU ANYMORE. THE ONLY ONES LEFT ARE DEAD OR DYING.

THIS HOUSE WILL BE PART OF OUR BASE CAMP...

BUT I GUESS YOU BOYS CAN STAY IF YOU KEEP THE JOINT CLEAN AND MAKE OUR BEDS.

WANT SOME CHOCOLATE?

M-MAYBE FOR LATER. THANK YOU.

SO WE WORKED FOR THE AMERICANS AND THEY LIKED ME THAT I CAN SPEAK ENGLISH.

THANKS FOR THE SHINE, WILLIE.

IT'S OKAY, SERGEANT. DON'T EVEN MENTION.

THEY GAVE TO US FOOD CANS AND GIFTS AND CALLED TO ME "WILLIE."

ONE TIME IT CAME A WOMAN WITH **OFFICIALS** TO THE HOUSE.

ARREST THOSE TWO **JEWISH** THIEVES!

THEY **STOLE** MY HUSBAND'S CLOTHES!

WE NEVER **LOOKED** ON WHAT CLOTHES WE TOOK!

ROB-BERS!

YOU'LL HAVE TO GIVE 'EM BACK, WILLIE.

"SO, LET HER TAKE," I TOLD. "WE HAVE STILL 3 FULL VALISES!"

ACH! LOOK ON THE TIME! WE HAVE TO **HURRY** NOW WITH MY WINDOWS.

BUT, BEFORE I FORGET— I PUT HERE A BOX WHAT YOU'LL BE HAPPY TO SEE.

I THOUGHT I LOST IT, BUT YOU SEE HOW I SAVED!

MOM'S DIA-RIES?!

NO, NO! ON THOSE IT'S NO MORE TO SPEAK. THOSE IT'S GONE, **FINISHED!**

BUT, BELOW MY CLOSET I FIND THESE SNAPSHOTS, SOME STILL FROM POLAND.

THANKS.

COME. YOU'LL LOOK AFTER THE WINDOWS!

IS THIS UNCLE HERMAN?

YAH. HE WAS ANJA'S OLDEST BROTHER. HE RAN, IN LODZ, THE FAMILY HOSIERY FACTORY.

Herman·Hela·Lodz 1928

IN 1939 HE AND HELA CAME TO SEE THE WORLD FAIR, AND STAYED HERE THE WAR. IN 1950-YOU WERE A BABY-WE CAME ALSO HERE, FROM STOCKHOLM TO HIS HOUSE.

I LIKED BETTER TO STAY IN SWEDEN-I HAD AGAIN A GOOD BUSINESS- BUT ANJA INSISTED TO BE WITH THE ONLY SURVIVING ONE OF ALL HER FAMILY.

AND -OY- WHEN HERMAN DIED FROM A HIT-AND-RUN DRIVER IN 1964, ANJA STARTED THEN ALSO TO DIE A LITTLE.

Herman. Norristown. PA. 1957

SO HERE IT'S THEIR TWO KIDS, LOLEK AND LONIA, WHAT STAYED BY US, IN SOSNOWIEC, IN THE WAR.

LOLEK, YOU KNOW HE THEN CAME OUT ALIVE FROM AUSCHWITZ, SO NOW HE'S AN ENGINEER AND A BIG-SHOT COLLEGE PROFESSOR.

THE LITTLE GIRL, SHE FINISHED WITH RICHIEU IN THE GHETTO.

Lolek·Hela 1946

THIS BROTHER OF ANJA, JOSEF, HE WAS A SIGN PAINTER, A COMMERCIAL ARTIST, ALWAYS SHE SAID YOU RESEMBLE.

Josef. Lodz. 1934

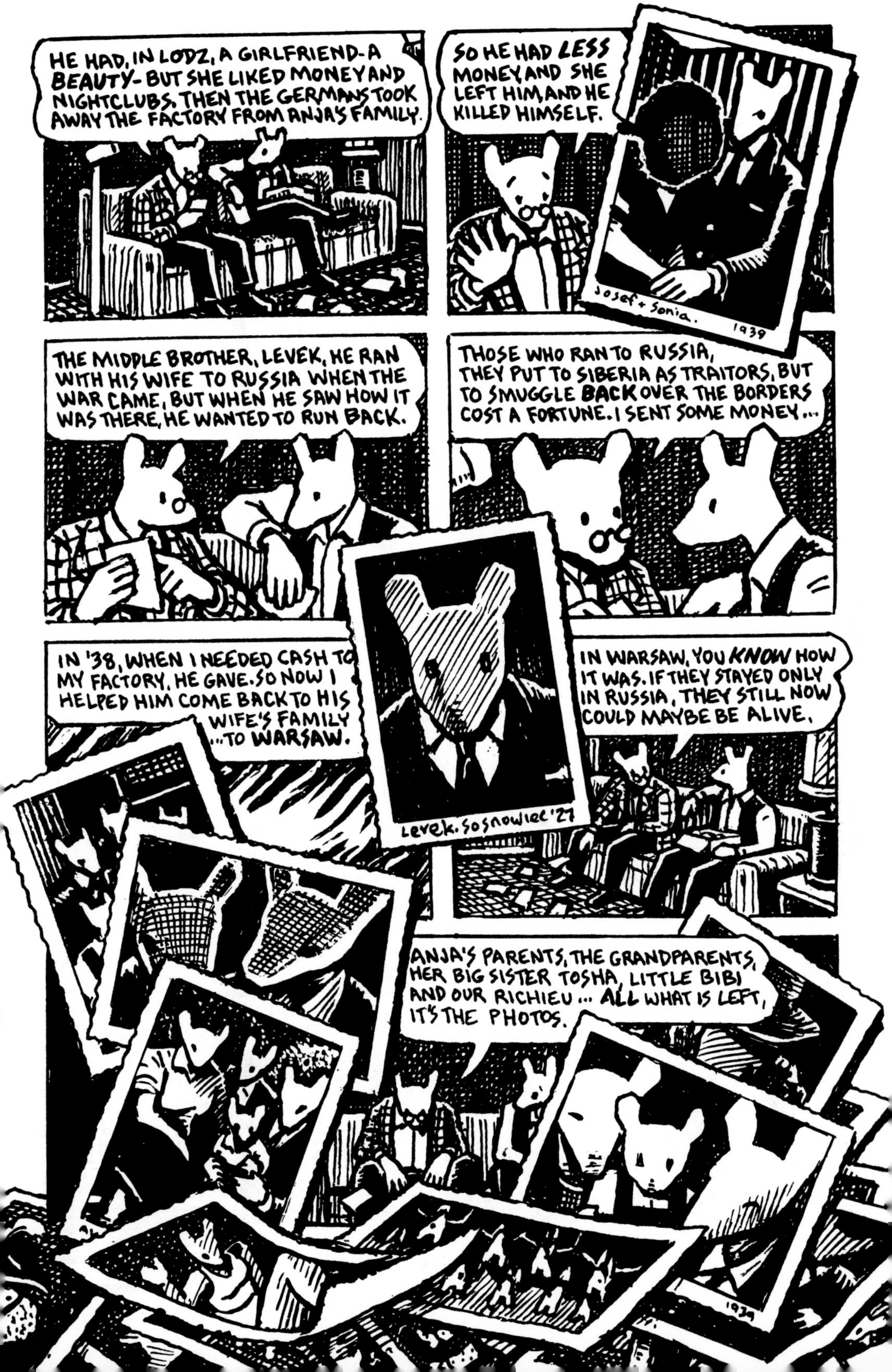
HE HAD, IN LODZ, A GIRLFRIEND - A BEAUTY - BUT SHE LIKED MONEY AND NIGHTCLUBS. THEN THE GERMANS TOOK AWAY THE FACTORY FROM ANJA'S FAMILY.
SO HE HAD LESS MONEY, AND SHE LEFT HIM, AND HE KILLED HIMSELF.
Josef + Sonia. 1939
THE MIDDLE BROTHER, LEVEK, HE RAN WITH HIS WIFE TO RUSSIA WHEN THE WAR CAME, BUT WHEN HE SAW HOW IT WAS THERE, HE WANTED TO RUN BACK.
THOSE WHO RAN TO RUSSIA, THEY PUT TO SIBERIA AS TRAITORS, BUT TO SMUGGLE BACK OVER THE BORDERS COST A FORTUNE. I SENT SOME MONEY...
Levek. Sosnowiec '27
IN '38, WHEN I NEEDED CASH TO MY FACTORY, HE GAVE. SO NOW I HELPED HIM COME BACK TO HIS WIFE'S FAMILY ...TO WARSAW.
IN WARSAW, YOU KNOW HOW IT WAS. IF THEY STAYED ONLY IN RUSSIA, THEY STILL NOW COULD MAYBE BE ALIVE.
ANJA'S PARENTS, THE GRANDPARENTS, HER BIG SISTER TOSHA, LITTLE BIBI AND OUR RICHIEU ... ALL WHAT IS LEFT, IT'S THE PHOTOS.
1939

WHAT ABOUT *YOUR* SIDE OF THE FAMILY?

MY SIDE?... MY FATHER, AND FELA, AND HER 4 KIDS, I TOLD YOU GOT TAKEN IN '42.

ZOSHA AND YADJA, MY *YOUNGER* SISTERS, HAD ONLY 1 KID EACH, AND CAME WITH ME INTO THE GHETTO BEFORE THEY ALL DIED LATER TO AUSCHWITZ.

MARCUS, MY *CLOSEST* BROTHER, AND MOSES, WENT TO A CAMP, TO BLECHAMER, SOON AFTER I CAME OUT FROM THE ARMY.

I SENT THEM MONEY BY THE RED CROSS... I HID IT INTO *BREAD*.

I WROTE THEM: "THIS BREAD, IT'S EXPENSIVE. EAT IT VERY SLOW AND CAREFUL." I MET AFTER THE WAR A GUY, HE SAW THEM DIE, BUT WOULDN'T TELL ME *HOW*.

MY OTHER BROTHERS, LEON AND PINEK, THEY *DESERTED* OUT FROM THE POLISH ARMY TO LEMBERG, IN RUSSIA...

A FAMILY OF PEASANT JEWS KEPT THEM SAFE. PINEK, HE MARRIED ONE OF THEM. BUT LEON GOT SICK. DOCTORS SAID IT'S *TYPHUS*, AND HE DIED OF A BAD APPENDIX.

Sarah + Pinek. Tel Aviv, 1963

SO ONLY MY LITTLE BROTHER, PINEK, CAME OUT FROM THE WAR ALIVE... FROM THE REST OF MY FAMILY, IT'S *NOTHING* LEFT, NOT EVEN A SNAPSHOT.

THESE PHOTOS WE GOT FROM RICHIEU'S POLISH GOVERNESS.

WE GAVE HER OUR VALUABLE THINGS TO HOLD UNTIL THE WAR IS OVER.

BUT AFTERWARD SHE SAID, "ALL THESE VALUABLES, THE NAZIS GRABBED AWAY."

WE DIDN'T BELIEVE, BUT THE PICTURES AT LEAST, SHE GAVE BACK.

CAN I TAKE THESE HOME?

YAH. IT'S FOR YOU. BUT, WAIT— I'LL PUT THEM TO AN ENVELOPE...

THE CIGAR BOX I CAN NEED FOR— AKKH!

WHOO— YOU SEE! MY NITRO-STAT HELPS ME RIGHT AWAY. BUT I TALKED TOO MUCH. I'LL LIE A LITTLE DOWN.

UM—WHAT ABOUT THE STORM WINDOWS?

ALONE YOU CAN'T KNOW HOW TO DO, AND I'M NOW TOO TIRED FOR THIS. MAYBE TOMORROW WE'LL DO.

IMPOSSIBLE. I'M TOO BUSY! I'LL COME OUT AGAIN NEXT WEEK.

ACH. THEN NOW WE MUST DO IT. I'LL—UNNF

GREAT— HAVE ANOTHER HEART ATTACK! LOOK, YOU'LL JUST HAVE TO PAY A BIT MORE FOR HEAT A FEW DAYS LONGER.

GROAN.

I'M —UH— SORRY I MADE YOU TALK SO MUCH, POP.

SO, NEVER MIND, DARLING. ALWAYS IT'S A PLEASURE WHEN YOU VISIT.

CHAPTER FIVE

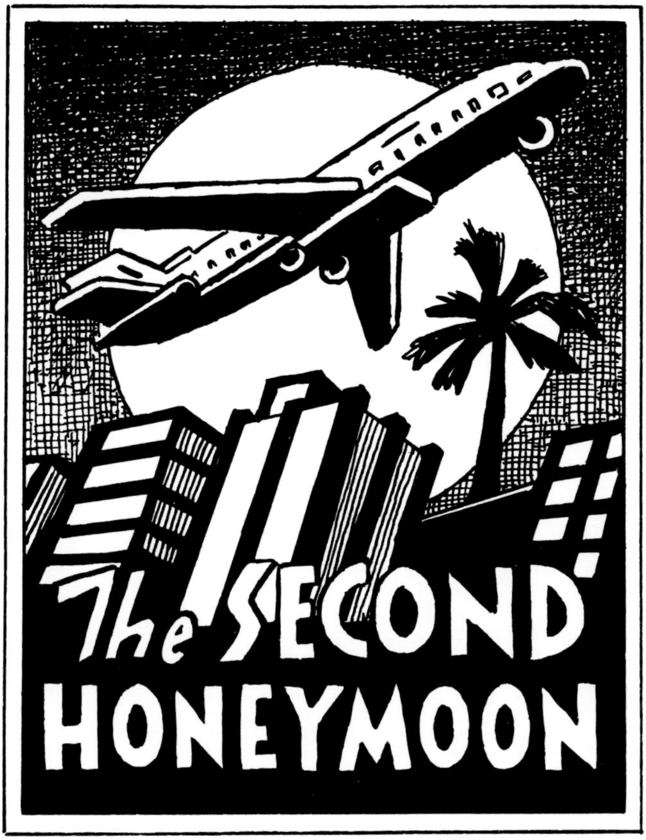
The SECOND HONEYMOON

Winter...

WANT SOME COFFEE?

AND SHE SAID: "NO! I WILL NOT GO IN THE GAS CHAMBERS. AND MY *CHILDREN* WILL NOT— CLIK

YOU BET!

Y'KNOW, I'VE GOT OVER 20 HOURS OF VLADEK'S STORY ON TAPE NOW. WE WERE JUST ABOUT *FINISHED* WHEN HE RAN OFF TO FLORIDA.

HE HASN'T CALLED US ONCE. I HOPE HE'S OKAY...

MALA IS DOWN THERE. MAYBE THEY MET AND KILLED EACH OTHER.

ACTUALLY, I THINK THEIR BATTLE KEEPS HIM GOING. HE'S BEEN A BIZARRE COMBINATION OF HELPLESSNESS AND MANIACAL ENERGY EVER SINCE SHE LEFT.

WHAT ARE WE GONNA DO WITH VLADEK? WE SURE AS HELL CAN'T MOVE OUT TO REGO PARK!

MAYBE HE COULD MOVE IN HERE WITH US.

ARE YOU *NUTS*? HIS HEART CAN'T TAKE OUR FOUR FLIGHTS OF STAIRS. IT'S THE BEST THING ABOUT THIS PLACE.

BESIDES, WHAT IF HE SAYS YES!

WELL...IT'S UP TO YOU... HE'S YOUR FATHER.

STOP! I FEEL GUILTY ENOUGH ALREADY!

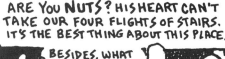

GREAT. THAT SOLVES EV- ERYTHING!

I WISH HE AND MALA COULD PATCH THINGS UP AND MAKE EACH OTHER MISERABLE AGAIN.

CLIK "AND MY CHILDREN WILL NOT GO IN THE GAS CHAMBERS." SO, TOSHA TOOK THE POISON NOT ONLY TO HERSELF, BUT TO *OUR LITTLE*

BRING RING!

HELLO. MALA?! WE WERE JUST— HUH? WHAT'S THE MATTER?

I DON'T KNOW IF I'M GOING OR COMING! YOUR FATHER IS IN ST. FRANCIS HOSPITAL.

CLIK

IT'S THE THIRD TIME IN ONE MONTH—WATER IN THE LUNGS! HE DIDN'T WANT ME TO WORRY YOU, BUT IT'S *SERIOUS!*

WHEW. WHERE ARE YOU?

IN THE CONDO. *SOB.* I'M BACK WITH HIM AGAIN, THOUGH GOD KNOWS WHY!

WELL, LOOK. I'LL CALL YOU BACK AFTER I CALL THE HOSPITAL.

HELLO, ST. FRANCIS? CAN I SPEAK TO MR. SPIEGELMAN?...HE'S A PATIENT... WHA?...YOU'RE *SURE*??

HI, MALA? THE HOSPITAL SAYS HE'S NOT REGISTERED THERE.

I KNOW... HE JUST CAME IN THE DOOR!

HE RAN OUT OF THE HOSPITAL AGAINST HIS DOCTOR'S ADVICE. HE SAYS THAT HE DOESN'T TRUST THE DOCTORS HERE.... IT'S CRAZY. HE LOOKS LIKE A GHOST!

HE WANTS TO GO TO HIS N.Y. HOSPITAL. I THINK HE WANTS TO BE NEAR YOU IN CASE, GOD FORBID ANYTHING HAPPENS! I CAN'T HANDLE THIS. COME HELP ME!

GULP.

FLORIDA

HEY! EVERYTHING'S ALMOST *PACKED*, MALA. THE MAIN REASON I FLEW DOWN WAS TO *HELP!*

PSSH. YOU KNOW VLADEK. WILD HORSES CAN'T HOLD HIM STILL... SO NOW HE'S EXHAUSTED, AND ME TOO.

GROAN

HI, POP. HOW ARE YOU?

TERRIBLE. SO WEAK... SO WEAK...

DID YOU ARRANGE EMERGENCY OXYGEN FOR HIM ON TOMORROW'S PLANE?

UH-HUH. AND I'VE GOT AN AMBULANCE TO TAKE HIM AND ME FROM J.F.K. TO LAGUARDIA HOSPITAL. I'LL CHECK HIM IN WHILE FRANÇOISE DRIVES YOU HOME.

HOW DID YOU TWO GET BACK TOGETHER?

I DON'T KNOW. I GOT A CALL FROM THE HOSPITAL AND FELT SORRY FOR HIM. I WENT OVER.

I *SWORE* I'D NEVER SEE HIM AGAIN, BUT I'M JUST A SUCKER. HE TALKED UNTIL I WAS BLUE IN THE FACE... AND HERE I AM.

MALA, MALA! COME QUICK!

ANJA MUST HAVE BEEN A *SAINT!* NO WONDER SHE KILLED HERSELF.

HE'S CALLING YOU.

IT'S JUST HIS *STOOL.* HE WANTS ME TO CHECK IT BEFORE HE'LL FLUSH. HE'S AS DIFFICULT AS EVER.

BUT NOW HE'S MORE CONFUSED AND DEPENDENT. ...WHAT CAN I DO? HE *TRAPPED* ME.

Next morning...

AT LAST! WE'RE DONE!

YEAH. ONE HOUR TO PACK, AND *FOUR* HOURS FOR VLADEK TO UNPACK AND REFOLD IT ALL!

I'M *DIZZY* NOW. LET'S GO SIT IN THE FRESH AIR.

YOU GO. I NEED TO CALL MY BROTHER, LEO, AND SAY GOOD-BY BEFORE WE LEAVE.

WHOOSH. A FEW YEARS AGO I WENT OUTSIDE HERE TO BUY FOR MALA BAGELS. I GOT DIZZY, SO LIKE NOW, I GRABBED TO A BUSH, AND I FELL...

I CRAWLED TO THE SIDE SO PEOPLE CAN *SEE* ME BUT WON'T *STEP* ON ME. FINALLY SOMEONE HELPED.

AAH. IT'S GOOD TO GET SOME SUN...

YAH. JUST IT'S TOO NOISY FROM THE HIGHWAY AND AIRPORT NEARBY. *LOOK,* ARTIE! YOU SEE IN THE SKY THAT TINY AIRPLANE?...

UH-HUH.

ON *SUCH* A TINY PLANE WE WENT OUT IN 1946 FROM POLAND TO SWEDEN. IT WAS MAYBE TEN OF US, REFUGEES...

WE NEVER WENT BEFORE IN A PLANE. THE OTHERS WERE *AFRAID* TO GO, BUT I WENT RIGHT AWAY INSIDE...

I SAID TO THEM, "SO DON'T WORRY. *LET* THE PLANE CRASH—AT LEAST WE'LL BE OUT FROM POLAND!"

WHY DID YOU WANT TO LEAVE POLAND?

PSSH. IT WAS **NOTHING** ANYMORE THERE FOR US AFTER THE WAR. NOTHING.

WE WANTED *HERE* TO COME, TO UNCLE HERMAN, BUT HERE WAS **QUOTAS**, SO HERMAN HELPED US TO HAVE A VISA OVER TO STOCKHOLM TO WAIT.

DID YOU WORK THERE?

AND *HOW* I WORKED-HARD LABORS...

I LIFTED AND CARRIED ALL DAY HEAVY BOXES. ONLY *SUCH* JOBS IT WAS FOR REFUGEES.

BUT I WAS *STRONG* THEN NOT SO LIKE NOW... AND I LOOKED TO GET IN A BETTER BUSINESS.

ONE DEPARTMENT STORE THERE, A JEW OWNED IT. I WENT TO HIM...

I'VE BEEN TRYING TO SEE YOU FOR *WEEKS!*

BUT MR. SPIEGELMAN— WE DON'T *NEED* ANY-MORE SALESMEN!...

BESIDES, YOU CAN HARDLY SPEAK SWEDISH!

IN YIDDISH WE SPOKE.

I SOLD TEXTILES AND HOSIERY IN POLAND, BUT I CAN SELL *ANYTHING!*

GIVE ME SOMETHING *NO ONE* CAN SELL—I JUST NEED A **CHANCE!**

HOSIERY? HMM...WE'RE STUCK WITH A WAREHOUSE FULL OF UNFASHIONABLE KNEE-LENGTH STOCKINGS, BUT *NOBODY*—

PERFECT!

IN THE U.S., UNCLE HERMAN AGAIN HAD A HOSIERY FACTORY. BY HIM I GOT FULL-LENGTH **NYLON** STOCKINGS.

THESE IT WAS **IMPOSSIBLE** TO FIND IN SWEDEN.

YOU WANT MY **NYLONS** TO BUY?

DO I?! MY CUSTOMERS WILL **KILL** FOR THESE. THEY'RE RATIONED!

HOW MUCH?

NORMAL PRICE. BUT TO EACH PAIR YOU MUST TAKE ALSO A PAIR OF MY **KNEE**-LENGTHS.

I'LL THROW THEM AWAY, BUT IT'S **WORTH** IT!

AND I SOLD OUT THE WHOLE INVENTORY.

I BECAME SO, LIKE A **PARTNER** TO THIS DEPARTMENT STORE AND VERY WELL-OFF.

WHEN IT CAME A FEW YEARS LATER OUR VISAS TO AMERICA, THE STORE MADE A BIG SURPRISE PARTY.

YOU CAN **STILL** RIP UP YOUR BOAT TICKETS AND STAY!

BON VOYAGE

REALLY I WAS SORRY TO GO.

I MADE IN THE STATES A LIVING DEALING DIAMONDS, BUT NEVER I HAD IT AGAIN SO GOOD.

SIGH. COME, WE'LL GO NOW INSIDE.

HUH? **WHY?** WE'VE GOT LOTS OF TIME.

IT'S TOO **SUNNY.** MAYBE IF YOU DIDN'T PACK AWAY MY **SUNGLASSES,** WE COULD STILL SIT.

Late that night...

PLEASE REMAIN SEATED UNTIL OUR SICK PASSENGER HAS DE-PLANED...

GROAN

SO THERE WAS A 6 HOUR DELAY BEFORE BOARDING. *THEN* VLADEK COMPLAINS THAT THE OXYGEN UNIT ISN'T WORKING AND HE CAN'T BREATHE.

THE CREW CHECKS AND SAYS THE UNIT IS FINE...

THEY SAY HE'S TOO SICK TO FLY, BUT WE REFUSE TO GET OFF. THEN VLADEK SAYS THE OXYGEN TANK *IS* WORKING, AND HERE WE ARE!

I'M GLAD YOU CALLED TO SAY YOU'D BE LATE.

THEY SET UP A FREE PHONE FOR DELAYED PASSENGERS. MALA CALLED EVERYONE SHE KNOWS IN AMERICA.

YOU SEE? I *LEARNED* FROM VLADEK!

A half hour later...

FINALLY! FRANÇOISE AND MALA MUST BE HOME AND DRY BY NOW. THEY COULD'VE DRIVEN US TO THE HOSPITAL.

DON'T WORRY, THE RIDE IS PAID BY MY *INSURANCE*.

EXCUSE ME. HE'S SICK, BUT I DON'T THINK HE NEEDS A STRETCHER.

REGULATIONS BUDDY.

SO, WHERE *IS* LA GUARDIA HOSPITAL?

ACH! GO ON QUEENS BOULEVARD 'TIL I SAY YOU TO TURN RIGHT.

THANKS, MISTER... BUT *PLEASE* STAY ON THE STRETCHER.

LaGuardia Hospital...

YAWN. WILL IT BE MUCH LONGER?

THE TESTS ARE DONE... YOU CAN WAIT FOR THE DOCTOR IN THERE, WITH YOUR FATHER.

HOW'RE YOU DOIN', POP?

MOAN
SO TIRED...
SO TIRED...

SORRY IT TOOK SO LONG, BUT BECAUSE OF WHAT YOU TOLD US ABOUT YOUR FATHER'S CONDITION, WE PLAYED IT SAFE AND RAN EXTENSIVE TESTS...

THE PILLS HE GOT IN FLORIDA ARE TAKING CARE OF THE WATER IN HIS LUNGS AND HIS HEART SEEMS TO BE DOING FINE...

YOU'LL BE GLAD TO KNOW YOU CAN TAKE HIM HOME WITH YOU!

WHAT?!

UM. IF HE'S A BORDER-LINE CASE, WHY NOT KEEP HIM UNDER OBSER-VATION FOR A FEW DAYS.

THERE'S JUST NO *NEED* FOR HIM TO BE HOSPITALIZED.

WELL, THE DOC-TOR SAYS YOU'RE OKAY. WE CAN GO HOME NOW.

YAH? THEN MALA AND I CAN STAY THE REST OF THE YEAR HERE IN REGO PARK.

IT'S BETTER IF NOTHING IS WRONG *HERE*, NEAR TO MY HEALTH PLAN HOSPITAL, THAN IN A *FLORIDA* HOSPI-TAL FOR HUNDREDS OF DOLLARS A DAY!

A month or so later...

ARTIE, WE HAVEN'T SEEN YOU IN AGES.

I NEEDED TIME TO GET OVER OUR TRIP FROM FLORIDA... WHAT'S NEW?

WELL, WE'RE GOING TO SELL THIS HOUSE AND MOVE DOWN THERE.

I'M AMAZED VLADEK AGREED. HE'S SO ATTACHED TO THIS PLACE.

HOW'S HE FEELING?

HE'S BEEN KIND OF LISTLESS. IT MAKES HIM EASIER TO TAKE, BUT HE'S NOT REALLY DOING TOO WELL.

HE GETS CONFUSED. LAST WEEK HE WENT TO HIS BANK AND ACTUALLY GOT LOST ON THE WAY HOME! ... ANYWAY, HE'S IN THERE RESTING.

SO, I HEAR YOU WANNA SELL THE HOUSE...

YAH? I WANT ONLY PEACE. IF MALA WANTS FLORIDA, OKAY, LET IT BE FLORIDA.

COME AND SIT. I'M SURPRISED TO SEE YOU!

HUH? WHY? I SAID I WAS COMING WHEN I PHONED YOU YESTERDAY.

YOU PHONED? I DON'T REMEMBER...

I CAME TO TAPE THE REST OF YOUR STORY, IF YOU FEEL UP TO IT.

I NEED TO KNOW WHAT HAPPENED AT THE VERY END OF THE WAR...

THE WAR. YAH, THIS I STILL REMEMBER.

288

YOU WERE LIVING ON A FARM WITH SOME G.I.S...

YAH. WITH MY FRIEND, SHIVEK.

SO, WHAT HAPPENED?

MANY REFUGEES STARTED TO BE EVERYWHERE...

SO, IT CAME AN ORDER...

WE ALL CAME OVER TO GARMISCH-PARTENKIRCHEN.

HEADQUARTERS IS SETTING UP A DISPLACED PERSONS' CAMP. YOU'LL HAVE TO MOVE THERE.

NAME?

VLADEK SPIEGELMAN.

COUNTRY OF ORIGIN?

POLAND...

HERE WE GOT IDENTITY PAPERS AND A PLACE WHERE TO STAY...

HEY, VLADEK. COME WITH ME TO HANNOVER TO SEE MY BROTHER. HE'S MARRIED TO A GENTILE WHO KEPT HIM HIDDEN. HE-

OW!

WHAT'S WRONG?

I DON'T KNOW, SHIVEK. I'VE GOT A FEVER, AND I'M ITCHING ALL OVER-IN MY THROAT, MY EARS, EVERYWHERE! AII!

I WAS FOR A GOOD FEW DAYS VERY SICK.

WH-WHERE AM I?

THE INFIRMARY. YOU'VE HAD A RELAPSE OF TYPHUS.

I FEEL FINE NOW.

SEE A DOCTOR REGULARLY. WE CAN'T DIAGNOSE IT, BUT SOMETHING IS STILL WRONG.

A YEAR AFTER, I FOUND OUT IT WAS NOT ONLY TYPHUS, BUT ALSO DIABETES.

IN THIS DP CAMP, I HAD IT EASY...

HURRY, VLADEK! WE CAN EARN SOME CHOCOLATES!

OKAY! WE SPEAK ENGLISH! OKAY!!

SHIVEK, HE COULDN'T SPEAK EVEN POLISH—JUST YIDDISH.

WE CARRIED MANY GOODIES WHEN FINALLY WE GOT OUR I.D. PAPERS TO GO.

WE WANT TICK-ETS TO HANNOVER.

TICKETS??...

I DON'T KNOW IF THERE ARE EVEN ANY TRACKS! THAT FREIGHT MAY BE HEADING NORTH.

TRAINS STOPPED AND STARTED AND HAD TO CHANGE OFTEN DIRECTIONS...

LOOK, SHIVEK—NUREMBERG.

I SCRUBBED STREETS HERE AS A P.O.W....

NOW IT WAS ONLY STONES AND NOTHING.

WE CAME TO ONE PLACE, WÜRZBURG—WHAT A MESS!

WE CAME AWAY HAPPY.

WHERE CAN WE FIND WATER?

HAH! WE HAVEN'T HAD ANY WATER IN THREE DAYS!

THE AMERICANS DESTROYED—SOB—EVERYTHING!

NOT ONE BUILDING WAS STILL STANDING.

LET THE GERMANS HAVE A LITTLE WHAT THEY DID TO THE JEWS.

WE ARRIVED FINALLY TO HANNOVER...

THE KIDS CAN SHARE ONE BEDROOM. YOU TWO CAN HAVE THE OTHER...

DO YOU KNOW WHERE ANY OF **YOUR** FAMILY IS?

I'LL GO TO POLAND TO SEE IF ANYONE'S LEFT. WE PLANNED TO MEET IN SOSNOWIEC IF WE GOT SEPARATED.

I SENT A LETTER TO THE JEWISH COMMUNITY CENTER THERE, FOR MY WIFE, BUT- SHE CAN'T STILL BE ALIVE... I SAW HER IN AUSCHWITZ LAST YEAR...

SHE WAS SO THIN... SO WEAK...

YOU MIGHT GET NEWS ABOUT YOUR FAMILY AT THE BIG DP CAMP AT BELSEN. JEWS ARE FLOODING IN FROM ALL OVER.

IT WASN'T FAR, SO I WENT FOR A FEW DAYS TO BELSEN. ONE MORNING A CROWD ARRIVED IN, WITH TWO GIRLS WHAT I KNEW A LITTLE FROM MY HOME TOWN...

JENNY! SONIA!

LOOK! IT'S VLADEK SPIEGELMAN!

WE JUST CAME FROM POLAND...

WE WERE LUCKY TO GET OUT!...

WHATEVER YOU DO, DON'T GO BACK TO SOSNOWIEC. THE POLES ARE STILL KILLING JEWS THERE!

REMEMBER THE GELBERS? THEY OWNED THE BIG BAKERY IN SOSNOWIEC...

"ONE OF THE SONS SURVIVED AND CAME BACK HOME...

WHAT DO *YOU* WANT?

THIS IS MY FAMILY'S HOUSE. I'M GELBER!

WE THOUGHT HITLER FINISHED YOU OFF!

GO AWAY, JEW! THIS IS *OUR* BAKERY NOW!

SLAM!

"HE DIDN'T KNOW WHAT TO DO. HE SPENT THE NIGHT IN THE SHED BEHIND HIS HOUSE...

"THE POLES WENT IN. THEY BEAT HIM AND HANGED HIM.

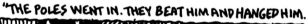

"...FOR *THIS* HE SURVIVED."

HIS BROTHER CAME FROM THE CAMPS A DAY LATER, AND ONLY STAYED LONG ENOUGH TO BURY HIM...

STOP IT!..I DON'T WANT TO HEAR ANY MORE!

JUST TELL ME, DID YOU HEAR ANYTHING ABOUT ANJA?

I *SAW* HER! SHE DIDN'T TRY TO GET HER PROPERTY BACK. THE POLES LEAVE HER ALONE.

ANJA IS ALIVE! MY HEART JUMPED! I COULDN'T BELIEVE.

ANJA IS ALIVE! MY HEART JUMPED! I COULDN'T BELIEVE.

ANJA WAS ALL ALONE THERE IN SOSNOWIEC...

SORRY ANJA. NO NEWS FOR YOU...

EACH DAY SHE CHECKED TO THE JEWISH ORGANIZATION, AND EACH DAY SHE CRIED.

SHE TOLD ME LATER, SHE WENT ONCE TO A GYPSY...

ANJA KNEW IT WAS FOOLISH, BUT LOOKED ONLY FOR SOME HOPE.

I SEE TRAGEDY...DEATH!... YOU'VE LOST YOUR FATHER... YOUR MOTHER...EVERYONE!

Y-YES. ONLY LOLEK, MY NEPHEW, CAME BACK—

I SEE A CHILD... A DEAD CHILD...

RICHIEU! MY LITTLE BOY, RICHIEU. SOB.

WAIT! NOW I SEE A MAN... ILLNESS...IT'S YOUR HUSBAND! HE'S BEEN VERY, VERY ILL...

HE'S COMING—HE'S COMING HOME! YOU'LL GET A *SIGN* THAT HE'S ALIVE BY THE TIME THE MOON IS FULL!

I SEE A SHIP...A FARAWAY PLACE... YOU'LL HAVE A NEW LIFE... AND ANOTHER LITTLE BOY.

293

ANJA WENT A FEW TIMES EACH DAY OVER TO THE JEWISH ORGANIZATION....

BUT NO SIGN CAME OF ME.

SO SHE SAT HOME EVEN MORE DEPRESSED, UNTIL...

KNOCK KNOCK

ANJA! GUESS WHAT! A LETTER FROM YOUR HUSBAND JUST CAME!

HE'S IN GERMANY... HE'S HAD *TYPHUS!*

IT'S JUST LIKE THE GYPSY SAID.

AND HERE'S A *PICTURE* OF HIM! MY GOD-VLADEK IS REALLY ALIVE!

I PASSED ONCE A PHOTO PLACE WHAT HAD A *CAMP* UNIFORM - A NEW AND CLEAN ONE - TO MAKE SOUVENIR PHOTOS...

ANJA KEPT THIS PICTURE ALWAYS. I HAVE IT STILL *NOW* IN MY DESK!

HUH? WHERE DO YOU GO?

I NEED THAT PHOTO IN MY BOOK!

294

INCRED-IBLE!

YAH. SO, WHEN I HEARD ANJA IS ALIVE I STOPPED EVERYTHING TO GO ONLY BACK TO SOSNOWIEC.

I TRADED MY THINGS TO HAVE GIFTS.

LOOK! I GOT SOME DRESSES AND A FUR COAT TO BRING ANJA.

Y'KNOW, IF YOU GO TO POLAND, I'LL GO TOO!

WE WENT, SOMETIMES BY FOOT, SOMETIMES BY TRAIN.

TO POLAND, MANY TIMES IT WASN'T ANY *TRACKS* LEFT.

ONE PLACE WE STOPPED, HOURS, HOURS AND HOURS.

STAY HERE WITH OUR LUGGAGE, SHIVEK. I'LL GO FILL OUR CANTEENS.

I MARKED OUR TRAIN CAR, BUT WHEN I CAME IN AN HOUR BACK, IT WAS GONE TO ANOTHER TRACK.

SHIVEK?!

I COULDN'T FIND MORE MY FRIEND AND MY LUGGAGE. I HAD ONLY MY THIN SHIRT AND MY WATER.

SHIVEK WENT BACK TO HAN-NOVER TO FIND ME AGAIN...

...BUT I WENT ONLY STRAIGHT TO POLAND. IT TOOK 3 OR 4 WEEKS.

WHEN I CAME FINALLY TO SOSNOWIEC, I HAVE SEEN VERY LITTLE JEWS AROUND.

THERE IT WAS PEOPLE WHAT KNEW ME.

BUT I FOUND OUT WHERE IS THE JEWISH ORGANIZATION.

LOOK WHO'S HERE! SOMEBODY FIND ANJA AND BRING HER RIGHT AWAY!

AND SOMEBODY FOUND HER...

GASP.

V-VLADEK!

IT WAS SUCH A MOMENT THAT EVERYBODY AROUND WAS CRYING TOGETHER WITH US.

ANJA, ANJA, MY ANJA!

MORE I DON'T NEED TO TELL YOU. WE WERE BOTH VERY HAPPY, AND LIVED HAPPY, HAPPY EVER AFTER.

SO... LET'S STOP, PLEASE, YOUR TAPE RECORDER...

I'M *TIRED* FROM TALKING, RICHIEU, AND IT'S *ENOUGH* STORIES FOR NOW...

SPIEGELMAN

VLADEK
Oct. 11, 1906
Aug 18, 1982

ANJA
Mar. 15, 1912
May 21, 1968

— art spiegelman — 1978·1991